# SIEGE

TOR BOOKS BY RHIANNON FRATER

*The First Days*
*Fighting to Survive*
*Siege*

# SIEGE

## · AS THE WORLD DIES ·
### BOOK THREE

WITHDRAWN

## *Rhiannon Frater*

TOR®

A TOM DOHERTY ASSOCIATES BOOK · NEW YORK

SIEGE: AS THE WORLD DIES

Copyright © 2009, 2012 by Rhiannon Frater

Foreword copyright © 2009 by Michael Carl West

A Tor Book
Published by Tom Doherty Associates, LLC
175 Fifth Avenue
New York, NY 10010

www.tor-forge.com

Tor® is a registered trademark of Tom Doherty Associates, LLC.

ISBN 978-0-7653-3128-1 (trade paperback)
ISBN 978-1-4299-8821-6 (e-book)

First Tor Edition: April 2012

Printed in the United States of America

10  9  8  7  6  5  4  3  2  1

*To all the fans of this trilogy*

## ACKNOWLEDGMENTS

Thanks to my mother and husband for their unwavering support.

Special thanks to Dr. Pus of the *Library of the Living Dead* podcast. Your encouragement and pimpage of this trilogy have been phenomenal. Thank you so much!

Special acknowledgment to my original test readers: Michelle, Kelly, Julie, Kody, and Helen, you are awesome!

A huge thank-you to my editor, Melissa Singer, for helping me wrestle the original enormous online serial into the ultimate versions of the story of Jenni and Katie.

# FOREWORD

*Dr. Pus of the* Library of
the Living Dead *podcast*

If you're reading this, you must be a fan of Rhiannon Frater's zombie epic that started with the incredible first book, *The First Days.* When I started reading *The First Days,* I didn't get past the opening chapter. It was so shocking, I had to go back immediately and read it again. And when I finished the book, I read it again!

Now, I have been asked to write the foreword to the third and final installment. This is just an incredible honor. Why? Because I *know* zombie novels. I live for zombie novels. My podcast is specifically for the zombies. My own Library of the Living Dead is jam-packed with almost every zombie novel that has ever seen print. It is overflowing with zombie goodness except for one spot. One area on the top shelf is reserved for one special book . . . the one you are holding in your hands.

*Siege* will answer all the questions you've been asking since you read *The First Days* and *Fighting to Survive.* Rhiannon addresses them all, but you won't like some of the answers. That's because she is such a talented writer that her characters are ones you have come to love, care about, have empathy and sympathy for. Her characters are us. And even though we all want them to live, it just isn't always possible in Rhiannon's universe.

Start reading *Siege* now. When you're finished, your heart will have been touched, and it will be a little bruised, too.

Undead love to you all,
Doc

*Somewhere in Texas*

**In the Hills**

# · CHAPTER ONE ·

## 1.
### *Return of the Tiny Fingers*

The tiny fingers under the door were missing. Jenni stared down at the dark crack under the front door, waiting for her toddler's tiny pink digits to appear. The gap beneath the door was far too big. She had told Lloyd that many times. It was too easy for a little hand to slip underneath.

Standing on the front porch of her home, she felt the cool morning air teasing her dark hair and ruffling her pink nightgown and robe.

"Benji?" she whispered.

The hard, steady thumping against the door was a terrifying reminder that her zombified husband, Lloyd, was just on the other side. She could barely discern the dim outline of his form through the blood-smeared, frosted glass panes set in the door.

"Benji?"

Jenni waited, but the tiny fingers did not emerge. Slowly, she squatted until her shaking hands touched the cold cement of the front stoop. "Benji?"

The crack under the door, ominous in its promise, did not give birth to tiny bloody fingers.

"Mom!"

Jenni rose swiftly to her feet. "Mikey?"

Her twelve-year-old son ran around the corner of the house, barefoot and in his pajamas, clutching his toddler brother in his arms.

"Mikey! Benji!" Jenni stumbled toward them.

"We got out the back door, Mom!"

Jenni embraced her sons, then lifted Benji onto her hip.

"Mommy! Daddy's scary!" Benji thrust one tiny thumb into his mouth.

Crying and thanking God for their survival, she pulled them away from the house.

"Mom, we gotta get away! Dad's crazy!" Mikey exclaimed.

"We'll get away! I promise. In a minute or two, Katie will be here," Jenni said, gripping his hand with all her strength.

"Who, Mom?"

"Katie's coming to save us." Jenni glanced warily at the house. Lloyd was now banging on the window next to the front door. "She'll be here soon."

Scowling, she tried not to think too hard about what had happened before. . . .

"Mom, where is Katie?"

Jenni cried out when the window shattered beneath Lloyd's fists.

In his fear, Mikey was crushing her hand. Benji sobbed loudly, his wet face against her neck, his tiny fingers gripping the collar of her nightgown.

"She should be here!" Jenni ran into the street, feeling the cold asphalt under her bare feet. The road was empty. Jenni whirled around, her dark eyes searching desperately for the white truck that should be their salvation.

"Mom! Mom!" Mikey's voice was high and terrified. He was pointing at Lloyd, who had crashed to the ground outside the house and was struggling to get up.

"Katie, where are you?" Jenni yelled.

Lloyd staggered to his feet. With an unholy screech, he began to race toward his wife and sons.

Jenni screamed and ran. Benji was a heavy weight in her arms and Mikey clung to the edge of her robe as they fled. Bare feet slapping hard against the pavement, Jenni ran for her life and the lives of her children. She could hear Lloyd gaining on them, his footfalls close behind her.

"Mommy! Mommy!" Benji sobbed while his warm urine soaked her robe as his fear unleashed his bladder.

"Katie! Hurry! Katie!" Jenni cried out.

The doors of her neighbors' houses flew open. Bloody mutilated figures raced in Jenni's direction, screeching, hands and teeth seeking human flesh.

"Mommy! Mommy!" Mikey and Benji chorused in terror.

The street filled with the hungry undead. Their horrible blood-stained teeth gnashed with hunger.

"Katie! Katie!" Jenni sobbed. "Katie, please come!"

The undead closed in around Jenni and her family.

## 2.
### *Hitchhikers of the Living Dead*

Jenni woke with a start, banging her head against the passenger-side window of the truck. "Ouch! Dammit!"

As she forced the nightmare from her waking mind, she looked up—and gasped. The badly mauled face of a zombie was pressed into the window, its tongue licking eagerly against the fogged glass, where her head had rested a few seconds before.

"Fuck," she groaned. She was groggy from sleep and fumbled for her weapon. Out of the corner of her eye, she caught a glimpse of Katarina's blue wool coat as the woman moved around the parked truck, her pistol in her hand.

"I got him, Jenni," she called out. The zombie, hearing Katarina's voice, ambled away from the window and howled. The homely redhead aimed and fired. The zombie's head burst, its body collapsing onto the road.

"Thanks!" Jenni said, rubbing her eyes. She had fallen asleep on the way back from a successful scavenging run with a large convoy from the fort. There had been no loss of life and they were returning with a lot of supplies.

Katarina climbed back into the truck's cab, slammed the door, shutting out the freezing wind, and sighed. "I don't know why Felix couldn't wait to pee until we were back at the fort, *away* from the zombies."

"Couldn't hold it, huh?"

"No. He said he was going to explode. I told him to hang it out the window. He laughed." Katarina frowned. "I was serious."

"I'm sure Ed loved bringing the convoy to a halt so Felix could pee." Jenni glanced through the blood-splattered window at the side mirror and saw Felix's reflection. He was just finishing. Another zombie lay dead not too far from him.

"He better finish the hell up so we can get home." Katarina rubbed her hands over the steering wheel, her knuckles bright red from the cold weather. "I want some nice hot coffee."

"I just want a nice warm bed with a nice warm Juan in it."

Katarina's deep blush, which almost matched her red hair, made Jenni giggle.

Texas winters were always unpredictable. Snow had fallen three times since Christmas. Barely a week into January, Jenni was already sick of the new year. It was so damn cold.

Felix wrenched open the back door and slid in. "I urinated on my shoes! Can't a man relieve himself without those damn things showing up?"

Jenni slid around in her seat and grinned at him. "Should have held it, huh?"

"When a man has to go, he has to go!" Felix folded his arms across his muscled chest and glared. He wore several layers of clothing under his usual tracksuit, and his black skin looked beautiful against the whiteness of the fabric. Felix dressed like a gangster, but spoke with a sophisticated air most of the time. He was the adopted son of rich white parents from Houston and would have graduated with a master's in literature if not for the zombie apocalypse. Jenni liked him a lot and they enjoyed teasing each other.

Despite her joking, Jenni could not get the final image of her nightmare out of her head. It had been so vivid. Her children had seemed so real. But Jenni knew that the boys never made it out of the house. Lloyd had killed them. And if Katie had not arrived when she did, Jenni would have perished as well.

Katarina lifted her walkie-talkie off the console and reported in. "Ed, he's done. We're moving back into position."

Jenni laid her head against the backrest and stared at Katarina as she drove the truck back onto the country road to continue the journey home. The rest of the caravan was waiting ahead. As their truck drew near, those vehicles slowly accelerated. Soon the convoy was speeding toward the fort.

"My trainers are ruined." Felix pulled a book from his backpack. "It will be difficult to find good replacements."

"You could try to clean them," Katarina suggested.

"I scrape zombie guts off my boots all the time," Jenni added.

Felix just grumbled something that they couldn't make out and began to read the words of Socrates.

"Boys are so moody," Jenni decided.

"And they say we are," Katarina scoffed.

Jenni felt odd riding shotgun with Katarina instead of Katie. Jenni suspected Travis, Katie's husband, had something to do with Katie's not being assigned to any of the scavenging or search-and-rescue groups lately. The announcement of Katie's pregnancy had been a shock to everyone. Some of the survivors were happy to welcome a new life into their barren world, but others felt a pregnancy was irresponsible under the circumstances. Negative comments were never made around Katie or Travis, the first couple daring to bring a child into the undead world.

Jenni's own feelings about the baby were mixed. On one hand, she was happy for her friend and ready to be an aunt, but on the other, she feared it was unwise to bring a new life into a world full of the hungry dead. How could she have raised her boys in this undead world? Her stepson, Jason, was almost an adult, but Mikey and Benji would have lost whatever remained of their child-hood innocence. The children of the fort bore deep emotional scars from the horrors they had witnessed.

Tears burned in her eyes as she realized she would rather her boys were with her than dead. Juan would have been a good father, and they would have worked hard to give the boys a good life. Instead, her little ones were part of the undead hordes.

"Something is going on," Katarina said, pulling Jenni away from her dark thoughts.

The caravan was slowing down.

"We got problems ahead," Ed's voice crackled over the CB.

Jenni snatched up the mouthpiece. "What's up?"

"Bunch of zombies have a van surrounded. Looks like people are on top of it. Whole way is blocked." Ed sounded peeved.

"We have to save them!" Curtis's voice cut through the static. Jenni could imagine the grim expression on the young policeman's face.

"Got any ideas on how to handle it?" Ed answered.

"Pull up," Jenni said to Katarina.

With a nod, Katarina shifted gears and moved their truck to the front of the convoy, idling it next to Ed's school bus. Jenni scowled as the scene below came into view.

"Fuck."

The undead were busily consuming someone near the side of the road. The van's side door was open and zombies were crowd-ing to get inside. On top of the van, a group of people was hud-dled near an open sunroof.

Ed, the driver of the bus, leaned out his window. Beneath his battered hat, his sun-wrinkled face looked pissed. Jenni pushed the button for her window and it slid down. "What do you think, Ed?"

"Got at least three dozen trying to get to those folks. I figure we can drive close enough to try to get them to come for us, then flat-ten them."

"They've got fresh food in front of them," Jenni reminded him.

"They're not going to come after us. What if we thin out the outer edge with the guns, then clear the rest with machetes, spears, and my trusty ax?"

Curtis walked up between their vehicles, his weapon in hand. The slim young man with the golden blond hair and blue eyes was bundled into a thick leather jacket with a wool scarf wrapped around his neck, nearly obscuring his mouth. "We need to hurry, whatever the hell we're doing. It's getting bad down there."

The van was rocking under the onslaught of the undead. Some-one on top of the van spotted the convoy and dared to stand and wave to get their attention. Jenni gasped as he tumbled off. His screams tore through the cold air, then broke off abruptly. Zom-bies moaned with delight as they swarmed him.

"We gotta move now!" Jenni shoved her door open, nearly hit-ting Curtis. Yanking her ax out of the truck, she gestured for Fe-lix and Katarina to follow. Shoving the ax into the specially made sheath on her back, she banged the door shut with her hip. Deter-mined to bust some zombie heads, she headed down the hill.

"We don't have a plan, Jenni!" Ed shouted after her.

Jenni stalked toward the undead swarm. "Kill the fuckers! That's the plan!"

## 3.
### *Sentries of the Dead*

The zombie slammed its mangled hand against the fort wall again, growling.

Katie observed it from her sentry post, her blond curls flowing in the wind. Rubbing her cold-reddened hands together, she stud-ied the creature's distorted features. Most of its flesh had torn off. One eyeball rolled up toward her in a gouged socket. How it could see her, she could not imagine. It had no lips, so its bloodied, decaying teeth looked hideously large as they chomped together hungrily.

"I can't even tell if you're a boy or a girl," Katie muttered, then blew on her fingers to warm them.

Stacey peered over the edge of the wall. The slim young woman leaned her elbows on the cement bricks and stared at the zombie. "I think it's a boy."

"That patch of hair on the back of its head is kinda long," Katie pointed out.

"Yeah, but lots of redneck boys have long hair. There were a lot of guys back in my old town with ponytails longer than mine." Stacey tugged on her short braid. When she and her boyfriend were first rescued, she had been terribly thin, her shoulder blades and collarbones sticking out of her tanned skin at sharp angles. Now she was fit and muscular.

Katie tilted her head as she studied the creature. "I think it's a girl. Still ugly as sin."

"Uglier. Guess we should put it down."

"Yep," Katie agreed.

She reached for the huge crossbow rigged on a sliding track that ran along the wall. It was one of Jason's creations, and it made killing the close-in zombies a lot easier. Mirrors attached to the contraption helped Katie see her target.

"I'm not saying I miss the big crowds of them, but lone zombies just seem so sad," Stacey said.

"Until they try to eat you."

"Well, there is that." Stacey watched Katie carefully use a lever to adjust her aim. "Jason is like a genius, huh?"

"Jenni says that he's always tinkered with stuff. Once he took apart his Xbox and put it back together and it still worked. I don't think she's surprised at some of the things he's come up with lately, but I'm pretty impressed." Katie checked her mirrors and saw that she had the zombie perfectly lined up. She squeezed the trigger.

The bolt punctured the top of the zombie's head and it fell, limbs askew.

"Penis! I see a penis! It's a boy!"

"That is so disgusting!" Katie made a comical face.

Stacey giggled. "It flopped out!"

"It's not funny! It's a poor dead guy." Despite herself, Katie was laughing. "My God, the gallows humor around here is thick."

"Freud would have had a blast studying us," Stacey agreed.

"Oh, well. Either we're a little crazy and laugh at the absurdities of life or we just give in to despair and die." Katie reset the crossbow, showing Stacey each step.

"I've done despair. It doesn't help anything." Stacey fell silent, obviously pondering a thought. "The fort hasn't really had anyone go nuts and commit suicide or anything, has it?"

"Well, in the first days, a city councilman tried to save his zombie family and ended up eaten. And the Vigilante pitches people over the wall." Katie slipped her hands into her jacket. Her swelling belly was straining the zipper.

"Who do you think the Vigilante is?" Stacey pulled the collar of her coat closer to her face and huddled down into it.

Katie bit her bottom lip, then shrugged. "No clue. I'm sure everyone has a theory."

"I think it's Nerit," Stacey confided.

"She wasn't here when the first guy was thrown over the wall."

"The meth dealer?"

"Yeah. Ritchie." Katie vividly remembered the young man's disfigured body staring up at her, duct tape still over his mouth.

"Well, there goes my theory. You know, a few people think the Vigilante is doing the right thing."

"I had no love for Phil or Shane, but what the Vigilante did to them was inhumane. Stranding them with gimped weapons in the middle of the zombie deadlands."

"They deserved it." Now Stacey shrugged. "I'm not gonna cry over them."

"What if the Vigilante gets mad at you, or Eric, or someone you care about? The Vigilante killed Jimmy because he panicked when we took the hotel. We all have our moments. We're human.

And zombies are so fucking terrifying—sometimes even the bravest feel afraid."

Stacey's brow furrowed. "When you put it that way . . ."

Katie pulled her cap down on her head, trying to keep the whistling wind away from her numb ears. "Life is hard enough without having to worry about someone's skewed sense of justice getting you or your friends killed."

"I just want to feel safe." Stacey's gaze was on the zombie below. "But I never really do."

They smelled Otis Calhoun before they saw him. The scrawny old man shoved them roughly aside and peered down into the road.

"Hey, Calhoun, watch it! Katie's pregnant, you know!"

"Checking something," Calhoun mumbled.

He scribbled in a battered pad, making quick notations with a stubby pencil. Katie craned her head to take a peek, but couldn't make sense of the marks. Stacey covered her nose with her gloved hands, trying not to gag. Calhoun was more ripe than usual.

Calhoun whipped out a strange contraption made of rulers taped together at odd angles. Grumbling something about the city planners being imbeciles, he studied the surrounding streets with the device.

"Calhoun, we're supposed to be guarding this area. You need to move along." Katie said, attempting to shoo him off.

"Dear God, woman! Do you understand the gravity of what I am doing? No, you do not! I am trying to make this fort safe from the messed-up clones." Calhoun pointed down at the corpse in the road. "They don't even have the decency to cover their junk. Heathens!"

Katie stared at Calhoun, one eyebrow arched.

"Fine! I will return later!" As Calhoun whipped around, his long coat slapped their knees. Katie watched as his skinny legs carried him down the stairs past Travis, who was just starting up to the sentry post. The cold wind ruffled his hair over his creased brow as he climbed up the wood steps.

Katie winced. "I'm busted."

"Oh, yeah. Without a doubt," Stacey agreed.

Stepping onto the platform, Travis looked amused and annoyed at the same time. He folded his arms over his chest and cocked his head. "Aren't you supposed to be helping Peggy with the inventory?"

"Yeah, but Stacey needed training, and the supply caravan isn't back yet so Jenni couldn't help her. . . ." Katie rolled her eyes. "Okay, okay. I'm just sick of being cooped up and not doing anything."

Travis kissed her brow. "Yeah, but you're pregnant, and after that bad cough you had, Charlotte told you to take it easy. You should pay attention to our resident nurse."

"Shooting zombies really isn't taxing," Katie insisted. "Anyway, I need to feel I'm doing something."

"Inventory is doing something," Travis insisted. "Plus it keeps you inside and warm until you're back to full fighting form."

Katie tried not to look as peeved as she felt. Her husband was damn annoying when he was being overprotective, but she really couldn't blame him. This was their first child, and the world had been turned upside down. Medicine was scarce and their food supply was limited. The processed food that made up the survivors' diet wasn't exactly rich in nutrients. There were plans for vegetable gardens that hopefully would have a good yield and generate healthier meals.

"You better not try to keep me off sentry duty when I'm feeling one hundred percent. I don't like being coddled." Katie gave him a grumpy glare, then let herself lean into him.

Travis briefly cuddled her. "You're so cold. You don't need to relapse. Please get in where it's warm."

Stacey smirked as she fiddled with the crossbow, pretending not to listen.

"Fine. You win. But you better let me know when the caravan gets back. They're running late and I'm starting to worry."

"Will do," Travis promised.

Katie waved to Stacey, then climbed down the stairs. She hoped Jenni and the others would be back soon. The sky was low and threatening, a sure sign that bad weather was on the way. She hurried into the hotel and out of the cold wind that moaned like the undead zombies in the world beyond the walls.

## CHAPTER TWO

## 1.

### *Battle of the Undead*

Her nickname wasn't Loca for nothing, Jenni thought as she slipped her gun out of her belt, flipped off the safety, and began to systematically shoot zombies. Gouts of decaying gore exploded out of their rotting heads.

"Jenni!" Behind her, Ed sounded pissed.

The zombies were so intent on their feast, they didn't even look up as she approached. The stench of fresh death combined with the reek of decay, and Jenni tried hard not to gag. The zombies were tearing at one another frantically, ripping away tattered clothes and rotting flesh as they tried to get to the living. Their moans were a terrible rumble.

Curtis slid into her peripheral view, firing his weapon. Jogging, Felix passed Jenni, using two pistols on the undead. Katarina had taken up a sniper's position and was picking off any zombie that got too close to the people huddled on top of the van. As one managed to snag the foot of someone on the roof, Katarina's shot severed the zombie's hand.

As Jenni drew closer, she could clearly see the zombies huddled over their victim, stuffing muscle and skin into their mouths with feverish delight. Dead, gray flesh was peeling off their bones, and their clothes were tatters. Many were missing limbs. A few had odd objects sticking out of their bodies, such as knives, pieces of furniture, tree limbs, and in one case, an umbrella.

Jenni felt her throat tighten as a small child-zombie staggered into view. It was gripping part of a bloody rib in one hand while trying to fight off much larger zombies. Jenni put a bullet through the little one's forehead.

"Reloading," she said, and Curtis moved in front of her to provide cover.

The old clip slid out with ease and she tucked it quickly into her jeans pocket before slamming a new one home. Looking up, she saw that their situation had taken a nasty turn.

The zombies were heading up the hill toward the people from the convoy.

"Keep the line," Ed barked.

Forming two lines that stretched over the width of the road, Jenni and her companions advanced on the undead. The first line unleashed on the zombies, then dropped back to reload while the second group took over. Then the second group dropped back and the first group went forward again. The walking dead jerked and tumbled in a bizarre dance as they were gunned down, bullets ripping through their mottled features and punching out the backs of their skulls.

"Nearly got them all now," Ed called out.

"Watch out! Watch out! They're coming out of the trees!" a deep voice thundered from atop the van just as Jenni was reloading again. "Running zombies!"

Six runners sprinted out of the tall, dry grass and naked trees lining the road toward the humans. Their freshly killed bodies glistened with blood in the cold sunlight. Gaping wounds, terrible and grotesque, decorated their torsos and throats, but their limbs were still intact and they moved swiftly. The group from the fort concentrated on taking down the runners; the slow zombies were a lot less dangerous than these fast ones.

"Don't panic! Don't panic!" Ed shouted, but people did anyway. Runners were so swift, it was hard to hit them with a kill shot. The lines shattered. Jenni yanked her ax off her back as her pistol clicked empty. She had no time to reload and shoved the gun into her belt before gripping the ax handle tightly with both hands.

"More runners!" someone was shouting.

Runners were now coming up off the side of the road. Men, women, children, their faces snarled into hungry expressions. The gunfire was rapid now. People were firing and reloading as fast as they could.

Jenni met the first runner as Curtis ducked out of the way to reload. She swung the ax as hard as she could; the blade struck deep into the thing's neck. It scrabbled at her, its fingers skidding along the leather of her jacket. She shoved it back with one foot, jerking the ax out of its flesh. Blood spewed over her as she slashed at it a second time, beheading it. The head rolled away as the body fell.

Another zombie was almost on her—a woman, her frizzy blond hair matted with blood. Her face was partially torn from her skull, and her throat was nothing but strips of flesh and spine. Jenni pivoted, bringing her elbow up firmly into the zombie's chin. The creature was screaming and the impact of Jenni's blow rammed her jaw up hard enough to clip off the tip of her tongue with her own bloody teeth. Shoving the dead woman away, Jenni got a little distance between them, then neatly decapitated the zombie with a single swing of her ax.

"Help! Help!" Curtis sounded terrified.

Jenni spun. He was on the ground, one arm lifted defensively. A zombie had his forearm in its teeth and was shaking its head wildly, trying to bite through the thick leather of Curtis's jacket. Jenni slammed the ax blade down onto its head, splitting open its skull. It fell, lifeless. Curtis scrambled to his feet.

Chaos surrounded Jenni, but the zombies were dying. She saw them falling under machetes, spears, and bullets. Nearby, she saw one of the fort people struggling to get a runner off his back as the creature gnawed at the back of his neck. Blood rained around the man's terrified face as he screamed.

"Dammit! They got Bob!" Jenni yelled.

The words had barely left her lips when two shots roared out, killing both the runner and Bob.

Something brushed Jenni's shoulder and she twisted around, ax ready to strike, but it was only Felix. He'd tripped over a body. Recovering, he fired into the face of a slower, more-decayed zombie grabbing at him. The runners were down, their blood making the road slick. The rest of the zombies were shambling toward the fort people and tripping over the remains of their former companions.

Felix kicked the feet out from under a zombie and shot it point-blank in the face. "I hate these things."

Feeling the heat of battle in her veins, Jenni marched toward the slower zombies, ax poised. Felix fell in beside her on one side and Ed on the other, and together they destroyed the stumbling creatures.

"We're done," Ed said.

Jenni looked up from the zombie she had just dispatched. A bit of its nose and brain stuck to the ax blade. The fighters congratulated one another on the swift victory and started cleaning off their blades and reloading their guns. Meanwhile, Ed and Curtis were checking everyone for bites before allowing them to return to the vehicles.

A bite was lethal. There was no cure. Whatever was carried in the saliva of the zombies always turned their victims if the brain remained intact. But bite victims didn't always die and come back. Sometimes people merely turned and attacked. No one knew why.

The road was littered with the dead. Jenni took a few deep breaths and instantly regretted it due to the stench. All of a sudden, Jenni felt her heart beating hard in her chest and became aware of her uneven breathing. Her arms ached from wielding her ax. During the fighting, she had felt nothing but the exhilaration of killing. Now she hurt all over.

"Anyone bit?" Ed's voice was hard. Glowering at the people milling around him, he made a point of cocking his shotgun. "I said, is anyone bit? Look yourselves over."

Jenni directed her attention to the van. The people they had saved were an older couple dressed in clothing native to India; two small children with the biggest, darkest eyes she had ever seen; a huge man with dark hair, a deep tan, and unruly muttonchops; and an older white woman dressed in a flowing skirt and blouse.

"You okay?"

"No one is bit up here," the big man replied. He was heavily muscled and looked like a wrestler.

The gore around the van was making Jenni's stomach heave. The man she saw fall from the roof had been consumed down to the bone. His skull gleamed under strips of flesh. She was drawing near when she saw his jaws open and close.

"That's fucked up," Felix said in a trembling voice just before he shot it.

"Its brain was intact," Jenni sighed. Her stomach roiled. Felix rubbed her back, and she closed her eyes and regained her composure.

"Let's get you guys down," she said.

When the huge guy jumped down from the van, he slipped on the blood and guts but caught himself. "Damn. Messy. Poor Jacob."

Jenni reached up for one of the kids, but the little girl shied away, hiding her face in the folds of the older woman's sari.

"Jenni, are you bit?"

She glanced at Curtis, shaking her head.

"I need to check. Fort rules, you know."

Sighing, Jenni lowered her hands and stepped away from the van. Holding out her arms, legs spread, she let Curtis check her. He even looked behind her ears. With a curt nod, he moved on to Felix.

Jenni lifted up her arms again to help the children off the van. This time, the grandmother whispered a few words to the little girl and scooted her to the edge. As Jenni's hands settled on the child's waist, she looked up into the enormous black eyes fearfully gazing at her. "It's okay," Jenni promised.

"Jenni, her hand," Felix said, his voice ragged.

Her eyes fell from the girl's face to the small hand clutching the thick leather of Jenni's jacket. Blood was seeping from a wound just below the little finger. A chunk of flesh was missing.

"No," Jenni gasped.

Looking up, she saw the little girl's dark eyes growing dimmer. Beneath her hands, she felt the tiny heartbeat growing fainter.

"Jenni!" Felix gasped.

"What is it?" the big guy asked, alarmed.

Jenni saw the spark of life fade out of the girl's eyes. With a scream of anger and fear, she threw the child away from her.

The little one hit the ground and rolled.

Her family cried out angrily in their own language.

The girl sprang to her feet, twisted around, and snarled.

## 2.
### The Biker from Hell

Rune had been on the road for a long time and was eager for a much-needed rest. The big Harley under him roared with power as it raged over the weed-infested road. He adjusted his goggles and tucked his long white braid into the collar of his leather jacket.

The darkened sky and barren hills were not welcoming. He had a bad feeling the day was going to get worse fast. He was on his way to meet up with his old buddy Dale and a bunch of people who had escaped from a rescue center outside Waco. Since the zombie rising, Rune had been on the road nearly nonstop. He had been past the rescue center twice before. The first time, it seemed safe enough, with barely any zombies stumbling around in town. But the last time, he was nearly dragged off his bike by a throng of zombies. A few grenades tossed into the crowd had cleared his way, and his helmet and leathers kept him safe from hungry mouths and grasping gnarled hands. It had been a fluke that he saw the spray-painted map and message, GOING TO THE FORT, on a billboard outside of town. Rune already knew where the fort was located, thanks to an unfortunate meeting with some bandits a few months back. The bandits had been targeting the fort. Rune hoped the place was still standing.

Rune never stayed long in any of the survivor encampments he came across. He didn't like trusting his safety to others. Most of the survivors had very little food or weapons and were just waiting for rescue. They didn't like it when he told them that they were damn fools. No one was coming to save them.

In a field next to the winding road, a herd of cows sauntered slowly toward shelter as the wind grew colder. It smelled like an ice storm, and Rune hoped to God in Heaven the fort was still there and that he'd be able to grab a cot for the night.

The Harley roared up a hill, and Rune quickly braked when he spotted a bunch of vehicles parked on the road. Sliding his Glock out of its holster, he weaved through the tangle of big vehicles. As the bike came out the other side, he saw a group of people milling around the remains of some pretty rancid zombies, and beyond them, a van with a few people on top.

A young man with blond hair and a worried expression looked toward him, surprise filling his features. "Hey, you!"

"Hey, yourself," Rune answered grumpily.

"Hey! You! Slow down! Who are you?" the young man persisted, jogging to keep up.

As Rune neared the van, a young woman suddenly hurled a little girl across the road just in front of his bike. He skidded to a stop, one foot planted firmly on the bloodied asphalt.

The child jumped to its feet, whirled around, and let out the terrifying screech of the walking dead. The little zombie hurtled across the road, heading straight for the startled humans. They raised their weapons but Rune was faster. His Glock barked. The bullet ripped into the side of the kid's head, blowing a pretty good-sized hole in it. The girl crashed to the ground.

As the gunshot echoed in the distance, the surviving humans all stared down at the small, sad figure. One by one, their gazes shifted to the new arrival.

"Name's Rune. Just passing through," he said.

"Good to see you, you son of a bitch," a gruff, familiar voice called out.

His gaze was drawn to the van, where an older woman with waist-length hair was being helped down by a big bear of a man who was none other than his buddy Dale.

"I'll be damned!" Rune said. "What the hell happened at the rescue center?"

"Got overrun when some people decided to try to get supplies from the grocery store and brought a whole mess of zombies down on us. The doors didn't hold," Dale answered as he helped the Indian couple down.

"Okay, people. Let's get back to the fort!" an older, grizzled man called out. "First we'll check you for bites and if you're clean, you can come with us."

The pretty woman with the black hair—the one who had thrown the child—was standing a few feet away, her head down. She was staring at the little girl's corpse. The Indian woman howled in agony as she was led away by a woman with red hair. Her husband looked stricken, but was mute as he carried the other small child with him. Rune wanted to feel for them, but he had seen too much to indulge in compassion. It was a fucked-up world, and fucked-up things happened in it.

The witchy older woman—Rune remembered she was named Maddie Goode—covered the child's body with her shawl. An older man took her arm and escorted her toward the bus.

"Good to see you, Rune," she said as she walked past his bike.

"And you, Maddie," he answered.

Dale lumbered over to him. "Heading for the fort?"

"Yeah. Need to find a place to crash before the storm hits." He shook Dale's hand firmly, their leather gloves creaking.

"You're going to the fort?" It was the gorgeous woman who spoke. He hadn't even realized she was eavesdropping.

Rune felt a little flutter in his belly as he eyed her. Her pale skin was splattered with blood, the ax in her hand still dripping. "Yeah."

"Can I ride with you?"

"Sure."

The woman slid the ax into the sheath on her back and climbed behind him onto the bike. Her fingers gripped his leather jacket. In his mirrors, he noted that she was still staring at the little girl.

"See you at the fort," Dale said, clapping him on the shoulder and winking before striding away to the waiting vehicles.

"Hold on," Rune said to the woman, glancing at her over his shoulder.

She didn't answer. The young man who had yelled at Rune earlier grabbed the kid by her ankle and dragged her shawl-covered body off the road. Finally, the woman looked away.

Rune gunned the engine and headed for the fort, leaving the convoy behind. He was strangely entranced by the silent creature behind him. She was beautiful. Her eyes were large and haunted, but the set of her jaw told him she was a fighter. He wanted to say something to her, but he observed that she was in her own head, dealing with her own shit.

As they rode, the woman let down her long hair and closed her eyes as the wind streamed through it. The tension around her jaw alleviated a bit and Rune tried hard not to keep looking at her in his mirrors. He felt her slowly relaxing and was pretty sure the ride was doing her some good.

The trip to Ashley Oaks was uneventful. He was impressed by the high walls surrounding the old hotel, newspaper building, and city hall. He was even more impressed with the gated entry. As he drove through, he looked up to see sentries on the walls watching with interest.

Behind him, the pretty creature smeared in blood was silent. He could almost believe she was a ghost, but he had seen enough of those to know she was flesh and blood. It was tough being a medium when the world was full of the dead, but he was slowly getting used to it.

The final gate opened and the bike roared into a busy paddock. The woman pointed, and he directed the rumbling bike over to an empty parking spot. She slid off the bike and patted his shoulder lightly.

"Thanks, dude. I needed that."

"No prob. Name's Rune," he said, extending his hand to her.

"Jenni," she answered, shaking it briefly. With her dark hair shifting around her blood-spattered face, she looked fierce. "Also known as La Loca."

"Loca is good," Rune said, giving her a rakish grin.

"Sometimes," she answered, winking and walking off.

He watched as she headed over to where people were cleaning spears, machetes, hatchets, and other weapons. A small, newly constructed building had steam rising out of it, and Rune guessed that was where returning citizens cleaned off the zombie gore. Halfway there, Jenni leaped onto the back of a tall, lean, Hispanic cowboy. With a grin, the cowboy carried her over to the others.

Rune sighed. Of course a fine woman like that was taken.

"Okay. Who the hell are you? And what's in the bag?" It was the old codger that reminded him of his deceased father. He probably only had ten years on Rune's forty-eight, but seemed older.

"Rune." He opened the bag to reveal the grenades. "And a whole lot of hurt."

"Mind leaving that in the weapon storage?"

"As long as I can reclaim it later, old-timer," Rune answered, handing over the bag.

The man chuckled. "Name's Ed. Welcome to the fort."

"Just staying until the storm blows over. Then I gotta move on."

"You sure?"

"Gotta keep moving," Rune answered. He discerned the ghosts around him, faint shimmering things. "Gotta keep ahead of the dead."

Ed looked at him strangely.

"There ain't no rest for the wicked, man," Rune joked. Or for mediums, he thought. Ghosts were everywhere, just like zombies.

"You can't escape the dead in this world," Ed finally said. "You're welcome to stay if you like."

"Thanks, man. I'll think about it." Rune shifted on his feet. "Like I said, we'll see how it goes." The man who could see the dead looked around, studying the fort, seeing the flickering of spirits all around him. "We'll see how it goes."

# 3.
## *Promises and Shadows*

Juan grimaced at the stink coming off the woman he loved. She was hanging on his back, covered in drying blood and gore, and reeked of death. In the first days, when they'd been under siege, he'd become used to the stench of the dead. It was strange how humans could acclimate to things like that. But once the dead throngs were cleared out and clean, fresh breezes filled the fort, and the smell of the dead was again sharp and repellent to him.

"You ruined my jacket, Loca," he grumbled, trudging toward the cleanup area.

"It's ugly anyway," she assured him. "Besides, I'm tired. Spoil me."

"As if I have a choice," Juan drawled, grinning and grimacing at the same time. "What did you do this time to get so messy?"

"Up close and personal decapitations of the zombie kind. I went whacky-whacky with my trusty ax."

"You're supposed to shoot them before they get too close." He felt his stomach clench at the thought of her fighting in close quarters with the ravenous dead.

"Yeah, well, sometimes runners see it differently."

"Shit!"

"Fresh and fast." Jenni sighed, laying her head against his shoulder.

He tried hard not to be angry with her. She had a tendency to act first, think later, and her rabid hatred of the undead often spurred her to insane acts of heroics. "I just wish you wouldn't take so many chances," he said at last.

"Well, a girl's gotta do what a girl's gotta do. Zombies need to be killed or they munch on us." Her voice was soft, almost petulant. "Besides, it works, doesn't it? Zombies die. I come home to you."

"I just worry."

"I'm not going to die without a fight," Jenni vowed.

"I don't want you to die."

"I'm not gonna!"

"Says the *loca*."

They reached the fenced-in area where the weapons were being cleaned and where Charlotte, the fort's nurse, was tending to the wounded. Her chin-length brown hair was pulled back from her round face with a pink headband that matched the nursing scrubs under her heavy coat.

Everyone knew a bite was deadly, but twice people had hidden their injuries and turned after entering the paddock. Nerit had implemented additional measures to keep the fort safe. Now, two armed guards stood watch as Charlotte finished bandaging a newcomer. A holstered pistol on the nurse's hip was an extra precaution.

Juan plopped Jenni onto a lawn chair and stared down at her, amazed again at her bloody appearance. "Seriously, you couldn't shoot them in the head before they reached you?"

"Well, I was trying, but they were kinda fast. And then it just got all crazy." A dark and frightening emotion briefly shadowed her countenance.

With a sigh, Juan slouched in his chair next to her, taking off his cowboy hat. There were moments when it was clear that Jenni was overwhelmed with grief, but he had learned she did not want his comfort at those times. His beloved rarely spoke of her past as an abused trophy wife and mother. Occasionally a snippet or two of information would leak out, but never on purpose. It was always worse when she saw something out in the deadlands that reminded her of her children.

Jenni flipped her hair over one shoulder and stared at him. He had a feeling she knew he was holding his tongue.

"What?" he finally said.

"A kid got bit. The new guy on the bike had to kill her. I saw the light go out of her eyes. I saw the hunger come into them." His eyebrows flew up. "I've never seen that before," Jenni continued. "I saw her life vanish, like a curtain falling. Then—*bam!*— hungry zombie." She pulled the ax off her back and tossed it onto the ground.

"Fucking scary, huh?"

Jenni slumped down in the chair. "It sucked." Jenni thought for a long moment, swinging her legs back and forth. "I don't want that to happen to me. I don't want you or anyone else to see the light go out in my eyes and the crazy, hungry, zombie look come into them."

"Jenni, that's not gonna—"

"You can't say that!" Jenni pointed at him, her voice vehement. "You cannot say that! You don't know. None of us know. Bob died today. I'm sure he didn't go out there thinking he was gonna bite it."

"Okay, okay. You're right," Juan said, hands raised in a placating gesture. "None of us can know. You just gotta be extra careful when you go out there."

"I want a bullet right here—" Jenni pointed to her forehead. "—if it ever goes down that way. I want it fast. I don't want to be one of those things, not even for a second."

Juan stared into her dark, luminous eyes, tinged with the madness that made him love her more than he thought possible. The idea of her not being next to him made his throat tighten with emotion. He didn't know what to say, though she seemed to be waiting for words to soothe her. At last, he managed to say, "Okay," his voice cracking slightly.

With a satisfied nod, Jenni curled up in her chair. She looked so small and so delicate, the blood splatter and the reek couldn't keep Juan away. He grabbed her arm and tugged her onto his lap. Holding her close, he nuzzled her cheek. Her body melded to his and she made a small, happy sound that made him smile.

# · CHAPTER THREE ·

## 1.
### *The Boring Things in Life*

Katie found the hotel's ground floor packed with weary workers, just off shift, making their way to their rooms. Tucking her hands into her jacket, she pondered if she should look for Jenni outside, or wait for her near the elevators in the lobby. Her friend usually headed upstairs for a nap after missions.

"Got Muslims now," Curtis said, joining Katie. He nodded toward an older man and woman dressed in traditional Indian garb being checked into the hotel by Ken.

"They may be Hindu," Katie answered.

"Still heathens," Curtis said, shaking his head. "Don't know if we should be taking in heathens."

Katie frowned at the younger man. "Really?" Her voice dripped with displeasure.

"We're a God-fearing group, Katie. Bringing in other kinds is gonna cause trouble." Curtis's boyish face flushed with emotion. "It's rough enough keeping things going as it is."

"Curtis, people are people. We can't start picking and choosing who we allow into the fort or we'll end up like the Vigilante, offing people because we don't approve of them."

A look of horror washed over the police officer's face. "I—I didn't mean . . ."

Feeling bad for the harshness in her tone, Katie patted his arm. "It's okay, Curtis. I know you're concerned."

He covered her hand with his own and squeezed, guiltily blushing.

Jenni stomped up to them. Her hair was damp, her face was flushed, and she was dressed in a big bathrobe. She had a bag slung over one shoulder and was holding her boots in one hand. "Charlotte declared my clothes totaled. I really liked those jeans!"

"Oh, c'mon. It's a great excuse to go dig a new pair out of the inventory."

"Yeah, but still . . . they looked good! I looked five pounds smaller in them!"

"You *are* five pounds smaller," Katie stated. Everyone was slimmer lately. The kitchen crew was careful not to waste food by preparing too much. Though people ate their fill at each meal, they usually did not overeat, and hard work was whittling the fat off beer bellies and strengthening muscles.

Curtis made his escape as they spoke and Katie let him go. The poor guy was so easily flustered. She felt bad for the young man. He had been the youngest member of the Ashley Oaks police force and its only survivor.

"I got stuff to show you!" Jenni patted the bag at her side. "I had fun out there until . . ." She waved her hand as if to wipe away the pain that lingered in her eyes.

Katie knew better than to push Jenni. "When do I get to see?"

"Let's go to your room. This is top secret stuff."

"I will not be treated in this manner!" A sharp female voice sliced through the drone of conversation. A big candle hurtled through the air into a painting, sending it to the ground with a loud crash.

Blanche Mann, a former beauty queen and the richest woman in town before the zombie rising, was the meanest bitch most of them had encountered. She stomped into the lobby, her high heels clicking loudly in the sudden silence. A beautiful woman dressed in a skintight red dress, she appeared younger than her thirty-plus years. She was carrying another candle, which she flung at the woman retreating in front of her.

Monica, one of Juan's cousins, ducked as the candle flew over her head. "You said you would give me the Imitrex if I cleaned your hotel room!"

"You call that cleaning? That's the most piss-poor job I have ever seen! You didn't even polish my shoes or iron Steven's clothes!" Blanche was in a fury.

"Look, bitch, give me the Imitrex! We need it for the clinic!" Monica wasn't about to be intimidated. "I did what you asked. Pay up!"

"I caught you going through my things, trying to find something to steal!"

"I was looking for the pills you promised me!"

"You're a thief and I'm going to report you to Bill!"

"Call him, you stupid bitch, and I'll tell him how you scammed me!" Monica kicked a chair with agitation.

"You stupid, thieving spic!"

That was enough for Katie. She stepped between Blanche and Monica. "Calm down, Blanche. We'll get this sorted out. You don't need to resort to insults."

"Get out of my face!" Blanche shoved Katie with both hands.

Chaos erupted. Jenni swooped in like an avenging angel, shouting in Spanish. Katie wasn't hurt by Blanche's push, but everyone seemed to think she should sit down, much to her chagrin.

It wasn't until Bill showed up that any semblance of order returned to the hotel lobby. The tall man with the kind face, sandy hair, freckles, and dwindling gut waded into the ruckus. He got everyone separated and ordered those not involved to move on.

"Okay, now what is going on?" Bill's voice was calm, but held a hint of authority.

"She said if I cleaned her pigpen of a room, she would give me some Imitrex. Manny is having really bad migraines and we ran out of the right meds a few weeks ago," Monica explained, her voice edged with anger. "None of the supply teams have found any."

"She did a shitty job and tried to steal from me! And then she had the nerve to lip off." Blanche glowered at Bill. "Besides, I don't have any Imitrex here. She'll have to go to my house to get it."

"You didn't say that!" Monica lunged forward. Katie caught Monica's arm before she could hit Blanche. Jenni grabbed Monica's other arm and whispered something to her in Spanish.

Bill sighed with exasperation. "Blanche, we already took everything we could use out of your house."

"How dare you!"

"Steven knew all about it," Bill said. "And you know that we take what we need for the fort wherever we find it."

"You stole from my home!"

"Fuck this." Monica pulled away from Katie and Jenni, shaking her head. "I can't believe I was fooled by that bitch." She stalked off.

Curtis fell in behind Monica, resting a comforting hand on her shoulder as they left the lobby.

Bill shifted his belt up over his belly. "Blanche, you best just let this drop. You did Monica wrong and everyone knows it. You ain't making many friends around here."

"I don't need friends. I should have left to meet up with my sister when the damn zombies showed up. I'd be with her, safe and sound, and not dealing with you disgusting hicks." Blanche whirled around on her high heels and stalked off.

Bill let out a long, slow breath.

"She's such a whore," Jenni said.

"Her sister is even worse. I had the displeasure of meeting her more than once." Katie rubbed her forehead, feeling very tired.

"I didn't vote for her," Jenni grumbled. "Of course, I never voted, but . . ." She shrugged.

Bill hooked his thumbs over his belt. "Blanche is not used to being ordinary folk and taking care of her own needs."

"I'm not going to feel bad for her," Katie replied.

"Don't expect you to." Bill hooked his thumbs on his belt. "But we need to remember she's a very unhappy viper. She's gonna strike out at whoever is closest to her at any given moment."

"We should make a suggestion box for the Vigilante," Jenni murmured. "I got a name to shove into it."

"Jenni, behave." Katie hooked her fingers through her friend's and squeezed.

With a sigh, Jenni relaxed her stance and tugged Katie to her feet. "Let's get out of here." The two women headed for the elevators. "Poor Bill," Jenni said softly. "He has to deal with all the crazy shit."

"What isn't crazy nowadays?" Katie asked, arching a brow.

Jenni snorted. "True dat."


# 2.
## *Rough Spots*

The small bonfire sparked and dark smoke rose into the graying sky. As Nerit watched Charlotte burn the blood-soaked clothing taken from some of the returning fort members, the slim older woman couldn't help but think of Bob, lying out there somewhere. Proper burial was a thing of the past.

"One loss," Ed said beside her, as if reading her thoughts. "Seven more people to feed and care for."

"It never balances out," Nerit said, flipping her silver braid over one shoulder.

Nerit was indulging in another cigarette, grateful the salvage team had found more cartons. She wasn't picky about the brand. Cigarettes calmed her nerves and were her one small luxury in this life. She missed her husband—murdered by bandits—every day, and she couldn't think too long about his death without feeling tired and old.

"Lenore brought back a whole bunch of beauty supplies for Ken," Ed added after a few beats. "Seems silly to me."

"People need a few pleasures."

"I think they're gonna set up a beauty shop." Ed seemed perplexed by the notion.

"Honestly, I think that might help morale. Life isn't easy nowadays."

In the distance, cold rain fell in a gray curtain over the hills.

"My boys were hoping I'd ask you out," Ed said casually. Nerit choked on her smoke. Ed continued, "I told them that you're too much of a man for me. That you could probably kick my ass ten ways till Sunday."

Half-coughing, half-laughing, Nerit grinned. "Probably."

Ed crossed his arms over his chest and planted his feet slightly apart. "I ain't gonna ask you out, Nerit. I admire you something fierce and yer my friend. But knowing my boys, they'll be dropping hints like crazy, so I thought you should know."

"That's fine, Ed. I am flattered." Nerit smiled a little, trying not to think of Ralph and her own adult offspring. She hoped that her children and grandchildren were still alive in Israel.

"Storm's going to hit hard by the looks of those clouds. Better sound the alarm and get everything tied down."

"Agreed. Please take care of it," Nerit said.

"You got it." Ducking his head down against the strengthening wind, Ed rushed off.

Nerit continued to stare at the small fire after he left. Her hip and leg were throbbing, and she was afraid that if she moved, she'd fall. The people in the fort had elevated her to legendary status, and she would not disappoint them by appearing fragile.

A few minutes later, Travis joined her. He slid an arm around her and gave her a light hug. Despite her resolve to be a hard-ass, she rested her head on his shoulder for a few seconds. He reminded her so much of her eldest son at times, and it was nice to feel comforted.

"What's the status?" Travis asked.

"One dead. Six permanent new members. And one guy with a bag of grenades passing through," Nerit replied. "The salvage team managed to get into that gun store in Emorton without bringing the entire town down on them. So we should be set for at least six more months as long as we don't get hit too hard. More boxed and canned food. Two generators. Fuel. And beauty supplies."

Travis smirked. "Let me guess: Lenore?"

"Lenore asked and I said it was okay if it wouldn't endanger anyone."

Travis swept his hand over his dark curls. "It won't hurt to get a decent haircut, I suppose."

"Bob died," Nerit said after a long pause.

"I know." Travis's shoulders slumped. "I spoke with that new guy, Dale. They were in a rescue station outside of Waco that got overrun. Two vans full of people got away, but someone in the lead van must have been bit. It went off the road and then they were swarmed."

"That area is badly infested thanks to Hackleburg." Nerit rubbed her cold fingers together and settled her gaze on Travis's somber face. "I have a suggestion. We should take a break during the bad weather to get our bearings. We've been in overdrive, and I think people are worn out and cranky."

"I agree. We need to take stock and plan."

Nerit admired Travis. He was not a natural-born leader, but he was doing his best. "Having people's attention focused on specific goals may help shake them out of their malaise."

"Better than having a horde of zombies show up on our doorstep to get the old blood pumping," Travis joked.

"Well, this old blood is going in before the sleet gets here," Nerit said, patting his shoulder. She was relieved when her leg moved without much of a limp.

"See you later, Nerit," Travis said, giving her a fond smile.

"God willing," Nerit answered.

It wasn't until she was in her room, listening to her old dog snore in the corner, that she realized Travis had been holding her up, giving her hip a rest until she could move again. Collapsing into a chair, a book in hand, she chuckled.

Maybe Travis was a better leader than she had given him credit for.

Cracking her romance novel open, she began to read.

## 3.
### *Dangerous Times*

Katie stared down at the baby clothes strewn across her bed and felt her heart beat a little faster. Her hand settled against her slightly swollen belly as her gaze slid to Jenni's anxious face.

"I did good, didn't I?"

"Amazing." Katie gently touched a blue Onesies outfit and her heart beat even faster.

"I got blue, pink, and yellow. That way, we have it covered whether it's Jenni or Travis Jr." Jenni set a little pink bonnet on top of her head, beaming.

"Jenni, huh?"

"It's only natural for the baby to be named after her auntie." Jenni posed cutely. "Why wouldn't she be named after my fabulousness?"

Katie plucked the bonnet off Jenni's head and traced the delicate lace with one finger. "Oh, God." She sat on the edge of the bed and tried to calm her abruptly unsteady hands.

"Hey, you okay?" Jenni crawled over the bed to Katie's side.

"I think so. I felt overwhelmed there for a second." Katie forced herself to take another deep breath, embarrassed by the tears brimming in her eyes. "Maybe it's hormones."

"You're okay with having a baby, right?"

Katie was surprised by the question. "Of course! Travis and I wanted this." Jenni kept silent. She was obviously waiting for Katie to go on. "We're trying to build a life together. Besides, someone has to be the first to have a baby in this new world." It was good to hear her own words, to be reminded that this was her choice.

"Despite the zombies?" Jenni said in a soft, worried voice.

It was an awful testament to the devastation of the zombie plague, but there weren't infants or pregnant women in the fort. Katie bristled slightly. "Yes. I don't see them going away anytime soon, do you?"

"No . . ." Jenni sighed sadly.

"So what are we supposed to do? Stop trying to build a future because the dead decided we taste really damn good?"

"Hey, you don't have to defend yourself to me!"

Katie rose, clutching the bonnet in one hand. "Are you sure?" She hated the swell of anger filling her. She was happy about the baby. It made her feel closer to Travis than she had ever expected. Before the dead began to attack the living, she had never seen herself as a mother. Her old life had not allowed much room for it. But this life, full of so much grief and terror, was also full of hope. The fort was secure now. It was a place of safety and community.

"My baby died. My baby was eaten," Jenni said in a dull voice, staring at her hands. "I just don't want anything to happen to yours."

Katie swallowed hard. Jenni's words reflected her own fears. "I don't want anything to happen to anyone I love. Every time you go out there, I live in terror that you won't come back. But I can't ask you to stop doing what you need to do to help our fort survive. And I can't stop my life because of those fucking zombies."

Jenni finally directed her gaze at Katie's face. "My old life feels so far away. The first day, it seemed like the world was suddenly empty. But it feels fuller now. Like . . . like . . . it's coming back to life."

Katie wrapped her arms around Jenni. "That's because we didn't stop living."

Jenni snuggled into Katie's embrace. "I know. Hell, I think I kinda went apeshit crazy trying to feel alive those first few months."

At the memory of some of Jenni's more insane shenanigans, Katie had to smile. "Oh, yeah. Definitely."

"Fuck zombies."

"Fuck 'em," Katie agreed.

Jenni smiled and squeezed her. "I'll teach the baby to be *loca*. And it will do fine, kickin' zombie ass."

Kissing Jenni's cheek, Katie felt love for her friend fill her completely. It was almost overwhelming. "I know you'll always be looking out for me and the baby."

"You mean Baby Jenni."

Katie rolled her eyes.

Jenni flopped onto the bed laughing, scattering the baby clothes.

# · CHAPTER FOUR ·

## 1.
### *A Little Taste of the Old World*

Ken was in a fabulous mood. The air was filled with a combination of the harsh scents of bleach and hair dye and the fruity fragrances of shampoo and conditioner. His dark hair now had blond tips and his fingernails were carefully manicured. He felt more like himself than he had in ages.

The conference room that had been reluctantly turned over to him for his beauty salon was buzzing. Music played softly from a big, ancient boom box in the corner. Next to him, Lenore twisted Yolanda's hair into a tight French braid that wound around her head while Yolanda flipped through a year-old copy of a fashion magazine. They were both sassing Felix, who was trying to ignore them as he read a book. Felix was good-looking but, Ken had discovered after flirting with him, painfully straight. Ken had been down in the dumps about being single, but now that his beauty salon was up and running, he felt better. He was much happier doing hair than working on the construction site, and he knew he was helping raise people's spirits.

Now, nothing could dampen his mood, not even the sleet pinging against the curtained windows. If only Curtis would sit still so Ken could give him a decent haircut, all would be well.

"I think you took too much off the side," Curtis complained.

"No, I didn't. Sit still!"

He was having a horrible time trimming Curtis's hair. The

boy kept fidgeting. Curtis had wanted Lenore to do his hair, but she was halfway through a ten-hour marathon, sewing in Yolanda's new extensions. Finally the young police officer had agreed to let Ken work on him. Ken had considered poking at the guy's homophobia, but decided against it. He was working hard to make friends and find acceptance in the fort. Riling Curtis wouldn't do him any favors.

Curtis squirmed around in his chair. "You're taking too much—"

Ken grabbed Curtis's head firmly between his hands and aimed his gaze straight forward. "Stop moving."

Yolanda flipped through the magazine for the fourth time. "When are you going to get the stuff so I can get rid of these damn press-on nails? I need some decent nails, Lenore. I've glued these onto my nails so many times, they're wearing thin."

"Maybe next time. I can't grab beauty stuff unless the coast is clear or I'll get in trouble. Don't need no Vigilante tossing my fat ass over the wall." Lenore's nimble fingers kept braiding as she spoke. Ken marveled at her patience and stamina.

"Your ass is fine," Felix drawled from behind his book. There was a pause as everyone looked at him. Aware of their attention, he peered over the well-worn pages. "I meant that it's not fat. Not that it's—"

"You saying my ass ain't fine?" Lenore shot him a cross look, her fingers still braiding.

"I didn't mean that!" Felix sighed heavily.

"So it *is* fine?" Yolanda arched both her eyebrows, gazing at his reflection in the mirror in front of her.

Ken giggled.

"Don't answer them, Felix. They got you trapped," Curtis advised. "They're just being wicked."

"You have no idea how wicked I can get." Yolanda winked.

Ken was amazed at how red Curtis's scalp turned under the golden strands of hair. "You made him blush, Yolanda!"

"That isn't hard. Curtis is our sweetie, aren't you?"

Curtis blushed even more.

"He's always making sure everyone minds themselves and he is always supersweet and gets me coffee when I'm on duty in the communication center." Yolanda smiled affectionately at the young man.

"It's no big thing," he answered awkwardly.

"Maybe he's sweet on you," Ken teased.

"Nah, he's sweet on Monica," Yolanda answered.

Curtis darted out of the chair so fast, Ken almost stuck him with his scissors. "Hey!"

"I . . . um . . . I can't pay nothing and can't tip you. I feel bad about that—"

Ken was done trying to be diplomatic. His wicked streak grabbed his tongue and he said coyly, "Just gimme a kiss and we're even."

Blinking hard, Curtis stammered, retreating to the doorway. "I think . . . I'll . . ."

"I'm just teasing, Curtis!" Ken burst out laughing. "I wasn't done. Sit your ass back down."

Curtis ran his fingers over his hair, fussing with it a little. "It'll do. See you later." He dashed out of the room so fast, he nearly shoved Peggy back through the doorway. Mumbling an apology, he darted past her and vanished.

Peggy screwed up her face, frowning. "What is up with that boy?"

"I just teased him a little about Monica," Yolanda confessed.

"Oh, Lord. You didn't!" Peggy looked aghast.

"Oh, so there *is* dish here. Spill it!" Ken cleaned around the chair, sweeping up the bits of hair he had trimmed.

"I caught him consoling Monica in the communication center." Peggy paused for dramatic effect. "They were naked."

Ken almost dropped his broom. "No!"

"Oh, yeah. They were buck-ass naked and going at it. Well, actually, Curtis's pants were around his ankles, but they were doing the naked tango just fine." Peggy smirked as she took a seat in front of Ken.

"I will never sit in that chair again," Yolanda declared. "Curtis's naked pasty ass is too much for me to deal with."

Lenore murmured in agreement. Felix sighed loudly.

"Were you next?" Peggy asked, turning to Felix.

"I have nothing better to do, so you might as well go first." Felix cracked his book back open with dramatic flair that impressed even Ken.

"I just need a little trim and some fresh bangs." Peggy showed Ken her abundance of split ends.

"Okay, I suggest taking two inches off the bottom, skip the bangs, and do a little bit of layering in the front instead, and let me put a lighter color in."

"Honey, I ain't got a man to impress no more. Just chop it so it's easy to deal with."

Ken frowned at the back of Peggy's head. He wanted to make her stunning. The thought of a mere trim was too terrible to bear. He was sick of her perpetual ponytail.

"Hey, you got an opening for me? I need a serious shave and some of this hair whacked off." The voice was big and booming, yet strangely comforting and warm.

Everyone in the room looked toward the door. A stranger stood there, tall and muscular, with a shaggy beard and a magnificent head of dark curls. Ken thought he looked like a big ol' cuddly bear. He wanted the big man to cuddle him right up. He felt his jaw drop, but didn't care.

"Twinkle-toes is gonna trim my hair, but you can take a seat," Peggy answered.

"I'll check back in, then. I gotta go find some guy named Juan," the big man said.

"I can make time for you," Ken managed to squeak out.

"When you're done with me," Peggy ordered, giving Ken a dark look.

He ignored her and took a step toward the newcomer. "I'm Ken and I'm more than willing to help you fulfill your grooming needs."

"If that ain't a come-on, I don't know what is," Lenore snorted.

"Um-hmm," Yolanda agreed.

Ken flipped them both off.

The big guy chuckled. "It's all good. I'll just come back. Name's Dale. I'm glad to meet all of you."

"I'm Ken. The rest of these bitches are Peggy, Lenore, and Yolanda, and that's Felix."

"I'll be back, Ken. Thanks." The big guy flashed a wide grin, then left.

"You could have let him go first!" Ken wailed, whirling on Peggy.

"Oh, no way am I supporting your sinning ways. You practically threw yourself at that poor man." Peggy folded her arms, giving him a disdainful look.

"Ugh! I hate you." Ken pouted. "I'm chopping off your hair and dyeing it, you old bat!"

"Fine! But make it snappy!" Peggy smiled slowly. "Besides, he was kinda cute. Maybe I should look a little more presentable."

"I'm going to shave your head," Ken growled.

Peggy rolled her eyes. "You'd like to, but you won't. 'Cause then I could tell everyone you ruined my hair."

"Ugh! You're evil!" Ken frowned, snatching up his scissors. Soon he was consumed in his task, but still thinking of the big, brawny guy with the great voice.

Hopefully, he would come back soon. Smiling, Ken snipped away as ice continued to ping against the window.


## 2.
### *Making Demands*

Travis sighed the second he saw Steven Mann walking briskly down the hotel hallway toward him. This wasn't going to be pleasant. The sleet was coming down hard, but for an instant he contemplated ducking into it to escape the tall man heading for him. The thought of being pelted by sleet was enough to keep him inside. He was trapped.

"We need to talk," Steven began. The imposing man resembled a cowboy, from his Wrangler jeans to the Stetson on his blond head, but his keen blue eyes held the shrewd gaze of a successful businessman. Steven had conceded the mayoral election to Travis, but he was very vocal in his opposition to some of the fort's policies.

"Make it fast. I've got a lot to do," Travis answered, heading down the hall with Steven at his side.

"It's about the situation with Monica and Blanche. I'm not pleased with how it was handled by Bill."

"Blanche lied to Monica. It's that simple."

"It's been very difficult for Blanche to adapt. She's trying to fit in and she's just not doing too well."

Travis stopped and regarded Steven with raised eyebrows. "You're joking, right?"

Steven crossed his arms defensively over his chest. "What do you mean?"

"Blanche does not try to fit in at all. She yells at everyone all the time and is a right, royal bitch. She lied to Monica and accused her of stealing. She also shoved my pregnant wife. So do not tell me that Blanche is trying."

Brow puckering, Steven averted his eyes, obviously weighing his next words. "Okay. So maybe she's not trying, but this has been difficult for her. She was raised dirt poor, but her mama always treated her like a princess. When she married me, I made sure she got everything she deserved."

"Steven, why are you telling me all this? What do you want?"

Steven met Travis's gaze directly and said firmly, "Blanche hates it here. She wants the Hummer back and anything you guys took from our estate. She wants to go home."

"If you want to leave, we can give you a car, a few days of food, and a gun, but then you are on your own." Travis hated what he was saying, but this was the law of the new world. As mayor of the fort, it was his responsibility to keep its inhabitants as safe and healthy as possible. "As for the Hummer, it is now an important part of our defense."

"You have to return what you took." Steven's voice was hard and clipped.

"Steven, we salvaged your place months ago. All the food and whatever else we took went into the fort's stores. There's no way to know exactly what came from your place, and as for the food, it's probably been eaten by now." Travis set his hands on his hips and gazed steadily at Steven.

"Then give us sufficient rations to make up for what you took and return our vehicle."

"Why are you so insistent on the Hummer?"

"It's our property, Travis. I don't see room for argument here."

"Chances are, we give you the Hummer, you take off, and we'll find you two moaning outside our walls in a few days."

"Don't underestimate us, Travis. We're country born and bred. Give us supplies, weapons, and our vehicle, and we'll be fine."

"Blanche won't even clean her own damn room. Who's going to cook?"

"That brings me to my next request. I would like to hire guards and other staff. We have jewelry and other valuables to pay them with. If you return our resources, we can maintain our own home safely."

The tone of Steven's voice told Travis Steven was growing impatient. He was used to being able to push local officials around and did not like being rebuffed. "Those 'valuables' are worthless, now that the zombies have risen." Travis shook his head. "I can't believe you're letting Blanche talk you into this."

"Why won't you let us leave?" Steven glowered at Travis.

"You can leave whenever you want to, but you're going to have to take the deal we offer everyone who wants to go."

"We are not to be trifled with, Travis. We own this town."

Travis gripped Steven's arm tightly with one hand. "Steven, you're just a human being, like everyone else. Who you were before the zombies is over. I wish to God that you two would settle down and adapt.

"Look, I get that you are used to having a lot of clout in this town, but those days are gone. All of us need to carry our own damn weight and help each other. Do you get that? Do you understand that? We can't afford to be selfish anymore."

Steven wrenched his arm away and stood in silence.

"Steven, the old world is gone." Travis tried again.

"You know, everyone keeps talking about the old world being gone. But it's not," Steven said shortly. "It's just waiting for us to push back the dead. Then everything will go back to the way it was before. You'll go back to being the foreman of a construction site. You'll be working for me, not strutting around being the mayor of a bunch of scared folk." His voice was cold. "All these people you want us to be *friends* with will go back to their pathetic lives. You think everyone is equal, but people with power, like me, have that power because we worked hard to get it."

"Steven, your great-grandpa was smart enough to take advantage of the railroad when it came through these parts way back in the day. He put this town on the map. Hell, this town is named after your great-grandma. So maybe you should follow his example and join us in making this fort a success. Let that be your legacy."

"You don't get it, Travis. I love my wife. I want her to be happy and she is *not* happy. She wants our supplies and our Hummer. She wants an armed escort and some people to work the estate. I think she deserves those things. Being here is hard on her. And being a good, decent husband, I plan to do what she needs to make her safe and happy." Steven clearly was not about to back down from the argument.

Travis shook his head, frustrated at not being able to get through to the man. "I can't let you leave with any of the fort's resources, Steven, and that's all there is to it."

"You may think this is over, Travis, but it's not." Steven stared at Travis for a long, piercing second, then stomped off without another word.

Travis rubbed his very tired eyes. When he lowered his hand, he saw Bill lingering near the archway to the lobby. "What's up?"

"You can't make Steven be what he doesn't want to be."

"You heard that, huh?"

Bill nodded, his hands resting on his belt, which was cinched tighter than it had been when he and Travis had first met. Like most people in the fort, Bill had lost weight. He had been a very big man to start and was still far from skinny, but he looked healthier. "They ain't never been easy people. I've lived in this county all my life and they've always acted like gentry. They don't wanna be here, Travis, because this is what they've tried to avoid all their lives—being common folk."

Travis inclined his head, acknowledging this was probably true. "Do you want to give them a bunch of supplies, the Hummer, an armed escort, and maids?"

"Nope. But if they really want to go, we should let them. Give them a decent car. A week's-worth of supplies. Weapons and ammo." Bill lifted his shoulders. "Either they'll get their asses eaten or show up in a week or two, begging to come back." Bill's expression was somewhere between amusement and anger.

"That's pretty much what I told him, but . . ."

"Let him simmer down, then tell him again."

"Never gets easier, does it?"

"It will. One day."

"As long as that's not when we're all dead," Travis said with a weary grin.

"I was lookin' for ya to let ya know Calhoun's got some specs for some kinda flamethrower weapons for the walls. I can't make heads or tails of his scribbling, but I figured you, Eric, and Juan could let him know if it's doable."

"Mind rounding up the others?"

"Can do."

"Thanks." Travis headed for his office, which had once been the hotel manager's office. He was not surprised to see Peggy at the front desk, as she often was, trying to contact the outside world on what was left of the Internet. Travis noticed that she had a cute new hairdo. "Looking good, Peggy."

She smiled and handed him a bottle of Febreze. "Calhoun is looking for you. I think he was rolling in dog shit."

"This day just keeps getting better."

# 3.
## *Tangled Webs*

Calhoun skirted around the lobby and ducked down one of the lesser-used hallways, dimly aware of two people holding a whispered conversation behind a large potted plant a few feet away. The voices in the lobby were echoing and mingling with the ones in his head, making his brain hurt. Clutching his head, he envisioned the thoughts moving through his mind as long, colorful threads, twisting and looping. Sometimes they made a beautiful weave; other times they became a jumbled mess. When that happened, his head throbbed and the threads sang in wild voices, demanding his attention. Gripping the wall with one dirty, gnarled hand, he tried to find the strongest thread and grab on to it.

His eyes snapped open and he realized that the blond bitch and Ray, one of the salvage crew guys, were staring at him with disgust.

"Blanche Mann, you're the Whore of Babylon!" He saw it so clearly. Her twisted soul was a black miasma of goo around her neck, and evil was vivid in her red eyes. With a cry of despair, he twirled around and ran from her.

He barely heard Blanche tell Ray, "Get the old fucker."

There was evil in the halls of the fort, and Calhoun had to rectify the situation. He raced through the lobby, wailing, his battered boots beating on the marble floor. Out of the fuzzy world around him, a face came sharply into focus and he skittered to a standstill.

"What's up, Calhoun?" Travis asked. "You're looking for me?"

Calhoun felt his mind slip off the thread he was clutching and swirl into the maze of brightly colored thoughts. It took him a few seconds to latch on to a new thread.

"Flamethrowers!" Calhoun snapped his fingers. "Flamethrowers to protect the gate! That's it!"

"You seemed a little upset there."

Calhoun tapped his chin as he tried to remember what had terrified him. "Don't rightly know why."

"Okay . . . are you ready to talk about the flamethrowers?" Travis regarded him worriedly.

Fumbling with his jacket, Calhoun managed to find the pocket he had made by sewing a kerchief into the lining. After tugging out his notebook, he waved it in front of Travis. "Got it right here! Let's go!"

The big red thread in his mind—full of fire and the destruction of messed-up clones—throbbed, pouring out all the information he needed to guide the young ones to prepare proper defenses.

For thirty minutes, he was vividly sane.

## 4.
### The Scales

It was nearly dinnertime when Travis finally made it up to the room he shared with his wife. He, Bill, and Juan had been walking the walls, compiling a list of supplies the fort would need to expand. Now Travis felt half-frozen and was dying for a hot shower. When he pushed open the door, he saw Katie sitting in a chair near the window, holding a baby blanket and staring wistfully toward the hills.

"Katie?"

"Do you ever wonder when it happened? When the tide turned against us?" Her voice was soft, thoughtful, and melodic.

"What do you mean?" He tugged off his heavy jacket, glad that the heater in the room was working.

"There had to be a moment when the future of the world was balanced between the living and the dead. And then the scales tipped in favor of the dead."

"I guess there was," Travis answered, unsure where the conversation was heading.

"I was just sitting here, wondering about our baby, and then it hit me. What if our baby never knows what it's like to live freely, outside these walls? And then it occurred to me that there must have been one deciding moment in all of this."

Travis knelt beside her chair and took her hand in his, rubbing her fingers lightly. "Maybe, but we'll never know what it was or when it happened. This insanity had to have started before what we call the first day. Jenni's no-good husband was bitten the day before. And there was that weird plane crash in Chicago and riots all over the place."

"Why didn't the government tell us?" Katie's green eyes were so big and beautiful with tears sparkling in them.

"Maybe they thought it was under control. Or maybe they didn't understand how fast it was spreading."

"Do you think they wanted it to happen?"

Travis pondered this, then shrugged. "I may sound like Calhoun, but maybe they wanted something to happen so they could seize full control of the people, but whatever it was went too far. I don't know. But if there was a moment when the scales tipped, then maybe that will happen again, and next time, those scales will tip in our favor."

Katie leaned her forehead against his and stroked his cheek lightly. "I want to believe you."

"Then do," Travis whispered, and kissed her gently.

"I'm sorry I'm being so hormonal," Katie said.

"Nah. You're just saying what everyone else is thinking. We're all in a weird funk. We need to focus on more positive things. Like the fact we're alive. We're inside fortified walls. We have food and supplies. We have each other." Travis felt better as he spoke. It was so easy to forget the good things when the days were cold, gray, and full of unexpected dangers.

"You're right," Katie said after a beat. "And maybe we will have a chance to reclaim the world. For our sake . . . and our children's."

Travis was in awe that his baby was growing inside her. It seemed like magic. His little family meant the world to him, and he would never have had it if not for the zombies.

"I'm going to take a hot shower, then take my favorite girl out to dinner."

"Oh, that sounds good! Where are we going?" Her bright smile washed away the shadows that had been haunting her expression.

"Well, there is this quaint little place downstairs that has some of the best food around."

"Sounds amazing! I can't wait!" Katie wiped the last of her tears away with the baby blanket.

"And then maybe we'll get crazy and go watch a movie. I hear there's a Burt Reynolds double feature tonight."

"Oh, wow! I don't think I can stand the excitement!"

Travis grinned, stood, and pulled her out of the chair. Holding her close, he kissed her tenderly on the lips. "You know you want to hear Curtis heckling the Bandit for his lawbreaking ways."

Katie snuggled up against him. "We're just one big crazy family, aren't we?"

Laying his cheek on her blond hair, Travis smiled. "Yeah. We are. And it will be okay."

Katie sighed. Her body relaxed against his, and Travis was glad that she trusted him so completely. He vowed that he would never let her down.

# 5.
## *No Peace for the Living or Dead*

Rune sauntered into the dining room and peered around cautiously. To his eyes, the hotel was full of shimmering patches of light and shadow. He was relieved to see that the dining room was full of living people lining up at the buffet. Rune smelled chili and his stomach rumbled.

The soft whisper of a ghost glided past him. He didn't acknowledge it.

"Hey, Rune!" Maddie and Dale waved at him from the food line. He nodded his head in greeting and joined the end of the line. He wasn't too surprised when Maddie and Dale dropped back to stand with him. Maddie's long hair was braided down her back and she'd found a flowing skirt and comfortable sweater to wear. Rune wasn't sure how old she was, but he thought she was pretty, wrinkles and all. Dale's curly hair was pulled back in a ponytail and his sideburns were razor sharp.

"How are you, Rune?"

"Good, Maddie. Slept all day. I was tuckered out."

"Figured you were taking the time to rest up. I volunteered to help with the garden."

"Good for you!"

"They actually got a beauty salon here. Can you imagine?" Dale stroked his smooth chin, appearing floored by the idea. "I was pretty fuckin' amazed."

An old man in a creaky manual wheelchair glided past them to the front of the line. His arms were covered in tattoos and he looked older than God.

"Maybe I'll drop by and get my hair properly done. Wind is hell on it after a while." Rune folded his arms over his chest.

"You could stay here, you know. It's so dangerous out there." Maddie shook her head sadly.

"Can't. Once they figure out I can see them, they won't stop badgering me," Rune said in a low tone.

"Oh, right!" Maddie's eyes widened. "Are they here now?"

"A few. Over by the bar," Rune said, not looking in that direction.

"Has to be a bitch having what you got with this shit going down," Dale growled. "Damn, man. Glad I ain't you."

"We all got our crosses to bear." Rune shifted on his feet, uncomfortable with the topic.

A tall, homely redhead walked into the dining room. Right behind her was the perfectly formed ghost of an old, angry woman. Rune caught himself before he shivered.

"More, huh?" Dale wondered.

"Whole world is full of the dead. Nobody, living or dead, ain't getting no peace," Rune answered.

A boy in his teens entered the dining room, closely followed by a big German shepherd. Rune felt a strong premonition hit him and spoke almost without thinking. "That boy is special. Real special. People gotta take care of him."

"You're weirding me out again." Dale winked. "All creepy and mysterious. That's Rune."

"I'm sure he doesn't have the name Rune for nothing," Maddie said, laying her delicate hand on Rune's arm. A huge moonstone glimmered on her finger, and Rune covered it gently with his hand. He smiled, feeling the energy in the gem.

"My mama nicknamed me that. When I was three, I got a bunch of rocks from the backyard and tried to draw on them with a marker. My mom caught me at it and started calling me Rune. We got old Nordic blood in our veins."

The dining room was filling with the energy of the living.

A black woman and a young man whose hair was tipped with gold walked by, both carrying trays heaped with steaming food. The man gave Dale a flirtatious smile and waved with his fingers. Dale waved back.

"That boy is sweet on you," Maddie teased.

"Yeah, but I'm sweet on her." Dale pointed across the room at a grumpy-looking woman.

"That's the city secretary, Peggy," Maddie told him.

"She's hot."

Rune nodded his head approvingly. "She ain't much to look at, but she's got that vibe."

"That hellcat vibe." Dale grinned.

An older black man stepped into the center of the dining room and loudly cleared his throat. He was impressively tall, with a lean face and gentle, dark eyes. "Before we start dinner, I would like to say grace and thank God for the blessings we have received. We have new people among us and a bounty of new supplies in our storeroom. I would also like to commend the soul of our brother Bob into the hands of God. Let us thank God for our lives and our safe home."

There was a round of amens. The man, obviously some kind of reverend, launched into a prayer that boomed through the room. Rune lowered his gaze, staring at the tips of his motorcycle boots. They were pretty battered and probably needed new soles. As the prayer continued, he began to glance around the room. He saw the pretty woman who had hitched a ride with him hugging the tall teenager while the German shepherd leaned against her legs. Behind her stood the tall Mexican in the cowboy hat. His eyes were closed and he had one arm around the shoulders of an older Hispanic woman. The leader of the fort and his pregnant wife were last in line. They were hugging each other. Her head rested on his shoulder and they looked so happy, it made Rune's heart twist in his chest.

The community around him felt unified and strong. He yearned to be a part of it. Moments like these reminded him that he was not alone and that there was a bit of hope left in the world.

The reverend finished, and people shouted "Amen!"

Then someone said, "Let's tear this chili up!"

Laughter filled the room and Rune smiled to himself. Maybe staying around a bit longer would be a good thing.

# · CHAPTER FIVE ·

## 1.
### *Rebuilding the World*

"Stupid freakin' Texas weather," Jenni huffed. In just a few days, the ice and snow had disappeared. It was eighty degrees outside.

She tossed a bag of garbage out the second-floor window of the old movie theater into the Dumpster below. She was clad in jeans and a tank top; sweat was pouring down her face.

Katie swept more debris into a dustpan, then dumped that into another garbage bag. Her hair was pinned on top of her head; blond tendrils poked out at odd angles. Her face was flushed and she was breathing hard.

Leaning out the window, Jenni craned her neck to look over the new wall that cut off the street just after the theater and stretched across to a clothing store on the other side. They'd reclaimed an additional block in every direction, and their world suddenly seemed much larger.

Restoring the theater was part of that expansion. Rosie, Juan's mother, put on social events every week to help the fort's inhabitants blow off steam and relax. But the town council knew that people needed something more, something that was closer to the world they had once lived in. The movie theater was a mess, having been closed for several years, but the cleanup team was making steady progress. Jenni and Katie, working through the upstairs, had almost died laughing when they found a hidden stash of porn magazines and fetish gear.

"Can you imagine the guy who owned this place hanging out here with all this stuff while his wife thinks he's working?" Jenni grinned at Katie as she shoved more fetish magazines into the trash.

Katie blew a strand of hair out of her eyes. "I hate to think what he might have been up to."

Jenni dangled some shackles and handcuffs in front of Katie before tossing them into a box for Bill to look at. "And who with?" She threw another bag out the window, then looked across the street. "Hey, Charlotte is still up on the roof watching the zombies."

Katie tied off the bag. "Really?"

"Yeah." Jenni adjusted her gloves, then grabbed another bag and hurled it out the window. "I wonder why."

"Scientific research, maybe." Katie leaned down to pick up a full, black trash bag.

Jenni lifted the big bag, shooing Katie away. "You're pregnant. No heavy lifting."

"Yes, Mom," Katie said, rolling her eyes. "I swear, between you and Travis, I don't know how I'm allowed out of bed. I'm five months pregnant, not nine!"

"You're just lucky we don't use those shackles on you!"

Jenni peered out the window to see the Reverend Thomas pulling up to the front of the building, riding on a power mower that was towing a large cart. The cart was loaded with sack lunches. He honked the horn several times, summoning the workers to eat. Jenni liked the reverend, who was always smiling and laughing. Plus, his sermons were actually good and not at all boring.

"People need God in times like these," he had said to her at lunch one day. "We're in the new Eden . . . just got more than that damn snake to deal with."

Jenni yanked off her gloves and tossed them onto a pile of cleaning supplies. "Let's go eat. I'm hungry and need a break."

"Sounds good," Katie answered. "I'm pretty tired, too." She

pulled off her own gloves, dropped them, and rubbed her baby bump absently.

Together, they trudged down the narrow staircase. The fading black-and-white pictures of old movie stars were strangely comforting. Jenni blew a kiss at Cary Grant as they passed his photo. She tried not to think about the fact that Hollywood was gone. Maybe someday humanity would get control of the world again and new movies would fill old theaters.

Outside, the workers gathered around the cart were cleaning their faces and hands with damp hand towels from a basket offered around by Reverend Thomas. Jenni grabbed one and pressed the moist cloth to her cheeks. It felt amazingly refreshing. After cleaning her face, she ran it over her hands and arms.

Katie tossed her used one into a second basket. "That felt good, but I'm dying for a shower."

Jenni draped her towel over the back of Katie's neck to cool her down. As she grabbed a lunch bag, the reverend said, "Make sure to drink plenty of water." He pointed at the cooler packed with water bottles. Sitting on the curb next to Katie, Jenni bit eagerly into her peanut butter-and-jelly sandwich.

"Oh God, when did water start tasting so good!" Katie gulped down a bottle.

"When peanut butter and jelly started tasting like manna from heaven," Jenni answered. "Everything just tastes better nowadays."

Three of the new people were part of the cleaning crew. They wandered over, looking for open spaces on the curb, and sat down. One was an older woman who reminded Jenni of the artist types who used to inhabit South Austin. She had a funky way of putting clothes together. With her were Rune and a massive guy with prominent muttonchops and unruly dark hair.

"Hey, Rune!" Jenni said, smiling.

"Hey, Jenni. Good to see ya."

"I thought you'd be long gone by now."

"Figured I might stay a short spell. Decided to help out some."

He bit into his sandwich. Watching, Jenni wondered if she'd be able to get another ride on his bike.

Charlotte sat down on Katie's other side and started to eat, looking thoughtful. Though she was a rather plain woman with mousy hair, her brown eyes were keen and her gaze intense.

"How are you today, Charlotte?" the reverend asked as he handed out more water bottles.

"Figuring it out, Padre," Charlotte replied.

"Figuring what out?" Jenni asked, watching Katie pull the crusts off her sandwich.

"The zombies. I've been studying them," Charlotte said while chewing. "I'm trying to figure out how they tick. We have to know our enemy, after all."

"True words for a sad time," the reverend agreed.

Jenni snagged Katie's crusts. "Just kill 'em."

"Notice anything helpful?" Rune asked, ignoring Jenni.

"Well," Charlotte hesitated, appearing to gather her thoughts, "I'm planning to put it all into a report for the council, but I can tell you the basics. The regular process of decay is just not happening. There's no rigor mortis, the bodies don't bloat as the gases inside build up, et cetera. I really expected there to be some exploding zombies. But not one."

"Exploding zombies?" Jenni blinked. "That would be awesome."

"Normally, gases build up in the body as it decays. Sometimes those gases burst out of the body. But not now. It's just slow . . . really slow . . . rot."

"And they're fast at the beginning. That is so breaking the rules," Jenni said with disappointment, then let out a huge burp.

Rune handed her another bottle of water. "I noticed that they kinda beat themselves ragged. They don't stay fast for long."

"Yes, they do slow down fairly quickly. The truly dangerous ones are new ones that are just turned, especially if they've only suffered minor damage to their limbs. That's why so many people died in the first days." Charlotte sighed sadly. "But you're right,

Rune. They don't feel pain, so they just go and go, breaking themselves apart as they try to get to prey. The older they get, the slower they are."

"Ha! I knew Romero had it right!" Jenni grinned with satisfaction, then saw that Katie rolled her eyes. "He *did*. C'mon. They're so much slower. Everyone knows it. And it's so much easier to kill them now."

"They seem fascinated by our Christmas lights. They will stare at the lights all night and only move when they are turned off." Charlotte opened a bag of chips. "I seriously don't think we should take them down."

"Really?" Katie lifted an eyebrow.

"Really."

The reverend whistled. "We could string up a lot of lights."

"Well, if there are enough humans in view, the zombies wake up, but otherwise they'll just stare. The fireworks on New Year's Eve had them completely stone-cold still."

"Why haven't you said anything about this to anyone?" Katie demanded, an edge to her voice.

"I wanted to make sure." Charlotte popped a chip in her mouth. "They don't really seem to think. I have a feeling their behavior is all instinct. On the first day of the rising, I saw a zombie try to mow the lawn at the school. I don't think it was a reasoning action, just something the man had done often in his life, maybe some sort of residual memory. A few days later, he was banging on the windows like the rest of them."

"So you think in the first few days after they change, they might have a memory of how to do things?" Jenni frowned, not really wanting to know what this meant.

"Not real memories, Jenni. I think their brains fire off in weird ways as they transform into zombies." Charlotte stuffed more chips in her mouth, then flicked crumbs from her fingers. "That could explain why some of the zombies figured out how to climb over the truck barricade in the beginning days of the fort."

"So, if a zombie tries to open a door on the day it turns, that doesn't mean it will be able to do that the next day?" Katie looked at Jenni. "Remember that girl who tried to open the truck door?"

"Oh, right!" The image was seared into Jenni's mind. She had been terrified that the zombies were actually thinking, and she knew others shared that fear.

Charlotte nodded her head. "I theorize that as their brains are dying or transforming or whatever, residual memory pathways may allow some zombies to perform mundane human actions. But after a day or two, those neural pathways die and we're left with a creature that has only an instinct to feed."

"So they're stupid," Jenni said with satisfaction. She drank more water, washing away the salty taste of the chips. Jenni liked Charlotte's theories. They made things nice and simple, just the way Jenni liked it.

"Do you think there's anything human left inside them? A spark of who they were?" Maddie asked.

From the expression on Katie's face, Jenni understood that this was a question her friend had been afraid to ask. She took Katie's hand, saying, "Of course not! Right, Charlotte? They're just dead things!"

"I haven't seen any of them acting remotely like they have any memory of who they were. Have any of you? Most of us saw friends and family turn. All they want to do is eat us," the nurse said calmly.

Reverend Thomas was nodding in agreement. "I haven't seen any of my old friends or family, my former parishioners, look at me as anything other than food," he said. "Their souls have moved on. They're free of this world."

"Actually, Reverend, not to correct you or nothing, but they haven't really moved on." Rune swept his gaze over the group as he spoke. "They're all around us, all the time. They're caught between the world of the living and the dead. All the dead rising like that, the natural order of things got screwed up."

"Kinda like that line in *Dawn of the Dead* when they said when there was no more room in hell, the dead walk the earth?"

Jenni felt Katie's hand trembling and knew she was thinking of Lydia. Jenni refused to think that her kids were not in heaven. Knowing they were there and safe was her salvation when the nightmares came.

"I don't know, rightly. All I know is that I see 'em. I see ghosts. Everywhere I go," Rune said, looking at them a bit defiantly.

The reverend seeemed to be about to respond, then apparently reconsidered and looked away.

Rune continued, "I think they're all waiting for something to happen so they can move on. Something big. I don't know what it is, but they're trapped here until it gets done." The biker took a big bite of his sandwich as if to say that he was finished talking for now.

There was an awkward silence as people pondered what had been said.

"I don't know if it's a consolation or not, thinking of our loved ones being ghosts while their dead bodies try to eat us," Katie said at last, "but it makes me feel a little bit better, knowing they're not trapped in those rotting husks."

"At least we know the zombies are stupid," Jenni said. "Stupid is good, right?"

"And they're afraid of fire. We've seen that when they are near our controlled burns," Charlotte added, as if the conversation had not taken a strange, metaphysical turn. "Another primitive fear of the reptilian brain."

Jenni envisioned bonfires all around the fort. The image appealed to her.

Katie said, "So, we have ideas for a few really weird new weapons." Her voice didn't sound shaky anymore.

"Christmas lights," the reverend said as a smile spread slowly across his face.

"Fireworks," Charlotte added. "And bonfires."

Jenni grinned. "Damn. That's just kinda funny."

## · CHAPTER SIX ·

### 1.
### *Jenni's World*

"And what do you do if you see a zombie?" Nerit asked in a loud, clear voice.

"Poke it in the eye!"

The chorus of children's voices drew Jenni's attention. She was helping lay cement blocks on top of the old wall, but now she stopped working to watch the fort's young inhabitants at their lessons. A group of twenty youngsters, ages four to ten, were gathered around Nerit and a dummy made of burlap bags, stuffed and painted to resemble a zombie. The students all held make-shift spears.

"And then what do you do?"

"Shake it hard!"

"Why?"

"To make brain soup!" a little wiseass called out.

The students broke into wild peals of laughter.

Nerit smiled, then ordered, "Okay, line up! Let's make zombie brain soup!"

Next to Jenni, Juan was also watching the children. He was sweating hard and his long, curly hair had slipped free from his ponytail.

"This looks so wrong." Jenni sighed.

"They need to know how to fight back."

A young boy, about Mikey's age, walked up to the zombie effigy. He rammed his spear into its cloth eye, then shook it violently.

The children laughed again.

Jenni sighed and spread more wet cement with a trowel. "I wish Mikey hadn't turned back to defend me."

"He didn't know, babe," Juan said softly.

"I know, but . . . you would have liked him," Jenni fought back a few tears and lifted the heavy cement block into place. She rarely spoke to Juan about her kids. It was hard, not being able to share that part of her life with him.

Juan kissed her cheek, causing the makeshift platform they were on to wobble a little. "I know, Loca. I know."

"If I could find a way to give you kids . . ."

"Loca, it's okay. Really. I got you. I got Jason, even though he kinda hates me, and I got Jack. And Jack is pretty badass. Kinda furry, but a great kid."

Jenni laughed despite the lump in her throat.

"Besides, Katie and Travis are probably going to be spitting out kids left and right and we'll end up with babysitting duty." He wiped the sweat from his brow, managing to get a little cement in his hair. "If we're together, I'm happy. Even if you are batshit crazy."

Jenni laughed and leaned against him. "Crazy is good."

"And fun in bed." Juan grinned at her lovingly.

"You're such a pervert," she teased, and kissed his salty cheek.

"And you like it." He pressed a kiss to her forehead, then moved to lay another brick.

Below, Nerit called, "Okay, who's next?"

A slew of young voices shouted, "Me!"

"Hey, Mom." Jason slid into the seat next to Jenni at lunch. He peered out at her from beneath his long bangs, seeming a little embarrassed.

"Hey, baby, what's up?" Jenni shoved a couple of home-style fries dunked in mustard into her mouth and ignored Jack, who was staring at her longingly from beside Jason's chair.

"I was wondering if I could have Michelle over to watch movies tonight?" the teenager whispered, blushing.

"You gonna make out?" Jenni asked.

"Mom!"

Jenni grinned. "Are you?"

Ducking his head, Jason muttered, "Maybe."

She playfully nudged him with her elbow. "My sexy son is getting some loving!"

"Mom!"

"Okay, okay. Have your make-out session, but she has to leave by eleven."

"You're so embarrassing, Mom," Jason grumbled.

"Hey, I gotta tease you when I can. You're always off with Roger and your crew, making crazy, mad-scientist, zombie-killing stuff." Jenni hugged him and pressed little kisses to his cheek. He squirmed with discomfort.

"Mom, stop! I get it, I get it, okay? And thanks, Mom," her stepson said, wiggling away. Moving quickly, he kissed her on the cheek, then stood up.

Jack laid a paw on her knee and looked at her plaintively. With a sigh, Jenni gave the dog her dessert—two peanut butter cookies. Graced with a doggy grin, she smiled back.

The boy and his dog jogged away, leaving her to finish her fries alone.

Jenni loved the aftermath of lovemaking with Juan. They lounged around in bed, naked and tired, smiling every time each caught the other's eye. She painted her toenails, one foot propped on his knee as he read a book. It had gotten cold after the sun set; Juan was nearly buried in blankets, but Jenni was nude to the waist, enjoying the feel of cool air on her skin.

"Blanche was giving me shit again today," Jenni said after a while.

"Yeah? Why?" Juan didn't look away from his book.

"She was on cleanup crew tonight and ragged on me for not putting my dinner plate into the proper bin. Then she ragged on me for a bunch of other stuff. I stopped listening after the 'stupid spic' comment."

Juan frowned. "I thought she just called me that."

"No, no. She calls everyone she thinks is Mexican a spic, including Rashi, the Indian guy we picked up the other day."

"That woman is such a bitch," Juan growled. Putting down his book, he rubbed Jenni's leg gently as she finished polishing her toenails.

"Too much drama," Jenni said, studying her handiwork.

Juan shook his head. "Gotta wonder if they realize what is really going on."

Flopping back on the pillows piled behind her, Jenni giggled. "Stupid people doing stupid things, huh?"

Juan flipped the book off the bed. "Yeah, but we're keeping them alive for some reason."

"Entertainment value!"

"Are your nails dry yet?"

"Um . . . no . . . why?"

Juan looked at her toes, then said, "Eh, fuck it. You can redo them." He leaned over and kissed her passionately, pulling her close.

With a grin, Jenni wrapped her arms around him and returned his kiss.

## 2.
### *Time to Go*

Rune awoke with a start. His hand automatically gripped his Glock as he sat up. He pointed the gun at the figure at the end of the bed as his brain sputtered into wakefulness. The room was dark, but the figure at the end of the bed was a black blot. He nearly expected the thing to moan and reach for him, then realized he wasn't facing a zombie.

Flipping on the lamp next to the bed stand, he stared blearily at the transparent man standing at the foot of his bed. Setting down the Glock, Rune groaned.

"What do you want, buddy?"

The man opened and closed his mouth, forming silent words.

"You need to speak up. I can't hear you."

The room grew steadily colder as the apparition tried again. It managed one word—"*Help*"—before it lost its tentative hold on the physical world and vanished.

Rune shivered as the room became even colder. His breath turned to mist. Standing, he grabbed up his jeans and boots, whispering, "Damnit." He felt the faint touch of the dead as they gathered around him and the room filled with shimmers of light and shadow.

"I can't help you," he said flatly. "I can't hear you. Stop pestering me." Frustration and despair filled him as he pulled on his leather vest and reached for his heavy jacket. The delicate touches of the dead fluttered over his skin. He tried to brush them away, but they were persistent.

The room was freezing. Cussing under his breath, he grabbed his motorcycle bags and headed for the door. Though he'd lived in the fort for two weeks, he'd never unpacked, always anticipating this moment.

Striding down the hall, he saw the air rippling around him. A few of the spirits had enough energy to actually grab his arms, but he shrugged them off.

In the beginning, Rune tried to help the ghosts he encountered, but over time, he'd realized that the spirits were simply trapped. Nothing he said helped to guide them on.

Ignoring the elevator, he headed down the stairs, his bootheels sounding like thunder rolling through the stairwell. The spirits were losing energy quickly, burning themselves out trying to hold on to him. He hit the bottom floor and cut across the lobby, heading for the construction site.

The exit was through what had once been a janitor's closet. Stepping in, he was startled when a hand grabbed his arm in an iron grip and a powerful stench wafted over him. Rune yanked himself away, his Glock already in his hand. Then he heard Calhoun mutter, "I can't remember!"

"What the hell, Calhoun?" Rune shoved the gun back into its holster, frowning. The old codger had given him a dreadful fright.

"I can't remember something important. And it's eatin' at me! I saw something long ago and then again a few days ago, and I know it was important." He faltered, obviously struggling to grasp a flitting thought. Abruptly he spun, shoved open the door, and plunged into the night, perhaps chasing that thought. Rune sighed and followed.

He didn't feel the ghosts right then, but he knew they would catch up. His only real hope for peace of mind was to head out into the deadlands and keep moving.

He was sorry to have to leave the fort. He would miss Maddie and Dale. He'd allowed himself the luxury of becoming a part of the community, maybe even deceived himself into believing he could stay for longer than a few days.

Ahead of him, Calhoun suddenly came to a stop and turned around. "The Whore of Babylon. That was what it was about. She was in cahoots with the one that ended up killed in a woman's dress. She . . . she . . ." His eyes rolled wildly in their sockets. Clutching his hands to his face, Calhoun wailed. "I can't remember. It was . . . it was . . ."

In the distance a rooster crowed, long and loud.

"Chickens!" Calhoun shouted. "Chickens!"

The old guy was sure in a tizzy. It must suck to have lost your mind. Rune climbed the stairs that led over the wall and into the fort's huge parking area. He'd left his bike in one of the old newspaper garages. The door was closed but not locked; he easily rolled it up and headed inside. As he pulled the tarp off his bike, he heard a noise behind him that sounded like a door opening. He turned to look, but didn't see anything through the gloom.

"Hello?" Rune called, not too loudly.

There was no response. Rune shook his head. The damn ghosts had him spooked. Securing his bags to the bike, he took a deep breath. It was time to move on again and that was all there was to it. No time for regrets or fear. He rolled the motorcycle into the open air and realized that the sun had begun to peek over the horizon.

Ed was standing nearby, holding a steaming cup of coffee. "Heading out, Rune?" the older man asked.

"Yeah," Rune replied, then pulled down the garage door.

Behind Ed, Rune saw the sentries changing shift on the wall. The early-morning crew was arriving to work on reinforcing the perimeter. The smell of Ed's coffee was incredibly tempting, but Rune didn't dare go back to the hotel for anything. That would only stir up the ghosts. It was hard enough to stay focused when he had to deal with only one or two. He couldn't handle a whole town's worth.

"Well, you're welcome to stay," Ed said.

"Yeah. I know that. But it's time to move on. I can't stay long in one place. My nature don't permit it." Rune felt that was explanation enough.

"I understand. I'll get the gates opened for ya." Ed moved off.

Rune straddled his bike and tugged on his thick leather gloves. His braid of white hair fell over one shoulder as he zipped up his leather jacket.

Glancing toward Ed, Rune saw a woman with short brown hair smiling at him. Her long black dress flowed down to shiny black boots, and ornate jewelry decorated her neck and wrists.

"Damn," he whispered, mesmerized by the spirit.

"We'll let you know when it's time to head back," she said in a clear, melodic voice.

Rune slowly bobbed his head. "Okay."

"You'll be needed later," she continued. "Stay alive."

"I'll keep that in mind."

Rune noticed that the edges of her figure were slightly blurred, but he was sure he could touch her if he tried. Ed stepped through the apparition and she vanished.

"Here's your grenades. Hope they serve you well," Ed said, handing over the bag he'd retrieved from the storage locker, where Rune had deposited the grenades when he first arrived at the fort. "Once the first gate is open and you're in the lock, we'll close it up, then open the second. Area's clear of zombies, but be careful. Got Katarina, the sniper, watching out for ya."

"Gotcha. And thanks, man." Rune clasped hands with the older man after slinging the bag of grenades over his shoulder, then gunned the motorcycle to life. He had to be rattled to almost forget his grenades.

"You're always welcome to come back."

"I think I will, someday. Kinda . . . got that feeling." He settled his goggles into place as Ed nodded.

Minutes later, Rune's bike roared down the abandoned streets of Ashley Oaks, away from the fort and into the deadlands.

## 3.
### The Whore of Babylon

For once, Jenni dreamed blissful dreams. Secure in Juan's arms, she slept deeply and did not awaken once. Juan left early in the morning. Jenni roused briefly when he kissed her before sliding out of bed, then fell back to sleep. When the alarm clock went off two hours later, she groggily climbed out of bed.

After a long hot shower, she pulled on her work clothes and fussed with her hair, thinking how wonderful the night had been. She felt amazingly happy and at peace.

There was a knock on the door. Jenni flung it open, expecting to see Katie. Instead, it was Blanche.

"Oh, hi, bitch." Jenni couldn't imagine what the woman wanted. Blanche smiled. "Hi, spic," she answered.

Jenni never saw what hit her, but suddenly the world swirled into darkness and she felt herself falling.

"Let's make this quick," Blanche ordered the two heavily muscled men standing behind her.

"You got it, babe." Ray gestured and the younger man, Brewster Johnson, moved to help him. Together, the men half carried, half dragged Jenni down the hall. Blanche walked swiftly behind them, still gripping the kid-sized baseball bat she had used to club Jenni.

Blanche felt that she had timed Jenni's abduction perfectly. Most of the rednecks were already performing their daily chores. She didn't anticipate any interference. She was finally going to be free of the fort and the idiots running it. She had given in to her husband long enough, and it was time to take matters into her own hands. She never should have let Steven talk her into coming to the fort in the first place, and now she wasn't going to stay there a moment longer than she had to.

"Ray, go get Juan," she told the big man with the thick wavy hair. Inwardly she smiled, remembering how good he was in bed. Better than her idiot husband. "Meet us in the garage near my Hummer."

"Gotcha," he said, and hurried off.

Brewster slung Jenni over one meaty shoulder as they hurried to the service elevator. "Why do we need Jenni?"

Brewster was young and handsome with his fair hair and skin, but a bit slow. "Because her spic boyfriend controls the gate and if we have her with us, he'll do what we say."

"Then we let her go?" Brewster asked.

"Of course not. I need someone to clean the mansion," Blanche said with a smirk.

The service elevator opened and Blanche stepped in. Brewster followed with Jenni. Blanche straightened her blouse under her leather coat and admired her snakeskin boots. Soon she would have all her lovely things back.

Including her car . . .

Blanche still couldn't believe Steven had let the fort leaders ransack their home and take her precious Hummer. She had fully expected him to become the fort's new mayor. Instead, he had bowed out of the race.

Her husband was an idiot if he believed she would forgive him for that.

The doors snapped open on a back hallway and Blanche strode quickly to a reinforced door that opened into the small enclosed courtyard between the hotel and the newspaper building. Brewster huffed behind her. After opening the door to the newspaper building, Blanche marched confidently past the old offices, now used for storage. She slipped through the doorway to the loading dock.

The bay doors were closed and the trucks were swathed in shadow, but she could still make out her beautiful Hummer, looking out of place among the shitkicker vehicles the fort's vermin had collected. The keys for the trucks, buses, and cars hung on hooks on a wooden board; Blanche grabbed the ones for the Hummer. Ray had hidden her overnight bag in the garage last night, and now she pulled it out from behind a pile of tires before heading for her car. A second car was hidden in town packed with items her men had sneaked over the wall for her. Blanche smiled, thinking how smoothly everything had gone. Her fingers briefly touched the gun in her pocket that Ray had salvaged for her. He'd even found a silencer for it.

As they reached the Hummer, Blanche reminded Brewster, "Don't say anything. I'll do all the talking. Set her down, but hold her upright."

He shifted Jenni off his shoulder and held her, drooping but as upright as possible, against his side.

"Blanche?" Ah, her lame duck husband had arrived on schedule.

"Over here, Steven."

She rather enjoyed the startled expression on his face when he rounded a truck and saw her and her companions.

"What are you doing?" His voice was sharp yet uncertain.

"What you don't have the balls to do," she answered with her prize-winning smile.

A brief flash of sunlight announced Juan and Ray as they opened the side door to the paddock. Juan jogged toward them, a frantic expression on his face. Blanche wondered what Ray had told him to get him to the garage.

"What happened? Is Jenni okay?" Juan asked as he drew near. "How did she get hurt?"

Blanche calmly drew her gun from her pocket and pressed the muzzle of the silencer against the underside of Jenni's chin.

Juan stopped cold. "What the fuck?"

"Blanche!" Steven shouted.

"We're leaving and you're opening the gate," Blanche said coolly.

Juan glared at Ray, who backed away, ducking his head. "What the hell is going on, Ray? What did you do to Jenni?"

"We're leaving, Juan," the big man said.

"You could have just asked," Juan said furiously.

"Oh, like you would have let us have the Hummer," Blanche said mockingly.

"This is about your fucking car?" Juan said, looking startled and angry at the same time.

"Blanche, this is uncalled for," Steven sputtered.

Blanche rolled her eyes. "What's been uncalled for is my fucking treatment around here. I am taking my car and my men, and I'm going home."

Steven appeared speechless as his eyes darted toward Juan.

"Fine, but you can't take Jenni!" Juan stepped forward, his hands clenched at his sides.

"I'll give her back to you once we're through the gate. I'll leave her on a corner somewhere in town and you can hurry your tight little ass to get her before the zombies do," Blanche lied.

"Blanche, you can't do this! I'll get us home safe if you give me enough time," Steven protested.

"I'm tired of waiting on you, Steven. Or maybe I'm just tired of you." Blanche dismissed him with a look of disdain.

"So you *were* fucking Shane," Steven growled.

"At least he was good enough to stock up our mansion with supplies and promise to help me get the hell out of here."

"Bitch," Juan spat. "I should have known you were up to no good."

Blanche flipped the safety off. "I have no problem shooting your girlfriend if you don't do as I say."

"You shoot her, I won't let you out." Juan's gaze was riveted on Jenni and the gun.

"Someone else will let us out because then *you'll* be our hostage," Blanche assured him.

"I don't believe you," Juan retorted. "You don't have it in you."

Blanche's eyes flicked toward her husband. Without another word, she shot him twice in the chest. She felt some satisfaction as his expression of surprise gave way to horror before he collapsed.

"Damn," Ray said.

"You're fucking crazy!" Juan shouted.

"Start the car," Blanche told Ray, tossing him the keys.

Having easily snagged the keys, Ray headed for the Hummer. Blanche noticed that Brewster was eyeing Ray uneasily, though he kept a firm grip on Jenni. Blanche wondered if she had read him wrong. She sighed. Stupid Shane. He would have had her back.

Juan held out his hands in a pleading gesture. "Just take me, okay? Let her go. I'll tell them to open the gate, and you can drop me off somewhere. Okay?"

Blanche considered it. It was a tempting offer, but she really needed a maid. "Now, Juan, don't go messing up my plans."

"Give me Jenni and then just go. Just go." She heard the strain in his voice and saw the fear in his eyes.

Anger flooded through her and she felt the heat of it rise in her face. He made it sound so easy, but she had a point to make. She hadn't clawed her way out of the trailer park to be forced to mop, dust, wash dishes, and put up with stupid people. She was a shining daughter of the fucking state of Texas. How dare they treat her like shit?

"Blanche, put the gun down and let Jenni go," Juan urged her, misreading her hesitation.

"Don't tell me what to do!" She swung the gun around and fired.

Juan staggered backwards and collapsed.

"Why the fuck did you do that?" Brewster demanded.

As Blanche turned to tell him to shut the fuck up, Jenni's head snapped back, breaking Brewster's nose with a loud *thwack*. Blood sprayed everywhere. Blanche twisted away, trying to avoid it. Brewster grunted and went down with a thud.

Something hard smashed into Blanche's temple and sent her spinning. The revolver flew from her hand as she landed, gasping, on the disgusting, oily floor. Before she could gather herself, she was flipped onto her back. She saw a blur of long black hair and a pale face; then something hit her cheekbone with a sickening thud. Pain splintered her thoughts as she was pummeled into senselessness.

## 4.
### *Winter Sky*

Jenni staggered away from Blanche, her hands and face splattered with red. Her hands were a mess—bruised and battered, her knuckles torn open—but she didn't care. The bitch was down and not moving. She grabbed Blanche's fancy gun and pivoted to take aim at Ray and Brewster. Brewster was unconscious, but Ray was nowhere to be seen.

Jenni cried, tears hot on her face. She stumbled forward, her head throbbing. She'd regained consciousness moments before

Blanche killed Steven, but had stayed limp, waiting for the right moment to try to escape. She'd been watching through her hair, with her eyes barely open, when Juan was shot. As anger swept through her, she had moved almost without thinking.

Juan lay slumped against the wall. Blood was pooling around his body, and his shirt was soaked. Falling to her knees, she whispered to him in Spanish.

Juan was barely able to lift his head. "Loca," he gasped.

Jenni put the gun down and quickly removed her sweater, then pressed the wadded-up garment against the wound in the left side of Juan's chest, trying to stanch the bleeding. She didn't want to think about the damage the bullet might have done.

"*Tengo frio,*" Juan whispered.

"We'll get you somewhere warm," Jenni promised.

"I . . . always . . . thought . . . she was . . . a stupid . . . bitch . . . ," Juan muttered.

"Shh . . . don't worry about her. I beat the hell out of her. No one messes with my man."

"That's . . . my . . . Loca. . . ." Juan smiled, but he looked too pale and his eyes were growing glassy.

His blood was hot against her flesh, soaking into the sweater. Jenni didn't want to leave him, but she needed help. "Baby, forgive me. This might hurt."

There were moments that would be forever seared into the memories of those who lived and worked in the fort. The terror of the first day, the raising of the first wall, the battle against the horde of zombies from the school, and countless others.

And the vision of Jenni, covered in blood, dragging a dying Juan into the winter sunlight.

Jenni would always remember her fear that she was losing the love of her life. But she would also remember how her screams brought others running to help.

And for some reason, until her last day on earth, she remembered the color of the white winter sky and the single bird flying overhead, riding the cold winds.

# · CHAPTER SEVEN ·

## 1.
### *Haunted Eyes*

Travis couldn't bear to look at Jenni when Katie had helped her into the hotel. He had seen the utter hollowness in Jenni's eyes and he went cold inside. She had appeared almost as lifeless as Juan.

Nerit and her people were looking for Ray. Bill had Blanche locked away. The bitch was still unconscious.

Travis stood in the hallway outside the fort's clinic—a series of repurposed conference rooms on the hotel's main floor. In one room, Charlotte was working feverishly to save Juan. Belinda had once been the town's librarian, but after long hours of studying medical books, she was now Charlotte's assistant. Peggy and Stacey were with Brewster in another room, trying to clean up his shattered nose. The reverend was leading a prayer vigil in the chapel at the far end of the hall.

Curtis strode up to Travis, looking very young and anxious. "I hear Juan's at death's door."

"Yeah," Travis said with a sad nod. How were you supposed to react when your best friend was dying? He wasn't sure. He felt numb yet furious.

"Seems like the Vigilante might have been Blanche and her goons all along." Curtis exhaled explosively. "Amazing, huh? It's kinda obvious now, dontcha think?"

Travis lifted an eyebrow. "Might have been her. But who knows? I don't think it's a closed case yet."

Curtis lifted his shoulders slightly. "I'm inclined to think that a mean viper like that might have done a lot more damage than we know."

"Maybe."

The young cop rubbed his hands together nervously. "So, what are we going to do with her and Brewster? And Ray if we find him?"

"I have no fucking clue," Travis replied.

Nerit came up to them, limping slightly. Her yellowish white hair was in a tight bun on her head, and her expression was severe. She said, "There's no sign of Ray. I suspect he went over the wall. Dixon swore he heard a car start up in the distance. I have a feeling this little group had some contingency plans."

"Dammit," Travis murmured.

"We should send out patrols!" Curtis looked fierce. His hands were clutched tightly at his sides and he kept pivoting back and forth on the balls of his feet with obvious agitation.

"For what purpose?" Nerit's gaze was cold. "We'd just set his ass back outside the wall again."

"But we need answers! A confession!"

"We have Blanche and Brewster. I think that is sufficient."

Travis thought about the reverend and his prayer group. "Nothing is sufficient anymore," he said bitterly.

"We gotta go after him and find out what was going on!" Curtis insisted.

"Curtis, it's obvious what was going on. Blanche wanted to leave," Travis said, "and she was stupid and crazy enough to kill her own husband and try to kill Juan in the process."

"It was more than that, Travis," Nerit said in a terse tone. "She was trying to make a point."

Travis didn't want to talk anymore. He stalked away from Nerit and Curtis and into the waiting room, where Jenni sat crying and whispering to Rosie in Spanish. Despite Rosie's pleas to be with Juan, Charlotte had told her to wait with the others. Katie immediately embraced Travis, and he allowed himself a brief moment of comfort in her arms.

Jenni looked up, her lips trembling. "Is Juan . . . Is he—?"

"No word yet," Travis said quickly.

Rosie was pale and her mouth was clenched shut. She and Jenni were holding hands, united in fear and grief. "My son is strong. He'll come through."

"I have no doubt that Juan is determined to live," Travis answered.

Jack was under Jenni's chair, his sad eyes looking at the humans. Jason was on guard duty and Jack had come to be with Jenni, almost as if he knew she needed him. Travis leaned down and petted the dog's head.

An exhausted-looking Charlotte entered the room, covered in blood. Letting out a desperate, horrified gasp, Rosie grabbed Jenni. Both women looked on the verge of collapse.

Travis and Katie clutched each other's hands. Travis forced the words out: "How is he?"

Charlotte let out a long sigh. "Stabilized, for now. I managed to stop the bleeding, but the bullet is still in there and it definitely collapsed a lung. I used an empty pen as a tube to get it reinflated, and Belinda is manually pumping air into his lungs. Peggy's looking for an oxygen tank that she swears she has in storage.

"I don't know what other damage was done. I do know that he lost a lot of blood. I've got Yolanda looking for donors so I can give him transfusions."

"Is my son going to live?" Rosie whispered.

Charlotte licked her lips, then said, "I did my best. But there's risk of infection, especially with the bullet still inside him. And he's in shock, but we're treating him for that."

Jenni pulled away from Rosie. "I need to go to him. He needs me."

For a moment, Travis thought Charlotte would deny Jenni,

but then she acquiesced. "He probably does. Just stay calm. Keep it soft. Encourage him to fight. He's not conscious, but he may hear you."

Holding hands, Rosie and Jenni went into the room where Juan lay. When the door closed behind them, Travis turned to Charlotte and asked, "What's up for real?"

"I need surgical tools and resources we don't have," Charlotte replied. "I need to get that bullet out. I need equipment to monitor him and keep him alive. I need medications to fight infections."

"Okay, get me a list. We'll get it."

Charlotte blinked. "Travis, you realize the hospitals are death traps."

"What choice do we have? It'll be volunteer only. He'll die if we don't go."

Charlotte grudgingly nodded. "All right. There's a small hospital about fifty miles from here. I used to work there in the ER. I know it very well. I can draw a map for the volunteers after I make my list."

"Excellent. I'll need it as soon as possible."

Bill knocked lightly, then entered the room. "Travis, Blanche is awake. Want to be there when I question her?"

"Yeah. I do." He kissed Katie and stroked her cheek softly. "Let me know if anything changes."

Katie nodded, her eyes full of love and desperation. "Of course."

Travis followed Bill, feeling fear and anxiety still clinging to him.

## 2.
### The Broken World

In the small holding cell in city hall, Blanche sat primly upon a cot as Travis and Bill questioned her from the other side of the bars. The longer they interrogated her, the more insanely confident Blanche seemed in her lies. She barely looked like herself;

her face was swollen and bruised and she was missing at least one tooth. Jenni had done a real number on her, and Travis was glad to see it.

"She attacked me and killed my husband! She's a crazy spic," Blanche said in a creepily calm tone.

"Blanche, we know that isn't true. You took Jenni hostage." Bill's voice was even.

"I think you're too stupid to know the truth." Blanche glared at them. They'd been talking to her for at least a half hour and she'd told them nothing but her warped version of events. "You stupid fucks. You have no freaking clue what is going on. You think you're so smart, but you're all just a bunch of dumb rednecks."

"Is that why you decided to kill off a few of us undesirables before striking out for your own promised land?" Bill asked.

"You think I'm your 'Vigilante'?" Blanche laughed. "If I was, I woulda killed a lot more people."

Travis felt his temper rising.

"You can't expect us to believe that Jenni attacked you and Steven when she discovered you were leaving, and shot Juan accidentally." Bill repeated Blanche's story back to her, staring at her incredulously.

Blanche smirked. "You are all so far beneath me that I shouldn't even waste my time talking to you. You can't see how dangerous that stupid spic is. Look what she did to my face!"

"What did you do to Calhoun? He's been reported missing, and I know you had a problem with him." Bill glowered at Blanche.

"Really?" She smiled, her bloody, swollen face a terrible parody of a clown. "Well, that's a bit of good news. Maybe he fell over the wall and got eaten."

"Is this really all about your Hummer?" Bill tried again. "Is that damn car why you killed two people, including your own husband?"

"Exile me. In my Hummer." Blanche cocked her head and fluttered her eyelashes; the flirtatious gesture was grotesque, given her battered features.

Travis stormed out of the cell area, Bill trailing behind him.

"What do we do now?" Bill asked.

"Send her home, since that's what she wants. Let the bitch go rot in her mansion. But not in the Hummer." Anger boiled in his chest. "Fuck her and that car."

"I'll have Curtis and Katarina escort her."

"Do it soon. We've wasted enough time on her." Travis shoved his hands into his jacket pockets. "We need to get hospital supplies to save Juan's life."

Bill arched his eyebrows and adjusted his belt nervously. "Really? A hospital?"

"I know. I know they're death traps, but . . . I gotta do something."

"I'm in. I'll go." Bill shrugged, as if to make light of his offer.

"Thanks, Bill. Get the word out that we're looking for volunteers, okay?"

Bill nodded. "You got it."

Travis wished to God he could restart the day.

Katie's eyes hurt from crying, and she felt a little sick to her stomach. Needing a small break from the clinic's waiting room, she went in search of her husband. She heard raised voices coming from inside Travis's office.

She knocked and the room went silent. Then Travis called, "Yes?" and Katie opened the door. Her husband was leaning back against his desk, glaring at Nerit and Peggy, who were seated in chairs near the wall. Bill was standing with his hands on his belt, glowering at Travis. Eric was sitting on the couch, legs crossed, cleaning his glasses and looking pensive.

"What's going on?"

"Your fool husband wants to go out and get himself killed," Peggy answered, her voice harsh with frustration. She quickly explained about the volunteer team being put together to find medical supplies for Charlotte.

Katie raised her eyebrows at her husband. "Travis, you can't go. We need you here."

"Your most trusted advisers, your friends, and your wife are telling you to stay." Eric donned his glasses and settled his eyes on Travis. "Don't you think you should listen to us?"

Picking up the volunteer sheet, Travis shook it. "There are only seven names on this list."

Nerit asked, "What is your point, Travis?"

"I'm closer to Juan than all of these people except Monica."

Katie stepped toward her husband. "Travis, we all know you care about Juan. Everyone in the fort knows you're willing to put your life on the line for him—for anyone."

"She's right, Travis. If you're trying to prove anything to us, you don't have to."

"Eric, it's not about proving anything to anyone. In fact, the Travis Fan Club freaks me the hell out! It's about—" Travis struggled visibly with his emotions. "—it's about me. How I feel. I want to help my friend. I want to help save him."

Katie ran her hand gently over his hair and let it rest on the back of his neck. He looked at her, his expression anguished. It hurt her to see him this way, but she couldn't let him act foolishly. "We understand more than you realize. I know what it's like to feel helpless in the face of death. But we need you here. You may not like it, but you make us believe we can survive and even flourish in this world. That may not seem like much to you, but it's everything to us."

"I'm the one who fucked up! I'm the one who didn't let that psycho take that damn Hummer and leave. She shot my friend because of me!"

"So it comes out. You feel guilty," Nerit said, lifting an eyebrow.

"Dammit, Travis! Blanche is unhinged. You can't blame yourself!" Peggy looked ready to smack him, and Katie couldn't blame her.

"So you're going to go out into the deadlands and risk not coming back to ease your guilt? You should feel guilty for wanting to put yourself at risk." Katie tried to keep her voice even and not let her own anger and desperation leak into it. "I need you. The baby needs you. We *all* need you."

Travis looked down at the volunteer sheet. His fingers were trembling and his jaw was clenched. After a long silence, he nodded and set the paper aside. He leaned forward, hands on his knees, and exhaled long and slow.

"It's the right thing to do, Travis," Nerit said reassuringly.

Eric said, "There's no question that it's a dangerous run, but it's being handled."

"Let us do our job and you do yours," Bill added with an encouraging smile.

Travis folded his arms over his chest, resigned. "You're right. But I hate to admit it."

Relief washed over Katie, and she felt the tension in her shoulders dissipate.

"Time is of the essence," Nerit insisted.

"Let's get moving. Charlotte should have the map and the list of equipment ready by now." Bill headed toward the door.

Katie watched their friends file out, feeling immensely grateful for each one. As the door shut, she tilted her head to gaze up at her solemn husband.

"I'm hardheaded, aren't I?" Travis granted her a sheepish smile.

"Oh, without a doubt. It took all of us to break through your thick skull."

"Forgive me?" Travis asked.

Katie kissed him firmly on the lips. "You're a loyal friend, a good leader, and a man with a huge heart. There is nothing to forgive."

"Katie, I'm so lucky to have you."

"Yes, you are. So there'll be no more talk of running off to do something stupid."

"Yes, ma'am."

Running her hand lightly over his arm, she reluctantly drew away from her husband. "I'm going to go check on Jenni."

Travis straightened, rubbing his neck. "Okay. I need to go to the briefing anyway. I love you, Katie."

"I love you, Travis."

It was nearly one thirty by the time the volunteers were finished being briefed on the medical supply run. While Charlotte explained exactly where they had to go, they studied the layout of the hospital she'd drawn for them. She'd also given them photocopies of pictures of the equipment and surgical instruments she wanted, in addition to the list of tools, medications, and other supplies.

Travis lingered in the back of the room, listening, wishing he could take away some of the teams' anxiety. The volunteers were divided into two groups: Monica, Dale, Ken, and Lenore in one; Roger, Bill, and Felix in the other.

Charlotte finished her briefing with, "Anyone have anything to ask?"

"Yeah," said a new voice. "When are we leaving?" Everyone turned to look at Jenni's pale, determined face.

"Shit," Roger groaned. The former science teacher and die-hard Trekker winced. As usual, he wore jeans and battered sneakers. His T-shirt read I LIKE TO PON FARR, and his thinning brown hair looked like he had slept on it. His plain face skewed into a grimace. "This isn't going to be good."

"Shouldn't you be with Juan?" Travis wondered if the sick feeling he had in the pit of his stomach was what the others had felt when he'd announced he was going on the mission.

"And do what? Watch him die?" Jenni shook her head. "Fuck that. I'm going. I'm good at this sort of thing. How many rescue teams have I been on?"

"You haven't done much scavenging," Roger answered. "Death rates on the scavenging teams are higher than for rescues."

Everyone eyed him, obviously wishing he hadn't spoken that particular truth aloud.

"Sorry, but seriously, there are a lot more red shirts on the scavenging teams," Roger said, a tad defensively.

Travis took hold of Jenni's arm and gazed down into her face. "You're a good fighter. But wouldn't you rather be with Juan?"

Jenni pulled away from Travis, her expression defiant. "I can feel myself going crazy in there. At least this way, I'm trying to do something to save his life."

"Jenni . . ."

"Travis, don't keep me from going out there. I'm begging you." Jenni lifted her chin. "I'm a big girl with a big ax."

"She has a point," Bill said gently, sorrow visible on his face. "Watching the one you love die slowly is a hell unto itself. I would have done anything to save my wife from cancer. I would have climbed Mount Everest to save her."

Travis knew that everyone in the room was waiting for him to do something. He tried again. "Jenni, if you go and something happens . . ."

Jenni's tear-filled eyes flashed with anger. "I won't be fucking helpless this time!"

"She's made her choice." Dale said, "Everyone's got the right to make a choice."

"We could use her," Monica said, nodding. "Juan is my cousin and I love him. Yeah, I'm scared knowing the risks, but he's always treated me like his little sister. I gotta do what I can to save him. I can tell that Jenni feels the same. Let her go, Travis."

Lenore and Ken were seated side by side and by their lowered heads and averted gazes, it was obvious they did not want to get involved. Felix just sighed. Charlotte fussed with her printouts, ignoring the ruckus.

Travis met Jenni's gaze. "Jenni, can you keep it together out there?"

She nodded vigorously. "Better than I can here." Squaring her shoulders, she stood straight, looking strong and sure of herself.

With a sigh, Travis made his decision. It was right that people who loved Juan tried to save him. "Okay, Jenni. You can go."

"Come here so I can catch you up," Bill ordered, waving her over to him.

Walking toward Bill and Charlotte, Jenni threw a smile at Travis that was both grateful and terribly sad.

Travis returned her smile uneasily and left the room.

## CHAPTER EIGHT

## 1.

### *Bless Me Father*

Jenni leaned over and gently kissed Juan's dry lips. Her fingers played over his curls and she took a deep, shuddering breath. Resting her hand lightly on his chest, she could feel the faint thudding of his heart.

"Keep strong, baby. I love you."

After one last kiss, she straightened and moved away from the bed. Rosie took her hand. They shared a quiet moment; then Jenni kissed the older woman on her cheek and departed.

Her long black hair fell freely around her shoulders as she walked toward the chapel. Her stomach was roiling with nerves, but she didn't care anymore. She was going to save Juan.

Ken stood near the open door to the chapel. "Bill says we got ten minutes before we roll out. Trucks are almost ready."

"That should be enough time. I just don't want to go out there without having God at my back, even if I'm a sucky Catholic most of the time."

Inside, Jenni found the reverend waiting with a Communion of saltines and red Kool-Aid. She had specifically asked for Communion and he had quickly agreed. Taking a seat, Jenni pulled out her rosary and threaded it between her fingers.

The reverend did his best to improvise a Catholic Communion service, even wearing a white robe made from a tablecloth. His

care for her—for everyone in the fort, no matter their religion—
touched her.

When it came time to partake of the Communion, she felt her
hands shaking. She wouldn't admit it to anyone, but she was pet-
rified. Juan's injury made her feel vulnerable. She hated that.

Taking the piece of stale saltine on her tongue, she closed her
eyes and tried to concentrate on the Risen Christ and the Blessed
Virgin. The Kool-Aid was a bit tart, but she downed it. Crossing
herself, she uttered fervent prayers.

"Just let him live," she whispered.


The stricken, worried expression Jenni saw on Katie's face as she
entered the staging area broke Jenni's heart. Jenni walked
straight to her and embraced Katie lovingly. She felt Katie trembling and she buried her face in Katie's soft curls.

"If you don't come back, I'll be really pissed," Katie said with
a catch in her voice.

"I'll be back. One way or the other. Nothing can keep me away."

"I know. I can't help but worry. You're my best friend."

Letting go of Katie, Jenni kissed her friend's cheek. "And you're
mine."

Jason ran up to Jenni and flung his arms around her. "Mom,"
he cried in her ear, "Mom, don't go."

She squeezed him so tight, it hurt. "I have to," Jenni said. "I have
to try to save him."

Jason swallowed hard; Jenni knew he was trying not to cry. He
said, "Be careful, Mom."

"I will be," she promised. She kissed him firmly on the forehead.
"I love you."

Jack pawed at her knee. Jenni kissed his furry head. "I love
you, too."

Trying to smile and not look scared shitless, Jenni strode to
Nerit's familiar red truck, where Roger and Bill were waiting for
her. She turned to wave to her small family: her best friend, her
stepson, and a dog.

She tried not to think of Juan, lying so still in that bed.
Climbing into the truck, she nodded at Bill. "Let's do this."
"Just like old times," he said, gunning the engine.
Jenni sighed. It felt nothing like old times.

## 2.
### Beer and Strawberries

Bill drove in silence down the unfamiliar weed-ridden road. Jenni
sat in the back of the truck's cab, staring out the window. He
doubted she was seeing anything other than Juan's face in her
mind's eye. Felix was asleep beside her, snoring lightly, while Roger
was deep into a *Star Trek* novel in the passenger seat. Looking into
the rearview mirror, he saw the second team's truck keeping pace
behind them.

Maybe it was good to be silent for a while. The drive would
take more than an hour and they were heading into a highly dangerous situation. They all knew that hospitals were death traps.

He gripped the steering wheel harder and concentrated on driving. He spotted a few zombies moving through the dried brush
beside the road. They seemed disoriented and sluggish. Charlotte
was right. They were slowing down as the elements got to them.
That didn't keep them from being fiercely terrifying if they got
close to you.

In the rearview mirror, he saw Jenni leaning her head against
the window, staring blankly.

Bill took a deep breath. He understood Jenni's distress and
why she had to be part of the rescue group. He would have done
the same for his wife.

Not for the first time, he admitted to himself that even every-
day living had been hard after she died. He had just gone back to
work when that dead little boy banged on his patrol car window.
Still mourning, he had almost given in and let the zombie take
him, but then he had started to worry about Ralph and Nerit and

that had been the end of that. His friends had stood by him through the thick and thin of his wife's illness, and he had to make sure they were okay.

Behind him, Felix snorted in his sleep and Bill smiled. To his surprise, he'd made incredible friends at the fort.

"Check that out," Roger said, pointing to one side of the road. Bill glanced over and saw a commercial plane rammed into the side of a badly charred barn. There was no sign of life or unlife.

"Bet they were trapped in there," Roger added. "What a way to go."

"I heard, right before the TV went black, that planes were going down into neighborhoods all around DFW. Just dropping right out of the sky," Bill said. "I'm sure that happened all over the world."

"So many ways to die," Jenni said with a sigh from the backseat.

"Yeah," Bill agreed, and they all fell silent again.

They passed an overturned car. Inside, a figure was flailing around. They drove on. Another figure darted out behind them and was flattened by the second truck.

How easy it was to kill them now. So very easy.

He thought of Katarina. He'd seen her right before they'd left, heading out of the hotel as she walked in.

"Good luck," she'd said.

"Thanks," he'd responded grimly.

"Come back, okay?"

"Try to," he'd said, then hesitated. To his own surprise—he still wasn't sure where he'd gotten the nerve—he'd said, "Hey, Katarina, want to have a drink with me when I get back?"

He was stunned when she'd replied, with a smile, "Yes, that sounds nice."

He kept thinking of that moment. He wanted to survive, go back to the fort, and have some of Rosie's home-brewed beer with Katarina. He was ashamed to admit it, but he wondered what her hair smelled like. He hoped he would find out. Maybe someday, if she could ignore his plain looks . . .

They hit the outskirts of the town that was their destination, passing closed restaurants, gas stations, and a trucking company. Up ahead, Bill saw the modern, two-story hospital.

The fort's trucks came to a stop.

Jenni leaned forward. "Looks like fun."

In the lobby, two zombies in wheelchairs clawed at the glass doors.

Bill sighed.

He bet Katarina's hair smelled like strawberries.


# 3.
## *Possibilities*

The moving van made its way down the country road, following the first team's truck. In the back, Lenore and Ken were jostled around as they sat side by side on a long bench secured to the interior wall. They tried to stabilize themselves by holding on to straps someone had mounted on the side of the vehicle.

"So why *did* you volunteer?" Lenore fussed with her hair, wishing her new weave wasn't jammed under a hat. It had been a relief to get some beautiful lush hair after months of having to deal with her own short hair without any decent products or styling tools.

Ken crossed his legs and gave her his most annoyingly cute look. "Guess."

"Dale."

"See, that was easy!"

Lenore scowled at him. "You do realize, twinkle-toes, that we are going into a highly dangerous situation where we will most likely get our asses eaten?"

"He's really cute, don't you think? All rugged and strong. Dreamy," Ken said, smiling widely.

"Eaten. By zombies. Not by a cute guy."

"You do realize I only heard the words 'eaten' and 'cute guy' just then."

"I hate you." Lenore tried to get comfortable on the bench, cursing herself for volunteering.

"Why are *you* here?" Ken fussed with the laces of his boots, retying them as he bounced around on the bench. He made it look easy. She would have landed on her ass.

"You volunteered, so I volunteered. Someone has to watch out for you. You'd be staring at Dale and some zombie would bite you. Then I would have to beat you for being stupid and then kill you for being a zombie. Which would be annoying."

Ken laughed with delight. "Besides, I'm your best friend and your fag."

"I ain't your hag."

"Oh, yes, you are."

"Do not make me feed you to the zombies!"

"Feed me to Dale," Ken whispered huskily, winking.

"Don't make me slap you," she groused.

"Fine. Anyway, the dish is that Felix volunteered because you volunteered."

"No, he didn't. He doesn't like me like that."

"He does."

Lenore frowned. "No, he doesn't." Yet the thought of Felix being interested in her made her pulse speed up.

"He likes you. Why else would he sit in our beauty shop for hours, waiting for you to trim his hair?"

"Because he knows that *I* know how to trim his black hair and that your white ass does not."

"No, no, he likes you. Which is kind of funny if you think about it. Dale signed up for this mission to be part of the fort. I signed up to impress him with my prowess. You signed up to save my ass. And Felix signed up to watch yours. It's the circle of life."

Lenore wasn't too sure about that, but she didn't want to think about much more than getting into the hospital, grabbing what they were after, and leaving. Soon Ken dozed off with his head against her shoulder. She loved the idiot, but she hated to admit it.

He was the most loyal friend she had ever had, even if he was annoying. Sighing, she checked her crossbow and the bag of bolts.

When the truck came to a stop outside the hospital, she mentally prepared herself for the worst.

The doors opened and Dale peered in at them. "It looks pretty clear except for some dead guys in wheelchairs inside the front doors. Weirdest shit I've seen in a while."

"Thank God for that!" Ken hurried over and leaped down, while Lenore pulled herself to her feet and grabbed her stuff.

"Let's get this done so we can go home," Lenore grumbled as she tried to get out of the back of the truck while maintaining some dignity.

Dale grabbed hold and helped her down with surprising ease. She flashed a grin at Ken's jealous expression and slung the bag of crossbow bolts over her shoulder.

Felix, Bill, Jenni, and Roger approached, their weapons out, looking around cautiously. Lenore swept her gaze over their surroundings, which were mostly zombie free. Monica came around from the front of the truck, tucking her braids under her hat.

"Kinda feels too easy all at once," Dale said.

"Never say that!" Ken chided him.

"It's bad luck," Monica added.

"Oh, sorry." The big man looked sheepish.

Bill pulled his belt up over his stomach. "We go in. We get the stuff. We come out. Alive."

"Sounds like a plan," Felix said as he fell in beside Lenore.

Feeling shy after Ken's assertion about Felix's intentions, Lenore cautiously stole a look at him. Felix flashed a big smile, took her hand in his, and gave it a soft squeeze. Startled, she ended up scowling at him, which elicited an even bigger grin.

"So, it's zombie-killing time," Dale said, stretching, his huge muscles flexing under his T-shirt.

"Yep. Better zip up your jacket and pull on your gloves." Bill gestured to Dale's exposed chest. "T-shirt ain't enough protection." The rest of the squad was wearing leather jackets and jeans.

Lenore made sure her thick wool scarf was tight around her neck and yanked on the thick, flexible leather gloves that would protect her hands while allowing her to fire her crossbow.

"We should use motorcycle helmets," Ken suggested.

"They'd limit our hearing and vision," Bill pointed out.

"But I'd look cool."

Lenore smacked him.

Jenni braided up her hair, looking far too pale. Monica cocked her shotgun and looked at Bill, waiting for the word.

"Let's do it," Bill said grimly.


# 4.
## Banished

Pain brought Blanche to consciousness. Sitting up sharply, she was first startled, then pleased to see that she was in her bedroom at the mansion. Her face was throbbing and the coppery taste of blood filled her mouth, but she was home.

Those fucking hicks had finally seen the light and sent her home.

The last thing she remembered was Charlotte coming in after Bill and Travis had left. The fat nurse told Blanche that she was going to give her a shot for the pain. It had been a lie, for almost immediately she felt herself falling into darkness.

But now she was home, so she supposed she could overlook the bitch's deceit.

Blanche rolled off the bed and set her feet down on the velvety softness of her Persian rug. She had to stand very still until she no longer felt nauseated or dizzy. Walking cautiously into the bathroom, she caught sight of herself in the mirror and a fresh surge of fury welled up in her. She had paid good money for her nose job, veneers, and cheek implants, and now they were all ruined. Hopefully there was a good plastic surgeon out there somewhere.

She was sure the rich and famous were somewhere safe. She had told Steven they should try to find an enclave of the wealthy, probably in Austin. But no, her stupid husband had dragged her out to the godforsaken town he had sunk so much money into.

Slipping into a silk robe, she opened her bedroom door and strolled along the hall to the grand staircase.

The house was very quiet. For the first time, Blanche wondered if she was alone. Reaching the main floor, she looked past the open doors into the dining room. The dining table was covered with good-sized cardboard boxes. A piece of paper was taped to one carton.

Relieved at the sight of the boxes of supplies Shane and his men had been stockpiling for her, Blanche grabbed the note.

*Thanks for the food, thanks for the liquor, thanks for the sex. If you ever make it back here, I took all the stuff. Good luck, babe. You're going to need it. Ray.*

Blanche growled in anger and grabbed the nearest box. Empty. All the cartons were empty. The things she had paid Shane good money to collect were gone. She stalked into the kitchen, hoping to find more supplies stashed there, hoping that Ray hadn't bothered to look around. There was a single can of chili sitting on the counter. Beside it, she saw her gun and another note.

*Here's dinner. Here's your gun. Hope you enjoy both.*
*—Curtis.*

"Dammit."

Furious, Blanche picked up the can of chili and hurled it across the kitchen. It shattered the lead glass of her china cabinet.

Spinning on her heel, she stormed to Steven's office. She would get money out of the safe and take Steven's car. It shouldn't be too hard to find another dumb-ass to do her bidding.

When she opened the office door, she blinked, then swore angrily. The safe was open and empty. *Dammit!* Shane had said that Ray was once in prison; now she had a good idea why.

Stomping to the back hallway, she headed for the garage. She already suspected that Ray had taken Steven's Mercedes, but she had to be sure. When she saw the empty garage, she screamed with frustration. The sun would be going down soon.

There were some jewels and money stashed in her closet. She could get the work truck from the stable. There was a gas pump on the grounds and she could fuel up and leave in the morning. She wouldn't be traveling in luxury, but she'd be on the way to it. Things would be fine.

Comforted by this thought, she began to look for something to eat other than the disgusting canned chili. Finally, she found some chocolates and a bottle of wine. She was halfway through the box of somewhat stale truffles when she heard yelling. Moving closer to the front door, she caught her own name in the shouts.

It was Ray.

"Blanche, open the door! Open the gawd damn door!"

She dashed into the kitchen and grabbed her gun, then peered out into the gloom and spotted Ray running up the driveway. She started to unlock the door, then remembered his note. With a snort, she backed away from the door.

He smashed into it. "Blanche! Open the door! I know you're in there! I saw Curtis drop you off!"

Blanche's anger blazed. "Oh, really? And why didn't you come to save me?"

"The car broke down, okay? I was stuck up the road, but I came back as soon as I could after I saw Curtis leave. Open the door! Blanche, open the door! They're coming!"

"So, you steal my things and my husband's car and then you come running back here when it breaks down because *they* are coming, huh?"

"Blanche! Open the door!" Ray sounded hysterical. He was pounding on the wood. "I'm out of bullets! Open the fucking door, bitch!"

Blanche lifted her gun and opened the door, revealing Ray's terrified face and, beyond him, figures moving through the growing darkness.

"Thank God, Blanche, I—"

She fired and Ray's head snapped back. He looked suitably shocked before his eyes went utterly blank and he fell. Mottled, decaying zombies were closing in.

"Stay off my property!" she screamed, aiming at the nearest one. When she squeezed the trigger, the gun clicked empty.

She was hit full force by the horrible reek of the undead creatures; then they were on her, knocking her back into the house and onto her expensive Persian rug. One of the zombies screeched at her and she slapped it. "Get off me!"

It grabbed her hand and bit down.

Screaming, she tried to get away, but then more were on her and suddenly she realized what Curtis's note had meant.

He had left her one bullet.

She had used it to kill Ray.

*Fuck!*

Her screams of fury filled the night until they finally gave way to screams of pain.

# · CHAPTER NINE ·

## 1.
### *Gateway to Death*

Jenni watched as the front door to the hospital swung open and the zombie in the pink housecoat growled and grabbed for Ken.

With a grunt, Ken shoved the spear into the dead old woman's eye socket.

The male zombie in the other wheelchair fumbled toward the open door, trying to reach the opening where the humans were.

Roger put his sneaker squarely on the zombie woman's gnarled knees and shoved her and her wheelchair back.

With a loud hiss, the old man launched himself toward Bill, but landed flat on his stomach. He clawed at the floor, trying to move, but Bill beat his head in with his boot heel.

"That was truly disgusting," Ken muttered as he watched Bill walk over to the lawn and wipe the gore off his boot on the dry, overgrown grass.

Tilting her head, Monica read the male's admission bracelet. "He's tagged as bitten."

"They took off and left the infected behind," Jenni said, pointing to the sign on the door. It read: EVACUATED TO MADISON RESCUE CENTER. DO NOT ENTER HOSPITAL. GO TO MADISON RESCUE CENTER.

"I wonder how many infected there were," Roger said, looking nervous.

Jenni checked her weapons one more time: her ax, a dagger in a sheath on her thigh, two revolvers, a rifle, and a short spear. "Enough to kill us," she said honestly.

Lenore snorted. "Same old, same old."

Moving back over to the group gathered in the hospital doorway, Bill said, "Okay, no guns unless absolutely necessary. Do not open any doors that are not in our brief. If you run into trouble, radio in immediately. We're here to get the supplies and get out."

Monica moved closer to the front door and peered past the two dead zombies, then shoved the old man to one side and stepped into the hall. Her large brown eyes looked terrified, but her chin was set with determination. In that moment, she reminded Jenni of Juan.

"We should hurry," she said. "The sun will go down soon, and we don't want to be wandering around here in the dark."

They walked cautiously down the hall, toward a large reception area. According to Charlotte's map, the hospital was divided into four areas. The doors straight ahead led to a long wing of patient rooms. To the left were the cafeteria and gift shop. To the right were the admissions area, doors to the ER, and the elevators and stairway. The operating rooms, exam rooms, and ICU were upstairs.

Jenni and Monica, who were in the lead, paused as they reached the end of the hall. The spacious waiting room was illuminated only by dim emergency lights. Most of the chairs had been overturned and dried blood was smeared over the walls. Behind a glass window, a woman dressed in nursing scrubs hissed.

"Someone ate that girl's arm," Lenore observed. "Nasty."

The nurse clawed at the window with her remaining hand, clearly unable to slide it open.

"Okay, no one goes into the receptionist's office," Monica said grimly.

Moving toward the stairs on the far side of the room, Jenni stepped over the body of a truly dead security guard who had been shot in the head. Roger followed Jenni, studying the room nervously. She grimaced at a headless corpse shoved under a pile of chairs. Bill let out a soft curse. Felix took up the rear, clutching his crossbow.

"Head," Roger whispered, jerking his chin to the left. Jenni glanced over and spotted a decapitated head snarling at her from a potted plant.

"I don't wanna know how that happened," Bill decided.

"Man, that's fucked up." Felix sent a crossbow bolt through the zombie's eye.

"Gross," Ken said from behind them.

Pausing before the doors to the emergency room, Jenni raised a hand to bring everyone to a halt. The stench of death was strong. That the doors were chained shut was not a good sign.

Fear flitted over the faces of her companions as they waited for her next move. Scrutinizing her surroundings, she pulled a framed picture off the wall. Holding it up, she used the reflective surface of the glass to get a look through the windows set in the chained doors. Adjusting it slowly, trying to stay out of sight, she finally managed to get a good look.

She almost dropped the painting.

Immediately, she slid down to the floor. *It's full of them,* she mouthed.

Lenore crossed herself and Ken gulped.

Bill signaled that they should crawl past the doors and stay out of sight. Ken and Lenore went first, with Dale and Monica right behind them heading for the patient wing. Holding her breath, Jenni followed, with Roger, Felix, and Bill right behind her. The stench was so bad, she found it hard not to gag. Keeping close to the waiting room chairs, she crawled to the stairwell. It appeared clear.

Across the room, the first team discovered that the doors to the patient rooms were not chained. After a wordless debate, Lenore stood up and peeked into that hallway, trying to do it without attracting the attention of the zombies in the emergency room. Motioning that all was clear, Lenore led her team through the doors.

Bill moved up beside Jenni and squeezed her arm gently. "We do this and go." They began to climb the stairs.

## 2.
### Death's Doorway

The patient wing seemed to be empty.

"I don't hear them," Lenore whispered. "It's all quiet here. I bet they're all stuffed in the emergency room."

"They can stay there," Ken groused. He winced as they passed a decomposing corpse, its shattered skull surrounded by dried blood and brains. "Whoever cleared this place shot everyone in the head."

"Smart move," Dale said in a hushed tone.

Lenore gingerly pushed an empty stretcher out of her way.

"Okay, let's start getting what we need." Monica blew her dark bangs out of her eyes. "Just what's on the list. No more."

Monica, Lenore, and Ken began to collect items, striking off entries on their "shopping" lists. Dale knocked out a window at the end of the hall and started to lower equipment onto the lawn. That seemed like a good idea to Ken, considering the danger in the emergency room. There were probably enough zombies in there to break the chains if they were provoked.

Lenore warily avoided closed doors while she shoved things into her tote bag. Ken wheeled equipment down the hall to Dale, sashaying as prettily as he could. Dale appeared amused.

Monica slid out the window and ran for the truck, gun in hand. Ken thought she was hot for a girl, but Dale . . . he was a big hunk of a man, just like Ken liked them. It was truly annoying that no one else in the fort was out of the closet. "Stop staring," Lenore chided.

Ken waved a hand at her and rolled the heart monitor to the window. He saw that Monica had backed the moving van closer to the hospital and was beginning to load it with the things Dale had placed on the lawn. Dale picked up the heart monitor and carefully set it outside, barely looking at Ken as he did so.

Sighing, Ken checked his map. There was supposed to be a supply room nearby, at the end of a short hall that branched off the main corridor. Charlotte had said that a number of the medications she needed could probably be found there. He peeked down the shorter hall and saw two more sets of double doors. The emergency lights made the windows in them glow an eerie red.

"Cover me," Ken ordered Lenore.

Holding his spear firmly in one hand and his map in the other, he moved along the hall, keeping close to the wall. The door to the supply room was near the very end. Beyond the double doors was another corridor that led to . . .

Ken unfolded the map just as he reached the double doors.

. . . the emergency room.

Heart pounding, he jerked his head up and stared into the snarling face of a zombie on the other side of the glass. Ken's gaze swept down the length of the doors. They were unchained.

The door burst open, smashing Ken into the wall and knocking his spear from his hand. Ken was trapped, wedged into the narrow area between the door and the wall. He was in a perfect little triangle of hell.

Ken cowered in the small sliver of space. The zombies growled at him through the window as they pressed against the door. His body barely fit into the space, and the pressure was beginning to cut off his breathing.

The twisted, dead faces squashed against the surface, teeth champing. Blood and spittle smeared the slowly cracking glass.

Struggling for breath, Ken knew he was going to die.

The first gunshot startled him. The volley made him hopeful. The distorted, gruesome faces turned away. Moaning, the zombies shambled down the hall.

Ken finally managed to take a full breath, relief filling him until he realized the door would swing shut without the zombies
holding it. He would be exposed. Grabbing the door's handle
firmly, he struggled to hold it in place. More zombies staggered
past him, moving toward his friends. His sweat-slicked fingers
slipped on the handle.

A zombie noticed him through the smeared glass. It was an
old man, one side of his face eaten away and his throat shredded
into dried strips of flesh. It gripped the side of the door firmly
and pulled.

"No, no, no," Ken whispered, struggling to hold on as his
adrenaline-fueled strength drained away.

The zombie persisted, its slow movements agonizingly frightening. Ken heard its bones cracking and its muscles tearing as it
hauled on the door, but since it didn't feel pain, it had no reason
to stop. Ken's grip failed and he tumbled into the corner, screaming as the zombie reached for him.

"Die, fucker," Lenore growled from behind the zombie.

Ken screamed again as the zombie toppled over onto him,
then realized the thing was truly dead. A crossbow bolt had shattered the back of its head. Rotting brains slid out in a slimy pile
as he shoved the creature away.

Grabbing Ken's arm, Lenore pulled him to his feet. "Run!"

They ran, stumbling and sliding over the dead bodies littering
the floor. Hearing moans, Ken glanced over his shoulder to see
zombies staggering after them. Lenore and Ken raced to the open
window, where Dale stood outside waiting for them. Dale lifted
him up and out. Ken clung to him, relishing the moment, until Dale
set him down and shoved him toward the moving van. Lenore was
heavier and the zombies had almost reached her when Dale wrestled her out of the window. Grabbing Lenore's hand, Dale tugged
her away as zombies filled the window and started to tumble out.

Standing next to the truck, Monica fired at the zombies, her
shotgun barking loudly.

Ken scrambled into the back of the truck.

"Hurry! Hurry!" His voice sounded shrill, but he didn't care.

Dale pushed and Ken pulled and Lenore cussed at them impressively as they hauled her into the back of the truck. Dale slammed the doors shut, securing them. Seconds later, the truck lurched off at top speed.

Lenore sat down on the bench beside Ken and took his hand. He was sobbing and was stunned to see that she was crying, too, her big body shaking.

"You are one stupid faggot," she finally said.

Ken threw his arms around her and wept into her large bosom. "I know, I know!"

Clutching him, Lenore rocked him. "I love you anyway."

"You saved me," Ken sobbed. "I thought I was dead, but you saved me."

"No zombie is eatin' my best friend," Lenore declared gruffly.

Ken lifted his head. "But what . . . oh, God . . . what about Jenni and the others? They're still back there!"

## 3.
### *Death's Doorway Opens*

It was evident from the chaos in the operating rooms that things had gone to hell fairly quickly. Dead bodies lay everywhere, each shot in the head. Someone had also meticulously killed every person in the ICU. Some victims, Jenni suspected, had not been zombies.

"Why kill all of these, but not the ones in the ER?"

"Ran out of time, I suspect," Bill said.

"Can we hurry it up? This place is making my skin crawl," Felix said from across the room.

"Yeah, it's damn creepy," Roger agreed.

Jenni unfolded her map and held it up against the wall to study it. "Bill, you and I can take care of the stuff in the OR. Roger, Felix, you get those drugs from the pharmacy," she ordered.

Felix gave her a brisk nod. "Let's roll."

The corpses in the operating rooms were terribly decomposed and the scavengers tried hard not to look at them too closely. Bill and Jenni loaded medical instruments into a bin, trying to collect all the ones Charlotte had requested.

Bill's walkie-talkie hissed to life.

"Sorry, Bill. Ken's my best friend," Lenore's voice said.

Bill fumbled to grab the walkie-talkie off his belt.

"What did she mean?"

"Hell if I know, Jenni."

Bill was about to call Lenore back when they heard gunshots from below, followed by the bellow of a hundred zombie voices rising.

"We're out of here," Bill declared.

Jenni grabbed the bin and followed Bill into the hallway just as Roger and Felix came running from the direction of the stairs.

"Just run!" Felix hollered.

Jenni heard footfalls on the stairs. "Shit!" She ran, clutching the bin.

Felix shoved open a door. They all piled into the room beyond, and Roger quickly locked the door behind them. Felix was already racing toward the windows on the far side of the room.

Looking around, Jenni saw that they were in some sort of dorm room, with several beds and curtained-off areas. It had probably been used by doctors working long shifts. Suddenly Jenni realized that something was moving behind a curtain at the far end. She could just make out its silhouette, highlighted by the fading sunlight coming through the windows.

"Felix, no!" Bill called.

Distracted, the slender young man glanced back—and ran straight into that last curtain. He and the thing behind it went down in a tumble of grunts and moans.

Roger ran to help. "Felix!"

Behind Jenni, the door shuddered as the pounding began. Bill pushed her aside and shoved a large metal wardrobe in front of the door.

Felix shouted as Roger grabbed the curtain and yanked it away. Felix gasped for air as he struggled to his feet. Behind him, a terribly mutilated, decaying soldier was chewing on something.

"Shit!" Roger yelled.

"Kill it!" Felix shouted, leaping away from the zombie with his hand clapped to the side of his head.

Jenni drew her weapon and fired as the soldier lunged forward. It jerked as the bullet tore through its chest. Her second shot blew off one side of its head and the zombie tumbled to the floor. When it hit, a bit of ear, with a diamond earring still attached, fell out of its mouth.

"Oh, shit, no!" Felix cried out. "No, no. He ripped off my earring!"

Roger raised his gun. "Sorry, Felix."

"No, the fucker ripped it off! It didn't bite me! I swear!"

Pushing a desk in front of the metal wardrobe, Bill swore under his breath. The door was starting to buckle. "We don't have much time!"

Jenni emptied the bin of surgical instruments onto a bed, then rolled the tools up in the sheet and tied the ends to make a backpack. With a sigh of regret, she yanked her ax from her back and tossed it away. Pulling on the makeshift backpack, she hurried toward the men, who were arguing fiercely. Felix screamed at Roger, clutching his torn ear, as Roger obviously tried to get up the nerve to fire.

"Don't do it! I swear it didn't bite me! I promise. Dear God, I promise!" Tears streaming down his face, Felix raised his gun, pointing it at Roger. "Put the gun down, Roger. I mean it! It didn't—"

Without a word, Jenni raised her gun and fired. Felix fell, silent and dead, on top of the soldier who had effectively ended his life.

"You make it fast," Jenni said to Roger in a ragged voice.

"God, Jenni. He was my friend."

"It doesn't matter. You make it fast!"

The pounding on the door was increasing.

"Roger, some help," Bill said from where he was still stacking things against the door. "Jenni, find us an escape route!"

Roger ran to help barricade the door. Decayed hands reached into the room as the door gradually inched open. Jenni looked out the window and saw the roof of the first floor about fifteen feet below. The red pickup was just within view.

She opened the window and punched out the screen.

"We gotta jump," she said, pulling a mattress off the nearest cot. She pushed it out the window and watched it fall to the roof. Satisfied with its position, she sent another mattress after it. "Let's go, guys!"

Bill and Roger abandoned the barricade, rushing to the window. The door gave way and the first of the zombies burst into the room. Jenni tucked her gun into its holster and climbed onto the windowsill, her trembling hands gripping the frame. With a deep breath, she lowered herself as far as she could, then let go. She dropped hard onto the mattresses, knocking the wind out of herself. Rolling onto her side, she managed to get to her feet.

Seconds later, Bill fell beside her. Despite his weight, he managed a better landing than Jenni had. He got up quickly and called to Roger to hurry.

Roger carefully perched on the sill. Jenni saw a gray, chewed-up hand reach out from behind him.

"Jump!" she and Bill shouted at the same time.

Catching a glimpse of the zombie hand, Roger screamed and jerked to one side. He fell wildly and landed feetfirst, hitting the hard gravel surface of the roof. Jenni heard his legs break and saw white splinters of bone erupt from his shins. Roger screamed in pain and collapsed.

"Fuck! I knew I shouldn't have worn this red shirt," he wailed.

Quickly, Jenni hooked her hands under Roger's arms. "Bill, help me!"

Bill stared at the window. "We need to go," he said in a desolate tone.

"Help me!" Jenni repeated, trying to drag Roger across the roof. The injured man howled in agony.

"Now, Jenni," Bill ordered. "We need to go *now*."

She looked up in time to see the first zombie plunge out of the window. Luckily, it landed headfirst, splitting its skull open. But the second landed on the first and immediately began crawling toward them.

Roger looked at her, terror in his eyes. "Make it fast," he said, his voice cracking. "It's over, Jenni."

More zombies were tumbling onto the roof and making their way toward the living.

"Jenni, do as he says!" Bill's voice was urgent and stricken all at the same time. "I lost my gun up there!"

"Make it fast!" Roger screamed at her, his gaze fastened on the zombies crawling toward him. "I don't want to be eaten alive! Do it!"

"Roger, I'm so sorry," Jenni whispered. She drew her weapon and pulled the trigger.

Bill grabbed her and they ran to the edge of the roof. "Roll when you land," Bill instructed.

With a nod, she sat down on the edge of the roof, her legs dangling. Taking a breath, she pushed off. She landed hard but managed to roll. A sharp, swift pain hit her and she felt blood on her hands, warm and sticky. Glancing down, she realized one of the surgical tools had sliced through the makeshift bag to cut a shallow, two-inch-long gash in her side.

Bill landed with a thud next to her and got to his feet, panting. "Just run," he said.

There were zombies all over the front lawn and more climbing out of a lower window. Slow, shambling figures grabbed at Bill and Jenni as they weaved quickly through the undead throng to the truck. Leaping inside, they slammed and locked the doors. Instantly, zombies began banging on the sides of the pickup. Turning on the engine, Bill floored the gas and broke through the wave of zombies pouring out of the hospital before they completely blocked the road.

Pulling off her jacket, Jenni tried to stanch the flow of blood from her wound.

"What happened?" Bill demanded tensely.

"Cut myself on something in the bag," she answered, lifting her sweater to show him the slash in her side.

"Okay," Bill said with relief.

The side mirror showed Jenni the throng of zombies crowding the front lawn of the hospital. There were far more of the things in the building than the scavenging teams had realized. They had been incredibly lucky to escape.

They fell silent as the truck roared into the hills. The sun was setting and the sky was ablaze in pinks and purples.

"We had to leave him," Bill finally said. "His legs were broken. We couldn't have carried him."

"I know."

"We all knew the risks," Bill continued.

"I know." Jenni was crying and her side was killing her, but she had the tools needed to save Juan. She hoped what she and the others had salvaged was enough. An hour back to the fort and then Juan would have his operation.

"Did you see the moving van?"

Jenni shook her head dismally. "It was gone."

"They must be ahead of us then." Reaching out, he snagged the CB mouthpiece. When he turned it on, a screech filled the cab.

"Shit!"

Bill tried to change the channel, but the electronic screech continued. Finally, he turned it off.

"Must be something interfering. A storm or something," he said in confusion.

Jenni checked her wound. The bleeding had slowed.

The darkness of the night washed over them, chasing away the brilliance of the sunset. Soon they were submerged in inky blackness.

"I liked them," Jenni said, a hitch in her voice.

"Me, too. Felix and Roger were both great guys."

Abruptly, the cab was filled with a bright, blinding white light. The red truck veered off the road, plunged through some brush, and slammed into a fence post.

Inside the cab, nothing stirred.

# · CHAPTER TEN ·

## 1.
### *Full Circle*

Jenni swam up from the depths of unconsciousness, her mind spinning and her body spasming. She fought to wakefulness, pushing her eyes open, straining to see. There was a loud ringing in her ears that made her feel sick to her stomach.

Something bad had happened, she knew, but the fragments of memory refused to form a coherent image.

Where was she? She'd been in a truck. . . . The truck had crashed! But she wasn't in the truck now; she was on a bed or cot. Was she in a hospital? She had been in a hospital, but they had escaped. Hadn't they?

Were there zombies around?

"Good to see you're awake."

It was a voice she didn't recognize. Struggling to sit up, she saw a handsome black man with the kindest green eyes she had ever seen sitting in a chair near the cot she was lying on. Dressed in fatigues, he was staring at her curiously.

"Fuck you," Jenni said, her fear quickly turning into angry defiance.

"We hardly know each other," the man answered, flashing a brilliant smile. "Let me introduce myself. I'm Lieutenant Kevin Reynolds. And you are?"

"I don't care who you are! You fucking kidnapped me!" Jenni nearly growled the words. Her fear for Juan was jumbled with the disaster at the hospital and the bright light blinding her and Bill. "Where's Bill?"

"Is that his name?"

Jenni clamped her mouth shut, determined to give nothing away.

"We've met before," Lieutenant Reynolds said. "You were wearing a pink bathrobe and you had this dog that looked exactly like one I had when I was a kid. There was a blond woman with you."

Taking a deep breath, Jenni glared at him and said nothing.

"I told you to come here, to Madison. But you went somewhere else."

The officer opened up a folder and began to show her photos of the fort and the people in it. The pictures had been taken from a distance, probably with a telescopic lens. One image showed Jenni and Juan. The sight of the man she loved brought tears to her eyes.

"Tell me about your home," Lieutenant Reynolds said in a soft, warm voice.

"Fuck you, *puto*. I'm not going to tell you a gawd damn thing," Jenni snarled. "You kidnapped me!"

"Our orders are to bring any civilians we find outside of the designated rescue center back here. It's for your protection."

Juan needed her, and these assholes were holding her prisoner.

"Please, talk to me. Tell me about your friends."

"Fuck you! I'm not telling you a damn thing! Let me go!"

With a sigh, Lieutenant Reynolds stood, closing the folder and tucking it under his arm. "Well, I see you don't want to cooperate. I'll give you a little time to cool off."

"I'm not going to tell you anything! You kidnapped me!" Jenni managed to pull herself off the cot. She staggered after the soldier as he slipped out the door. She heard the metallic click of the lock. Banging on the door, she screamed, "Let me out of here! You can't keep me here!"

\*   \*   \*

Bill looked at the photos, then at Lieutenant Reynolds. He sat in a chair, his hands folded on his lap. So far he'd been treated well, though he had heard Jenni screaming. But in a way, that was to be expected. Even if she was being treated kindly, she would kick up a fuss.

"We're just survivors making our way," Bill said.

"Are you a militia of some kind?"

"No, no. We're just trying to stay alive."

"Any religious affiliation?"

"You mean like a cult? No. We're all kinds: mostly Baptists, some Catholics, a few Hindus, a Jewish person, an agnostic or two . . . maybe even an atheist. And one guy who believes in aliens," Bill answered honestly.

Lieutenant Reynolds looked thoughtful. He tapped one of the photos that showed the walls of the fort. "And you did all this on the spur of the moment? There was no preplanning?"

"It was all done out of necessity, sir. Really. I mean, you gotta survive somehow when the dead come back." Bill shrugged a little.

"Back at the beginning, did you hear the order to report to Madison?"

"Honestly, no. I was hiding, just trying to stay safe."

Lieutenant Reynolds nodded again, looking thoughtful. "Well, martial law was enacted and all civilians were ordered to report to rescue centers." Bill stared at him. The soldier went on, his expression grim. "It is our responsibility to ensure the safety of the civilian population and keep our nation alive in any way possible."

"Yeah, so?"

The lieutenant studied Bill's expression intently as he said, "My superiors plan to take over the fort."

Bill blinked slowly, then lowered his head. He thought long and hard, swallowed a few times, then looked up. "The fort people won't take kindly to that."

Lieutenant Reynolds stared at him, then gave him a curt

nod. "Thank you for your time." Gathering his things, he left the room.

As the guard shut the door behind the officer, Bill sat back in his chair, exhaling slowly. "This ain't good."

## 2.
### *The Pendulum Sword*

From the window of her hotel room, Katarina watched a single truck near the fort, its headlights slicing through the blackness of the night. She had been waiting nervously for the last few hours for Bill to return. Dressed in her best jeans and blouse, she was ready for their date. She was still stunned that he had asked her to join him for a drink. Men did not usually take notice of her as anything more than a friend.

A few more minutes ticked by without any sign of the second vehicle that had been dispatched to the hospital.

"Shit," Katarina swore.

With a sinking heart, she feared the worst. Grabbing her coat, she rushed out of her room. In the hallway outside the clinic, she caught sight of the crew, led by Monica, carrying medical equipment.

"Monica, where are the others?" she asked.

"We don't know. We got overrun," Monica replied sadly before wheeling what looked like a heart monitor into the clinic.

Breaking into a run, Katarina headed for the garage, where she found Nerit, Travis, and Ed standing near the moving truck.

"Where are the others?" Katarina asked as she joined them. "Have we heard?"

"We don't know. We can't raise them on the CB," Nerit answered.

"Monica told us that there was a horde of zombies in the hospital. They broke out of a secured area and attacked the teams."

Travis took a deep breath, obviously trying to steady his nerves. "Lenore said it got bad really fast."

Katarina hesitated, then said, "I'll take a crew and go look for them."

"The airwaves are full of static, so we won't be able to talk to you. A norther is blowing in." Travis's tone was miserable. "We can't chance a bad storm and losing more people. We'll wait until morning."

Katarina swallowed hard. "What if they need help?"

Travis folded his arms over his chest and lowered his head slightly. He was obviously torn, but finally he shook his head. "We can't risk it."

"Everyone heading out knew there was a chance they weren't coming back," Ed added grimly. "No use risking other people to get them back when the conditions ain't good."

"Chances are, they are fine," Nerit said with a smile that didn't reach her eyes.

Katarina knew Nerit was trying to keep her calm and give her hope. But Katarina didn't feel calm or hopeful. "I'll go alone. I know the roads around here. I can handle it."

"No," Travis said simply. "We can't risk it. Lightning is flashing on the horizon. We still got those zombies on the outskirts wandering around. If something went wrong—"

"Something has already gone wrong," Katarina reminded him. "Those are our people out there!"

"You and I will go look for them in the morning," Nerit said in a tone that was all ice. Her fake smile was nowhere to be seen.

With a slight bob of her head, Katarina headed back to the hotel. She struggled to breathe and regain her composure.

The thought of Bill being lost to the zombie hordes hurt her more than she'd thought possible. Raising her eyes to the night sky, she prayed silently for his safe return.

# 3.
## *Revelation*

Jenni was surprised when Bill came to claim her from the holding cell. After giving him a hug, she asked, "What's going on?"

"They're having us join the rest of the people here in the rescue center. Got work and sleeping assignments."

Jenni gave him a wary look as he guided her out the door and down a long corridor. "So they aren't letting us go home? Shit."

"That's not the worst of it," Bill confessed.

"What is it?" Jenni frowned, not liking his tone.

"You're not going to like this," Bill warned.

Bill and Jenni stepped through the door and onto a walkway, then gazed over the railing into the world of Madison.

"Fuck," Jenni groaned. "It's a mall."

# · CHAPTER ELEVEN ·

## 1.
### *Waiting*

Peggy slammed her coffee cup down on the table; a little liquid sloshed out. The people gathered around the large table in the dining room regarded her curiously. "No word. Nothing." Grimacing, she tucked herself into a chair next to Dale. He gave her a short, comforting squeeze and she relished the moment.

Across the table, Lenore reached for a biscuit and grumbled, "That ain't good."

Ken gently rubbed her shoulder. "It'll be okay. They'll come back."

"We shouldn't have left them," Monica whispered, pouring whiskey into her coffee.

"We had to get out of there and get the equipment back," Dale stated. "Plus, the damn zombies were coming out of the woodwork."

Maddie ran her delicate hands down over her long tousled hair, which was a pretty mix of white, silver, and strawberry blond. "You can't second-guess yourselves. You did what you felt was right."

Peggy was torn between being spitting mad and succumbing to despair. She was tired of losing people. Tired of grief. Tired of the whole damn mess.

She grabbed a biscuit from the Tupperware container and reached for the butter and the peach jam. She was all about comfort eating. Rosie had put out coffee and hot tea as well as the day-old biscuits for a late-night snack. "Well, there ain't nothing out there tonight but static. Storm is kicking up a lot of wind, and the lightning isn't helping."

Monica passed the liquor bottle to Dale, then set her elbow on the table and rested her chin on her knuckles. "They just came at us so fast—I still don't know how we got Ken out of there."

"It was a blessing you did," Maddie said, patting Ken's hand.

Ken shook his head. "Not if it got the other team killed."

"I did what I had to," Lenore said hotly. "I was not letting my best friend die."

"No one is blaming you," Dale assured her. "I would have done the same damn thing."

"Felix, Jenni, Bill, and Roger all kick ass on a regular basis," Monica said. "If anyone can make it out of a hospital full of zombies, it's them."

Unexpectedly, tears spilled down Lenore's cheeks. "If they died . . ."

"Oh, Lenore, don't cry!" Maddie slid to her bare feet and rushed around the table to hug her. "You did what you thought was right."

"I may have gotten Felix killed," Lenore whispered. "And Jenni. Bill. And stupid ol' Roger, always going on about *Star Trek* . . ."

"It's my fault, Lenore, not yours! I shouldn't have gone down that hall!" Ken was adamant.

"But you were supposed to go there. It was your part of the mission. And you didn't know the zombies were there. What else could you have done?" Monica finished her coffee, then took the whiskey back from Dale and poured more into her cup.

"It's okay, little buddy. You were a tough *hombre* out there and you did good. I was damn proud of you." Dale raised his cup to Ken.

"Really?" Ken perked up.

"Really."

Monica gulped her drink and poured more. "We know the risks. Every time we go out there, we know the freaking risks."

"Should I cut you off?" Dale eyed the Latina thoughtfully.

"Try it." She gave him a sly smile.

"No flirting!" Ken pointed at her accusingly.

"You stop first!"

Dale chuckled as Ken sputtered.

Peggy sighed and stuffed a whole biscuit in her mouth. Dale looked at her, obviously impressed. When she'd finished chewing its floury goodness, she stared at him and said, "I was hungry." The truth was she was about to say something that would have pissed everyone off. She was in a bad mood and knew it. Yet she didn't want to be alone.

Curtis walked into the dining room and headed over, one hand shoving his thin blond hair back from his face. Peggy thought he looked about as harried as she felt.

"Monica, there you are. I thought you were going to join me in the communication center," Curtis said.

"I'm getting drunk," she answered, clicking coffee cups with Dale.

"Oh," Curtis said. He shot a peeved look at Dale, then sat down on Monica's other side.

"Felix was such a great guy," Monica said. "He was my buddy. And Roger, that fucking perv, taught me how to swear in Klingon. And Bill . . . man . . . Bill . . ."

"We don't know what's happened. We shouldn't start having their wake just yet," Maddie said gently.

"You don't know how we feel. You didn't know them." Curtis crossed his arms over his chest and glared at the older woman.

"Don't get in Maddie's face," Dale said shortly.

"I'm just saying she has no idea—"

Peggy put her hand on Curtis's arm and squeezed. "Shut up."

"What?" He looked at her in surprise.

"Just shut up. We're all upset, tired, and pissed off, and we're just trying to get a little comfort from each other. We don't need you wagging your badge or your dick in our faces."

Monica snorted whiskey out of her nose as she laughed. Curtis shot her a hurt look.

Slamming her hands down on the table, Lenore glowered at no one in particular. "I did what I thought was right."

"I wouldn't be here if not for you," Ken said, hugging her arm.

"But maybe the rest of the team *would* be here if you hadn't fired your gun," Curtis snapped.

"That's it!" Peggy stood up, grabbed Curtis's wrist, and dragged him out of his chair. "Go back to the communication center and do your job. Now!"

Curtis sputtered, but the look on Peggy's face shut him up. With a dark scowl, he stomped off.

Monica downed the last bit of whiskey and stood up, swaying on her feet. "I'll go calm his ass down."

"Is that what they call it nowadays?" Peggy felt a sharp pang of disappointment as Monica started after Curtis.

With a shrug, Monica kept walking.

"I'm not going into the communication center until tomorrow," Ken proclaimed.

"As long as they're still listening for our people," Peggy said, and sighed.

"Nothing wrong with comforting each other in our time of need," Dale said.

"Nothing at all," Maddie agreed. She was sitting next to Lenore and gently stroking her hair.

"You remind me of my grandma," Lenore said quietly.

The people at the table lapsed into silence and Peggy began to butter another biscuit. She couldn't stay much longer. Cody was sleeping over in a friend's room and she wanted to make sure he was okay before the friend's parents turned in.

She took a deep breath. Maybe it was the manly scent of Dale next to her or the smell of the biscuits, but she felt a little more relaxed.

# 2.
## *Choices Made in Haste*

It was nearly dawn when Travis finally climbed into bed. Katie was curled up with Jack, who gave Travis a petulant look as the man scooted the dog to the end of the bed. Spooning his wife, Travis kissed her shoulder.

"Are they back?" Her voice was thick with sleep.

"No," Travis sighed. "Nerit is taking a team out to look for them once the sun rises."

Katie rolled over and studied her husband's face, her green eyes glistening with tears. "You think they're dead, don't you?"

"No," Travis said, trying to keep the uncertainty from his voice. "I think there's a good chance that they're okay."

"I don't want to lose Jenni," Katie said, her voice quivering. "When I saved her, she saved me, too. She gave me a reason to live."

"Katie, we'll find her." Travis gently tucked her hair back from her face and kissed her brow. "It won't do you any good to upset yourself by thinking the worst."

Katie pressed her palms against her red eyes, nodding. "I know you're right. I just can't bear to lose her."

"Jenni won't leave this world without a fight. We both know that." Travis yawned loudly.

"Didn't sleep, did you?"

"I didn't mean to wake you." Travis pulled the covers over him as he kicked off his boots. They hit the floor with a resounding thud. Jack again gave him a disapproving look.

"How is Juan?" Katie spoke hesitantly, as if she wasn't sure she wanted to hear the answer.

"Stable, for now. Charlotte's doing the best she can. At least she now has some good monitoring equipment and some drugs to help control the infection."

"Thank God, he's still alive." Katie wrapped her arms around Travis's neck and kissed him lightly.

He sighed with weariness and contentment as she snuggled against his side. He felt her rounded tummy pressing against him. "I felt wired, so I stayed up working on some ideas. Plus, Ed gave me shit for not allowing the fort to vote on Blanche's fate." He looked at Katie, expecting her to be angry, but she looked pensive. "I was pissed. I was done with her. People had been killed and my best friend was dying. All over that damn Hummer."

"You knew leaving her at the mansion was a death sentence," Katie said flatly.

Travis moaned and covered his face with one hand. "Yes, I knew."

"Ed was upset?"

"He said we should have taken it to the fort."

"But it's done now."

"I should send someone out to check on her, shouldn't I?"

With a weary sigh, Katie said, "I don't know. I don't give a damn what happens to her, but if it adversely affects the fort . . ."

"Maybe we should bring her back, let everyone have a say, like we will with Brewster." Travis groaned. "Just when I thought I would get some sleep . . ."

"You're not going out there yourself, are you?"

"Nah. I'll find a volunteer." He glanced at the clock. "I'll go meet Nerit's team, see if anyone wants to look in on Blanche instead. They should be heading for breakfast."

"Then you'll come back for a few hours of sleep?"

"Yeah. Unless something else happens." Getting out of bed and reaching for his boots, he gave the reproachful-looking German shepherd a pat on the head.

# 3.
## *Walking Hamburgers and Helicopters*

The morning was very cold and misty. The Hummer sped along the back roads. Occasionally Nerit spotted a dark figure in the wispy haze, but mostly the world seemed sadly empty. The few houses they passed were desolate looking. Before winter set in, nature had begun dismantling the buildings; the season's damp weather had accelerated the process.

She stared out at the dead world thoughtfully. Behind the wheel, Katarina yawned as she drove past a herd of cows gathered around a pond. Nerit observed that they appeared relatively healthy, considering how long they had been on their own.

Curtis and Dale sat in the back, quiet and half-dozing.

"It won't take too long," Nerit commented.

"Huh?" Katarina asked, glancing at her before returning her attention to the road.

"For nature to take back the planet." Nerit motioned to the fallen fences alongside the road and a farmhouse with a listing front door.

Katarina glanced over. "Yeah. It's already going to hell. We never built anything to last."

"Hopefully humanity can outlast the disposable world we created." Nerit's thoughts lingered briefly on her family in Israel.

"Some of us are still here," Katarina asserted.

"The lucky and the too damn stubborn to die," Nerit said with a wry grin.

"I know which category I'm in."

"Me, too, Katarina."

"Damn lucky?"

"Absolutely." Nerit chuckled.

"Weird how it worked, huh? If you made it through the first day, it got easier somehow." Katarina steered the Hummer around a discarded tractor. She gestured to the zombie stumbling along the side of the road. "This feels normal now."

Nerit inclined her head in agreement. "People are beginning to move on. We're expanding our home . . . planting gardens . . ."

"Falling in love . . ."

Nerit studied Katarina suspiciously. "You like Bill."

"He's nice," Katarina said after a second.

"Nice is good. Ralph was nice." She felt the smile on her face soften at the thought of her dead husband. She missed him dearly. Then Nerit stiffened as she caught a flash of red ahead. "There," she said, pointing.

Katarina pulled over and stopped. The red pickup that had once belonged to Nerit's late husband, Ralph, was smashed into a fence post. Its deer guard had absorbed most of the damage, so it might be drivable. Both doors were wide open and it was obvious that the truck was empty.

"Shit," Curtis said sleepily, straightening up. "This isn't good."

Dale woke in mid-snore and sputtered incoherently before saying, "Hey, cows."

"They must have got out when the truck took the fence down," Katarina said.

Nerit gestured toward the crashed vehicle. "Get out slowly. Cover all sides. Let me examine the area around the truck." Opening her door, she slid out.

"You got it," Dale said.

Katarina jumped out of the truck, holding her gun easily in her hands. Curtis stumbled and worked a crick out of his leg as Dale strode in a slow circle, keeping his eye on the cows.

"Them's good eating," he said finally.

"Keep to the objective," Nerit responded as she moved toward the red pickup. With a little groan, she squatted down to squint at some shoe prints in the mud by the rear wheel. Curtis joined her, appearing perplexed.

"Jenni and Bill always wear cowboy boots. What do Roger and Felix wear?"

"Roger wears those nasty sneakers," Curtis said, "and Felix always has on those white trainers."

"What do these look like to you?" Nerit pointed at the impressions in the mud.

"Honestly? Combat boot prints."

"Exactly." Nerit stood up slowly, feeling her hips and back protesting. Gazing inside the pickup, she saw drying blood, sticky in the humidity of the morning, smeared along the passenger side.

"Military?" Dale asked.

"Possibly," Nerit replied. "Someone was hurt."

Curtis was instantly at Nerit's side. "Think they got bitten and went at each other?"

Nerit lifted a makeshift bag out of the truck. The white fabric was stained with blood and it clinked as she set it on the hood. She showed the others the tear in the fabric. "I think Jenni was stabbed by something in here."

"You can tell who was hurt by looking at the blood?" Dale asked in surprise.

"No, sweetheart, by looking at her wadded-up, bloodied leather jacket," Nerit answered, gesturing to the article of clothing lying on the floor of the truck.

Katarina pointed. "There are drag marks in the grass."

"And along the side of the truck," Curtis added.

"A helicopter set down in the pasture," Nerit said after looking around once more.

"How can you tell?"

"Look at the grass, Curtis. It's flattened in a circle. And it's not one of Roger's crop circles." Nerit moved around the truck slowly.

"Only two bodies," Curtis said from behind her as he studied the drag marks.

"Yes," Nerit answered. "Just two."

"So they, whoever they are, got Jenni and one other person." Katarina's voice was devoid of emotion, but Nerit knew the other woman was devastated by the turn of events.

Nerit climbed into her familiar old truck. Turning the key, she furrowed her brow as the engine tried to turn over. Suddenly it roared to life.

Katarina was stoic, but Nerit knew she was in pain. Curtis looked bewildered. Dale was still staring at the cows like they were walking hamburgers.

"What do we do now?" Curtis asked.

"We go back and tell everyone that we're not alone. And that they, whoever they are, have Jenni and one other survivor."

Curtis shook his head. "Fucking shit! If Lenore hadn't tried to save Ken—"

"She did what I would have done, fucktard," Dale growled. "You don't let friends die right in front of you."

Curtis recoiled from the harshness in Dale's voice. "Okay, okay."

"We do what comes instinctively. Lenore saved her friend. But we lost two others. That is the nature of this world," Nerit said grimly. "There are no second guesses, Curtis. We just do our best."

"Yeah, but Bill, Jenni, Roger, and Felix . . . they're gone," Curtis said in a low, tight voice.

"Yes, they are," Nerit answered calmly. "Now, let's go home."

Wordlessly, Katarina returned to the Hummer and climbed in. Curtis joined her, hunching down in his seat.

"Can I have a cow?" Dale asked.

Nerit snorted. "No."

Dale sighed, then climbed into the red truck with her, heedless of the drying blood. Nerit backed up slowly, relieved when the truck responded without a hitch.

"So you think the fucking military is out there?"

"Yes," Nerit answered, falling in line behind the Hummer. She gripped the steering wheel tightly. "The combat boots could have been anyone, but the helicopter signals military."

"Great. Fucking great. And who do you think controls them?"

Nerit lifted her shoulders. "People of power."

"Dammit," Dale cussed. "I was kinda hoping Congress got ate."

# 4.
## *Only Questions*

Katie hurried across the lobby, avoiding some of the old-timers who were taking up their morning bingo spots. Her blond curls were pulled up into a ponytail, and she was clad in one of Travis's shirts. Her swelling belly was beginning to pop out the bottom of her tops. Though she felt sheepish to admit it, she loved her baby bump. Instinctively, she placed a hand against her stomach as she ran, almost as if she could protect the baby from whatever news Nerit and the others had brought.

When she'd woken not long ago, Katie groggily realized that Travis had never returned to bed. She'd called down to the front desk to see if Peggy knew where her husband was located. Grumpy herself, Peggy told Katie that both teams Travis had sent out earlier were on their way back to the fort. After changing her clothes, Katie had rushed downstairs.

Entering, she could tell by the expression on Nerit's face that the news was not good. Nerit looked calm, but her gaze was fierce. She stood talking with Travis, whose expression was likewise serious as he rubbed his brow.

"What happened?" Katie asked as she reached them, her voice raw. She feared the worst.

"We found the truck and they weren't in it," Nerit answered simply. Shocked, Katie recoiled at the bluntness of the statement. Before she could say anything, Nerit went on, "They were taken, apparently by the military. We think it was Jenni and one of the men." Nerit's tone was gentle, despite the steel in her eyes.

"So we lost two people at the hospital," Katie said sadly.

Travis nodded, his mouth pressed into a grim line. "And the military is out there somewhere."

Nerit explained how she'd figured out that Jenni was one of the missing, then added, "We brought back the surgical equipment they'd found and gave it to Charlotte. She says it will help save Juan." Nerit smiled bitterly. "The mission was successful."

Dizzy at the thought of Jenni being hurt, being carted off by some unknown military force, Katie leaned against Travis. His arm snaked around her and he held her briefly, releasing her as Ed and Monica approached.

"What did you find at Blanche's?" Travis asked. His voice was weary; Katie suspected he didn't want to hear any more bad news.

"A wrecked Mercedes, packed to the gills with supplies. We think Ray busted the axle trying to drive off-road, maybe to keep from being seen by Curtis and Katarina yesterday," Ed replied.

"We saw someone's remains on the mansion's porch. It looked like a man, so it was probably Ray. Gunshot wound to what was left of his head." Monica shivered. "The front door was open. Zombies inside. We didn't go in."

"We didn't stick around. There were no signs of life," Ed added.

"Think she got away?" Katie wasn't sure if she wanted Blanche to be alive or not. She wasn't happy about the choice Travis had made about the woman's fate, but it was hard to feel sympathy for Blanche.

"Nope." Ed's keen eyes looked toward Travis. "I think she's dead."

Monica snorted. "I don't feel bad for the bitch. She shot my cousin and killed two men."

"Justice has got to be fair for everyone or it ain't justice," Ed said, biting off each word.

Travis bristled under his words and started to retort, but the phone rang. He picked it up, listened, said, "Okay," then hung up. "That was Peggy," he said. "She said word's getting around about the military, and people are asking questions. We should go see what's going on."

The little group left the office and went into the lobby, where a group of excited people had gathered near the front desk.

"Is it true that the army is coming to rescue us?" asked Harry

Gilbreath eagerly. He was the father of a young family who had been saved in the early days of the fort.

"We don't know. They took two of our people," Travis answered.

"Yeah, but they know we're here now. Our people will tell them where to find us. Right?" Harry said.

"Is that true?" asked Belinda hopefully.

"We don't know anything. Two of our people are missing. It looks like they were taken away in a helicopter by military personnel," Nerit responded.

"But if it's the army, that means we're saved!" This from an older black woman named Tamara. Her expression was rapturous.

"Maybe it's not the army at all," Reverend Thomas suggested.

People were becoming agitated; voices swelled and arguments broke out. Some seemed almost desperate to believe this was good news while others looked dubious. Katie counted herself among the doubters.

Nerit held up a hand and gradually things quieted somewhat. "The truth is, we do not know enough about the situation to draw any conclusions."

"We shouldn't get excited," Travis added. "We don't know what this means for the fort."

"But they'll rescue us," said Janet, a local. Her face was flushed and anxious.

"Save us how?" Travis asked her, point-blank.

"Take us to where it's safe," Janet answered.

"But it's safe here," Katarina said, stepping out of the crowd.

"But they'll have real weapons," a voice called from the back.

"All we really know is that we don't know what's happening," Travis said loudly. "And that is where things stand." He looked at Peggy. "Gather the council, please."

She nodded and began working her way through the crowd. Travis said to the group, "The council's going to talk about this and try to figure out what it means. Please try to stay calm and not spread any rumors."

He lowered his voice and spoke directly to Katie and Nerit. "Let's go back to my office." Katie took his hand as they headed down the corridor with Nerit close behind.

Travis closed the office door firmly behind them, then stalked over to his desk. "I don't like how this feels," he said soberly, not sitting, just leaning on his hands, which were flat on the desktop.

"People are going to go apeshit," Katie stated. "The idea of being rescued is going to drive some folks completely nuts."

A few minutes later, Peggy slipped into the room, followed by Curtis; Katarina, who was standing in for Bill; and Eric, who adjusted his glasses as he took a seat. There was a moment of tense silence as they realized how many of the council were gone. Katie even missed Calhoun whipping out his camcorder.

Nerit quickly filled everyone in.

Sitting near Katarina, Curtis was twitchy. "Can we trust them? When the world went to hell, they were killing people left and right in the streets."

"Killing infected people," Katie reminded him.

"We don't even know if it's the real military," Katarina said sullenly. "What if they're like in the movies? What if they're rogue?"

"Just because the zombie movie cliché is that the military are the bad guys doesn't mean that that's the case here and now. More likely these men and women are just doing their jobs, rescuing civilians," Nerit interjected.

"Maybe they're from the Madison Rescue Center," Peggy suggested. "Since all this started, they've been broadcasting the same message on a loop, telling us to stay in our homes and wait for rescue."

Katie raised her eyebrows, remembering. "Back on the first day, some soldiers told Jenni and me to go to Madison."

"Where *is* Madison?" Eric adjusted his glasses on his face.

"'Bout seventy-five miles or so to the northeast. It's a pretty large town." Curtis was toying with a bust of Lincoln on the table next to him.

"Haven't we avoided that area because we heard of a large zombie infestation out of the Dallas–Fort Worth area?" Eric asked. "Could that rescue center still be operational?"

Peggy looked doubtful. "We know it got ugly out that way. When we lost phone service, there was speculation it was because that area went dark."

"What was so special about Madison? Why did they send people there?" Katie asked. "Is there an army base there?"

"Naw, there's no base there." Curtis stopped fiddling with Lincoln. "There ain't nothing special there."

"There's a convention center and a mall." Katarina shivered. "Damn. A mall. Just like the movies."

"I figured the rescue centers were all gone long ago," Peggy admitted.

"But this one might still be there and operational." Eric looked thoughtful. "Perhaps they've established a safe haven just like we have."

"A helicopter would allow them to come and go safely if they are surrounded. Madison is also close enough for them to have taken our people there." Nerit fell silent. Katie could tell from the sharpness in her eyes that she was assessing the situation.

"So what do we do?" Eric asked.

"Try to contact them?" Katie offered.

"Military channels are not accessible to civilians," Nerit reminded them.

"Maybe we should send a message of our own," Katie suggested. "Requesting the return of our people. They must be monitoring us."

"If that's true," Travis said with a sigh, "I gotta ask why they didn't come knocking before."

"Too many questions with no answers." Katie raised her eyes to the ceiling and wished she could make sense of it all.

"Back when the world had order and things worked properly, we might have found each other quickly. But we can't apply old-world norms to our current situation," Nerit said.

"They're the United States military. Sworn to serve and protect.

I don't see why we should fear them, right, Nerit?" Eric directed his gaze at Nerit.

"Caution will always serve us best," Nerit answered. "But I agree."

"I think we should start by asking for our people to be returned," Peggy said. "Maybe now that they know we're here, they'll be listening for us. And we can talk like civilized people instead of freaking out."

Katie felt a twinge of hope. Perhaps Jenni would soon come home.

"We gotta find out what is going on out there. I say we send out an invite." Katarina pushed her heavy red hair out of her face. "Won't do us no good worrying and not doing."

"I got no issue with calling them up and asking for our people," Peggy declared. "I am so sick of this bullshit."

Travis took a deep breath. "Then let's do it."

# · CHAPTER TWELVE ·

## 1.
### *The Mall, Zombies, and the Alamo*

*Damn lot of zombies,* Bill thought.

He'd spent about an hour getting a tour of the mall from Major General Knox. Knox had spoken passionately about building a new tomorrow and a greater America. Then he'd escorted Bill onto the roof of the mall.

"What do you think?" the major general asked, sweeping his hand across the panorama of the dead town of Madison.

A tall white wall surrounded the mall. Inside the wall, the mall's parking lot was full of cars, trucks, buses, and army, marine, and national guard vehicles of every shape and color. Every entrance into the mall parking lot was heavily fortified, with multiple guards on duty.

And beyond the wall . . .

Zombies . . . a whole lot of zombies . . .

"We can eradicate them if we work together," Knox said decisively. The older man was dressed in fatigues, and his graying brown hair was cropped close to his head. Bill thought he wore his uniform as if it were a costume.

"Or just get eaten," Bill replied.

The major general frowned.

"It's happened before," Bill said. "In at least two movies. Malls. They're just bad news."

"I'm not sure what you are talking about, but I can assure you, we can overcome the undead scourge," Knox declared.

Bill wasn't too sure. It looked like a lot of Madison was outside the walls. He glanced at the mall defenses, then back over toward the throng of decaying, gruesome zombies clawing at the walls.

Yep, that was a whole lot of zombies. . . .

Damn.

Now he knew how the people in the Alamo felt.

Shit. He hoped he died well.

"First Lieutenant Reynolds reported that you felt that the people of the fort would not welcome our leadership, but certainly you must see now that we need to work together. We can provide the guidance you need."

For a moment, he wondered if the major general, who spoke with a thick East Coast accent, would understand if he paraphrased Davy Crockett's famous words, "You can go to hell—I'm going to the fort."

"Once we take control of the fort, we can make things better for everyone. Senator Brightman has a plan for a new society built on the ashes of the old one. My forces will take over security for the fort so your people can get out into the fields and start preparing for a new future."

Bill squinted at the guy, wondering if he realized what the hell he was saying. "You want us growing crops?"

"And starting a cattle ranch and whatever else will be needed to create a new tomorrow. The women will maintain the households and have the children."

"Really?" Bill knew he sounded skeptical, but from the major general's reply, the other man didn't notice.

"Oh, yes, every woman will need to produce at least one child every two years. We must increase our population and keep moving toward a secure future." Knox gave Bill a warm smile.

"So you're saying that after we built the fort, provided for ourselves, and fought off bandits and zombies, we should just turn it all over to you and let you tell us what to do?" Bill was incredulous.

"It'll be rough at first, but good, old American know-how will get us through. Your people won't have anything to worry about. You'll have an experienced senator governing you and a trained military force protecting you. Sounds good, doesn't it?"

Tilting his head to one side, Bill took a deep breath, eyeing the throng of decaying dead outside the walls. Despite the general's friendly tone, the words he was saying brought a chill to Bill's innards.

In a deep Texan drawl that he deliberately emphasized, Bill answered, "Born, raised, and live as a Texan, sir. Aim to die as one. America was good to me, but she's as dead as those people out there. This is frontier land again. And if you don't see it that way, yer fucked. This is Texas. We don't take kindly to being told what to do."

The major general blinked at him. "I don't understand."

"This is *Texas,* sir. Folks here aim to do what's best for themselves and their families. Your government, your military, they don't exist anymore as far as we're concerned. We'll do our own thing, find our own way."

"You're saying the people at the fort won't welcome our leadership?"

"No, sir. I am saying that they will tell you to fuck off."

The military man's eyebrows lifted in surprise.

"Think I'm done now," Bill said firmly.

Major General Knox slowly nodded and ordered a soldier to lead Bill back into the mall to rejoin the rest of the population.

Bill was more than glad to get out of the view of the zombies outside the walls, but the mall didn't make him feel much safer. The blacked-out windows and dim lighting made the interior very gloomy. People were bundled up in sweaters, jackets, and jeans since the heat was off. Most of the survivors were in their late twenties to early thirties, but pain and despair had visibly aged them. Bill had seen only a few children and a handful of elderly people during his tour, and no laughter or joy. The mall felt more like a prison than a home.

Spotting Jenni at a table, eating breakfast, he headed over to her. She flipped her long dark hair over one shoulder and smiled at him as he sat down next to her. "What's the big deal with that guy wanting to tour you around the mall? I saw y'all walking around."

"We're in the gawd damn Alamo," Bill said gruffly, then filled her in on what he'd just seen.

"Seriously?" Jenni asked when he was done.

"Only difference, Mexicans didn't eat the people in the Alamo," Bill said with a wry smile.

Jenni leaned her head into his beefy shoulder. "Damn. We sure are good at getting ourselves into trouble."

"Yeah, tell me about it. This place makes the hospital look like a cake walk." Bill exhaled long and hard. He slid an arm around Jenni's shoulders and hugged her. "It'll be okay, Jenni. We always figure something out. We'll get out of here."

"I don't think my usual method of whacking zombies with my ax is going to work," Jenni said, moping. "Especially since I left my ax at the hospital."

Bill grinned briefly, then said, "Our friends are going to be looking for us and hopefully something can be done."

Jenni lifted a spoonful of oatmeal and slowly turned it over. The thick, gloppy stuff clung to the spoon. "Ugh. I hate the food here. Tasteless and gross. I miss Rosie's breakfast tacos."

"Me, too." Bill sighed. "Have you really looked at the people here? They've given up hope. They're like ghosts, just wandering around empty. If they're not doing their cleaning chores, they just sit and stare."

Jenni slowly swiveled in her chair, examining the people seated around them. There was barely a whisper of conversation among them and few smiles.

"I want to go home," Jenni said in a soft voice.

"We will, Jenni," Bill vowed.

## 2.
### *Speaker of the Dead*

Travis sighed and tried hard not to look at the clock hanging over the clinic's check-in counter. He hated waiting. It was sheer torture and always made him feel as though someone had decided to churn butter in his gut. Charlotte, Belinda, and the reverend were operating on Juan in an attempt to remove the bullet.

It didn't help that Travis hadn't slept a wink the night before. Rubbing his gritty eyes, he yawned. At least he wasn't alone—Juan's friends and family were all gathered in the waiting room.

Rosie sat nearby, clutching her rosary and whispering softly, "Hail Mary, full of Grace . . ." Nerit sat next to her, eyes closed, one hand resting gently on Rosie's arm. Jason was sprawled on the love seat next to the couch Travis was sitting on, reading a *Star Trek* novel he'd borrowed from Roger before the ill-fated hospital trip. The boy looked absolutely morose, and Travis couldn't blame him. His mother was apparently in the hands of whatever remained of the U.S. military, his friend and teacher was missing, and his stepfather, near death, was having surgery. Jason may have acted the surly teenager around Juan, but Travis knew that covered real affection for the man.

Travis looked down at Katie, who was asleep with her head resting on his thigh. He slowly drew his fingers through her hair, marveling anew at the softness of her silky curls. He was glad she was sleeping soundly; the stress of the last twenty-four hours had worn on her.

Picking up a pad and pencil from the end table next to him, Travis started to sketch a possible extension to the fort. Working made him feel more in control. He hated feeling helpless, feeling that there was nothing he could do to remedy a bad situation.

It wasn't until the fort had risen from the ashes of the former world that he felt he had found his place. People in the fort saw

Travis as a leader. He saw himself as a helper, doing his best to build a new life and make sure it was safe. He was Katie's husband and their child's father, and that was good enough for him. All the rest of it, the looks of admiration, the looks of disdain, the arguments, the accolades, were meaningless when he looked down into Katie's face.

"I always loved looking at her when she slept," said a silky, deep voice.

Looking up, Travis saw a very tall, slim woman gazing down at Katie. The newcomer wore a long-sleeved black dress that brushed the toes of her black boots. She sat down next to Jason, who ignored her, and smiled at Travis.

She had amazing cheekbones, shining dark eyes, and close-cropped brown hair with auburn highlights. Ornate exotic jewelry decorated her throat and wrists.

"She looks so innocent when she sleeps, though every once in a while, she gets this furrow right here," the woman said, leaning over to point between Katie's eyebrows. "That means she's arguing a case in her sleep."

"Lydia," Travis whispered.

"Yes," she answered with a dazzling smile.

Her hands were long and elegant, he saw, and she wore a diamond wedding band.

"I must be asleep," Travis said.

"You are," Lydia confirmed. She watched Katie, her eyes glimmering with unspoken love. She smiled bittersweetly. "She looks beautiful pregnant."

Even though he knew he was dreaming, Travis felt awkward. Meeting his wife's former wife was very odd. He didn't know what to say, and Lydia must have seen the confusion on his face, because she laughed and said, "Don't worry, Travis. Life goes on for the living. I know that. I don't want to hold her back from loving again. But I will always love her and I want her to be happy."

"But," Travis said, rubbing his brow and wincing with embarrassment, "I'm a guy."

"Yes, you are." Lydia reached toward him but didn't quite touch him. "It's all right, Travis. The heart loves without boundaries. It is the mind that can trap the heart with cages constructed by society's rules. Katie always had a beautiful open heart."

"Why am I dreaming about you, Lydia?"

Lydia's smile faded a little and she sat back, crossing her legs. "I'm here to give you a message."

"About Katie?"

"About you." She gazed at him with a serenity that was both comforting and disconcerting. "You need to understand that the world has changed. The veil between the living and the dead is very thin. Many have died and more will die as the world tries to regain its balance. The dead are all around you. Not just the empty shells that are trying to kill you, but the spirits of those trapped when the dead seized the world from the living."

"Like you," he said softly.

"Yes. I have yet to move on. But soon the world will find a new equilibrium and I will."

"I'm sorry about what happened to you, Lydia."

"Being a Good Samaritan sometimes gets you killed. Trust me." A shadow of pain flitted over her features before she swept it away with a wave of her hand. "This is something you need to learn."

"What are you saying?" He narrowed his eyes.

"You want to save everyone, Travis. But soon you will fully understand the fruitlessness of trying to control everything around you. You will need to make choices for yourself, Katie, and the baby."

Frowning a little, Travis looked down at his wife, then up at Lydia. "Katie and the baby are my priority, Lydia."

"Are they?" She stared straight into his eyes.

He swallowed hard, remembering how eager he'd been to risk his life to try to help Juan. Tears filled his eyes and his voice caught in his throat and he said, "You're right. I just want to help everyone."

Lydia smiled at him tenderly. "I know, but it's time for you to begin to let go of all the reins you have been holding and concentrate on your family. Other people will have to make choices for themselves. And sometimes even the right choice will lead to death."

"Who's going to die?"

Lydia gazed at Katie for a long, tender moment.

Travis held his breath, then repeated, "Who will die, Lydia?"

The dead woman hesitated. "The future isn't set. It's constantly changing, evolving, based on people's actions."

"But you know something."

"Juan is going to be all right. The operation was a success," she said softly; then suddenly she was gone and Charlotte was standing over Travis, shaking him gently by the shoulder.

"Did you hear me, Travis? Juan is going to be all right. We got the bullet and he's stable."

Katie was stirring and when she heard Charlotte's words, she leaped up and hugged her with joy. "Thank you, Charlotte!"

"Oh, thank God!" Rosie said, sobbing.

Then everyone was crying and hugging one another. Travis felt relieved but weirdly disconnected from his friends. His dream still felt tangible, and despite himself, he looked around for Lydia.

"Are you okay? You look a little odd," Katie said.

"I had a weird dream."

"Yeah, me, too. I dreamed you and Lydia were talking while I slept," Katie said. "Strange, huh?"

# · CHAPTER THIRTEEN ·

## 1.
### *The Return of the Living Dead and More*

The fort was completely enshrouded in fog and the fading darkness of the new day.

"Hate it when it's like this," Katarina groused as she stood watch on the wall, shivering in the early-morning chill.

"Should clear up once the sun is fully up," Monica, her partner on watch, offered.

"Just makes me nervous."

". . . if it was really her, then it means she's not trapped in a rotting corpse out there . . ." Katie's voice trailed out of the mist.

Katarina felt the floor beneath her quiver as the joggers approached. The extensive catwalk that had been built around the interior of the walled-in fort was finally finished, and several people used it as a jogging path, especially in the early-morning hours. Katie and Travis emerged from the mist, huffing and puffing, jogging slowly at an even stride.

"I don't know if I believe in ghosts," Travis said to his wife.

Everyone nodded hello to one another as the joggers shot by.

"Look, we live in a zombie-infested world. . . . I think that ghosts are not that much of a stretch anymore . . . ," Katie replied, and then they were gone.

Katarina wasn't sure what Katie and Travis were talking about, but on a morning like this, she didn't want to think about zombies and ghosts. She had a rough enough time dealing with her mother's ghost glowering at her at the worst times. Already, her skin was pricking and she didn't dare look behind her.

"This is the kinda thing that goes down in horror movies right before the monsters show up." Katarina lit a cigarette.

Monica laughed. "Oh, c'mon, you're not going to get all spooked out by some mist?"

Katarina gave Monica her coldest eye.

Monica grinned in response. "Zombies exist. I think we have the major spook factor covered, huh?"

The Christmas lights blinked on and off, small halos of red and green light illuminating the mist. As the fog parted slowly, at least a dozen zombies staggered into view. Decayed and gruesome, they pounded on the fort wall with low, rumbling moans.

Once again, Katarina was grateful for the wall. "Not too bad a group."

"Bullets or spears?"

"Save the ammo," Katarina answered. She and Monica grabbed long spears and braced themselves against the railing. The first group of zombies looked up and froze. They stared with wide, glazed eyes and slack mouths at the Christmas lights above. Some of the zombies behind them either didn't notice or weren't affected by the lights; they shoved past the staring ones to beat on the wall.

Katarina took a breath, ignoring the stench, and began to carefully plunge the spear into zombie skulls. She'd killed three of the creatures before a fourth grabbed her weapon, which she instantly released.

She was reaching for another spear when Monica shouted, "Katarina, they're pulling back!"

Whirling around, Katarina saw most of the zombies trudging back into the mist. Only three remained, staring at the Christmas lights.

"Someone's alive down there, close by. That's the only thing that would make them back off."

"Shit!" Monica pulled out her walkie-talkie. "We have a situation outside the wall. Possible human survivors approaching."

Moving swiftly, Katarina raised her rifle and dropped the last three zombies with a single shot each. All around the fort, spotlights were switched on, blazing out over the walls. Katarina cursed—nothing was visible except the now-gleaming mist. Hopefully whoever was out there could see the lights.

In the distance, Katarina heard the rumble of what sounded like an engine. Monica swung her spotlight back and forth, trying to see through the fog. A new sound broke through the moans of the unseen zombies—the barks and growls of what sounded like a good-sized pack of dogs.

"Hello!" Katarina called out.

Travis and Katie reappeared out of the fog. "What's going on?" Travis asked.

"The zombies that were attacking the wall just took off," Monica answered.

"We think someone is alive down there," Katarina added. "Just listen."

A huge chunk of mist floated down the street even as the sun's rays began to slowly disperse the fog. The area outside the walls crept into view. The engine sound grew louder.

"I'll be damned!" Monica said.

A huge tractor was slowly coming down Bowie Street, towing two flatbeds. A strange, cagelike contraption surrounded the driver's seat of the tractor. The first flatbed was piled high with chicken coops and pet carriers; the second carried bales of hay. Behind this, following at a slow walk, was a small herd of black and white cows. Weaving in and out of the parade were dogs of many sizes and breeds.

And zombies.

It was almost comical, watching the zombies try to get to the driver of the tractor. Some were bouncing off the cows, which they completely ignored. Others were being attacked by the dogs.

Even the littlest Chihuahuas seemed almost rabid in their apparent hatred of the zombies. They clamped their jaws onto the dead and tore at them viciously. As the stunned onlookers on the walls watched, the pack took down a zombie with primal savagery. When a little terrier walked out of the fray carrying the thing's head by an ear, Katarina began to laugh.

"I'm going to start picking off the zombies on the outer edge," Katarina said. There were at least a dozen struggling to get past the dogs and cows to the driver.

A male zombie scrambled up onto the side of the tractor and shook the cage. It suddenly stiffened, then tumbled over dead. The zombie of an elderly woman tripped over a dog, fell, and was trampled by the cows.

The mist rolled back as the grayish light of dawn filled the streets. The driver of the tractor could now be clearly identified as Calhoun, complete with foil jumpsuit and cowboy hat. Katarina and Monica shot the zombies as Calhoun turned the tractor to run alongside the wall.

Spotting the fort people, he slowed down and shouted, "Got dairy cows for milk and chickens for eggs! Nobody eats 'em or I keep driving."

"Okay, Calhoun, just get inside!" Travis shouted back.

With a salute, Calhoun shifted gears and the parade continued.

Katarina could now see that the pet carriers on the first flatbed were filled with snarling, hissing cats.

Meanwhile, the little dog was still dragging the zombie head while a bigger dog attempted to steal it.

"Leave that nasty ol' head alone, Pee Wee," Calhoun called.

The little black dog heard its master and dropped the head. It hesitated, then lifted its leg and peed on the head before trotting after the rest of the dogs.

Katarina thought she would die laughing.

## 2.
### *John Wayne, the Alamo, and the Republic of Texas*

"Calhoun, seriously, I want to talk to you," Travis called from outside the rope corral. He peered through the milling cows, looking for the older man.

"Can't talk . . . milking," Calhoun answered from somewhere in the herd.

Travis sighed, climbed over the rope, and pushed through the cows, which barely acknowledged his presence.

Calhoun was seated on a short stool beside one of the black and white beasts, milking away. He still wore his foil suit and smelled of sour milk and sweat. Three cats and two dogs waited patiently for their master to send a squirt of fresh milk their way.

"So you went for your animals," Travis commented with a wry smile.

"Yep. Figured the feeders were about empty," Calhoun answered. "Had them rigged up to last half a year."

"I see."

"We need milk and eggs anyway," Calhoun said. "Keeps our brains sharp against the aliens. 'Sides, army's been circling my farm. Don't need them taking my stuff," Calhoun said darkly. "Don't take kindly to martial law. Didn't vote for that yokel in the White House."

"I think that yokel is dead," Travis said. "We're glad you're back, even though now we have to figure out how to handle the animals." He looked down at a Chihuahua that was busy sniffing his foot. "We thought Blanche had killed you."

"That bitch? Hell no! I saw her wandering around on the roads. Almost feel bad for them zombies that ate her. Must have given 'em a bad case of indigestion," Calhoun said with a snort.

"Calhoun, seriously, we got to talk," Travis said, trying to redirect the conversation.

Calhoun looked up at him through the long, crazy threads of his thick eyebrows and said, "You wired?"

"By who?"

"That old woman with the devil's eye."

"Nerit?"

"I figured it out. She's the *real* Amazonian queen."

Travis considered this, then shrugged. "Probably, but no, I'm not wired."

"What do you want to know?" Calhoun asked as he sprayed a cat with milk. The tabby licked the rich white liquid from its whiskers with relish.

"How long have you known about the army?"

"Army's been around for a long time," Calhoun answered. "Started back when we fought against the alien overlords that were possessing the English king."

"I mean, recently. The helicopters."

"I *told* you the government was kidnapping people for cloning. Then the clones got fucked up and now they're zombies."

"Do you know where the helicopters are coming from?"

Calhoun studied Travis long and hard before saying, "Madison. I monitor the military channels all the time. I will not be caught unaware again!" Calhoun squirted two dogs, muttering about zombies, clones, Ashley Oaks' former mayor, and the possessed government.

"You've been listening to military channels on the radio?"

"Yep," Calhoun said, nodding vigorously. "Madison Mall. They're all holed up in there, and some she-devil overlord is running the whole shebang. Talks all high and mighty to some nitwit in someplace called Central Government. They keep telling her that they want her to stay put."

"Why doesn't she take a helicopter to Central Government?"

" 'Cause they'd shoot her ass down. *Bam bam bam!*" Calhoun made a great show of this happening, complete with a demonstration of how the helicopter would fall to earth. "Zombies would have barbecue."

The old man was making sense, in a way. "Okay, so this she-devil overlord is at this Madison Mall place and she has the military working for her?"

Calhoun made a face. "Guess so. Mostly I listen so I know where they're gonna be. Don't want them near my stuff. Bad enough dealing with the aliens and the zombie-clones. Don't need to be dealing with the she-devil's helicopters. I seriously think she has mental powers to control people." Calhoun pointed to his hat made out of foil. "She ain't gonna gct me."

"Do they have Jenni?"

"Yep. And Bill. Heard that this morning." Calhoun milked in earnest now.

"Bill?" Travis felt an unpleasant combination of relief and despair, knowing that Roger and Felix had to be dead.

"Yep. They are a-coming to visit. That's why I brought the animals in. Figure if we're gonna pull an Alamo, might as well have fresh eggs and milk." With a grin, the old codger picked up the bucket and stool and headed for the hotel, a trail of kids, dogs, and cats behind him. "Y'all should have listened to me when I first told you all this. Now we're gonna have to fight down to the last man."

Katie and Nerit watched Travis's conversation with Calhoun with some amusement.

"We have cows," Katie observed.

"Yep." Nerit smirked.

They stood at the guard post on the edge of Main Street, looking down into the corral that had been thrown up on a cleared lot near the hotel. The cows were comfortably munching on hay and apparently enjoying the attention they were getting. People were lined up around the roped-off area, trying to pet them.

"And cats," Katie said, pointing to a cat walking daintily across the old construction site.

"And dogs," Nerit added. She gave the Chihuahua trying to mate with her boot a dark look. It grinned up at her and kept going.

"Did we want him back?" Katie asked, scrunching up her nose.

"Unfortunately, I think we did."

"We're on crack," Katie decided.

"Absolutely," Nerit answered.

Travis joined them, a somber expression on his face.

"Well?" the Israeli woman asked.

"He's plumb nuts, Nerit."

"Yes, Travis, but did he say anything enlightening?"

"He says the military is at the Madison Mall like we suspected. He's been monitoring the military channels." Travis hesitated and took Katie's hand gently. "He says they have Bill and Jenni at the mall."

Katie took a deep breath and let it out slowly. Nerit merely nodded.

"He said something about a woman being in charge and that she's evil. I'm not sure how much to believe. He sees the world in a really warped way. He's convinced we're about to do another Alamo."

Nerit tilted her head thoughtfully. "I have a feeling that a lot of what he is telling you is true, just twisted to fit his theory of how the world runs."

Katie cocked her head. "Okay, what do we do now?"

"I guess, get ready for the military to come knocking," Travis said. "Calhoun says he heard them talking about coming to see us."

"And I get to be John Wayne," Nerit stated with a gleam in her eye.

"Oh, no, no, Nerit. I want to be John Wayne," Travis protested.

Nerit considered this, then shook her head. "No. *I'm* John Wayne."

Katie knew that these moments of teasing concealed serious concerns. She had read somewhere that John Wayne once said, "Courage is being scared to death—but saddling up anyway."

They were going to have to saddle up.

Sweeping her hair back from her face, she wondered what Bill and Jenni were experiencing.

Were they saddling up?

## 3.
### *The Twilight World*

Jenni couldn't believe she was in a freaking mall. At least the damn "mall music" wasn't on.

Grumpily, she tried to get comfortable, but it wasn't easy on the hard canvas cot. Bill was snoring loudly in the next cot, and she was surrounded by the gentle breathing of other sleepers. It was hard to believe she was spending another night in this godforsaken place. She missed Juan with all her heart. She firmly believed he was still alive and waiting for her.

Staring up at the high ceiling, she sniffed back tears. The mall's emergency lights were on, keeping her awake. She needed to sleep in a pitch-black space. She needed Juan next to her. She rolled over, putting her back to Bill.

Mikey was lying on the cot on her other side. He was fast asleep; his sweet face, slowly transitioning from little boy to teenager, made her heart beat faster.

No, Mikey was dead.

Yet there he was, deeply asleep, mouth hanging slightly open.

She pressed her eyes closed.

When she looked again, Mikey was still there.

"No!" Jenni woke with a start, gasping. Where her son had been a moment before, she saw a little girl clutching an oversized teddy bear.

Her heart was thudding so hard, she could barely stand it. Tears flowed as Jenni covered her face with both hands and wept silently.

She hated the mall. Hated it! It made her feel helpless. It made her think of that horrible day. She should have found a way to save her son. But she'd been scared. She had run, and she didn't turn back to see if he was behind her. Not once.

"It's about choices made and not made. It's about what we do with our life and the impact we have on others," a soft voice said. "Do you understand?"

She raised her head and saw Katie's dead wife, Lydia, sitting at the end of the bed. She recognized Lydia from the cell phone photo Katie had shown her, months earlier.

"I . . . ran. . . ."

Lydia nodded. "I know."

"Was Mikey the one who was supposed to survive? Did I steal his life from him?"

"Right or wrong, you made a choice that day and because of it you had a second chance to find happiness. To fight to survive with those who love you. To live a new life."

"Why are you here?" Jenni asked.

"Because very soon, Jenni, you are going to have to make that same choice again."

Jenni nodded. "I know. I've been feeling it. Will I make it back to the fort? To see Juan?"

Lydia smiled gently. "Yes, you will."

"Then I am not afraid now."

The ghost's expression became tinged with sadness. "I know, Jenni. But you will be."

Jenni woke with a start. The mall was full of light, and voices drifted around her. The smell of weak coffee and something close to oatmeal wafted in the air. Sitting up groggily, she looked across the store at the people gathering in line for breakfast.

Tears ran down her cheeks. It was time to finally let go of the past. She could no longer be haunted by the choice she had made that dreadful morning. She had conquered the ghost of her dead husband, and now it was time to release the ghosts of her dead children.

Sniffling, she lowered her head and whispered, "Good-bye, boys. I will always love you."

She felt the ugly tendrils of guilt slowly dissolving inside her until nothing was left but peace. She wiped away her tears and stood up, ready to face whatever came next.

# · CHAPTER FOURTEEN ·

## 1.

### *Tales of the Madison Mall*

Jenni poked at the lumpish gray stuff in her bowl. It smelled like oatmeal—a little—but sure didn't look like it.

"Army food," a woman said, sitting down across from her.

Jenni was surprised that someone was talking to her. The day before, everyone seemed to watch her with suspicion. But she was grateful for the company. "It's not all that great, is it?"

"Makes me really appreciate the army," the woman said with a wry smile. Her pale blue eyes flicked to a soldier strolling by in full battle fatigues. "I'm Amy, by the way."

"Jenni."

"Pleased to meet you. Where did they rescue you from?"

"I wasn't rescued. They kidnapped me," Jenni said with a frown, looking at her table mate for the first time. Amy was probably only a few years older than Jenni, but those had been hard years. Her dark blond hair was in a messy bun and she was clad in gray sweats under a quilted blue coat.

Amy regarded Jenni with confusion. "What do you mean?"

"We were returning to our fort after gathering supplies when a helicopter swooped down on us. We had an accident and woke up here. To me, that's kidnapping." Jenni shrugged.

"A fort? Do you mean a real fort?"

"Well, more like four walled-in blocks of a small town," Jenni explained.

Amy gasped. "Are there lots of people there?"

"Maybe two hundred and fifty? I'm not sure of the exact number. We're mostly living in a big hotel."

Amy exhaled slowly. "Wow. We really thought we were the only ones still alive out this way. But why would the army take ya if you weren't in trouble?"

"I think whoever runs this place wants the fort. That's what my friend Bill says." Jenni shoved her bowl away and instead tried to eat something that looked like toast. "How long have you been here?"

"Since the first day. When it started, I didn't pay much attention to the crazy talk on the TV, but then this man started trying to get in our back door. Troy, my husband, he shouted at the man to get lost, but the guy kept hitting the door. Hitting it so hard, he busted his hands open. We saw him through the window. My kids started screaming. Troy got the shotgun and threatened to shoot the guy, but he just kept banging and making these noises."

"Oh, God, what did you do?"

"Troy opened the door and waved the gun around, but the guy just lunged into the house. And then I saw that his guts were falling out. So me, Troy, and the kids ran out the front door."

Jenni shivered.

"We get into the truck and we see Mabel, our neighbor, running to us with some nasty folks after her. Troy reaches out to her. And she bites his hand!"

"Oh, gawd! That's awful!"

"I know. Only I didn't know he was bit, right then." Sadness stilled Amy's tongue for a few seconds; then she continued, "So he coldcocks her and we see her back is all tore up. Troy gets into the truck and we haul ass to the Civic Center. That's where FEMA told us to go on the radio."

"So how'd you end up here?" Jenni was enraptured by the story and reached for another piece of stale toast.

"Soldiers came and got us after FEMA took off."

"FEMA took off?"

"Yeah. They gave us milk and cookies and told us to sit down in the auditorium. They took the worst of the injured people into another room, where there were volunteer doctors and nurses. Troy showed them the bite, but they said he wasn't hurt enough to go back there." Amy fastened her blue eyes on Jenni, sadness filling them.

"It was real scary. Nobody in charge was telling us anything, but there was plenty of gossip. I heard someone was gonna come and give us all shots so we wouldn't get rabid. Troy got a fever and the kids were all antsy and so was I. Then the damn FEMA people started packing up their stuff and told us that we needed to sit tight and wait for the army to come get us and take us to another place. And then they bailed."

A few other people moved closer to listen. One older black woman, who was vigorously nodding, said, "Oh, yeah. I remember that!"

"So Troy and some other people get sicker. Finally the army does show up, but it's just a few guys, and one of them comes in saying that the doors to that other room are locked and there are those *things* in there."

"FEMA just up and left us with a whole bunch of those zombies in that back room. All those doctors and nurses got ate up," the black woman cut in.

Remembering Katie's decision not to go to the rescue center in Madison, Jenni was grateful once again for her friend's intuition.

"More soldiers show up, in little groups, looking for a place to be safe, and it's clear to us that none of them know what's going on. When that handsome one finds out about the back room, he says that we're all going to the mall.

"The soldiers start asking people if they are bit or not, and all the bit people are put in another room. Including my Troy." Amy took a gasping breath, as if she was about to start weeping. "The kids cried so hard. . . ."

"It was real bad," the other woman said.

"We got into lines and filed outside. The trucks started taking people to the mall, old folks first. It was only like two blocks away, but they wanted us to be safe. You got a ride on a truck, didn't you, Ethel?"

"Thank you, Jesus, yes, or I wouldn't be here today," the black woman answered, sitting down next to Amy.

"My kids kept crying for their daddy. We were in the last group, and just as the trucks drove away with the people before us, the doors of the Civic Center started shaking. We looked back, and the place was full of zombies. The soldiers shouted, 'Run!' And, girl, we ran.

"We were running like crazy down the street, us and some soldiers. Then the doors got knocked down and those things came after us. Everyone was screaming and crying. People were tripping. The soldiers were trying to shoot—" Amy's voice rose, on the brink of hysteria.

Ethel took her hand. "Take a breath, Amy, take a breath," she said softly. The table was now packed with people, and others had drawn near. Most were clearly remembering the horrors of the first day.

Amy visibly steadied herself. "My little boy said, 'Look, Mommy, Daddy is coming, too,' and I looked back, but he wasn't my Troy anymore. He was all messed up and screaming. One of the soldiers grabbed my kids and ran. I was running so hard, I could barely breathe. And people . . . started . . . to fall back . . . and we could hear them getting . . . ripped up—" She turned and sobbed into Ethel's shoulder.

A big black man leaned forward, taking over the story. "When we made it to the mall, the soldiers were already closing the gates. The city council had ordered the gates built to keep vandals from doing graffiti on the mall."

"Probably the only thing they ever did right," someone huffed.

"Other soldiers were shooting at the zombies, and once we got in, they shut the gates and shoved cars up against them to keep them closed and those things out. And later, the helicopters came," the big man added.

"Those soldiers didn't know what they were doing at first," Ethel said. "They almost ran out of ammunition, shooting the zombies. Later, they fed us and started making things safer. Kevin started figuring things out."

"So this wasn't the rescue center?" Jenni asked. "They just brought you here and made do?"

"Exactly," Ethel said.

A middle-aged white man said, "Every time new people showed up, there was lots of shooting. I heard the helicopters brought in more ammunition and more soldiers. Then the National Guard base got taken by the dead things, and they had to shoot the people who got bitten."

Amy nodded sadly. "They had to. 'Cause they'd die and just get right back up."

Hearing what these people had been through brought back Jenni's memories of the first day. When someone touched her back, she jumped, then almost sighed with relief when she saw that it was Bill. He slid onto the bench next to her, looking very solemn.

"So you folks have been here all this time with the soldiers taking care of you?" Bill asked.

"Yes," Amy responded. "After a week, Senator Brightman and Major General Knox came with their troops. They made Kevin step down, even though he'd been doing such a good job." She lowered her voice. "They brought a lot more zombies with them, too, just dragged them down on us."

"So you don't like the senator?"

Everyone glanced around warily. A Mexican woman who looked like she was about a hundred years old said, "*Tonta! Pendeja!* Stupid. She makes the Mexicans do the . . . the . . . work of the gutter. She don't like us 'cause she says we're wetbacks. My family has been in Texas since it was Mexico!"

"I agree, Guadalupe. A total bitch," a woman who was probably in her early fifties said briskly. Unlike many of the other people, who were just clad in jeans and sweaters, she was wearing makeup, jewelry, and high heels. "She makes us all do menial chores, like mopping, dusting, and that sort of thing to keep us busy. She doesn't talk to any of us, just stays up on the second floor. We all had to fill out this weird questionnaire about our skill sets, health, and education. I know she was behind it, because her campaign manager, Raleigh, told me later that I would have to learn how to be something other than a real estate agent. How could he know my profession if he hadn't read my questionnaire?"

"Yeah. That was kinda weird and scary," Amy agreed.

"*Esta tonta! Pendeja! Tocha*," Guadalupe grumbled. Jenni giggled, reminded of her own late Mexican grandmother.

"Things are not good here," Amy stated. "We're all hungry. We're all scared."

Bill folded his hands and regarded the people gathered around the table. "The fort has room for everyone, but I don't think the senator will just let y'all go there. I think she's gonna try to take it over."

Murmurs of discontent spread through the group.

"Is it really better there? Really?" Amy's expression was hopeful.

Jenni smiled at the tired, smelly, desperate people. "Yeah. It is."

Guadalupe hit the top of the table with her cane. "Then we go with you. The *puta* stays here."

Everyone laughed until the senator appeared on a walkway above them. Silence fell and a few people scurried away.

"I'm not sure what's going on," Bill said once the senator had moved on. "But I'm sure that if we can get you good people to the fort, you will be more than welcome there."

Hope appeared on the faces around them and Jenni looked at Bill nervously. She leaned toward him and whispered, "Bill, how are we going to get all these people to the fort?"

"Dunno . . . but damn . . . they gotta have hope," Bill answered.

At his words, Jenni realized that that was what was missing in the mall: a sense of hope. Now it was spreading like wildfire and she felt warmth growing in her belly.

"Gotta have hope, Jenni," Bill repeated.

# 2.
## *Preparing the Way*

Travis could always tell when his wife was on edge. She'd stand with her legs slightly apart, arms crossed, hip shifted to the side, chin set firmly. Walking into the lobby of the hotel, he saw her in that pose and thought, *Crap*. Moving up behind her, he looked over her shoulder to see at least fifteen people sitting on the sofas and love seats, surrounded by backpacks, suitcases, and even bulging pillowcases.

"Do I want to know?" He spoke softly, for her ears only.

"They're waiting for the army," Katie answered tersely. "Ingrates."

"Katie," Travis said in a chiding tone.

"We risked our asses to rescue them, and this is the thanks we get? They've ditched their chores to sit around and wait for the army." Her eyes flashed with indignation.

"You know," Travis said with a slow smile, "you're kinda sexy when you're angry."

Katie frowned, narrowing her eyes. "Don't make me hurt you."

"Hormones," Nerit whispered, walking by.

"I am not hormonal!" Katie protested vehemently.

Travis chuckled. "Right."

Katie pointed at him with one long finger. "You're just lucky I love you." She stomped away.

"Pregnant lady coming through! Step aside!" Calhoun shouted as Katie walked toward the dining room. "She's loaded and dangerous."

Katie flung up her hands before vanishing down the hall.

"She's really cute pregnant," Travis stated to no one in particular.

"I can't believe they're pulling this shit," Curtis said, walking over. "There are more on the way, all excited that the army is coming."

"I'm a little peeved, too, but I figure they hope things are better somewhere else."

"But it's bullshit. After everything we've done for them!" Curtis's young face was red with anger. "Rescuing them, giving them shelter, giving them food—"

"I expect some of the latecomers don't realize how much the original group did to build the fort." Travis tucked his hands into his jacket pockets and watched the little crowd grow larger. He noticed some dark looks among those walking by.

"They're not country folk. They're not used to working together to beat the odds," Curtis grumbled.

Studying the gathering, Travis realized it consisted mostly of people from either larger towns or the cities. He spotted only a few locals in the mix. "Well, I'm from the city and so are Katie and Jenni and a few others."

"Exceptions. City folk are just lazy," Curtis scoffed.

"Curtis, you're too young to be so bitter," Travis said, shaking his head.

Looking flushed and anxious, Yolanda emerged from the hallway that led to the offices. "Travis! Travis! The military is calling!"

"Told you!" Calhoun whooped. "I told you!"

Travis ran across the lobby as the waiting people applauded. Curtis threw a nasty look at them, then followed Travis to the communication center.

# 3.
## *The Dead World*

First Lieutenant Kevin Reynolds felt dread as he soared above the streets of Madison. Staggering figures grasped hungrily at the helicopter. The lightweight UH-72 Lakota swooped over the besieged mall. His handpicked team fit comfortably in the spacious chopper. Private Tom Franks was trying to sleep, stretched out across from Kevin.

"It never gets easier to see," Valerie Rodriguez said into her helmet mic.

Kevin silently agreed. He and Valerie had spent a good chunk of the night curled up together, comforting each other. Kevin tried not to think of his wife and kids, and he knew that Valerie struggled with memories of her boyfriend, a mechanic at the base in San Antonio. It was difficult to think of a future when the past haunted them both.

Months earlier, right after they had secured the mall and managed to feed all the people they saved from the Civic Center deathtrap, Kevin had found himself alone for the first time since he had woken next to his wife early that horrible first morning. Overcome, he had collapsed in a service hallway. Valerie had been nothing more than a fellow soldier until she'd stumbled across him and sat with him until his tears subsided. Since then, she had been his main source of comfort—and he had done his best to be hers.

They flew over a highway. Kevin spotted a semi-truck flipped onto its side and a few cars scattered haphazardly on the road. One or two zombies stared up at the helicopter. Kevin shuddered, remembering his escape from the city along clogged highways. This scene was a relief compared to that horror.

The Texas sun was muted by dark clouds moving into the area.

The weather was definitely wetter in February. The helicopter began to make a long turn, preparing to head for the fort.

"Do you think the fort's leaders will listen to what you have to say?"

Kevin rolled his shoulders. "I hope so. We can't hold the mall much longer. Supplies are low and we're running out of ammunition."

Valerie ran a hand over her skimmed-back hair. "I just don't know how easy this is going to be."

Kevin didn't want to make a promise he wasn't sure he could keep, but he had to say something reassuring. He settled for, "It'll be okay."

They lapsed into silence as the helicopter flew over the dead world.

Twenty minutes later, they crested a hill and the hotel appeared, standing tall and imposing over ranches and farms. As the chopper drew nearer, Ashley Oaks slowly emerged from the trees.

"Make a pass," Kevin said into his headset. "I want to see the fort."

The pilot made a slow turn over the mostly abandoned town. Kevin saw zombies plodding toward the fort. With the trees stripped of foliage, it was easy to spot old-fashioned houses nestled in weed-ridden yards. The downtown area was encircled by a high wall. In the middle of the fort, Kevin was startled to see a small herd of cows munching on hay. Children were running around and riding bikes. As the helicopter roared overhead, the kids looked up and waved.

"We've been instructed to land in front of the hotel," the pilot's voice said in his ear. The block between the hotel and the wall was nothing more than an empty lot.

Kevin chuckled. "We won't be able to make a hasty escape, will we?"

"Or snatch their leader," Valerie added. "Nice move."

As the chopper swooped around the hotel and started to land,

Kevin automatically said, "Watch out for zombies," though he knew it was an unnecessary reminder.

Valerie, Kevin, and Tom zipped their jackets, straightened their helmets, and double-checked their weapons as the chopper landed. Once they were down, their pilot, Greta, did the same. She wasn't pleased about having to leave the helicopter, but the leaders of the fort had insisted that everyone come inside.

As Kevin had expected, the sound and sight of the aircraft attracted the dead, who came staggering and crawling toward the helicopter. As the machine's rotors slowed, Kevin thought briefly of the original *Dawn of the Dead*, where a zombie had the top of his head whacked off by helicopter blades.

"I got four on this side," Tom reported.

"I got nine," Valerie said.

"Just sit tight. They should be out here with a vehicle in a few," Kevin promised them.

Unexpectedly, the zombies began to collapse, plumes of bone and brain exploding out of their heads.

"Snipers?" Valerie looked shocked.

Greta whipped her head around to stare at Kevin. "Think they got military here?"

"Maybe. That sniper is a dead-on shot," Kevin answered, impressed.

Another zombie tumbled to the ground even as more appeared from the side streets.

"We're drawing a crowd," Valerie said, her voice tense.

Abruptly jets of flame erupted out of the street. The zombies retreated, scrambling, some of them on fire.

"Fire traps," Tom said in awe.

"They have a formidable setup. Better than we realized," Kevin said.

"These people are not going to want to turn over their fort to us," Valerie said somberly.

"No, they're not," Kevin agreed.

A civilian Hummer raced around the corner at top speed,

running over a few crawling zombies as it roared up to the helicopter.

"Out," Kevin ordered.

They slid the doors open, leaped to the ground, and ran for the SUV as the sharpshooter continued to pick off the zombies. Piling into the Hummer, they were surprised to hear country music coming from the car's speakers.

"Hi," said the driver, a woman with bright red hair. "Hold on." She floored the gas pedal and the Hummer smashed into a few more zombies before spinning around and heading back in the direction it had come from.

"My name's Katarina," the redhead said, aiming the vehicle at a lurching zombie. The impact flung the creature's broken body into a tree.

"First Lieutenant Kevin Reynolds," Kevin said, gripping the dashboard for stability.

The Hummer swerved sharply and slid through an opening in the wall. Turning around in his seat, Kevin saw a set of heavy metal gates closing behind them. A few zombies attempted to follow, but more jets of flame sent them fleeing. There was a second set of closed gates in front of the Hummer. Kevin realized the fort's entrance was some kind of lock system.

Once the gates had closed behind the vehicle, a man and a woman who were standing on the walls on either side of the Hummer used long poles with mirrors mounted on their ends to inspect the car's undercarriage. Satisfied that all was clear, the guards signaled and the second gate opened.

"Are you all civilians?" Kevin asked, marveling at the efficiency of the fort's operation. It felt like a military op, but no one was in uniform.

"Yes, except for Nerit," Katarina answered. "She was a sniper for the Israeli army." She hit the gas and drove into a large courtyard, coming to a stop near an open set of garage doors.

Waiting there were a tall, handsome man, a blond woman who was visibly pregnant, and an older woman. Studying the welcoming committee, Kevin pegged the woman with the silvery yellow hair as the former Israeli sniper. Her keen gaze reminded him of a hawk.

Katarina got out of the SUV first, but Kevin quickly followed. His crew climbed out behind him, falling into formation.

The tall man walked over to Kevin and held out his hand. "I'm Travis. This is my wife, Katie." He smiled at the pregnant woman. "And this is Nerit, our head of security. Welcome to our home."

Trying not to stare at their surroundings, Kevin gave the man's hand a brief shake. "I'm First Lieutenant Kevin Reynolds. I've been serving at the Madison Mall Rescue Center since the first day." He introduced the rest of his team.

"So, how can we help you?" Travis asked.

"I was sent by my superiors to ask you to surrender the fort." Travis's face grew solemn and Katie's eyes narrowed. Nerit looked calm and deadly. Kevin continued quickly, "But I'm really here on behalf of the people at the Madison Mall and the men under my command. We want permission to relocate here and join you. My superiors can go to hell."

Travis was clearly surprised. "Sounds like we got a lot to talk about."

Kevin nodded solemnly. "You have no idea."

## · CHAPTER FIFTEEN ·

### 1.
### *The Bridging of Worlds*

This world was far different from the one he knew.

Glancing over the cars and trucks in the fort's garage before Travis led the group away, Kevin could not help but think of the vehicles in the mall's parking lot. His troops turned on the engines once a week to make sure their batteries didn't die, but no one drove anywhere, since the lot's gates were blocked by the wailing dead. In contrast, this fleet of vehicles seemed ready to go at a moment's notice.

The fort people escorted the newcomers up a staircase that led over the wall that separated the parking area from the rest of the fort. Levers at the top and bottom of the staircase made it clear the stairs could be collapsed at a moment's notice. As they climbed, Kevin noted that armed guards scrutinized his every move.

"Is this the only way in or out?" Valerie asked as they followed Travis and the two women.

"When the garage doors are down, yes," Nerit answered in an Israeli accent. "And those are reinforced."

Reaching the top of the stairs, Kevin froze, mesmerized by the sight of the reclaimed downtown of the small town. Tears sprang into his eyes and he fought them back. Children played in the streets, shouting and laughing. Old people sat in a gazebo, chatting. Young people walked down the sidewalk outside an old movie theater, talking and sipping sodas. The theater's marquee read, TUESDAY FAMILY NIGHT DOUBLE FEATURE. MONSTERS INC. AND SHREK. A pack of dogs ran around. A cat sat calmly in the sun near the gazebo, cleaning a paw.

Some of the people in the street began to notice the soldiers. Some waved; others just stared. An older man, arms covered with navy tattoos, saluted. Kevin saluted back, smiling.

"Are you going to kill all the zombies, mister?" called out a boy who was playing with toy soldiers in the dirt.

"We're working on it," Kevin answered.

Travis led the group to the hotel. While most people they passed seemed happy or surprised to see the newcomers, Kevin saw one woman, who was holding a little boy's hand, eyeing them suspiciously. Inside the hotel, a large chalkboard mounted on an easel in the hallway announced, LUNCH: EGG SANDWICHES, HOME-STYLE FRIES, AND CHOCOLATE MILK SHAKES.

"Eggs," Tom gasped.

Kevin could barely swallow past the lump in his throat. He'd never imagined the fort would be anything like this. Not after the mall. The world he'd known for months was one of near-starvation, mindless tasks to keep people busy, people dying from the flu, and zombies moaning endlessly outside. Life was all about power struggles. Life was hell.

As they walked through the lobby of the hotel, Kevin was startled to hear applause. He looked around and saw a group of people clapping. Focusing on them, Kevin realized that they were surrounded by luggage.

"What the hell is this?" Valerie muttered behind him.

In his peripheral vision, Kevin saw Travis sigh and rub his brow. A middle-aged man rushed over to their group.

"It's so good to see you! We're all ready to go!" the man said as he pumped Kevin's hand.

"Go where?" Kevin asked, confused.

"To your base, of course. Away from here!"

Tom, Greta, and Valerie laughed, and Kevin patted the man's shoulder. "Trust me. You don't want to go to where I came from."

The gathered people whispered among themselves, confused.

An older black woman stepped forward and said, "We want to go where it's safer!"

"Ma'am, this is about as safe as you are going to get." Kevin glanced at Travis and Katie and saw the amused expressions on their faces. He opened his hands and said, "Trust me, they don't want to go there."

Travis nodded like he wasn't surprised and led the group from the lobby to a large office. The woman who had given Kevin a suspicious look entered the room and sat down, still obviously uneasy. As Travis introduced the woman as Peggy, Kevin wondered where the little boy had gone. Travis perched on the edge of the desk; Katie sat on the desk as well, next to her husband. Nerit took the chair closest to the door, crossing her legs as she observed Kevin and his people.

There were several unoccupied chairs set in a semicircle facing the desk. Feeling nervous, not to mention awkward in his helmet and body armor, Kevin lowered himself into a creaky leather chair and took off his helmet. His companions followed his example.

Arms folded across his chest, Travis said, "So, what can we do for you folks?"

"Like I said, we were ordered to come here and demand that you surrender the fort. But we don't want to do that," Kevin said earnestly.

"Why are we supposed to believe you?" Katie arched an eyebrow.

Kevin pulled a letter from his jacket pocket. "This is from Police Chief Bruce Kiel. Recon photos revealed that his daughter is here. If she reads this, she'll be able to vouch for me."

The blond woman's face paled and her hand shook as she reached for the letter. "Give that to me."

Travis laid a hand on her shoulder as Kevin passed Katie the folded bit of paper. "You're Katie *Kiel*?"

"Yes," she answered. She let out a gasp as the familiar handwriting came into view. Covering her mouth with one trembling hand, she read quickly. Then, with tears shimmering in her eyes, she took a deep breath. More composed, she read aloud,

*Katie-girl, it's Dad. I'm alive and safe in the Madison Mall. Safe for now, at least.*

    *Senator Brightman wants your fort. Don't let her have it. The way she treats people is despicable. Listen to Kevin. He's a good guy and what he says is the truth.*

    *Love you, baby.*

                               *Your Dad.*

Katie sniffled, but kept her tears in check. Kevin respected her composure.

Nerit smiled at her warmly. "It is good to know that ones we love survived."

Kevin lowered his gaze. He knew in his heart that none of his loved ones had made it. That was part of why he wanted to give the people at the mall a chance.

"So what do you have to tell us?" Travis asked.

"I guess I should start at the beginning," Kevin said as images of the first day unfolded in his mind.

## 2.
### *Kevin's Story*

The phone woke him. His unit was being mobilized to deal with civic unrest and he had to report immediately.

He'd just returned from overseas, and he and his wife had been hoping to live a normal life for a while. They'd planned to see his son play basketball that evening, followed by dinner at their favorite barbecue dive. Kevin remembered but didn't speak of the look of sadness in his wife's eyes when she heard he was being deployed again.

Kevin was still glad that he'd taken the time to step into the bedrooms of his three children. He knew he would never forget how their skin and hair felt, how sweet they smelled as he kissed them good-bye while they slept. He promised his wife that he would contact her as soon as he could, not knowing that he would never speak to her again.

The briefing at the base was quick. A riot had broken out at a truck stop near a small town. The local police and sheriff had responded and been overwhelmed. The military was being sent in to quell the violence. There were rumors of more riots breaking out all over the country.

A convoy of trucks departed the base, headlights sluicing through the darkness. When they arrived at the truck stop, which was like a small city unto itself, they found a scene out of hell. Vehicles were smashed into one another, a truck had been overturned, and fire was spreading inside the restaurant. As soon as the convoy came into view, it was rushed.

The next minutes were a blur: weapons firing; bloody, mutilated people grabbing at the soldiers; and a horrible chorus of screams, growls, and *chewing*. He'd had to stop more than once to wipe blood from his face mask. Somehow, the soldiers managed to tear a swath of destruction through the horde of crazed rioters. Kevin saw an armless man running toward him and a woman with an empty chest cavity ripping the eyes out of a soldier. In that moment, Kevin realized what they were fighting: zombies. Then someone had shouted to aim for their heads.

The soldiers swept through the truck stop, bullets ripping through undead skulls, blood and gore splashing the pavement and the sides of trucks like gruesome graffiti. Some of his troops fell to the zombies, but eventually the survivors stood wearily triumphant among the truly dead.

Horror swept over Kevin when the wounded suddenly attacked the living. He unleashed four bullets into the face of one of his best friends to save himself. Clearly, a bite was lethal.

Reporting in, Kevin tried to make his disbelieving superiors understand what was happening. As the sun rose over the hills, he was ordered to help the National Guard in a nearby city.

The world was already dead, but no one knew it.

They had taken the back roads to the city, occasionally stopping to eliminate zombies or infected people. He hadn't known at the time that he was fighting a losing battle, that the number of undead probably already outnumbered the living.

As he recalled that nightmarish journey, Kevin recognized Katie as the other woman he had seen with Jenni and the German shepherd. They had looked so shell-shocked, yet determined to survive. He remembered petting the dog and thinking of his family.

Entering the city had been like driving into hell—snarled traffic, abandoned vehicles, makeshift barricades, and rampaging zombies. They had reached the police station just as it was overrun. The police chief and some of his surviving officers had leaped from the roof of the station onto one of the army trucks. It was terrifying to see how few people survived. The soldiers found what remained of the National Guard and headed out of the city to save their own lives. Nearly half their vehicles and people had been lost to the waves of zombies that filled the roads.

Shattered, overwhelmed, and near panic, a few men and women went AWOL, trying to rescue their families. Kevin understood the temptation, but knew that they would fail. The world was dead. Their families were dead.

His own family would have taken refuge in the hospital where his wife worked. He'd seen enough to know the hospitals were deathtraps. There was no hope for them, but he could try to save others.

He had let those soldiers go. The world was ending, and every man and woman deserved to make a choice as to their own fate.

Most of the troops followed him into the hills and made their way to Madison. They'd found the Rescue Center, and Kevin had almost immediately decided to move everyone to the mall. It seemed like a secure location, thanks to the high wall around the parking lot.

For a week, he had run the mall as best he could, using his troops, plus the National Guard and the police to secure the place and keep the zombie population down. National Guard helicopters began arriving on the second day, bringing in supplies and ammunition until their base was overrun. More survivors showed up and sometimes made it to safety, but more often than not, they were torn apart trying to scale the walls.

Working hard and keeping focused on what needed to be done kept him from thinking about his family. But he always felt as though he was about to lose his mind, and when he was alone, he would sometimes weep until he thought he would die.

Then Senator Paige Brightman and Major General Gordon Knox arrived. The major general carried orders from the president putting him in charge of the rescue centers, so Kevin had stepped aside. Now he wished he had never relinquished authority.

"I just want to do what's right," Kevin finished. "I want to give those people a good home. I failed them once. I don't want to fail them again."

"You won't," Travis said, standing. "Let's bring your people home."

# 3.
## A Terrible Thing

Katie listened to Kevin, her fingers slowly tracing the edges of the letter from her father. The first lieutenant looked tired, discouraged, and worn; his shoulders were stooped as if the burden of protecting those people in the mall weighed them down. Travis looked like that at times, too; Katie knew that Kevin, like her husband, took his responsibilities seriously.

"I appreciate this more than you know. We are getting low on ammunition, and the gates won't hold forever against the zombies," the soldier said.

"The crowd gets a little bigger every day," Valerie added.

"Have you considered trying to get the people out before?" Nerit asked.

"Yes. Every time we went out in the helicopters, we'd try to find a safe place to go, but nothing was really viable. And the major general and the senator were more interested in staying put and keeping the zombies out than in relocating."

"We sent out scavenging parties. We lost people when we went east, so we started coming west. We found one group making a meth lab in the back of a grocery store. Their leader told us about your fort. He said his group had tried to join yours and that you had attacked them instead of helping them."

"The bandits," Curtis hissed.

"We could tell his story was fishy, but the minute the senator heard about the fort, she got very excited."

"Why?" Katie asked. "What does she want with us?"

Kevin drew a deep breath. "The truth of the situation is this: No one knows what happened to the rest of the world, and nothing remains of the United States government except Vice President Ramón Castellanos and a few other members of Congress. Castellanos is calling himself the president these days."

"Wow," Katie breathed, surprised. She had assumed nothing was left of the former government.

"I thought all those bozos got eaten," Peggy drawled.

Kevin chuckled lightly. "No. The vice president was hunting in East Texas when the world went to hell. He's holed up in Galveston. The military and civilians worked together to blockade the bridges to the mainland, and Galveston Island is now the location of what is called the Central Government of the United States.

"Eliminating all the zombies from the island took months and exhausted most of their resources. We know that there are a couple of other enclaves on the coast and that those people are sending supplies to Galveston by boat." He paused.

"The area is heavily infested because of Houston. The only way on or off the island is by sea or air. The senator's been trying to make the mall seem like an asset to the president so that we would receive more assistance—"

"And make her life cushier," Valerie grumbled.

"—but it was clear that the powers that be consider us a lost cause. Not long ago, Central informed the senator that the mall is on its own."

"Why doesn't she just ask us for help? Or put us in contact with Central?" Travis's tone was wary.

"She considers the fort to be a tool that she can use to secure a power base. Then she'll have leverage with the new government." Kevin sighed somberly. "I read her entire plan without her knowledge. Bruce Kiel smuggled a copy of the senator's plan for your fort to me. She had given it to him for feedback. What I read both saddened and horrified me. Basically, she intends to enslave everyone from the fort and the mall. Based on skill set, education, and health, a person would be given a specific task to perform and receive shelter and a specific amount of food in return."

Katie saw that everyone in the room looked shocked except Nerit, who nodded as if what she was hearing simply confirmed something she already suspected.

"The military will not only defend the civilians against the zombies, but enforce martial law. Curfews would be enacted, and in general people's movements and freedom of choice will be heavily restricted. Even reproduction will be regulated."

Katie gasped, her hands holding her tummy protectively. "What do you mean?"

"All women between the ages of eighteen and forty-five have been designated as breeders. One child, every two years."

"How does Major General Knox feel about the plan?" Nerit asked.

"Brightman sold the whole idea to Knox by skewing it as a return to the values of the founding fathers. She claims it will restore the American family and society by encouraging hard work and a close-knit community."

"Has she proposed it to the Central Government yet?" Travis's voice was pensive, matching his expression.

Kevin shook his head. "No. She wants to create a seat of power before dealing with them again. I serve the American people. And the people deserve better."

"What do you suggest we do?" Katie asked. "Do you think the senator will try to invade or stop people from leaving the mall?"

"She probably has about twenty military people on her side, but we have more soldiers on ours. She may try to order them to attack us. Considering what I've seen of the fort's defenses, a successful invasion by twenty men would be very difficult, if not impossible."

Valerie agreed with a curt nod of her head. "It could get nasty. Everyone is under extreme duress. Tempers might flare. Shots could be fired."

"Do you think she'll just back down from her plans?" Travis asked.

With a weary sigh, Kevin answered, "No. I don't."

Katie took a deep breath. Her father was alive but trapped. She wanted him here, with her. She wanted him to know and love Travis as he had once known and loved Lydia, to hold her child—his first grandchild—in his arms. She wanted Jenni and Bill to come home and to have Jenni at her side when she gave birth. She wanted her family to be whole again.

She stood up and said, "I'll go to the mall and speak with the senator." At Travis's startled look, she continued, "I was a prosecutor before, and I can be very persuasive. I can make the senator see that the fort is open to everyone who is willing to work hard."

"Katie, no," Travis protested.

"I may personally despise the woman, but if Ashley Oaks is all that remains of the American dream and Texas's independence, we need to fight for our freedom."

Everyone was staring at her.

Determined, Katie said, "I've argued Paige Brightman into corners before. I had the displeasure of meeting her at more than one dinner party. She had a real issue with me being married to a woman, and we've had words about that."

The "married to a woman" line elicited raised eyebrows from Peggy and looks of curiosity from the mall's representatives, but Katie had no intention of explaining.

Travis kissed her temple, his lips warm against her skin. "Okay, then I'm going, too." He pointed at Nerit. "And you are not stopping me this time!"

Nerit inclined her head. "I agree with you. This time."

"If the senator agrees to relocating, how do we get the people away if there's a big horde of zombies outside the mall?" Peggy sounded uncomfortable. One foot was rapidly tapping on the floor.

"Airlift. We got three other helicopters," Greta answered.

"We've been using an abandoned commercial airstrip for refueling. We keep it clear of zombies," Kevin explained. "It'll take a lot of trips to bring everyone out, but it's the safest option."

"As long as the helicopters don't attract any zombie mobs, that should work fine," Nerit said.

The tension in the room was being swiftly replaced by a tentative sense of camaraderie. It would be rough bringing everyone here, Katie knew, but they could do it. And perhaps they could use the senator's contacts with President Castellanos to their advantage.

"Sounds like we have a lot of planning to do before we get this ball rolling," Travis said, taking control of the conversation. "I say we get to it."

## CHAPTER SIXTEEN

## 1.
### *Entering the Parlor*

*This is hell,* Jenni thought. She'd just spent hours scrubbing toilets and sinks along with five other women. The mall stank of fear, sweat, and unwashed human beings. According to one of the people on her work crew, there were only a few working showers in the mall and most of them were upstairs, where the senator and her entourage lived. Most people were allowed a two-minute shower once every four days.

The mall's lower floor was shaped like the letter *A*. The corridor that connected the two legs held the food court and public area, complete with a two-story waterfall. Today there were a few kids running around in the playscape near the waterfall, but most people were just sitting at the tables in the food court, silently eating what looked like beans with bits of hot dog mixed in.

The scene was depressing. Word had spread that the senator wanted to seize control of the fort, and hope had slowly fizzled out of everyone.

An enormous skylight let in the outside light and illuminated the area. Looking up, Jenni noticed that a crisscross of catwalks sprawled over the entire food court. A fire escape–like metal stairway snaked up the back wall and over the empty fast-food stalls.

She fell in behind other people waiting for food and let her hair down from its ponytail. After a few minutes she was handed a bowl of beans and wieners. Turning, she spotted Bill at a table and went to join him. He was eating, watching the children with a sad look on his face.

"They're just waiting to die," he said as she sat down.

"Aren't we all?" she answered flippantly.

"No, not really. At the fort we were actually living. Finding love, making babies. Movie nights and dances. We *live*."

With a sigh, Jenni started eating. She heard the sound of the helicopter returning. Its shadow filled the food court as it flew over the enormous skylight before settling somewhere outside the mall.

"You're right. It's different at the fort," she admitted. "This is just existing. It's not right."

Bill sighed. "Katarina and I were going to have a beer together after the hospital run."

"Really?" Jenni grinned. "Good for you!"

"I felt kinda guilty at first, liking her. My wife died a year ago, so . . ." Bill let out a slow breath. "You know what I mean."

Jenni didn't, but nodded anyway. She had hated her abusive husband. She felt no remorse or guilt about her relationship with Juan.

"Then I figured that in this world, you gotta take your chance at happiness." Bill glanced at the people all around them. The mall people were muted, shadows, living on what little remained of their normal energy.

"I just hope we can get these people a better life," Jenni said with a sigh.

"We just got the military and zombies standing in our way," Bill answered. "Piece of cake."

Jenni stood up to return her bowl and spoon to the cleanup crew. She saw movement out of the corner of her eye. Pivoting around, Jenni saw Kevin leading a group of people through the food court. Her bowl and spoon clattered to the floor when she saw Katie and Travis among them.

"Katie!" Jenni rushed toward her friend. Katie saw her and called her name. As if they were in some stupid movie, they ran to each other and flung their arms around each other. Katie squeezed her so tight, Jenni could hardly breathe. Pressing kisses to her best friend's cheek, Jenni felt her tears of joy falling down her face, hot and fierce.

"How's Juan?" Jenni asked.

"He's fine," Travis answered as he joined them and gave Jenni a comforting hug. Jenni exhaled with relief.

"What are you doing here?" she demanded. "It sucks here!"

Katie grinned before throwing her arms around Bill, who had also come up to the group. "We came to take you guys home."

Travis gave Jenni a little squeeze. "And everyone else here."

"We're game." Bill answered with a grin, "Just tell us what to do!"

Jenni glanced at the soldiers around them. She frowned.

"They're with us," Katie assured her.

"Honestly?"

"Yes," Travis said with a grin.

For the first time since she'd entered the mall, Jenni felt a sense of hope.

## 2.
### *The Spider and the Fly*

Those around him would make decisions, Lydia had said, that might lead to their deaths.

Travis sat solemnly beside Katie in the food court as they waited for Kevin to return with the senator. Kevin was certain the senator would want to make a grand show of welcoming the fort's leaders to the mall.

Katie's decision to go to the mall had terrified Travis, but one of the things he loved about Katie was her strength. She looked at him with her clear, beautiful green eyes and smiled at him reassuringly. Jenni sat on Katie's other side. Their fingers were intertwined. Travis had been relieved to see Jenni and Bill. Not that he didn't mourn Roger and Felix, but it was hard not to feel relieved when those closest to you survived.

The people seated at the nearby tables kept stealing looks at the newcomers. Some stared openly. Even the workers who were mopping the floor of the food court were watching them.

The daylight spilling through the enormous skylight above was somewhat comforting. All the mall doorways were blacked out. Travis supposed it was to keep the people from seeing the hordes of zombies outside the gates. He had been horrified when he'd seen the mass of the undead as the helicopter swung over the mall. How the soldiers had kept them at bay so long was beyond him.

A tall man with white hair and an imposing face rushed down a frozen escalator. At the sight of him, Katie let out a cry and jumped to her feet. Travis realized who the man must be: her father. Without a word, Bruce Kiel took Katie in his arms.

"Dad!" Katie gasped as they embraced.

"Katie-girl, it's so good to see you. I'm so sorry about Lydia, baby. I can't believe you're here!"

"Dad, I can't believe *you're* here!" Katie pulled Travis closer. "This is Travis, Dad, my husband."

The stern man looked startled, then smiled, took Travis's hand, and pumped it in a handshake. "Good to meet you, son," Bruce said in his deep voice. "If Katie chose you, you have to be one helluva person."

"It is a pleasure meet you," Travis answered, feeling a bit overwhelmed.

"And as you can tell, you're going to be a grandfather, Dad."

Bruce grinned and put his hand gently on his daughter's abdomen. "I'm thrilled, Katie. Surprised, but thrilled!"

A group of people appeared at the top of the escalator; Travis saw Kevin and eight other soldiers, a man Travis recognized from CNN as the senator's campaign manager, and Senator Paige Brightman. Her campaign manager wore a suit, but the senator was clad in a bright red dress with diamonds glittering in her ears. She descended the steps at an even pace; there was a beautcous smile on her face. She and her entourage stopped near the base of the escalators while Kevin walked briskly to Travis and the others. Looking again at the group, Travis realized that one of the soldiers probably outranked the others, judging by his uniform.

"It looks like it's time for you to deal with the senator," Bruce said grimly.

"Don't worry. We're ready," Katie assured him.

"That's my girl." Bruce glanced at Kevin, who inclined his head slightly. Katie's father fell back, joining Jenni and Bill.

"She believes this is a transfer of power, so she's in a good mood." Kevin escorted Travis and Katie to the senator. "She wants a bit of a show."

The senator's personal guards swooped down to keep the mall's inhabitants at bay as the fort's delegation approached.

"Welcome to the Madison Mall Rescue Center," the senator said, projecting her pleasant voice and extending her hand. "I'm Senator Paige Brightman. The gentleman behind me is Major General Gordon Knox."

"Travis Buchanan," Travis answered, shaking hands briefly.

"A pleasure to meet you. It's good that you have agreed to move forward for the benefit of the American people," the major general said.

Travis hesitated, then decided not to rock the boat just yet. "This is my wife, Katie."

Senator Paige Brightman clearly recognized the younger woman. She laughed, a bright, amused chuckle, and lowered her voice to a more conversational volume, one that the onlookers could no longer hear. "Katie, I see you came back to the right side of the fence."

Travis sensed Katie's cold anger rising like a wave.

"My wife died the first day," Katie answered tersely.

"Oh, I see. I'm sorry," the senator answered in a sorrowful tone that Travis pegged as false. She flashed a smile at Travis, winking. "But you found a strapping, handsome man, I see."

He observed Katie's eyes glittering with anger and unexpected tears. "And I was lucky to find a wonderful woman who has no prejudices," Travis responded, taking his wife's hand.

"I meant no offense. It's a shame about Lydia. She was one of the best interior designers in Texas." Paige Brightman displayed a fairly convincing mournful expression, and Travis felt Katie's hand clench into a fist inside his grasp.

"I'd love to catch up on old times," the senator said in her Texas drawl, "but there are matters of great importance to be discussed." A crowd of people was watching from the food court, and the senator gave them her best campaign smile. Raising her voice, she said, "Why don't we go upstairs to my office?"

"Very well," Katie said. "Let's get this over with."

### 3.
### *Showdown*

As Katie walked up the unmoving escalator, she felt the hundred or so people gathered in the corridor below staring up at her. The irony of the rescue center being a mall made her smile to herself. And of course, Kevin was a black hero. Romero would be proud.

That she was a blond, pregnant woman was also amusing, but unlike the heroine of *Dawn of the Dead,* she was a former prosecutor who had no trouble stepping up to the plate. Add in the fact that she was bisexual, and she pretty much blew the stereotype.

She loved that.

Katie saw the strain in Travis's face and knew that he was worried sick about the risks they were taking. Every time she looked at him, his gaze seemed to wrap around her protectively. Their love for each other gave her strength. Strangely, being brought up by the senator had given Lydia strength as well. The memory of her wife made her feel more determined and strong. There was no way she was going to let the senator enslave these people.

Entering the office behind the senator, Katie saw that the desk was flanked by large American and Texan flags. A map of Texas was tacked to the wall; the locations of the fort and the mall were marked and labeled. The senator took her seat as the major general positioned himself behind her chair. Katie remembered that Kevin had pegged this man as someone who had joined the military to enhance his political résumé. Compared to her father, he did appear a little soft. The campaign manager and armed guard remained outside.

Kevin took a seat, but Travis did not. Instead, he closed the office door and leaned against it, arms folded over his chest. His gaze was direct and encouraging.

Katie remained standing. She took a breath, readying herself.

The senator crossed her legs and rested her folded hands on her lap. "Let's get down to business. I take it you are speaking for the fort, Katie?"

"Consider me their ambassador," she answered.

"Very well, Ambassador. We will be relocating to the fort immediately. I expect for you to have the Governor's Suite ready for us," the senator said. "I will meet with the fort's former leadership for an in-depth debriefing within an hour of my arrival."

Katie arched her eyebrow. "I see."

"We expect full cooperation on all levels. Major General Knox will oversee all security matters with the assistance of First Lieutenant Reynolds. Armed troops will be dispatched to my sister's estate. Unless Steven and Blanche Mann are already at the fort?"

"Blanche was there," Katie said, "until she shot one man and killed two others. To the best of my knowledge, she is now most likely a zombie, staggering through the countryside."

"What?" The senator rose sharply to her feet.

"Your sister is not the subject of discussion right now," Katie said firmly. "I'm here to deliver a message to you."

The senator's eyes narrowed as she recognized the defiance in Katie's tone. "Really? And what is that?"

"We are not giving up the fort. The people of Madison Mall are welcome to join us. We're more than willing to take them in.

If you want to come as well, you need to realize that we are building a community based on respect for the individual and freedom of choice."

"What the hell are you talking about?" The senator looked confused.

"We are determined to give people a chance to have a good life. If they don't value hard work, loyalty, and the basic ideals of the U.S. Constitution, they can leave."

"How dare you tell me how to live my life," the senator snapped.

"Oh, but you can tell us?"

"I am an elected official. It's my job to make the hard decisions," the senator retorted. She came around the desk in a streak of red.

Katie didn't shy away as she was sure the senator expected, but crossed her arms under her breasts and stood her ground. The curve of her belly, pressing against her arms, made her feel even stronger.

"I am in charge here!"

"That is where you're mistaken. You're supposed to *represent* the people who elected you. To help them, not hamper their lives. Kevin told us about your plans. You call people *assets* and *breeders,* and you've estimated how many of us can die without negative consequences."

The senator shot a venomous look at Kevin. "You were supposed to convince them to turn over the fort."

Kevin stood up slowly. "I told them your plans so they wouldn't."

"First Lieutenant Reynolds, how dare you disobey a direct order?" Major General Knox finally spoke up, looking furious.

"Easily. I realized you meant to make people into slaves." Kevin's eyes blazed.

"Slaves?" The senator barked a sharp, sarcastic laugh. "The people need to be guided firmly or we're doomed." She glared at Katie. "How long before your people fall into chaos without experienced leadership? Let's be frank here. You have no clue what you're doing.

"The citizens of this country can barely take care of themselves. Why do you think there are so many social programs? The *people* have no idea how to make good choices." The senator was speaking in the quiet, persuasive voice she used so well during debates.

"Bullshit," Katie answered angrily. "You are completely underestimating the people who helped build this country. If folks want to stay here, then they can. But we are offering them a chance to come to the fort, where circumstances are better than they are in the mall." She looked the senator straight in the eye. "We make you the same offer: Stay here or come with us. But if you relocate to the fort, you'll be one among equals. You'll have to find a way to make yourself useful."

The senator laughed again. "You are completely delusional. I am a proven leader and an elected official. I know that government and the law bring order to the people. They trust us, and without us, they don't know how to think or act for themselves. Only the educated and powerful truly understand what it takes to run society."

It shocked Katie to realize that the senator fully believed what she was saying. "I'm not here to debate politics. I'm here to tell you that we are not turning over the fort and we are not going to follow your orders. We are leaving, with whoever wants to go with us."

"My men will not follow you into mutiny, Reynolds," the major general declared.

"Most will," Kevin answered. "Frankly, sir, you are a disgrace to the uniform you wear. The minute you fell into bed with this woman, you lost the right to give orders to any of us."

The senator's mouth opened in shock. "Well, I never—"

"Oh, please," Katie said, rolling her eyes.

"The worst thing I ever did was to allow you to take command of the mall," Kevin continued. "I should have trusted my instincts. I've learned my lesson. I'm leaving and taking these people and my men with me."

"There is no room for debate on this," Katie said firmly. "We're leaving in the morning. We're going to start organizing people for the airlift right away. You are welcome to join us, under the terms I've already stated."

"Gordon, you can't let them do this!" the senator exclaimed.

"Try to stop us," Katie answered.

"We outnumber you," Kevin added. "Don't make this ugly."

Travis opened the door. He, Katie, and Kevin left without a backward glance.

## 4.
### The Last Hours

The fissure among the members of the armed forces was immediate. The senator's supporters retreated to the second floor as Kevin's troop claimed the downstairs. There were a few tense moments, but it was clear that no one wanted to start a skirmish. Despite their differences, these men and women had served side by side and had no desire to start a firefight.

"Come with us, Ben," Kevin urged one of the senator's men. Sergeant Ben Constantine was a good man and a superb soldier, and Kevin knew if Ben joined him, the rest of the dissenters would follow.

"I won't turn my weapon on civilians, Kevin, but I'm sticking with the senator. I want to get home. She's my best shot to do that once she gets to Central," Ben answered.

Kevin appealed to the others as well, but the loyalists would not be shaken. It was easy to understand why they were unwilling to turn against the authority they had served for so long. When the first lieutenant finally, reluctantly, retreated down the escalator, he was heartbroken, but felt that the possibility of an armed response was minimal.

Using the mall's public address system, which was located in the offices on the main floor, Kevin announced that anyone who wanted to move to the fort should line up in the food court and register for the airlift.

The line began forming immediately. Jenni and Katie scrambled to get organized. They settled on using separate notebooks to keep track of different groups: families, orphans, and single people, separated into under and over sixty-five years of age. Bill, Valerie, and Greta joined Katie and Jenni in signing up the desperate residents of the Madison Mall.

Jenni carefully translated for any Spanish speakers who were confused and promised them that they were not going to be reduced to noncitizens. Meanwhile, Katie assured the elderly that they would be taken care of and the helicopter ride wouldn't be too bad.

The complete list held a little over four hundred names. All of the civilian population was leaving, along with most of the military personnel.

Meanwhile, Travis and Kevin worked out an evacuation plan with Nerit via the radio, carefully planning each stage of the withdrawal from the mall.

About an hour before dinner, the senator addressed the mall from the top of the escalators. Beautifully dressed and coiffed, she was a vision of sophistication.

"I realize that many of you have chosen to depart for the fort. This is understandable, since you are desperate to escape the zombie scourge and the conditions here are difficult. But you must consider that you may be exchanging a haven that you are not completely happy with for one that you know nothing about, one that may be in far worse condition than you have been told.

"I want to take the reins of the fort to ensure that all surviving citizens of this great state and our great country are given a fair and equal chance to fulfill their patriotic duty. To ensure that all citizens benefit from strong and capable leadership.

"I have worked hard for the people of Texas for many years. Help me appeal to the untried leaders of the fort and help them see that true leadership—experienced, strong leadership—is best for everyone."

Listening to the senator, Jenni rolled her eyes.

"I am in regular contact with the president and what remains of the U.S. government. They have assured me that they will do all they can to assist us."

"We've heard that lie before," Amy whispered to Jenni.

"Together, united, we can withstand all that comes against us. Do not give up hope. America will rise again, and President Castellanos is dedicated to helping you."

Bill shook his head. Katie sighed.

"Come stand with me and let the leaders of the fort see that you want a strong, powerful new home. That you want to be part of the rebuilding of America and the great state of Texas. Join me and we will begin a new world together." The senator ended her speech with a bright smile. She stood at the top of the escalators, looking expectantly at the crowd below. The people dispersed, ignoring her completely. At last she retreated out of sight.

Ten minutes later, no one had left the ground floor.

"I think that's a pretty good answer," Katie said.

Gordon Knox sat on the king-sized bed he shared with Paige Brightman in the partitioned area of a store they had claimed as their own. Staring into the bottom of his empty glass, he considered pouring another shot from his precious liquor stores. But he was exhausted to the marrow of his bones, and the bottle on the dresser seemed too far away to reach. Instead, he lifted the glass and drank the last few drops of the burning liquid.

He hoped to be unconscious when Paige returned from making her patriotism-driven speech. He knew she would be in a foul mood and he didn't want to endure it. When she had those dark moments, he wondered why he loved her so much, but his doubts always slipped away when she was happy and loving. They were dating for nearly a year when the zombies had risen. They'd been riding high on Paige's reelection to the Senate and his new job with FEMA and were planning their wedding.

They'd each been married before, and Knox knew that most people thought marrying a senator was a savvy political move on his part. All his life he'd done exactly the right things to advance his career. He'd never tipped the boat too much, always made the right friends, toed the line, and produced a solid record that was perfectly suited to a transition into politics.

But Gordon's marriage to Paige wasn't about advancing his career. He loved her madly.

"You need to talk to your men," Paige said angrily as she swept back the heavy curtains that served as the door. Their home was part of a furniture display, with three standing walls. It was a good facsimile of a home, almost convincing until he looked at the curtains blocking the view of the store.

"What do you mean, Paige?"

"Go *talk* to your *men*, Gordon!" Her face twisted into the angry expression he loathed and he averted his eyes. "I spoke with Sergeant Constantine, and he refuses to take armed action against the soldiers siding with Kevin. He is also refusing to stop people from using *our* helicopters to leave tomorrow."

"Paige, you can't expect soldiers to fire on their own people. Those are *Americans* down there." Gordon shook his head in agitation. "Paige, are you even hearing what you're saying?"

She strode briskly over to his side of the bed and glared at him. "I know exactly what I'm saying. Our perfect opportunity to rise to the top of this new world order is being stolen away, and you're just sitting here drinking instead of mobilizing your men!"

Gordon stood up as unexpected anger filled him. "Paige, if this was a general election, you just lost. Hell, I guess it was a general election, because the people down there are your constituents and you were just ousted in a landslide."

Paige's mouth opened, but not a word slipped past her bright red lips.

"Don't you understand, Paige? The old world is done. It's over."

He brushed past her to the dresser and picked up the binder that held her extensive plans for the future. "This is a fool's dream! The people of the fort have already rebuilt their world. We can't take that away from them. This plan isn't about restoring order, it's about suppressing freedom. Freedom I used to fight for. I don't know what the hell I was thinking when I agreed to it." He threw the binder at her feet.

"You were thinking we needed to restore America!"

"Maybe," Gordon said, nodding. "But now I see that it's all about restoring you to power!" He grabbed Paige's arms, staring into her beautiful eyes. "Paige, we're not in charge anymore. If we believe in the true American spirit, then we must accept that we serve the people, not vice versa."

"You're drunk. I can smell the brandy on your breath," she said scornfully, pulling away.

"Paige, please."

"Oh, shut up, Gordon." She set her hands on her hips and leveled her furious gaze on him. "I came from the fucking trailer park. I know what imbeciles those hicks are. I had to fight my way out of poverty. I plastered on a fake smile, taped up my tits, teased my hair, and wore gobs of makeup just so I could win enough beauty pageant scholarships to attend college. I used the assets God gave me to get me and my sister out of that backwater hellhole, and I am not going back there. If we lose the fort, then we're nothing more than another fucking idiot trying not to get eaten."

Dizzy from the alcohol, Gordon sat down hard on the bed. "Paige, we've already lost. Let's go with them tomorrow. Let's start over. We can get married and work with those people to make a new America. Darling, I have every faith that when the next election rolls around, you will win."

Tapping her foot, Paige stared at him incredulously. "I am not starting over."

"Paige, please."

"Go to bed, Gordon. You're a drunken idiot."

Gordon lowered his head, anger and disappointment filling him. "Paige, we should leave tomorrow."

Without a word, she stalked out of their room, the curtain swishing back into place behind her.

"Don't do anything foolish, Paige," Gordon called after her, then passed out.

## CHAPTER SEVENTEEN

## 1.

### *Exit the Wickedest Woman in Texas*

In the gray dawn, the senator and her people quietly rushed down the employee staircase. A guard swung open the double doors at the bottom, and the group stepped into the mall's main entrance at the top of the *A,* just in front of the blacked-out doors that led to the outside world.

"Take care of the front gate guards, Sergeant Constantine. They're Kevin's men and won't let us leave peacefully," Paige ordered Ben.

Giving a brisk nod, Ben signaled two other guards to follow him and hurried outside. The door opened and shut quickly, but not quickly enough—they could all hear the zombies moaning beyond the walls.

Raleigh, the senator's campaign manager, stared into the mall, at the darkened stores where people were sleeping. "If we blow the front gate . . . ," he said uncertainly.

"The zombies fear fire. We'll be okay."

"I would hate for these people to end up dead," Raleigh continued.

"I didn't know you were such a bleeding heart," the senator said teasingly.

"Where's Major General Knox?"

"He's had a change of heart. He turned out to be a coward," the senator said dismissively. The truth was, she was done with him. His words the night before had been an unforgivable betrayal. So she'd left him. If she could not claim the fort directly, then she would make her way to Central and get them to help her. One way or the other, that fort would be hers.

A paint-blackened outer door swung open, and Ben and his soldiers rushed inside. Ben said, "Okay, the guards are neutralized and we've moved two trucks into position. I don't think we were spotted."

"Good," the senator said with a smile. "Well done, Sergeant Constantine."

"We should pull the guards inside," Ben continued. "So they won't be killed."

"Excellent point. Go ahead," Paige said, trying not to let her annoyance show. How many more delays must she face?

The parking lot was shaped like a trapezoid, with the main entrance at the narrowest end. The securely locked gate was solid metal, unlike the three wrought-iron gates behind the mall. The rear gates had been heavily barricaded and the two narrow parking areas along the sides of the mall blocked off months earlier. If the zombies broke in on one side of the parking lot, the other side would still be protected.

When Brightman and Knox had taken over the mall, the main gate was wired with explosives. Additional explosive devices had been tossed over the gate; wires connected them to triggers inside the parking lot. The plan was to blow the gate, then set off the bombs in the crowd of zombies to clear a path for the escaping vehicles.

The unconscious guards were carried into the mall and laid carefully on the floor.

"None of this feels right," Raleigh protested.

"Do you want to go to Central, or do you want to go to the fort and be led by those hicks?"

"I just want to get out of here." His hands were shaking.

Paige was disappointed in his weakness. She knew that mistakes had been made here at the mall. But she would learn from her mistakes and move on. Once at Central, she would make sure the president understood her determination to stand with him and rebuild America.

"Ma'am, you ready?" Sergeant Constantine asked.

She flashed her perfect, beautiful smile once again. "Yes, I am."

He opened the door for her and she walked out to the waiting truck, ignoring the sounds of the undead.

The gate slid open soundlessly. The explosives detonated with a loud thump. Flames erupted, setting the zombies near the gate on fire. A stampede spread quickly as their primitive fear of fire sent the undead scrambling away. The secondary explosives went off, setting more zombies on fire. The two military trucks roared out of the gate and down the street, crunching burning zombies under their tires.

"I hope the doors hold," Raleigh whispered as the trucks roared into the gray dawn.

## 2.
### *The Floodgates Open*

Standing guard in the mall's rear parking lot, Tom jerked his head up when he heard a distant thud that seemed to come from the main gate. The zombies outside the gate they were watching went into a frenzy at the sound. A few stumbled away.

"Did you hear that?" Tom asked Arnold, the soldier next to him.

The young private with the shocking red hair tilted his head. "Yeah. What the hell was that?"

Tom scanned the huge back parking lot, which was full of parked vehicles and several National Guard helicopters. When he turned toward the front of the mall, he spotted smoke and flames.

"Shit!" He began running for the mall, shouting at Arnold, "Get the trucks ready!"

The first zombies tottered cautiously past the remains of their burning comrades, heading for the front of the mall. They staggered to the doors and clawed at the unyielding glass. The zombies jostled one another, their masticated limbs sometimes breaking off.

In the melee, one zombie stumbled hard enough into the bright, blue, wheelchair-access button to activate the motorized door.

The door opened silently.

Several zombies immediately lurched through the opening and into the mall beyond.

Zombies poured into the first two stores. The first people died silently, in their sleep.

Then the screams began as people woke to the invasion of the undead.

People ran, trying to escape.

Chaos descended.

In the Left Corridor, Valerie woke, dived off her cot, and grabbed her gun and flak jacket. Struggling to clear her mind and her vision, she stumbled into the corridor and spotted zombies at the far end of the mall, greedily devouring their victims. Frightened people ran past her. More soldiers appeared out of side stores.

"Stupid *puta* bitch," Guadalupe hissed as her wheelchair zipped past Valerie, propelled by a teenage boy running at top speed. "She did this!"

Valerie called out to the other soldiers. "We need to stop them! Barricade the hall!"

Frantically, they shoved cots and anything else heavy or bulky into the corridor, trying desperately to slow down the zombies.

At first, the newly fallen dead distracted the ravenous zombies, who greedily stuffed their ruined mouths.

Then, slowly, some of the zombies rose and trudged toward the mall's defenders.

Valerie opened fire.

Major General Gordon Knox heard the screams and gunfire. He scrambled out of bed, shocked to find Paige gone. Confused by her absence, he snagged his holster and hurried down to the main floor. Quickly realizing that the mall was being overrun, he ran to the nearest exit, determined to reach the escape vehicles in the front of the mall.

The doors were locked, but Gordon always carried a set of keys to all the outer doors. He'd fallen asleep fully dressed, so the keys were still in his pants. He intended to pull a truck up to the doors and start evacuating people.

He unlocked the door and hurried outside, weapon in hand. Before he took more than a step, he was shoved to the ground and his throat was torn out.

The zombie that had killed Gordon Knox bent down to eat him and was shoved aside and trampled by the undead throng. Soon the Right Corridor began to fill with the undead.

The first people out of the mall were Kevin's soldiers. Bunked down near the entrances, they were quick to run to their assigned vehicles. Greta and another pilot ran to their helicopters. Other men and women leaped into driver's seats and began to rev up the engines of the big trucks and buses.

Soon survivors began to flood into the parking lot.

"Get into the trucks!" Arnold shouted. He wasn't sure anyone really heard him, but they did what he ordered. People ran past him, all screaming in terror.

The crush of people in the Right Corridor was almost unbearable. As those in the back of the mob fell to the zombies, panic swept through the crowd.

In the Left Corridor, soldiers blasted the zombie throng as people streamed into the rear parking lot. The zombie corpses tripped their shambling comrades, but the horde just kept coming.

Three minutes after the initial breach, a soldier in the Right Corridor was dragged down by zombies. As he fell, he pulled the pin on the phosphorous grenade he clutched in his hand.

The explosion resounded through the entire mall. The surrounding zombies were engulfed in flame. They staggered about, setting anything they touched on fire.

Black smoke quickly began to fill the corridor.

Travis, Katie, and Jenni wrestled their way out of the store where they'd been sleeping and into the smoky chaos of the hallway. They'd almost immediately lost track of Bill in the struggle to get out of the store and barely managed to hang on to each other in the tussle of panicking people.

# · CHAPTER EIGHTEEN ·

## 1.
### *Trapped*

Jenni felt like she was being squashed. She could barely hold on to Katie's hand. Luckily, most of the smoke was rising to the mall's high ceiling, but the fire continued to spread, and the crowd of survivors pressed at her from all sides.

"Jenni! Jenni!" called a newly familiar voice. Amy was struggling to maneuver through the crowd with her three children. No one was trying to help the terrified family.

"Keep moving, Amy!" Jenni cried out encouragingly.

A second later, Jenni was shoved into the wall. The impact broke her grip on Katie's hand, and Jenni glimpsed Katie's horrified expression as they were swept apart. Catching herself against a store window, Jenni managed to stay on her feet. After a breath, she plunged back into the stream of people, trying to find her friends.

The first of the would-be escapees in the Right Corridor reached the exit only to find it locked. Panicking, unable to escape, the people tried to turn back, but were smashed into the doors by the flood of panicking survivors. Many would die, crushed to death at the exit, forming a second barrier in front of the sealed doors.

Travis heard the shouts of "The doors are locked!" and immediately reversed direction, dragging Katie with him. Skirting the crowd and keeping close to the wall, he managed to reach the food court. Other people followed his example and soon a large group was running in the direction of the food court and the other side of the mall.

"Travis, I lost Jenni!" Katie pulled on his hand, trying to turn back.

"Keep moving, Katie; she'll catch up!" Travis was determined to save his wife and their unborn child. Lydia had said there would be choices to be made and, dammit, his choice was for his family to live.

By the time Jenni neared the food court, the smoke had thickened and lowered and she was coughing violently. It was difficult to see as she struggled to keep up with the fleeing mob while avoiding the advancing zombies. Behind her, zombies were dragging people down, but instead of completely consuming their victims, they were now taking a few bites, then lunging after fresh prey.

Two miniature figures emerged out of the black smoke: Amy's youngest children, Holly and Troy, who were clinging desperately to each other. Jenni knelt and swept them into her arms.

"Where's your mom?"

The little boy pointed back into the haze. Just then, the swirling smoke parted and Jenni saw Amy struggling with a zombie. Her elbow was up under its chin as she attempted to push it away from her throat. Sobbing hysterically, her eight-year-old daughter clung to her mother.

"Margie, run!" Amy shouted, but the little girl held on.

The staggering zombies closed in on the mother and child.

Desperation on her face, Amy yanked Margie up into her arms and tossed her toward Jenni. The act sealed her fate, as the zombie she had been holding off bit down into her throat.

The throng of zombies was almost upon the little girl.

"Stay right here!" Jenni ordered the little ones before darting through the grasping, shambling creatures.

Shoving a zombie away from Margie, she grabbed the girl's hand and ran back to Troy and Holly. She set Margie down and hoisted Troy onto one hip. Clutching the girls' hands, Jenni ran ahead of the zombies with renewed vigor, determined to save Amy's children.

The first fast zombies appeared, racing past the soldiers to feast on the people fleeing toward the rear parking lot. Tom, who was guarding the exit doors, opened fire and fell back into the mall, joining Kevin, Valerie, and six other soldiers who were attempting to protect the escaping citizens.

Realizing they were on the verge of being overrun, Kevin ordered his troops into the corridor that led to the food court. "We'll exit through the Right Corridor!"

More sprinting zombies appeared.

The soldiers turned and ran. The only thing that saved them was that the new zombies, ravenously hungry, dived onto the already-dying to feast.

Greta swung her helicopter low, trying to literally blow the zombies off their feet outside the mall. Cursing, she wished she had a nice bomb or machine gun, but the helicopter was intended for medical evacuation and general transport and was unarmed.

Below her, the zombies stumbled and fell beneath the rotor wash. Then they got up and kept going.

Travis reached the thundering waterfall just as Kevin and his men did.

"We have to go out the Right Corridor," Kevin said.

"It's blocked!" Travis yelled in frustration.

"What?"

"We couldn't get out!"

The two men stared at each other in shock.

"Fuck, we're trapped!" Valerie exclaimed.

A doughnut shop saved the last people in the Right Corridor. The fire was spreading quickly; when the flames reached the shop, the oil used to make the doughnuts ignited. The resulting fireball killed a few of the living even as it flattened all the zombies in the immediate area and set them on fire.

The resulting inferno brought the zombies to a halt. They cowered in fear, allowing people to escape into the food court.

## 2.
### Fall to Grace

"Where the hell do we go now?"

Travis's question hung in the air. Kevin looked around quickly, assessing the situation. He spotted the maintenance stairway that snaked up the side of the building toward the skylight overhead.

Pointing to the metal stairs, Kevin said, "Up. We go up. There's a fire escape that leads down to the parking lot from the roof. It's our only way out." He turned to his squad. "Bette, you go first and open that door up there."

With a nod, Bette obeyed. Tom swung open the gate at the bottom of the stairs, and the female soldier quickly climbed the three stories to the top.

Valerie and Kevin began steering the crowd to the stairway, and soon a jumble of men, women, and children began streaming up toward the roof.

Katie's gaze swept over the food court, anxiously examining each fleeing figure, hoping to see Jenni emerge from the smoke.

"Katie, let's go," Travis said firmly, pulling her toward the stairs.

"But Jenni," Katie protested. "We need to find her!"

Travis looked at her. Katie saw the anguish in his eyes. "Katie, I love you and you know I care about Jenni, but we need to get out of here now! Think of the baby."

Tears streamed down Katie's face as she let her husband guide her into line.

Valerie and the other soldiers began creating a barricade in the Left Corridor, tossing chairs and tables into the hallway. The zombies tended not to pay attention to anything but their victims and were easily tripped.

"Target the fast zombies first," Kevin ordered as he and his team took up a position looking down the corridor.

"Where the fuck did the fast ones come from?" Tom yelled angrily.

"They're fresh," Kevin answered grimly.

"Oh, shit," Tom said in an agonized tone.

Valerie didn't want to think of how many fresh zombies there might be.

People continued to flee the smoke-filled Right Corridor. Some had been badly burned by the explosion of the doughnut shop, but others were unscathed. Among the last to appear were Jenni and Amy's children. Half-carrying and half-pulling Amy's kids, Jenni ran to the line of people ascending the metal staircase.

Running zombies appeared from the Left Corridor, howling with hunger.

The soldiers opened fire, their bullets slicing through the air. The zombies were eliminated, though several managed to get close enough to trip over the tables and chairs before they were cut down.

"I'm running low on ammo," Valerie informed Kevin.

Kevin checked on the progress of the evacuation. "We have to keep them covered until they are up the stairs," he said somberly. "The zombies can't climb."

The soldiers all nodded gravely.

The stumbling, slow dead were moving toward them in a great wave.

Valerie grimaced, reloading her weapon.

Nearly halfway up the stairs, Katie glanced downward and saw Jenni pushing some children onto the first steps of the narrow staircase. Clinging to the rails, she shouted over her shoulder at her husband, "Travis, she made it!"

"Thank God!" Travis whispered fervently.

At the bottom of the stairs, Jenni's attention was attracted by renewed gunfire. She glanced over her shoulder to see the slower zombies lunging for the soldiers who were defending the staircase. She looked up, hoping to spot Katie, but her gaze was drawn to a single black bird soaring high above the skylight. Instantly, she understood what she had to do.

"Keep going," she told Margie, setting the two younger children on the stairs behind their older sister. "Get your brother and sister out of here!"

Jenni abandoned the stairs and her hope of escape as she shoved past the last few survivors on the stairs. Running up behind Tom, she grabbed his revolver from its holster and raced past him, toward the zombies.

Behind her, she dimly heard Tom and Kevin calling her name.

Amy had given her life for her children. Katie and Travis were going to have a baby and be a family. They had to live.

This was Jenni's time. Her *choice*.

"Hey, fuckers!" Jenni waved her arms. "You stupid, gawddamn, muthafuckin' zombies, c'mere!" She screamed at them, jumping up and down and waving like mad to draw their attention. "Look at me, you fuckers! C'mon, you fuckin' cannibals. Prime rib Jenni right here!"

"What the fuck is she doing?" Kevin gasped as the black-haired woman danced terrifyingly close to the slowly advancing zombies.

Valerie glanced at the people on the stairs and understood.

"The right thing," she said to Kevin before running after Jenni. "Hey stinkbags, follow us!"

"Oh, shit, I don't want to die," Tom growled as he followed the women.

"Awwww, hell . . ." The last soldier, William, hesitated for an instant, then joined Jenni and the others in their suicide run.

Kevin almost set off after them, but instead became the rear guard for the people ascending the stairs. The runners were vanquished for now, but the slower moving zombies flowed relentlessly into the food court. He had to make sure all the civilians escaped.

Jenni and the soldiers created a powerful diversion. They teased, taunted, and lured the zombies away from the staircase. Low on ammunition, they held their fire, moving ahead of the mob, keeping them away from the stairs.

Jenni screamed at the undead, releasing her hate and her joy, yelling her lungs out. She knew she was doing the right thing. Glancing briefly at the stairs, she saw Katie and Travis near the top and Kevin at the bottom, with Amy's children in between, slowly making their way to safety.

"Hey, you stupid shits, come get me, you stupid muthafuckas!" Jenni shouted with glee.

Their grisly faces and clawed hands reached for her, grasping at empty air as she dodged away. She moved toward the waterfall, thinking maybe she could circle it and then head for the stairs.

It was then that the zombies from the Right Corridor made their appearance. None of the people in the food court had realized that the sprinklers had finally gone on in the hall, quenching most of the fire.

Jenni whirled about as the dead began to fill the space around her. "Oh, hell," she said sadly but calmly.

William went down first, firing until the last moment. Laughing hysterically, Tom was next to fall, also still shooting at the dead.

The waterfall rose to Jenni's left. Glancing about in search of another way out, she was surprised to see a narrow staircase cutting through the rocks. Without hesitation, she began to climb the fake stone façade.

Valerie tried to follow Jenni but was cut off by a running zombie and then grabbed from behind. Without a second thought, she lifted her revolver to her temple and fired.

Jenni ascended swiftly as the zombies struggled to chase after her, moaning and wailing. More runners were moving through the horde. She paused once or twice to aim and fire the revolver, watching with satisfaction as disgusting, rotten heads exploded. Reaching the top of the waterfall, she stood on the edge, next to the rushing water. Looking down, she was horrified to see that almost all the dead were reaching for her.

Even above the roar of the water, Jenni heard Katie screaming her name.

*I've done the right thing,* she thought as she saw Kevin push the children through the doorway to the roof.

The zombies had yet to go near the staircase. Her diversion had worked perfectly. Everyone was safe.

She felt completely calm. Gazing down, she wondered if the water was deep.

A growl—close by—startled her. Turning, she saw a horribly scorched, reanimated Amy step onto the platform. Freshly reborn, the zombie's residual memory had enabled it to ascend the staircase.

Raising her gun, Jenni fired at her zombified friend.

The gun clicked empty.

Amy lunged forward, her teeth snapping shut.

Jenni jerked her hand away in shock. A surge of rage hit her and she slammed the gun down on Amy's head until the dead woman's skull shattered. Cursing, Jenni reached into Amy's head and ripped out chunks of her brain, throwing them to the zombie horde below. Amy's corpse slid to the ground, truly dead.

*I made the right choice,* she thought again. Bending down, she washed her hands in the rushing water, which turned red with her blood.

On the catwalk at the top of the stairs, Katie was waving and yelling, telling Jenni to jump into the pool of water below. The zombies had yet to entirely encircle the waterfall pool and at the moment, there was a chance Jenni could reach the stairs the others had used to escape. Katie didn't understand, Jenni realized.

She straightened and raised her arm, displaying her hand. Blood, hot with her life, trailed down her arm.

"No!" Katie's shout rang out over the roar of the water and the cries of the dead.

Jenni kept her hand up in victory as she watched Katie turn to Kevin. The first lieutenant handed Katie his rifle. Jenni knew she had done the right thing. There was no running away this time. She had faced the monsters and she had saved the people she loved.

She had won.

*I love you, Juan. I love you, Jason. I love you, Benj. I love you, Mikey. I love you, Katie.*

Katie raised the rifle.

*Yes, I did the right thing. This is how it should be. Absolution is good. I can face God and myself once more. I saved the children. I saved those people. I saved the ones I loved.*

Jenni smiled beatifically as peace filled her. She clenched her bitten hand into a tight fist over her head, the blood pouring down her arm.

*It's been one helluva ride.*

The muzzle flash of Katie's rifle was bright and brilliant. It just didn't flash. It exploded toward her, a blast of dazzling, pure white light that swept over her. Warm and beautiful, it filled her senses. The smell of death disappeared; the pain disappeared. All she felt was love.

# 3.
## *Beyond the Light*

Juan's eyes flickered open and he took a deep breath. Something felt different. Cold gray morning light filled his bedroom in the fort's makeshift clinic.

"Hey," Jenni said as she sat down next to his bed.

"Jenni," he whispered, tears unexpectedly filling his eyes.

"Hey, baby." Her long, dark hair was dripping with water.

"Why are you so wet?" he asked as her hand closed around his. Her skin felt cold and damp.

"You know me. A total klutz." She grinned.

Juan's mind felt jumbled. He tried to focus on the woman he loved, but the morning light streaming around her made her appear blurry around the edges.

"You were kidnapped," Juan said unsurely.

"It totally sucked. We were stuck in this awful mall and there was this bitch of a senator and it was just bad." Jenni rolled her eyes. "A mall, can you believe it?"

"But you're here now," Juan said with relief. "Oh, Jenni, I was so worried."

"Juan, you should know me by now. Nothing, not even death, could keep me from coming to see you," she said with a laugh.

Her kiss was soft and wonderful and he touched her wet hair tenderly.

"Loca, I missed you."

"I missed you," Jenni whispered.

"You're hurt," he said with concern, looking at her bloody hand.

"You know me. I do crazy shit sometimes." She giggled, then tucked her hand out of sight.

"Are you okay?" he asked, worried even though he knew they wouldn't have let her into the fort if she were infected.

"Yeah, I'm fine now. I promise." She smiled lovingly.

"But you're so wet." Something didn't feel right.

"You make me wet, baby," she teased.

"Loca, I'm shot and you're beat up, and you're thinking about sex," Juan teased right back.

"Uh-huh. Well, mostly thinking about how much I love you," Jenni said, more somber now.

Juan sighed. "I promised myself that I would ask you to marry me when you got back. I know this really isn't romantic, but—"

Jenni kissed him again, then gazed deeply into his eyes. "In my heart, we were always married."

Juan tried to focus on her, but his vision was dimming. "You're getting me wet, Loca."

"I know. I have to go now anyway and you need to sleep."

"Loca," Juan gasped, suddenly feeling very emotional. "Loca, I love you."

She stood up, still holding his hand. She felt so cold and wet. He was worried about her.

"And I love you."

To his chagrin, he felt himself fading into slumber. "Jenni, stay with me."

"I'm here," Jenni assured him in a soft voice.

As his eyes closed, the light behind Jenni seemed to brighten.

"Jenni," he sobbed as he finally understood.

Her fingers slipped from his hand.

She was engulfed in the light as she whispered, "I love you."

And then he was asleep.

## CHAPTER NINETEEN

## 1.

*Exodus*

Trembling, Katie lowered the rifle. Hot, angry tears flowed down her cheeks and she choked back sobs as she watched Jenni's body tumble into the pool at the base of the waterfall. Jenni's body drifted on the waves, her black hair fanning out around her face like a dark halo. Relief filled Katie as the zombies abandoned their pursuit of Jenni now that she was dead.

Robbed of living flesh, the zombies' attention was drawn to the people on the stairs. The runners fought the slower creatures, attempting to be the first to reach the escaping humans.

"Katie, we need to go," Travis said urgently.

"Katie, she's at peace," Kevin said soothingly, reaching for his weapon.

Feeling numb, Katie walked onto the roof and into mayhem. People were climbing down the fire escape and then racing toward waiting trucks, guided and guarded by surviving members of the military. Above, two of the helicopters attempted to lure the zombies away from one of the back gates. In the parking lot, sobs of despair and cries of desperation filled the air, mingling with the hungry moans of the zombies.

Travis led Katie across the roof to the rickety fire escape. The climb down was frightening; the thin metal shook under her feet. Her body was trembling so hard, her teeth were chattering.

As Katie and Travis ran across the parking lot, Katie glimpsed

Bette lifting the children Jenni had saved into a truck. All around, people scrambled into trucks and buses. Kevin ran to the lead truck, and Arnold directed Katie and Travis to a different one.

"We're almost out of here," Travis said. "We're going to be okay."

The National Guardsman at the wheel shouted for them to get into the cab. Katie had trouble making the climb; the cab was far off the ground. Her pregnant body felt awkward and heavy. Travis boosted her up, then climbed in next to her.

Black smoke billowed out of the mall. The helicopters continued to try to herd the zombies away from one of the gates, taking turns gliding over the undead as one brave soldier hung out the side, waving and yelling.

Safely secured in the truck, Travis took Katie's hand. Frowning, he said, "I'm sorry I hurt you. I was afraid I'd lose you in the crowd."

Bruises were already appearing where he had gripped it tightly during their escape. She understood his concern, but the physical pain was nothing compared to her broken heart. "It's okay. I was afraid I would lose you, too." She lapsed into silence, not wanting to remember the horrible moment when Jenni's hand had slipped out of her fingers.

Pressing a kiss to her brow, Travis held her in his comforting embrace.

Slowly, the buses and trucks moved forward, making a huge loop around the parking lot, building speed.

"We're going to blow the gates, then set off charges to push back the zombies," their driver informed them.

Katie nodded mutely and braced herself for the explosion.

The redheaded soldier who had been directing traffic dived into a big Ford truck just as the center rear gate blew open. Immediately, the secondary bombs went off.

Katie gasped and Travis flinched beside her.

Fire and smoke filled the street outside the mall as the first truck barreled out of the parking lot. Military and civilian trucks, plus several metro buses and a school bus, roared out of the parking lot into the town of Madison.

Helicopters swooped overhead, attempting to distract the zombie throng. Behind the convoy, the doors of the mall shattered from the heat of the fire. Burning zombies staggered into the abandoned parking lot as the last bus rolled through the gate.

Katie held on to the dash for dear life as the motorcade roared through Madison. Zombies rushed at them, but the drivers never faltered. They smashed into the zombies, crushing them or hurling them into nearby buildings. In minutes, the vehicles were past the city limits and heading into the countryside.

As the sun broke completely free of the horizon, the unrelenting dead followed the convoy.


# 2.
## *Long Road Through Hell*

The country road swerved through the barren hills, the cracks in the asphalt already thick with gnarled weeds. Juniper and cedar trees stretched twisted limbs up toward the low, gray sky. Occasionally, the convoy passed a zombie, which immediately began struggling toward the vehicles.

Staring out the window, Katie wondered if the trees were praying for the survivors of the mall's destruction. She dimly remembered, from her Bible school days, a verse about trees praying when no one else had a voice. Katie closed her eyes, and fresh tears slipped silently down her cheeks.

The convoy had taken a long, roundabout route to make sure that any zombies tailing them from Madison would end up wandering away from the fort. Now the trucks and buses were driving along back roads, past long-dead farmhouses and ranches, heading for Ashley Oaks at last.

Fleeing the zombies in the mall, clutching Travis's and Jenni's hands, had been the most terrifying event of Katie's life, worse even than the first day. She'd been overwhelmed by the sight of so many zombies. The moans and screams of the dead and living had formed a mind-shattering cacophony.

As long as she lived, she would never forget the despair that had filled her when Jenni's fingers slid from her grasp.

"Fuck!" The driver swore as he wrenched the wheel to one side; the truck swerved, tossing Katie and Travis to the side of the big cab. Katie watched through the windshield as the truck in front of them also veered wildly. The tarp covering the rear of the truck swung open, revealing a young boy, his face covered in blood. Screaming, he reached toward them, before someone pulled him back inside.

"They're infected," Katie gasped. Nervously, she glanced over her shoulder, wondering if any of the people in the back of their vehicle had been bitten.

"We didn't have a chance to check everyone before we left," Travis said in anguish. "It all happened so fast."

As they watched in horror, the truck sped off the road, down an incline, and into some trees, shattering branches and slender trunks before colliding with the thick bole of an enormous oak. Katie saw the driver thrashing wildly in the cab and wondered if he was infected. People began to pour out of the back, bloodied and screaming. Horribly, it was impossible to tell if they were turned, infected, or still safe.

The truck Katie and Travis were in sped up, closing the gap that had opened in the line of vehicles. Katie watched in the side mirror as soldiers riding farther back in the motorcade opened fire on the people rushing toward the road. Two of the soldiers hurled something into the back of the crashed truck; then there were two loud bangs.

"Grenades," their driver said solemnly. "All according to plan."

Travis sighed and pulled Katie back into his arms. Kissing her brow, he whispered, "We'll get home soon."

Katie nodded mutely. She still wasn't sure if her father or Bill were alive. She knew that Jenni was dead, and now so were all the people in that truck. All those poor people who thought they had been saved.

When the line of trucks and buses reached a stretch of road bordered on either side by large fields, Kevin used his walkie-talkie to order a stop. The open spaces would make it easy for his troops to see any zombies in the area. Sliding out of the lead truck, he felt bone weary and numb. In just thirty minutes, they had lost hundreds of lives, including that of his best friend, Valerie. He couldn't bear to think about her right now. He had a job to do.

Kevin stood solemnly, watching the convoy come to a halt. Bette emerged from a Dodge truck, her face pinched and tired beneath the close crop of her blond hair. Joining him, the lean woman with the dusky complexion said, "What's up?"

"We lost a truck back there. We need to search the rest of the vehicles for any infected," Kevin said.

"And if we find some?" Arnold asked, walking up to the first lieutenant along with several other soldiers.

Kevin rubbed the back of his head with one hand. He studied the eight grim faces of those gathered around him. They had never had to kill infected civilians before, just people who were already zombies, and it made his heart ache to ask this of them. At last, he said, "We have no choice. Bette, check our people out first."

For several tense minutes, there was silence as the medic thoroughly searched each man and woman for bites. Cleared, they moved out, Kevin behind them. If he expected his people to do the shit jobs, then he better damn well be willing to do them himself.

They began with his own truck, opening the flaps and explaining what was going on to the people inside. The passengers climbed out slowly and stood close together. One woman hesitated, then held out her arm, showing a clear bite. Those around her immediately withdrew.

"I'm sorry," she said softly, then sniffled. Her eyes welled up.

Kevin said very gently, "It's okay, ma'am. Just step over there."

"I'm really sorry," she said again. "It doesn't hurt. Maybe—"
She broke into sobs.

Bette carefully led the weeping woman to the side of the road.

"Anyone else?" Kevin asked.

No one volunteered, so the soldiers began inspecting all the passengers. To everyone's relief, no one else had been bitten. Once they had been cleared, the men and women got back into their vehicle.

The procedure was repeated with the next truck and the next. Each time, people were allowed to volunteer that they were infected before everyone was searched. No one protested.

The next several vehicles were clear and Kevin felt a pang of hope. They had already lost so many people, he just didn't feel he could deal with much more death.

Behind him, he heard the infected woman still crying.

The passengers from a metro bus were given the all clear. As they reboarded, many looked at him desperately, seeking some kind of reassurance. Kevin forced a smile he did not feel, and several hollow-eyed people looked relieved.

Moving on to the next truck, he saw Travis drop to the ground then reach up to help Katie out of the cab. Bette and two other soldiers quickly examined them and the driver and cleared them. They moved on to the back of the truck and began unloading the passengers.

Kevin strode up to the couple. "Good to see you're safe and sound."

Travis glanced at the infected woman, who had collapsed to the pavement, sobbing. "I wish everyone was."

"Me, too. She probably won't be the only one," Kevin said with a sad shake of his head.

Travis gripped Kevin's shoulder briefly. "I'm sorry about your friends back in the mall. They were brave."

"So was Jenni," Kevin said with a slight smile. "Helluva a feisty one, wasn't she?"

"You have no idea," Travis responded with a bittersweet chuckle. "No idea."

Katie smiled thinly at this comment. She looked exhausted and was holding tightly to Travis's arm.

"You really should kill her now," Katie said in a tremulous voice, looking at the bitten woman. "She could turn at any second."

"What do you mean? She's not dead yet," Kevin said, startled at her words.

"Sometimes infected people turn without dying," Travis answered.

"Are you serious?" Kevin asked incredulously. He rubbed his brow and looked back at the woman, who had fallen silent.

The woman lurched to her feet and whirled on the guard. Without flinching, the soldier shot her point-blank in the head.

The people in the parked vehicles cried out in horror.

"You should kill them immediately," Travis recommended.

"I'd rather give them the dignity of a choice while they are still alive," Kevin answered grimly. "I can't ask my people to murder living beings."

"It's what you have to do," Katie said. "It's what I did for Jenni."

Kevin stared into Katie's tormented eyes, then turned away, shaking his head.

"It's what we do at the fort," Travis said somberly.

"We're not at the fort yet," Kevin answered grimly. *Fuck. Could this get any worse?*

"Katie!"

Kevin looked up to see Bruce Kiel being helped from a truck. His wrist was heavily bandaged. Kevin felt his heart sink.

"Dad! No!" Katie rushed toward her father.

Bruce held up a hand, motioning her back as he joined the line to be inspected. "It's okay, baby. Stay right there, okay?"

Katie obeyed him, stopping in her tracks. "Dad," Katie said in a calmer, yet shaking voice, "did you get bitten?"

"I'm not sure it's a bite," Bruce replied. "I punched a few of them while escaping, but I also climbed through a broken window to get out of a store."

"Let's see it," Bette ordered.

Bruce unwound the bandage, which looked like it had been made from a shirtsleeve. The bloody cloth fell away, revealing a bad wound. Bette held his hand and studied the gash.

Katie was trembling as she waited in agony, Travis resting his hand on the small of her back.

Bette sighed, then wrapped up the wound. "I see some glass in the wound, but there are also clear teeth indentations."

With a shivering breath, Bruce closed his eyes. "I understand."

"Oh, God, no!" Katie's legs buckled, and Travis caught her.

Kevin lowered his head, feeling sick of it all.

A soldier guided Bruce toward the side of the road.

Bruce smiled at his daughter as he passed her. "It's okay, Katie-girl."

Katie reached to touch him, but her father shook his head.

"Bruce, I'm sorry." Travis's voice was full of grief.

"I'm not. I got to see you and my daughter and know about my grandchild. I got to say good-bye." There were tears in Bruce's eyes. "I love you, Katie-girl. I'm damn happy you're going to be a mother and you're going to have a good life. I'm proud of you."

"Dad, I love you. I love you so much," Katie said passionately, struggling not to cry. She would be strong for her father.

Bruce blew his daughter a kiss, then stood on the side of the road with his head down. Travis and Katie clasped hands and watched him in silence, tears glimmering in their eyes.

"This day can't get much worse," Kevin whispered to Bette.

But it did. By the time every truck and bus had been searched, they'd found seven infected people: four men and three women. Two were teenagers; the rest were adults. The oldest was in his sixties.

"You have two choices," Kevin said as he walked down the line of infected. "We leave you here and you turn. Or, we can put you out of your misery and save you from the fate of the rest of the world. I know it doesn't seem fair and it's not, but I want to give you the dignity of the choice. I'm truly sorry."

"I'll do it myself," one girl said through chattering teeth. The eighteen-year-old was having spasms, and Kevin was sure she was on the verge of turning.

Kevin studied her, then glanced at the soldier standing behind her. The soldier stepped away. Kevin handed the teenager his revolver.

People in the buses and trucks behind him were watching. The soldiers had tried to make the people look away, but he knew there was something innately human in not being able to tear their eyes away from the drama.

The girl's breathing was shallow, her eyes milky.

Gazing at Kevin, she whispered in a voice that was barely human, "Take my mom to the fort." Then she shoved the gun in her mouth and, without hesitation, pulled the trigger.

Her blood splattered the others. One infected man screamed and ran into the pasture.

"Let him go," Kevin ordered. "He made his choice."

"I can't do it myself," one of the women said, staring at the dead teenager at her feet. "I can't."

"I'll do it," Bette said gently. She walked behind the woman and shot her.

"Me, too," a man said, looking at Bette. "Me, too."

Kevin looked into Bette's green eyes and saw her sadness. He moved to stop her, but she had already fired.

The teenage boy turned and ran.

"I can't," the last woman whispered, then raced into the field.

Bruce slowly and deliberately reached for the gun at the dead girl's side. "I don't want to ask you to do what I can do myself," he said in a wavering voice. His hand was shaking.

Kevin pressed his lips tightly together and gave a curt nod.

"You did a good job, son. Just some of us were a little slow. And a little foolish," Bruce said with a sigh. He looked at his daughter and son-in-law, in the cab of their truck. "Katie, I love you. Travis, take care of her. I got to say good-bye, and that makes this all worth it."

"Dad," Katie said emotionally, "I love you, too."

"I know, honey, I know. Take care, y'all." His hand steady now, Bruce pressed the gun to his temple.

The gunshot made Kevin jump even though he knew it was coming.

"One of them is coming back," a soldier said. He raised his weapon.

A shot rang out. Then silence ruled the world again.

"Let's go home," Kevin said at last, wiping his tears away.

## 3.
### *Home*

The sparkling Christmas lights were the first thing many of the evacuees saw as the convoy crested the hill and sped down toward the fort. Perhaps because of the gloomy, drizzly weather, the lights seemed very bright, twinkling in the grayness of the day.

Amy's children, huddled together in a metro bus, stared with wide, shell-shocked eyes at the glowing decorations. Margie leaned over and whispered to her brother and sister, "Maybe Christmas is here."

Guadalupe broke down crying, burying her face in her gnarled hands. Those around her laid comforting hands on her.

In one of the lead trucks, Bette sat in silence. Tired to the core of her being, she wanted to be somewhere safe and warm. Once she'd been a medic who tried to heal the sick. Now she was an executioner. Exhausted, she rested her head on the seatback.

The convoy drew up outside the fort's gates. Vehicles were admitted through the lock one at a time, the sentries examining them for any unwanted zombie stowaways. Overhead, the helicopters hovered watchfully. To everyone's relief, no zombies attacked while they waited.

When the truck Katie and Travis were in passed through the gate, Katie wiped away a few silent tears. They were home, but their world had been changed forever once again.

Her best friend was gone.

Her father was gone.

Kevin saw Nerit, the Israeli woman, standing on the wall, watching the proceedings with keen eyes. Their gazes met and something unspoken passed between them.

Having received word of the inspection for bites on the road, Charlotte waited with Belinda and other volunteers to treat the people who had been wounded during the escape.

Peggy and Yolanda feverishly took down the names of all the evacuees, realizing quickly that it would be a huge job to make sure everyone had lodging.

As the survivors poured into the courtyard that had once been a construction site, the citizens of the fort rushed to greet them.

There were moments of incredible joy as family members were reunited. Friends who had not seen each other in years wept as they embraced. Weary soldiers found themselves hugged and kissed by strangers. Newly arrived members of the reverend's flock were stunned to find their spiritual leader waiting for them, and he, in turn, shed tears as they greeted him.

These and many other unexpected reunions filled the dreary day with cries of happiness that were mingled with tears of sadness.

Finally, the last truck rolled in. A beleaguered middle-aged man, his hair messy and his face drawn, trudged through the crowd toward a redheaded woman who was staring at him in disbelief.

With infinite gentleness, Bill put his arms around Katarina and kissed her, then said, "I really need a beer."

# · CHAPTER TWENTY ·

## 1.
### *Moments*

"We must remember that our loved ones have moved on to a place where there is no fear or pain. It is we, who are left behind, who feel fear and pain. We must take comfort that their suffering is over; we must love one another and live the best life we can to honor their memory," the reverend said to his gathered flock, lifting his voice in prayer.

Katie moved past him, her legs feeling heavy and leaden. Travis walked behind her, resting a hand on her waist. She felt dizzy and tired, and her body ached from the long, bouncy ride in the truck. Her hand pressed protectively against the swell of her stomach as she walked toward the hotel.

As one man moved aside to let her pass, Katie saw Jason directly ahead of her. He was standing very still with Jack pressed to his side. Michelle stood a half step behind him, her face pale. Katie's heart broke all over again as she gazed into the boy's eyes.

"Jason," Katie managed to say before he flung himself into her arms. Shaking, he buried his face in her neck as he cried. Clutching him, she whispered, "I'm so sorry." Tears filled her eyes, then spilled over. Jack began to whine.

The teenager sobbed desperately. Travis wrapped his arms around both of them and said, "We're here, Jason. We're here."

"Mom! Mom! Mom!" Jason's voice was a screech of pain.

Michelle wrapped one arm hesitantly around Katie, who

pulled her into a four-way embrace. Jack squeezed between their legs and howled.

Rosie was in a feverish rush to get lunch on the table for the newcomers. The kitchen was filled with delicious smells as she and her crew worked hard to make a feast. She pulled dozens of fresh biscuits, golden and hot, out of the oven, then wiped her hands on a towel and went to check on the fried chicken. She had decided to break out the last of the frozen poultry for the new people. They needed good food, from the sight of them.

"Hey, Rosie," Calhoun called from the doorway.

"What is it, Otis?" Rosie asked.

"Your mama is in the lobby," the old man said.

Rosie looked up, startled. "What did you say?"

"Your mama, Guadalupe, is here. She hit me with her derned cane," Calhoun said as he sauntered none-too-casually toward the biscuits.

She waved her metal tongs at him to warn him off. "My *mamá* can't be alive. She went to the hospital for a checkup on the first day. Hospitals were deathtraps."

"Well, she's alive," Calhoun answered, reaching for the biscuits.

Rosie smacked him and he grunted, but snagged a biscuit. She hesitated, then handed the tongs to one of her helpers. "Don't let him get another one."

Calhoun shoved the entire biscuit in his mouth and grinned as he went for another.

The thought of her nearly one-hundred-year-old mother being alive was too much to even hope for, but when Rosie entered the lobby, she saw the hunched-up old woman in a wheelchair, banging on the check-in counter.

"I want a room with a view that doesn't include zombies!"

Rosie fainted. Guadalupe turned to look as people cried out. She was stunned to see her daughter lying on the floor. "*Dios mío!* My baby is alive!" She began to cry.

\* \* \*

The dining room had never been so full. People were crowded in, eating feverishly. The reverend had blessed the meal, and some people had wept at his words.

Bette sat with some of the survivors and a few fort residents. It had been a long time since she had eaten such good food. She picked at the biscuit on her plate, eating slowly so that she could relish the flavor. Across from her, a pretty Latina kept giving her furtive glances.

Finally, Bette put out her hand and introduced herself.

The younger woman smiled shyly and said, "My name is Monica."

Under Monica's intense gaze, Bette continued to eat. The heaviness inside her grew a little lighter every time she met the other woman's eyes.

Bill and Katarina ate together, holding hands under the table. Despite the pain around them, they were enveloped in a bubble of happiness. Bill was home and they were together. What exactly that meant, they weren't sure yet, but so far, it felt right.

Kevin and Nerit sat side by side in a corner of the dining room. They ate in silence. As people relaxed and laughter began to be heard, tears came to Kevin's eyes. He put down his fork and began to cry, his wide shoulders heaving. He had worked so hard to save the people at the mall and he had failed. He'd seen the list of names Peggy compiled. Close to half the four hundred people in the mall had died.

But two hundred had lived, and they were now safe, so perhaps he had not entirely failed. He didn't know what to think anymore. His family was gone. Valerie was gone. His soul was tired.

Nerit touched his shoulder, offering wordless comfort. A man on Kevin's other side did the same. Other people stopped to thank him. Somehow Kevin found himself on his feet.

"I wish I had done more. I wish everyone had made it. I'm so sorry," he apologized.

The people around him were shaking their heads.

"You did well."

"Good job."

"Thank you."

Without realizing it, Kevin moved through the dining room, surrounded by grief, faith, and love. People held him, kissed him, and cried with him.

At last, Nerit took his hand and led him to her own room. Kevin lay down on her bed, which smelled of lavender and sage.

"Sleep," she told him. "Your job is done. Now you can rest."

He closed his eyes and felt her cool fingers rest on his forehead. He was certain he would never be able to sleep.

He did not wake up for two days.

Katie slipped into Juan's room and found his mother visiting, along with Guadalupe.

"Katie," Juan said emotionally. He reached out and drew her down into a tight hug. His unkempt beard scratched her cheek.

"Juan, I came as soon as I could," she said, sitting next to him.

"Have you met my grandma yet?"

Katie smiled at Guadalupe. "We've met. I helped sign her up for the evacuation."

Guadalupe returned her smile. "We hung out at the mall together, right, *chica*?"

Katie struggled not to lose her composure. "Juan, about Jenni—"

"I already know," Juan said quickly. "Jenni came to me."

Rosie dabbed at her eyes. "He told me about his dream and I thought maybe it was just a nightmare, but now . . ."

"She came to you in a dream?" Katie said.

"I don't think it was a dream. I *saw* her. I felt her touch. She was wet and her hand was hurt. At first I thought she had come home, but then I realized . . ." Juan faltered and his voice grew hoarse as he continued, "I realized she was telling me good-bye."

Katie could not hold back her tears. "She's not one of them."

Juan sighed with relief and covered his eyes, trying to compose himself. "Was it you, Katie? You . . . did . . . it?"

Katie nodded. "I did."

Juan hugged her again. "Thank you, Katie . . . thank you . . ."

"I saw my mom," Jason whispered in a slurred voice.

Considering the strength of the sedative Charlotte had given the boy, Travis was surprised that he was awake. Next to him, on the bed, Jack continued to sleep, his tail wagging slightly.

Jason looked at Travis groggily and repeated, "I saw my mom. She's okay." Jason's eyes drifted shut, his breathing slowed, and he was asleep. Travis looked cautiously around the room. Feeling foolish, he whispered, "Hey, Jenni, don't go too far. We still need you."

He sat back in his chair, took a deep breath, and closed his eyes, feeling better.

# · CHAPTER TWENTY-ONE ·

## 1.
### *The Season Ends*

Some of the new arrivals slept for days. Others were hyperawake, afraid that if they fell asleep, they'd wake up back at the mall. Many people walked along Main Street, staring in awe at the buildings; others were astonished just to be outside after months indoors.

The fort's long-term residents helped the newcomers settle in and find their niche.

The two helicopters and their crews were temporarily grounded until new fuel supplies could be located. Kevin and the soldiers who had followed him joined fort security. Any ruffled feathers between the fort sentries and the soldiers were soon smoothed out as Kevin and Nerit worked together to create a cohesive defense unit.

With Bill back in the mix, the situation with Brewster, the last of Blanche's henchmen, was resolved. He was allowed to stay in the fort—under probation—after he stringently denied having any foreknowledge of Blanche's murderous plans.

Meanwhile, the fort monitored the communications between Senator Paige Brightman's convoy and Central. It quickly became evident that the Central Government did not have the resources to rescue the senator and the people who had left the mall with her. Within two weeks of the fall of the mall, all communication between Brightman and Central ceased.

The decision as to whether or not the Central Government should be contacted was placed in the hands of the fort's inhabitants. They voted nearly unanimously to continue on their own.

Spring arrived and bluebonnets sprang forth to color the hills as the trees regained their green regalia.

Life moved on.

## 2.

### *Happy Anniversary*

"I can't believe it's March already," Peggy huffed.

Stacey looked up from the ledger she was studying and lifted her eyebrows. "It is?"

"The new people arrived in mid-February, and that was a month ago. I guess we've all been so busy, it got away from us. Lord knows I've hardly slept." Peggy was busily making a homemade calendar on the back of a used piece of paper.

"We missed Valentine's Day when all that stuff went down at the mall," Stacey said sadly. She marked off a few items on her ledger before reaching for the next form in her pile.

Peggy snorted. "Zombies rise and we're still doing paperwork."

Lenore knocked lightly on the door to Peggy's office. Clad in jeans and a blue Eeyore hoodie, she looked as dour as ever. "I'm heading out with a scavenging crew. I took twenty more bolts for my crossbow. They're looking low." She handed Stacey a slip of paper.

The blond woman nodded and said, "I'll let Jason and his crew know they need to make more."

"Thanks."

"How are you doing, Lenore?" Peggy asked.

"A girl can only cry so much over a boy," she answered in her usual dour tone.

"You know, that handsome Kevin Reynolds is single," Peggy said, hoping that maybe Lenore would smile and start feeling happier.

"You do realize that just because you put a black woman and a black man in the same room, that don't mean they're gonna hook up, right?" Lenore scowled.

"I was just saying—"

"Crazy-ass white people." Lenore rolled her eyes.

"You'd make cute babies," Stacey offered helpfully.

Lenore growled and stalked off.

"What got into her?" Peggy arched an eyebrow.

Stacey lifted her shoulders and updated her ledger again. "Who knows? We're getting low on sweet peas."

"We're getting low on everything. Hopefully, all the scavenging will help." Peggy finished her calendar and circled the present date. "Well, I'll be damned."

"What is it?"

"It's been a year. Today." Peggy laid a trembling hand over her heart. "It's been a year exactly since it all went down into zombie hell."

"Should we tell everyone?" Stacey's face had drained of blood beneath her ever-present tan.

"I don't know. What good would it do?" Peggy studied the calendar again. "It seems so much longer."

"A year." Stacey thought of all that had happened and was amazed. "A year."

# 3.
## Out with the Old

The first bulldozer tore into the old house with frightening ease. The structure quivered, then folded in on itself in splintering splendor.

Standing on one of the hotel balconies, Nerit watched through binoculars as bulldozers destroyed all the houses on a single block. The fort's scavenging teams had already removed everything useful from the homes.

There had been relatively few encounters with zombies. Nerit thought that it was likely most of the area's resident zombies had been eliminated. There was still a chance that there were zombies trapped in some of the homes, but they hadn't found any in months.

Despite the influx of newcomers, things were running more smoothly in the fort. Maybe it was the beauty of dawning spring, but people seemed less restless than they had during winter, more willing to help out.

Nerit had been pleased to add Kevin and his troops to the fort's defenses. The soldiers helped train the fort's civilian guards, creating an even more effective force. Kevin's tactical abilities surpassed Nerit's, though he deferred to her as the senior officer.

In one of their first strategy sessions, they'd decided to have one of the helicopters make a flyover of the National Guard base. They needed more ammunition and wanted to assess the potential threat from the zombie-occupied base.

To everyone's surprise, Greta reported that there were no zombies visible on the base or in the surrounding area. After several more recon flights, it was decided to send in some of Kevin's troops. After several nerve-racking hours, the soldiers had returned and reported that they'd found a few slow zombies inside the buildings. They'd put them down easily. The two helicopters returned full of additional equipment and weapons.

"How's it going?" Travis asked, stepping onto the balcony beside Nerit.

Nerit gave him a tight smile. "So far, no trouble."

Travis gripped the railing and stared at the bulldozers. "I wonder if we'll ever live in houses again. Go to the grocery store. Drive to a movie."

"In time, perhaps. Most likely not you or me. But your children's children, maybe."

A haunted look flitted across his face. "We can hope and plan to make it happen."

Nerit smiled ruefully. "We are pioneers in a new world. We

were so unchallenged by the old world, so spoiled. Now we are back to hunting and gathering."

They saw several large trucks heading back into town, loaded with dead deer. Winter had taken a harsh toll on the cattle on the neighboring ranches, but the deer population seemed to be up. A group of men were now taking care of the cattle. Once the herd was healthy again, beef would be back on the table. But until then, venison was the meat of choice.

"At least we got big guns and ammo," Travis said after a beat.

Nerit laughed. "Yes, at least we have that."

They both watched another house crash to the ground. Birds sang in the trees. Wildflowers covered the hills. The sky was bright blue, and fluffy white clouds glided overhead.

Below, the bulldozers continued to reshape the old world into the new.

# · CHAPTER TWENTY-TWO ·

## 1.
### *When All Is New*

Everything had changed.

Katie slowly jogged down Main Street, her ponytail swinging back and forth behind her head like a pendulum.

Overhead, a helicopter was veering off toward the north, probably running field-workers out to a nearby ranch the fort was attempting to secure, or heading for the farm, taking someone to check on the water station, or just refueling at the nearby airstrip.

Helicopters . . .

Who would have thought the fort would ever have helicopters? Jenni had joked about a handsome black leading man and helicopters when she and Katie were first on the road. She'd tossed out Romero film facts as if they were quotes from the zombie bible.

Katie's eyes suddenly stung and she tried not to think of Jenni in her pink bathrobe, riding shotgun in that old white pickup.

Turning the corner, she saw Nerit strolling down the street, hands in her pants pockets, her old hunting dog ambling along beside her. The older woman looked more relaxed than Katie had ever seen her. The influx of soldiers had made Nerit's job much easier. Recently, to Katie's surprise, Nerit had allowed Ken to give her a makeover. Gone was the long silver braid, replaced by a more youthful, sassy hairdo that barely brushed her shoulders. A rinse had taken the yellow tinge from her silver locks.

Katie almost resented Nerit's ease at moving past Ralph. She knew that was unfair of her—she was finally at peace with Lydia's death, and even with her father's. She'd assumed he was dead for months, so to have had a chance to hug him, talk to him, and say good-bye was a gift.

But it was hard to let go of Jenni.

She trudged along the interior of the wall. Above, on a sturdy platform, Jason and some other teenagers were building a catapult. Jack was up there, too, securely leashed in case he tried anything crazy like diving over the wall at a zombie.

Jason had wept for Jenni for days, but even through his tears, he kept saying that he knew his mom was all right, that she had come to comfort him. Soon, he had gone back to designing defensive weapons for the fort.

He was healing.

On the next street, Katie spotted Bill in his new uniform. The police force had grown to five, all former officers in their hometowns, now unified by their common purpose—to protect the citizens of Ashley Oaks—and by matching uniforms, recovered on a scavenging mission. Though crime was not a common occurrence, there was the occasional petty theft or fight, and sadly, some domestic disputes.

"Tell your husband the poker game is at eight tonight," Bill said as she drew near. "I plan to demolish him, Juan, and Eric."

"Okay. Will do," she answered, laughing. Between the new uniform and the glow of his fresh relationship with Katarina, Bill looked almost handsome.

Monica and Bette were standing outside the theater, holding hands and staring up at a newly hung old poster announcing the premiere of *Jaws*. The bloom of their brand-new love was fresh and beautiful. Unfortunately, a group of fundamentalists was taking strong issue with the fort's minuscule gay population.

Seeing Monica made Katie think of Curtis. He never smiled

anymore. Never did much of anything other than sit in the communication center or patrol the streets. He avoided any social gathering where he might see his former lover. Katie felt bad that he couldn't move on, but she understood his pain.

She was having trouble moving on herself, where Jenni was concerned. But how could she? Their life together seemed unfinished.

She turned through the gates into the old construction site. In one corner, Juan was building a small garden as a memorial to Jenni and others who had died. Though he wasn't well enough yet for heavy work, he'd roped off the area and begun breaking ground. Bags of rich soil and fertilizer sat nearby, and a statue of the Virgin Mary leaned against the wall, intended to be the garden's focal point.

Katie stopped near Juan to warm down. Her seven-month pregnancy bump was a little bit of an issue, but she was learning to work with it. She was having a very easy pregnancy according to Charlotte, though her aching back, swollen feet, and bladder did not seem to agree.

How could she have gained and lost so much in just a year?

Standing with her hands resting on her swollen belly, she studied Juan. His ponytail kept falling into his face and he kept flipping it back. Slowly Katie realized he was crying as he worked.

Refusing the release tears might give her, Katie walked away.

She wasn't ready yet. Despite the changes in the world around her, she couldn't let go of Jenni. Not yet.

## 2.
### *Daddy One*

It started slowly, as all love stories do.

It began with one lone man working long hours on a small garden in a corner of what had once been a construction site. Day by day, he toiled slowly and painfully, rarely looking at the people strolling by.

Silence was what he craved and silence was what he received. Everyone seemed afraid to talk to him and he was relieved. He didn't want to talk about her.

Jenni.

His *loca*.

His heart and his love.

So he labored on the memorial garden, the last thing he could give her.

True love comes slowly, they say.

In Jenni's case, it had hit him so hard, he never saw it coming. He had relished every moment with her. In his mind's eye, he saw her laughing until she fell over in a heap or dancing with wild abandon to some awful song. Then there were the quiet times, when she lie in his arms and her smile made this horrible life feel beautiful and good.

Now she was gone and he could find no beauty around him. Everything was gray and dark.

So he was planting flowers for her. Something beautiful to remind him of her beauty.

One morning, a shadow fell over him while he worked. He did not look up. He didn't want anyone to see the tears in his eyes.

"Whatcha doing?"

"Planting a memorial garden." Standard reply. Neutral voice. He stayed focused on the tray of flowers waiting to be planted. Monica and Bette had salvaged them from yards around town.

"What does that mean?" The voice was tiny. Female.

"It's for those who died. To remember them."

"Oh." A long pause. Then, "My mommy and daddy died."

At this, Juan looked up.

He saw three children. The speaker was around eight or nine years old, with long blond hair trailing around her face. Her eyes, dark and vivid, reminded him of Jenni's. Holding tight to the girl's T-shirt was a little boy, around four or five, and another girl, maybe six. The little boy had masses of dark hair and big, chestnut brown eyes. The second girl was blond with clear blue eyes.

The children Jenni gave her life for. He'd heard the story from Katie and Kevin and others who'd witnessed Jenni's sacrifice.

Juan had been avoiding the youngsters. He almost hated them. They were alive because Jenni had died. He knew Peggy had been trying to look after them, but mostly they drifted aimlessly through the fort like miniature ghosts.

The little boy leaned down and gently ran his fingers through the earth at the base of the freshly planted violets.

"I have a lot of work to do," Juan finally said.

"Can we help?" the oldest girl asked.

"No, I don't think so."

The middle child, her lips pursed, touched the features of the face of the Virgin Mary statue. "She's pretty."

Juan felt the beginnings of panic. Why wouldn't they leave?

The oldest girl squatted down and began to dig another hole. "We used to do this with Mommy," she said.

A lump rose in his throat and Juan fought not to cry.

The children clustered around him. The younger girl began to lay bits of pink granite in a little row along the walkway Juan had already laid down. People had been writing the names of their deceased family members on each stone. The little boy dug holes for his oldest sister, who carefully set flowers into the earth. Unable to speak, his throat clogged with anger and grief, Juan kept working. After several minutes, the boy asked in a raspy voice, "What's your name?"

As far as Juan knew, this was the first time the little one had said anything to anyone since arriving at the fort.

"Juan," he managed to choke out.

"One," the little boy said.

"No. Juan."

"One," the boy said again, smiling with satisfaction.

Juan started to correct him, then reconsidered. The boy was talking and that had to be important.

Despite his pain, he let them be. To his surprise, they were good workers. The next morning, they were waiting for him beside the garden. He hesitated, not sure if he could deal with them for another day, then set to work without a word.

They all worked hard, sweating, getting dirty. The children chattered quietly, in hushed voices. A few passersby tried to talk to the little ones, but at each approach, they drew close to Juan as if seeking his protection.

He wanted to scream and send them running, but he refrained.

Peggy made sure they had breakfast and were dressed appropriately, but otherwise they were Juan's responsibility. They called him One and asked him countless questions about the garden, but when others spoke to them, they fell silent.

Slowly, his anger faded. The garden began to look lush and beautiful with its redbrick walkways edged with pink granite and a plethora of blooming flowers.

"I like bluebonnets," the oldest girl, Margie, told Juan, and tickled his nose with one.

"Why?"

" 'Cause they're pretty," she answered with a giggle.

Juan smiled.

He started having lunch with them and then breakfast. Every evening, before they went inside to be with Peggy and her son, Cody, they would hug and kiss him.

The pain slowly lessened inside, and from time to time, Juan caught himself smiling.

One morning, as a helicopter ascended into the sky, he realized that the garden was complete. The bench beneath him was cool and the breeze was fresh. The three little ones sat smiling on the bench across from him.

"You are now our daddy," Margie informed him. The other two nodded in agreement, grinning happily.

Flustered, Juan said, "What?"

"The lady with the black hair told us," Margie answered. The other two nodded again.

"Which lady?" He already knew the answer.

"The lady from the mall. The nice lady who took care of us after Mommy . . ." The girl hesitated. "You know."

"When did she tell you this?"

"Last night. In our dreams," Troy answered. "She's pretty."

This was so like Jenni. She was making sure the kids were fine and that he was, too. He laughed, tears in his eyes, and whispered, "Oh, Loca . . ."

Then the kids were leaping on him, hugging and kissing him. He held them tight.

"Daddy One! Daddy One!" they chanted.

Juan felt his pain lift and he threw back his head and laughed. He was so full of love, he felt as if it must be bursting out of him. He leaped to his feet and danced around with glee, the kids dangling off him.

Somewhere, he knew Jenni was smiling down on them.

## · CHAPTER TWENTY-THREE ·

## 1.
### *The March of the Dead*

Nights in mid-April were still brisk, so Rune slept under a thick blanket in the hunters' blind he had discovered off a back road. His bike was parked right next to the trapdoor, and his hand grenades were close at hand. The wooden blind was sturdy enough, but the canvas roof was torn and not much protection from the cool wind and light rain. Rune was huddled against the wall, snoring lightly, when he was awakened by a simple touch on his knee.

Waking with a start, he drew his Glock and aimed at the figure kneeling next to him. "Don't move," he ordered.

There was no zombie moan in response. The dark figure didn't move.

With his free hand, he lifted his Maglite flashlight and flicked it on, revealing a pretty face with huge dark eyes.

"Jenni!"

"Hey, Rune."

Rune lowered the gun slowly, his hand beginning to tremble. He swallowed hard, then said, "Sorry."

She lifted her shoulders under her red sweater. "I'm okay with it."

"You go out good?"

"Hell yeah! I'm proud of how I died! I saved a bunch of people I love. It was good." Jenni grinned with satisfaction.

"Good for you. You went out a warrior." Rune began to holster his Glock, but she held out a hand to stop him, her smile fading.

"Don't. You need that. In fact, you need to get moving," Jenni said urgently.

"Shit. What's going on?"

"They're coming out of the east. They started walking this way a few weeks ago. You have to warn the fort."

"Damn, Jenni, that don't sound good!"

"There's a lot of them. You need to go *now*." Jenni's aspect was beginning to blur around the edges.

Rune fought to keep his teeth from chattering as the air around him grew colder. That she had appeared so realistically was impressive, but she was drawing all the energy from the air around him.

"I'm going," he said, getting to his feet.

Jenni didn't answer. She was already gone.

Whipping open the trapdoor, Rune dropped his motorcycle bags onto the ground next to the bike. It looked clear under the blind. Heaving the bag of grenades onto his shoulder, he swung his legs onto the ladder.

Faint moans made his skin crawl. He couldn't tell how far away they were.

Gripping his gun securely, he dropped to the ground. Swinging quickly in a circle, he didn't see any dead things. He secured the motorcycle bags to his bike as the first few figures emerged from the stand of trees to his right. They moved slowly, but when they saw him, their moans grew louder. The answering moans of what sounded like thousands of zombies made Rune's bowels heave.

Swinging his leg over the saddle, he gunned the engine and flipped on the headlight. The bright beam revealed countless zombies spilling into the valley.

"Shit!"

Rune raced the motorcycle away from the shambling dead. His heart was beating fast and the Glock felt slippery in his moist hand. Zombies reached for him as he zoomed past, but none were close enough to snag him.

The night was full of the moans and stench of the dead. Rune prayed hard as he drove—too slowly—along the rutted and nearly overgrown path. He was beginning to fear he was lost, when he saw Jenni standing near the path, light streaming through her as she pointed urgently to his left. That was not the way he'd originally come, but he obeyed. The new route led up a hill and was not easy going. Another rider might not have been able to traverse the terrain, but Rune managed to reach the top, breaking through a line of trees.

He paused to look back. The moonlight illuminated what looked like thousands of zombies filling the valley. If not for Jenni, he would have ridden straight into the teeming mass of the undead.

Yanking on his gloves and goggles, he looked around and saw a dirt path leading down to a country road. Both were clear of the undead.

Feeling like Paul Revere, he revved the engine and roared off toward the fort.

## 2.
### The Long March into the West

It began when a handful of zombies ignored the unexpected feast in a military truck that had crashed while trying to break through Interstate 35 and instead pursued a second truck escaping up a hill. Fifteen zombies had followed the truck, stumbling and struggling over miles of fields and roads.

The moving pack attracted their fellow undead as they walked through the south side of Fort Worth, then headed west, past dead towns and farms. A few of the creatures fell by the wayside as the weeks passed. Some became caught in fences and languished there until crows plucked out their eyes and vultures ate their flesh. Others toppled off overpasses, cracking their heads open.

A tornado swirled into their ranks one dark night, sucking hundreds into the air, pulling them apart, and smashing them to earth again. Bits of the undead littered a mile-long swath of countryside.

The zombie horde took no note of its losses, but continued forward in pursuit of flesh.

Slowly, relentlessly, the undead wandered west, toward the fort.

## CHAPTER TWENTY-FOUR

## 1.
### *The Dead Are Coming*

The new road signs were the first surprise. They gave clear directions on how to safely approach the fort. Rune also noted some nasty-looking traps along the way.

When he finally reached the gated entrance, the guards recognized him and immediately let him in. Ken and Lenore checked him for bites. It was good to see so many familiar faces.

"Can you let the Big Boss and Nerit know I need to speak to them right away?" Rune asked Lenore.

"Sure thing," she answered, and pulled out her walkie-talkie. "Is Dale still around? And Maddie?"

"Yeah, they're still here," Ken answered, his smile brightening at the mention of Dale. "It's been kinda rough since you left. A lot of people died. But a lot of new people came to join us."

"Fort grew in other ways, too," Rune said as an outgoing helicopter caught his eye.

"You have no idea," Ken said.

"Go on in, Rune. They'll meet you in Travis's office," Lenore instructed.

"Thanks. See you around."

Rune easily found his way to the hotel. When Maddie spotted him, he got an enormous hug, then excused himself.

It was strange to be among the living after being around the dead for so long. What was even stranger was the disconcerting lack of ghosts. He'd noticed that in the deadlands also. Something had changed, and the spirits had begun moving on again. Rune didn't know why.

Travis greeted him warmly when he entered the office. "Hey, Rune. Good to have you back."

"Good to be here. Nerit, like your hair. Looks good." He shook their hands. Nerit smiled at his compliment.

"What do you have to tell us, Rune? Lenore made it sound urgent." Travis sat on the edge of his desk as Nerit took a chair.

Rune remained standing. "I've been riding since last night to get here. I need to warn you about something big."

His smile fading, Travis said, "Go on."

"Jenni woke me up last night before some zombies could get me. I know she's dead, but ghosts talk to me." When neither person interrupted him, he continued, "She asked me to warn you."

"I believe you. The dead don't seem to stay dead in this world," Travis said, surprising Rune. "What's the warning?"

Rune took a deep breath. "Last night I saw a whole mess of zombies. They're heading straight for the fort. It will take them a while to get here 'cause they're slow and they're going over every hill and through every forest and pasture along the way. But they're coming."

"Thank you. We'll look into it immediately," Travis assured him. He offered Rune his hand again. "Welcome back, Rune."

Despite the terror of the night before and the dangers he knew were coming, Rune was glad to be back at the fort. It was like coming home.

## 2.
### Family Life

Juan wasn't sure he could deal with this. He felt dizzy, his stomach was clenched in a tight little ball, and his heart didn't seem to be beating right.

Slowly, he lowered the little pink panties into the dresser

drawer, gently straightening one of the pink bows decorating the waistband.

Margie, Troy, and Holly were moving in. Peggy had done a good job, taking care of the children for the last two months. That was obvious from the collection of clothes and toys she had compiled for each child. But the three kids were part of Juan's family now, and he was happy to bring them home.

Since Jenni's death, the suite they'd shared had been a sad place. Not wanting to upset his adopted teenage son, Juan had delayed the decision to bring the three orphans into their home. He was pleased when Jason made an effort to get to know the children. The teenager had explained to Juan that Jason felt passionately that his mother wanted him to love the little ones she had given her life to save.

In the end, it was Jason who had suggested that the kids move in.

Now their home was filled with laughter and loud, young voices. Jason was smiling from beneath his thick bangs as Margie talked his head off while he helped her unpack. Holly was conversing with her toys as she stuffed them onto the shelf in the side table.

The ever-faithful Jack lay on the bed between Jason and the trash bags full of clothes and toys Juan was unpacking. The dog was edging toward a stuffed bear, doing his best innocent look.

"My bear," Juan's new son said to the German shepherd, and grabbed the teddy bear. Jack whined and looked as pathetic as possible.

"Bad dog," the little boy said.

"Troy, don't be mean to Jack," Margie scolded.

Troy pressed his forehead to Jack's brow and received a sloppy lick in response. The boy laughed, crawled onto the bed, and tackled the dog. The tussle that ensued had Juan half-annoyed, half-amused as he tried to get the clothes tucked away.

A knock on the door of the suite's main room startled them. Holly yelled, "I'll get it!" and ran out of the bedroom.

A minute later, Travis walked in behind Holly, looking confused.

"Uh, you have little ones. Not just a surly teenager, but munchkins," Travis said, eyeing his old friend thoughtfully.

"I took over custody from Peggy," Juan said with a sheepish yet proud grin.

"Daddy One," Troy said. He was cuddling his teddy bear and using Jack as a pillow.

Travis chuckled and sat down on the edge of the bed. "Well, fatherhood suits you. You sure beat me to the punch."

"Hey, don't I count?" Jason frowned from across the room. His relationship with Juan since Jenni's death had grown much closer, and Juan beamed happily at his son's words.

"Travis is just a little slow," Juan said with a grin in his friend's direction. Noting his friend's distracted air, he said, "You have that look. Something's up."

Travis sighed. "We need you at a meeting in a few minutes. I hate to bug you in the middle of a major life change, but this is urgent."

"About the stinky people?" Holly asked. Leaning against the bed, she was playing with a battered Barbie and studiously not looking at the adults.

"Yeah, about the stinky people," Travis answered.

"I don't like them," Troy said softly.

"They killed our mom and dad," Margie added.

"They killed a lot of people," Travis said gently. "But we need Daddy One to help us make plans to get rid of them."

Margie was frowning. Juan already knew she was the chief worrier. He kissed the top of her head and said, "It's okay. I'll be back soon. Jason, can you watch them?"

"Sure," Jason answered with a smirk, "I can do that . . . Daddy One."

"Make sure they eat dinner and that they don't feed Jack too many cookies." He couldn't believe how much he sounded like a father.

▼

Jack gave him a reproachful look.

"Dog farts in the middle of the night are no fun, Jack," Juan informed the dog, who whined a little in response.

Kneeling, Juan was engulfed by little arms. He kissed the kids one by one, feeling his throat tighten with emotion.

When he stood, Jason got up, too, and gave him a quick, light hug before flopping onto the bed next to Jack. "Don't worry about the kiddies. I got it covered, Dad."

As he had so many times in recent weeks, Juan felt tears in his eyes—but now they were of joy, not sadness.

He and Travis headed out for the meeting.

"Daddy One, eh?" Travis said.

"I blame Jenni."

Travis grinned. "Ornery even beyond the grave, ain't she?"

Juan laughed as they headed down the hall. "That's our Loca."

### 3.
### *Facing the Truth*

"We are looking at around fifteen thousand zombies heading our way," Nerit said as the aerial photos were passed around the table in the conference room that was now the fort's command center.

"Possibly twenty thousand," Kevin added.

Travis frowned. "Where did they all come from?"

Greta lifted a shoulder. "Who knows? Does it matter? They're there and moving straight toward us. Rune was right."

Curtis and Bill studied the photos gravely. Katarina looked ill.

Dressed in a white shirt and navy trousers—as casual as he ever got—Eric went pale. "Could they be from the National Guard rescue center? Wouldn't that be from the right direction?"

"It *was* completely empty when we went there," Greta noted. "If so, what got them headed our way?"

"We haven't heard anything about the senator's crew for some time," Nerit said. "But that doesn't mean they aren't out there somewhere. They could have stirred up the zombies."

"Where the zombies come from doesn't really matter, does it?" Katie said tersely. "We all know that once they get started in a direction, they keep going until they find human flesh."

"Will the walls keep them out?" Bill asked abruptly.

Juan fidgeted in his chair, then finally rolled his shoulders. "I can't say."

"That's not very reassuring," Curtis snapped.

"Yeah, well, we've been building pretty damn fast, without calculating how much stress the walls could take. Up until now, we only had to hold off a couple hundred of those things at a time."

Eric nodded. "We haven't done any stress tests—"

"Well, we better hurry the hell up and do some!" Curtis shouted, smacking his hand down on the table. "'Cause they're fucking coming."

"We could always fall back to the inner areas," Kevin suggested.

"Less to protect," Nerit agreed. "And the walls are thicker around the hotel and entry lock."

"You're talking like we're going to get overrun," Bill commented softly.

The tension in the room was growing. Katie laced her fingers through Travis's.

"That's always been a possibility," Eric said calmly.

"Why are you such a gawd damn Vulcan?" Curtis yelled. He jumped to his feet and backed away from the table, eyes wide and terrified.

"Curtis, calm down," Bill ordered in a soothing tone, holding out one hand to the younger man, who was perspiring heavily. "Just calm down."

Curtis backed into a corner of the room, shaking his head.

"We're going to get overrun. I knew it, I knew this would happen when we brought in all those people from the mall."

"This has nothing to do with the mall," Nerit said sharply. "These zombies most likely came from the National Guard base or from Fort Worth or Dallas."

"It doesn't do any good to panic," Eric said.

"But people *are* gonna panic," Peggy said in a quivering voice. "Fuck, I'm panicking right now! That's a damn lot of zombies."

"Should we evacuate?" Eric wondered.

"Absolutely not. We worked hard to build this fort," Travis said vehemently.

"We figure out how to defend ourselves, then tell everyone," Nerit said.

"Yeah, well, how fucking long do we have, Nerit? How long before they're at our fucking walls, moaning and screaming for our guts? Huh? How gawdamn, fucking long!"

"End of the month," Greta said calmly, every inch the professional soldier.

"How do you know that?" The hysterical note in Curtis's voice was sharp. Bill stepped toward his fellow officer. Curtis avoided him and glared at Greta.

"Number of miles divided by a rough estimate of their walking speed, which is very, very slow," Greta said, regarding him coolly.

"So today we plan," Travis said.

Eric nodded. "Agreed. Before we terrify people."

"They're going to be terrified anyway," Peggy scoffed.

"Let's try to give them less to be terrified of, then," Kevin said with a small smile in her direction.

Juan shook his head. "It's not going to be easy to get rid of that many zombies. We're talking a total siege."

Nerit said sternly, "We have no other options."

Katie's fingers were trembling in Travis's grasp. He leaned over and kissed her cheek.

Juan said, "We gotta do this. We can't afford to lose all we've fucking gained."

Eric rolled out the schematic of the fort, and the council began to plan. Unnoticed by the rest, Curtis left. He started to run and did not stop until he reached the roof of city hall, where he sobbed until he collapsed.

No one came to soothe him.

# · CHAPTER TWENTY-FIVE ·

## 1.
### *Judgment Day*

Travis had never been so scared in his life. He had faced many chilling events in the last year, but this had to be the worst. He had to explain the dire situation they were now facing to the fort's residents. His heart was pounding. Though he'd been mayor for half a year, he still hated public speaking.

The hotel's ballroom was packed. People's voices blended into a loud rumble. In one corner, a small pack of dogs encircled Calhoun. Travis tapped the microphone lightly, and the booming sound that filled the room made everyone focus their attention on him.

He swallowed hard and glanced at Katie, seated in the front row, who favored him with a slight, encouraging smile. The tension in her face made him want to hug her, but he had a job to do.

"Okay, let's get started," he said, the volume of his amplified voice startling him. He cleared his throat again and took a deep breath before continuing. "I want to start by thanking everyone for their hard work on construction and in the gardens, the fields, and on the farm and ranch. And, oh yeah, thanks to the grub patrol. Last night's cobbler was awesome."

There was a smattering of applause as people settled down to pay attention.

"I'm going to be straight with you. Things have taken a turn for the worse," Travis said.

"And it ain't the toilet paper supply running low again," Peggy drawled, folding her arms grumpily across her chest.

This drew a bit of laughter and broke a little of the tension.

Travis continued, "There's a large group of zombies heading this way. And not just a few hundred, like we've seen before. It's around fifteen to twenty thousand."

It felt as if no one in the room drew a breath for a few seconds; then everyone began talking at once. The cacophony frightened the children and sent Calhoun's dogs into a barking fit. Travis held up his hands. "Please, calm down! Calm down! We are not defenseless. We have a plan!" Despite the microphone, he felt as if his voice were inaudible in the midst of the panic.

"Please, listen up! Please!" Travis heard his voice getting hard and angry. "I need you to fuckin' listen!"

"Language! There are children here," a woman snapped.

"We got zombies out there and you're worried about swearing?" Lenore scoffed.

"Please listen to the man," Reverend Thomas called out. "Please, listen, before you let fear overwhelm you."

There was much grumbling, but the din slowly lowered in volume.

Travis gripped the podium with both hands and plunged back into his speech. "The task before us is daunting. We need to get the horde moving away from us. We've sent the helicopters to buzz them, to try to get some of them to peel off, but it's not working. So we're going to use the six Durangos we confiscated a few weeks ago."

The uneasy gathering was silent now, listening intently to his every word.

"Each truck will carry two people—the driver and one passenger. They will try to lure as many zombies as possible off track. We're going to try to divert as many as we can before they reach the fort. We have plans to defend the fort from however many of the dead reach us, and we'll be moving people to safety inside the original wall."

When he paused for breath, someone in the ballroom shouted, "It's suicide to go out in those trucks!"

"It's volunteer only," Travis responded, abandoning his planned speech.

"And if no one volunteers?" a man asked.

"I'll go," Bette said, standing up, her expression somber.

Next to Bette, Monica got to her feet instantly. "I'll go with her."

"Count me in," Bill said as Curtis scowled angrily at Monica from Bill's other side.

"Me, too," Katarina said, resting her hand on Bill's shoulder.

Mary West stood. A dour woman with a pinched mouth, she was the leader of the self-styled Baptist Coalition. Her blue skirt and pale blouse were heavily starched and very neat. Her hair was swept into a chignon on top of her head, and Travis thought she looked a little like Peggy from *King of the Hill*.

Travis felt his pulse quicken slightly as he acknowledged her with a brief nod.

She spoke calmly, loud enough to be heard over the murmuring crowd. "Your plans are for naught. The sins of this fort have offended God, and as He passed judgment on the earth, He will pass judgment on the fort." The nodding heads around her and the chorus of *amen*s made Travis feel cold inside.

"Many of us feel that God has brought us here to begin anew," Reverend Thomas responded swiftly. "He has shown us grace in our time of need."

Mary's tight smile had no mirth or kindness to it. "You have fallen away, Pastor, and your congregation is full of fornicators, idolaters, and homosexuals."

"Hey," Ken cried out, jumping to his feet. "Hey, I'm a Christian, too!"

"A homosexual cannot be a Christian," Mary responded coolly.

"I love Jesus!" Ken shouted. "I read the Bible. You can't tell me that I'm not a Christian!"

"An unrepentant sinner cannot enter the Kingdom of Heaven,"

Mary bitingly answered. "This fort will fall, for sin runs rampant between its walls." She pointed at Bette and Monica. "Lesbians and gays in open displays of affection." She pointed at Travis and Katie. "Children born out of wedlock."

"We're married!" Katie protested.

With a cold look at Reverend Thomas, Mary answered, "Are you, really? By a holy man of God?"

"Oh, that is going too far," Yolanda said sharply as she rose to her feet. "Just because we may not believe as you do—"

"Catholics! Worshiping idols," Mary said dismissively.

"That's a tribute to those who fell," Juan snapped. "It's Jesus' mother, for God's sake."

"Taking the Lord's name in vain. Is it any wonder that God has sent this horde of demons to destroy you?"

Travis took a breath to steady his temper. Voices were rising in anger and frustration.

"If we die, you die with us!" Ken shouted.

"We must repent and throw out the fornicators, adulterers, idolaters, and homosexuals. Then God will deliver us." Mary's confidence was impressive yet disturbing.

To Travis's dismay, more than thirty people rose in support, calling out, "Amen!"

## 2.
### Trouble in Paradise

Horrified silence filled the room for a long moment.

"Look, I don't agree with gay people or what they do. I think it's wrong," Peggy said loudly, getting to her feet. "I think it's a sin, just like you do." Travis saw Katie stiffen in shock at Peggy's betrayal. "But I don't believe in putting anyone outside these walls just because we don't like how they live!" The former city secretary's voice trembled with emotion. "Death is outside those walls, and even if we don't all agree on what's right and what's wrong, we all got a right to live! It was bad enough when we had Blanche and her people tossing people over the wall, being vigilantes. We can't let that happen again."

"How do we know Blanche was the Vigilante? Maybe it was her!" Ken said, pointing an accusing finger at Mary.

"God is going to smite you, sinner!" Mary snapped at Ken.

"God is a God of love, not hate!" Reverend Thomas intoned. "You have no right to put words of hate in His mouth."

Mary's face was full of cold fury. "Jesus will judge you harshly for leading His people astray."

"Well," Bill's big, booming voice rang out. He adjusted his belt around his diminishing beer belly and fastened his eyes on Mary. "As a good Southern Baptist boy, son of a minister, and former summer missionary, I gotta say I don't remember Jesus saying anything about being so damn hateful."

"Fornicator! You have a serpent's tongue," Mary shot back.

Katarina's face was as red as her hair. "Bill and I have not had sex! We're waiting until we get married!"

"Lying harlot," Mary snapped.

"That is *enough,*" Travis said loudly into the microphone. "You have no right to judge anyone here. Didn't Jesus say, 'Judge not lest ye be judged'?" His voice was stern.

Mary lifted her chin and her eyes narrowed. "A sinner needs correction."

"Jesus said to love one another," someone called out.

"The devil himself turned the Scripture to his purposes," Mary hissed.

"Is that where you learned it from?" Ken asked smartly.

Laughter rang through the room.

"We will not stay and be slaughtered with the sinners!"

"Then leave," Kevin said. He'd moved forward to stand next to Travis. His voice was calm, but his eyes glittered with distaste. "Take your followers and leave. We won't hold anyone against their will."

"Agreed," Nerit said, joining the men at the front of the room.

"Your sin will be your downfall!" Mary shrieked harshly, beginning to lose control as the resistance in the room became clear.

"If that happens, it will be by our choice," Travis replied. "What is yours? Are you staying or going?"

Mary clenched her hands at her sides. Around her, the rest of the Baptist Coalition shifted about uneasily, their faces reflecting uncertainty.

"We will not stay and be judged with the fornicators, idolaters, and pagans," Mary said firmly.

"Fine," Bill said. "We can give them some supplies and a few vehicles, can't we?"

"I don't see why not," Nerit said calmly.

"Any objections?" Travis asked. Now that most of the fort had sided against the extremists, he felt the situation was a little more under control.

There were no objections.

"We will leave immediately," Mary said, and led her group out of the room.

Kevin gestured to Arnold and Bette, who hurried after the group. "Better keep an eye on them," he whispered to Travis.

It took a few minutes for everyone to settle down. While calm returned, Juan helped set up the large maps and posters the council had prepared. His three little ones never took their eyes off him.

When everything was ready, Travis said, "This fort is about life. It's about a new beginning, about building a new world out of the old and not making the same mistakes. We may not always get along or share the same opinions, but we gotta respect one another or we're going to end up destroying everything we have achieved.

"I am not a perfect man. I fall short of the mark a lot. But I believe in a God who will honor those who work hard to do what is best for everyone. I think He . . . or She . . . whatever you believe God is . . . has been helping us. I'm not a highly religious man, I admit to that, but I believe in the goodness of the human heart and the integrity of the human spirit. And I think God does, too."

Tears stung his eyes as he finished and he took a deep breath as applause filled his ears. Katie was smiling proudly and he felt himself blushing.

"I'm going to turn this over to Kevin now," Travis said, relinquishing the podium to the first lieutenant.

The handsome soldier stepped forward and began, "Now, this is what we have to do. . . ."

## 3.
### *The Unexpected Guest*

Nerit felt bone weary as she entered the small hotel room that she now called home. Tucker, her old dog, was asleep next to the bed, snoring loudly. Kevin lingered in the doorway, watching her with visible concern. It had been difficult to hide her limp today.

When she was in public, she made sure that no one witnessed how much her arthritic hip hurt. It was important to her that people see her as indestructible, to trust in her and her abilities.

"You need pain meds," Kevin said after a beat.

"Those are for dire injuries, not old bones," Nerit answered as she eased herself into the large recliner tucked into the corner of the room. Relaxing a bit, she exhaled slowly.

Leaning against the open door, Kevin smiled wryly. "You're a bullheaded woman."

"Yes, I am." Nerit smiled.

Tucker woke up, tottered over to her, and laid his head on her knee. Scratching him behind the ears, Nerit relaxed farther into the chair.

Kevin stepped into the room and the door shut behind him. "Makes it hard to take care of you."

"You don't have to watch over me."

"I know, but it makes me feel better," Kevin responded. Despite herself, Nerit appreciated the care she noticed in his green eyes. "Think the fort took the news well?"

"As well as could be expected."

Kevin was silent, his expression thoughtful. He seemed about to say something, but appeared to reconsider. He hesitated, then leaned over to kiss her on the cheek before retreating to the door. "Good night, Nerit."

"Good night, Kevin."

She watched him walk out, his shoulders slumped. She reached for a pack of cigarettes, then retired to her smoking chair by the window. She didn't have a fancy balcony, so if she wanted to smoke, she had to open the window. Having slid back the glass, she eased onto the simple wooden chair with a small grunt.

Lighting up, she felt her sore muscles protesting. Exhaling slowly, she rested her forehead against her hand and gazed into the silent courtyard below.

"Strange things happening since the dead all stood up," Ralph's voice said.

Turning, Nerit saw her deceased husband sitting in the recliner, one hand stroking Tucker's floppy ears.

"Things are all messed up now," he continued, looking straight at her. "Nothing's right no more."

"Ralph!"

"Crossing over ain't hard, for now," Ralph said. "You look real pretty, Nerit. I like yer hair."

"Ralph, why are you here?"

With another familiar, crooked little smile, he said, "Came to take you home with me."

"Ralph, no!" She stood up sharply, the cigarette falling from her hand. "I have too much to do here!"

Slowly standing up, Ralph reached out to her. "Honey, I know. You're a good woman and a good soldier. You were supposed to go when I did, but you're too damn stubborn."

For the first time in her life, Nerit feared her husband. She was not ready to move on. "Ralph, please, I'm not done here."

266 · RHIANNON FRATER

He embraced her gently. He felt like real flesh and blood, but she knew he could not be. "I know, but you're sicker than you think, Nerit. You got the bone cancer. That's why you're hurting so bad."

Nerit clung to her husband, feeling the roughness of his shirt and firmness of his grip. "Ralph, if you can ask for me, please . . ."

Kissing her cheek, Ralph drew her closer. Nerit felt tears sliding down her cheeks. The old dog whined at her feet.

"I miss you, Nerit. Is it so bad to have peace?"

"But I won't have peace, Ralph, knowing that these people need me. I won't have peace unless I help them. Tell Him that for me." She drew back to gaze into her dead husband's warm, loving eyes. "Please."

"I love you, Nerit," Ralph whispered, kissing her.

Nerit felt a delicate pop in her head, as if someone had switched something off. Then she was falling, slipping from Ralph's arms.

She thought, *Not now,* as the world faded into comforting black.

Kevin had just started to open the door of his room when he had a strong urge to go back to check on Nerit. As a soldier, he'd learned to trust his instincts. When he reached Nerit's door, he heard the mournful wail of her dog and the sound of something hitting the floor.

Without a second thought, Kevin kicked in the door. Nerit was lying on the floor, a lamp overturned beside her. Tucker was licking her face and whining loudly. A cigarette lay smoldering on the carpet.

Heart pounding, Kevin tossed the cigarette into the nearby ashtray, then knelt beside Nerit, who looked frail and young. The lines had been smoothed from her countenance, and her hair gleamed gold, not silver, in the light. He felt for a pulse in her wrist and found a faint beat.

Grabbing the phone, he dialed down to the clinic. "Bette, it's

Kevin. Nerit has collapsed. She has a pulse. I'm bringing her down." Before the startled nurse could answer, he hung up.

Picking up Nerit's surprisingly heavy form, he rushed toward the door, whispering fervent prayers all the way.

## 4.

### *Faith*

Travis walked briskly through the hotel lobby, looking for Bill. People were already signing up to defend the fort, taking on even the most dangerous tasks. He sensed their strong determination to defeat the oncoming undead army.

In the midst of the commotion, the Baptist Coalition was getting ready to leave. Bill was overseeing their departure.

"Okay," Bill said as Travis found him in the lobby. "I've got them set up in the extra short bus. Put extra fuel in the back and just about anything I could think of that they might need, short-term. Long-term, they're on their own."

"Did you give them something to use to siphon gas out of cars?" Travis asked.

"Sure did, and plenty of MREs. Gave them hunting rifles and some spears."

"Sounds good," Travis said approvingly.

"They're leaving tonight," Bill continued. "I tried to get them to stay until morning, but they just want to go. It's like they think God's about to hurl lightning bolts down on us."

"Wasn't that Zeus, not Jesus?" Travis said with a wry smile.

"You know how Fundies are. Hellfire and brimstone, God is gonna getcha."

Travis sighed.

Mary walked up to them. "Travis, I felt it best to give you one more chance to repent your sins and do what is right. Cleanse the fort and return to godly ways."

"If that means casting out the people you consider undesirable, I think I'll stay with my sinner ways," Travis stated.

Mary's face darkened. "A proud heart belongs to the fool," she responded tersely.

"Yeah," Travis said, looking at her pointedly. "It does."

The elevator doors slid open. Travis gasped as he saw Kevin stumble out with Nerit limp in his arms.

"God is already striking down the sinners," Mary said with a vindictive gleam in her eye and a smug smile.

"Get the hell out," Travis snarled at her over his shoulder, already moving toward the clinic. Katie appeared out of the crowd, reaching for Travis's hand. They were only steps behind Kevin.

"What happened?" Katie asked.

"I don't know. I found her on the floor of her room," the soldier answered.

Bette was standing in the clinic doorway, waiting for them. "I called Charlotte. She's on her way," she said, guiding Kevin to an examination table. Switching into full nurse mode, Bette checked Nerit's vital signs as Kevin stepped away.

The door opened and Charlotte charged in.

"All of you! Out! Go to the waiting room," Charlotte ordered.

Obediently, they filed into the adjoining room that served as a waiting area.

"Oh, God, we can't lose Nerit," Katie whispered as she took a seat.

Travis slid an arm over her shoulders, feeling her body trembling. Kevin sank into a chair and buried his face in his hands.

Reverend Thomas entered, his Bible clutched in one hand, his expression bewildered. "They're saying Nerit is dying."

"We don't know yet," Kevin answered darkly.

"Well, if you don't mind, I would like to say a prayer."

"Thank you," Katie said. "I think we would all find it a comfort."

The reverend joined hands with Katie and Kevin, as did Travis. With a voice full of warmth and faith, the reverend began,

"Dear Heavenly Father, be with us now in this most terrible hour of despair and rest your hand upon your child and our dear friend, Nerit. Bring her comfort in this time and heal her body. . . ."

## 5.
### *Where the Dead Aren't*

Juan crept into his hotel suite, hoping not to wake the children, but found them gathered around his mother and grandmother, clutching rosaries. The three little ones were in pajamas; Jason was still dressed in a T-shirt and jeans, with Jack asleep at his feet.

"Hi, Daddy One," Holly said with a somber expression on her face.

"Why are you children still up?"

"We're praying for Nerit," Margie answered, her hair falling around her face.

"How is she, Dad?" Jason asked.

"Coma, but no one knows why. Charlotte says she's stable but critical." He sat down on the sofa. Holly and Troy promptly climbed onto his lap. He cuddled them, sighing into Holly's hair.

"We're asking God to make her well," Margie said.

"And Jesus, too," Holly added.

"And his mom," Troy said in a soft voice. "I never prayed to Jesus' mom before. Can we pray to my mom, too?"

"I am sure your mama hears your every word," Guadalupe assured Troy.

"Does she?" Troy asked Juan, expecting the truth.

Juan thought of Jenni appearing to him after her death and nodded. "Yes, I know she does."

## CHAPTER TWENTY-SIX

## 1.

### *Good-byes*

Three shiny new Durangos were being checked over before the start of their mission. Curtis was watching from his post on the platform that straddled the wall between the hotel courtyard and the entry gates. Two days had passed since Nerit's collapse, and she was no closer to life or death. Reverend Thomas was holding an around-the-clock prayer vigil for her. Curtis wondered if God was listening anymore.

Curtis shifted nervously from foot to foot, staring at the back entrance of the hotel, where Monica and Bette were saying emotional farewells to Rosie, Guadalupe, and Juan's four children. It bothered him how accepting Monica's family was of her relationship with Bette. His scowl deepened as Rosie gave Bette a hug.

Finishing their good-byes, the two women started across the former construction site in Curtis's direction. Bette was dressed in army fatigues; Monica wore hunting clothes, her hair pulled back in a ponytail. To his disgust, they were holding hands. As they climbed the stairs, he took a breath and stepped in front of them. Bette's face registered surprise, but Monica just looked annoyed.

"Monica, I would like a moment of your time," he said calmly, trying very hard not to glare at Bette.

"I don't know, Curtis," she said.

"It's okay, hon. You take care of this," Bette said, giving Monica's hand a squeeze before heading into the paddock.

Monica put her hands on her hips. "What is it?"

"Look, I . . . uh . . . know I fucked up . . . somehow . . . you know . . . with you," he sputtered, trying to remember his well-rehearsed speech.

"Curtis, we were just fuck buddies," Monica answered tersely.

He winced, then plunged on. "You're going out on a dangerous mission. You could die. I don't want, you know, bad blood between us."

Monica folded her arms over the breasts he had loved to touch. She looked away from him, then said, "Okay, that's true. Look, I just wasn't clear enough with you, but I thought you understood. That I needed you to relieve all that stress, that it was just sex."

Curtis felt his temper rising and knew his face was getting red. He closed his fists and tried not to scream at her that she was a dirty whore. "Monica, I love you," he managed to say through clenched teeth.

She took a deep breath and exhaled very slowly. "Curtis, I'm sorry. I just don't feel that way about you."

"I know I did something wrong. But I'm young, and if you just gave me some time—"

"Curtis, I wasn't looking for a relationship when I was with you. I wasn't looking for one with Bette, either, it just happened. I've never been with a girl before, but I love her. I'm sorry that it hurts you. But if we could be friends and let our past go, Curtis, that would make me so happy. I really don't want bad blood between us."

Hurtful, angry words danced on the tip of his tongue. Forcing a smile, he said, instead, "Friendship is good." Even as he spoke, he imagined the women together, naked and sweating, touching and kissing each other. He wanted so badly to hurt them, he felt the desire as a pain in his gut. "I can live with friendship."

For the first time in weeks, Monica smiled at him. "Thank you, Curtis."

He kissed her awkwardly on the cheek, tasting her skin, hating her as much as he loved her.

Monica moved on, toward the woman who now got to touch her breasts and the other places Curtis had considered his. Fury rose in him.

"Hey, Curtis, ready to go?" Greta asked from behind him.

He started, his sheepish grin wiping away the tension in his young, handsome face. "Sure. Yeah. I'm ready."

"Great! Let's go zombie hunting."

"You die out there, I'll kick your ass," Lenore told Ken firmly.

"Do it now," he said, presenting his rear.

She gave him her sternest look. "You shouldn't go without me."

Dale, tattooed and intense, stood nearby. "I'll take care of your boyfriend."

"I'm her girlfriend," Ken said, putting on his best flaming gay routine.

Lenore growled. Finally, reluctantly, she hugged him. "Take care, you crazy faggot."

"Will and can do! Dale will protect me, won't you?"

Dale just grunted and donned his sunglasses.

"I love it when he does that," Ken whispered to Lenore.

"He's straight," Lenore chided him softly.

"For now!" Ken then heaved his rifle over one shoulder and jauntily strode over to Dale. "Let's be off, my good man."

"I'm gonna punch him," Dale said with a grin.

Lenore snorted. "Get in line."

"I think I have this memorized now," Katarina said, scanning the map and the notes from their briefing. She looked nervous, but her hands were steady.

"You better. That's our asses." Bill heaved himself up into the fancy Durango and adjusted the seat. What was he thinking, running off to lead a zombie parade? He wasn't sure whether he was brave or a damn fool.

Katarina shut the passenger door. "We'll be safe, I promise. Just do what I say."

"Oh, God, is this what our marriage will be like?" he said jokingly.

She laughed, smacking his arm.

Ahead of them, Bette and Monica shared a kiss. Behind them, Ken was tapping out some obscure song on the Durango's horn.

Dale leaned out of the truck and shouted, "Lesbians kissing, oh yeah! A good day to die!"

At a signal from Juan, the gates began to open.

"Here we go." Bill gripped the steering wheel, trying not to let his nerves get the better of him.

"I wonder what twenty thousand zombies looks like," Katarina said.

"Dunno, honey," Bill answered. "But we're gonna find out."

## 2.
### *Facing Death*

The helicopter flew low over the three Durangos as the SUVs sped down an old farm road. Taking advantage of the fall of humanity, crabgrass spread tendrils across the unused road, and weeds poked through the asphalt. Weather ate away at the structures along the way as foliage rose up and shrouded them in leafy robes.

Curtis despaired. How easily humankind was being erased from the face of the earth.

Beneath the helicopter, one by one, the Durangos came to a stop at their designated crossroads. Ken and Dale were the first to pull over. A few miles later, Bill and Katarina's truck came to a stop. Bette and Monica continued on, heading to the location Kevin had decided would be the best spot to first intercept the zombies.

"Almost there," Greta's voice said in Curtis's headset.

Shifting in his seat, Curtis gazed ahead, but saw no sign of the mobs of undead. "I don't see anything. Do you, Ed?"

"Nothing yet," came the answer. Ed was perched on the opposite side of the helicopter, scanning the terrain below.

Kevin sat in the back of the helicopter, flipping through papers on a clipboard—their plans. Curtis resented him to no end. Kevin was not one of them—he was an interloper. He was even arrogant enough to insist on flying out to run strategy from the air.

Curtis watched the Durango as it raced along the road below. Monica was down there with that slut, Bette. Whatever happened now, she deserved it. He'd hoped that she would see the light, that she'd realize he was the one for her. The Southern Baptists had it right. Two women together was not natural.

"Bette," Kevin's voice said in Curtis's headset.

"I'm here," Bette answered.

Kevin hesitated, then said, "You're nearing your rendezvous point. Good luck."

"Roger that," Bette answered.

Curtis watched the Durango. The windows of the SUV rolled down and the two women stuck out their hands to wave and give the thumbs-up.

Bette closed her window and drove on with a savage grin on her face. "Let's do this!"

"Woot!" Monica shouted, closing her own window.

"Scared?" Bette asked, reaching for Monica's hand without taking her eyes off the road.

"Shitless."

"Me, too. I swear my insides are quivering."

Monica pushed up the brim of her beat-up cowboy hat and exhaled slowly. "I think my stomach exploded."

"You didn't have to come. I got this gig because I'm a badass soldier," Bette said, her tone light and playful despite the dire situation.

Monica rolled her eyes. "Where you go, I go. I'm a badass, too, you know."

Tears flashed into Bette's eyes as she pressed a kiss to Monica's knuckles. "I'm lucky to be with you."

"Let's hope your luck keeps up. We need it. I've never been so scared in my life."

"You'll be happy to know I always won in Vegas."

Monica smiled at the woman she loved. "In more ways than one, I bet."

"Slow down right now," Kevin said through the CB radio tucked into the dashboard, his voice surprisingly calm. "They're not where they're supposed to be."

Bette immediately pressed on the brake. The Durango crested the top of the hill, and both women gasped.

Shuffling toward them was a multitude of undead. The walking corpses filled the road and spilled over into the countryside. They slogged relentlessly forward with mindless determination.

The plan had been to wait at the crossroad until the undead came into view, then lure them onto the side road and draw as many away as possible. If the zombies headed west, they would eventually hit the desert, where hopefully the elements would destroy them.

Now that plan might not be possible. The vanguard of the zombie horde had already reached the intersection that was supposed to be the first rendezvous point.

"Take a breath," Bette said, and Monica exhaled, realizing she had been holding her breath. "We can do this."

Monica lifted the CB's mouthpiece to her lips. "Bette says we can do this."

After a minute, which seemed more like an hour, Kevin's voice said, "Proceed with caution."

"I feel like Thelma and Louise," Monica grumbled.

"We'll have a happy ending," Bette promised, and pressed a soft kiss to her lips.

Bette shifted gears and floored the Durango, sending it speeding down the hill. When the zombies became aware of the vehicle, they raised their arms almost in unison and moaned loudly.

"We're going to have to slow down to make the curve," Bette said. "Don't freak."

"Okay." Monica gulped. Usually she was racing away from the mangled creatures, not toward them.

Bette decelerated only enough to keep control of the vehicle. A wall of gray, mottled creatures rose up before them like a nightmare. A few of the undead lashed out at the Durango, their rotting hands leaving smears of gunk on the windows.

Monica let out another gasp as the Durango slammed through a small knot of the undead, sending the creatures flying in all directions. Bette fought to stay in control of the car, her expression grim.

The Durango sped past the cluster of zombies at the intersection. Bette lifted her foot lightly off the accelerator, keeping the truck just in front of the pursuing dead. Twisting around in her seat, Monica looked back at the creatures.

"They're following!" she shouted, both scared and jubilant.

# 3.
## Running with the Dead

"Runners!" Greta's voice was so sharp and loud in their headsets that Curtis yelped.

Kevin scrambled to the window and looked down at the swiftly moving zombies pursuing the Durango. "Shit! Where the hell did they come from?"

"They're gaining fast," Curtis cried out.

"Ed." Kevin's tone held a silent order.

"Got it," Ed answered.

The older man double-checked his harness, then slid the door open. Wind buffeted everyone; Kevin pressed his clipboard tightly to his chest. Flipping off the safety on his rifle, Ed took aim as Greta flew lower so he could get a good shot.

"What do I do?" Bette's voice crackled over the radio. They could also hear Monica screaming, "Runners! Runners!"

"Go! Go! Go!" Kevin ordered. "Gun it!"

Below them, the runners were racing alongside the Durango, smashing their hands against the SUV, howling with hunger. There were at least thirty of them.

The Durango accelerated.

Monica fought down her growing panic, but her hands kept shaking. She twisted around in her seat to look out the back window. The runners were keeping pacc on the winding road. Bette couldn't speed up much without increasing the possibility that the car would flip on a turn.

A disgusting, bloody figure ran along the passenger-side door. The entire lower half of its face had been torn away and its gaping maw was the stuff of nightmares. Its head suddenly exploded and it fell, tumbling along the roadside and landing in a bush.

"They're shooting them from the helicopter," Monica said, feeling the knot in her chest loosen.

Bette nodded once, concentrating on her driving while keeping a diligcnt eye on the throng behind them. As the Durango entered a long, slowly arcing curve, Bette's eyes widened as a large portion of the zombies ran straight through the field, ignoring the road.

"They're going to cut us off," Bette said anxiously.

The helicopter zoomed as low as possible over the zombies in the field. Monica wasn't sure how many were knocked over by powerful blasts from the rotors and how many were taken out by sniper shots from above, but quite a few of the zombies fell into the deep grass, disappearing from view. The less-damaged ones kept racing toward the road.

"Shit! Shit! Shit!" Bette's knuckles were white as she gripped the steering wheel. The first of the runners reached the road in front of the Durango and charged at them.

Monica grabbed the handhold over the door and braced herself.

The Durango slammed into the zombies and lurched sickeningly to one side as something caught in one of the wheel wells.

The undead were tossed away from the front of the truck like chaff in the wind. Some darted out of the way but then leaped onto the side of the SUV, hooking their gnarled fingers around the luggage rack.

Monica screamed as one snarled at her through the window, pounding his free hand against the glass.

The banging of bloodied fists against the windows and doors was terrifying. The zombie outside Monica's window was getting more and more agitated, his blows growing in strength. Monica took a deep breath, raised her gun, flicked off the safety, and placed her finger on the button that controlled the window.

"Babe," Bette said, "what are you doing?"

"I got it," Monica assured her, pushing the button.

As the glass slid down, she shoved the gun through the gap and fired point-blank into the zombie's face. The zombie tumbled away into the ditch. Having forgotten that the window would fully roll down if she didn't stop it, Monica panicked as it continued to scroll. Gray, bloodied, shredded arms thrust through the open window.

Curtis watched in fascinated horror as one zombie tried to climb into the Durango. The SUV swerved abruptly and went airborne for a long moment before it crashed into the field. It slid across the ground, shedding zombies as it went, then hit something hidden in the wild grass and flipped over. It tumbled a few times before coming to a stop, zombie free, but a mangled wreck.

"Dammit," Greta grunted. She swung the helicopter around, aiming for the runners pursuing the fallen vehicle.

"Look for survivors!" Kevin ordered.

The zombies were closing in on the Durango. The helicopter buzzed low, and both Kevin and Ed fired.

Curtis saw the two women scramble out of the ruined SUV and begin running away from the zombies. Monica's face was smeared with blood, and Bette was holding her arm at an odd angle. He started to speak, but his voice caught in his throat.

"There they are!" Ed shouted.

Greta tried to move in for a rescue as four runners darted toward the women.

With looks of terror on their faces, Monica and Bette darted into the tree line.

"Don't lose them!" Kevin ordered.

Curtis leaned out the open door, looking for the women. The wind buffeted him as he tried to see beneath the tree canopy. Beside him, Ed swore up a storm.

"I don't see them," Greta said, her voice stricken.

"Keep looking," Kevin answered.

The helicopter hovered over the forest as zombies continued streaming into the trees. Suddenly Curtis caught sight of Monica and Bette in a small clearing. They had climbed into the loft of a broken-down tin and wood barn. The women huddled under the partially collapsed roof. They were trapped. The first runners had reached the clearing and were looking around, with hawklike movements, for their prey. The women curled against each other, trying to keep out of view of the zombies; that made them hard to spot from the air. Curtis could barely glimpse them between the tree branches, especially in their green-colored clothing.

"Does anyone see them?" Kevin's voice was strained. The helicopter slowly drifted away from the barn. Zombies clustered in the clearing. It probably wouldn't take long for them to bring down the building and rip Bette and Monica apart.

"Anyone see them?" Kevin's persistence ate away at Curtis's resolve to stay silent.

"Nothing," Greta answered dismally.

"I ain't got 'em," Ed answered. "No sign."

Curtis wanted Bette gone, but not Monica. Then again, Bette had corrupted Monica, hadn't she? They were lesbian whores. Sinners. Just like Mary had said.

"Curtis, do you see them?"

Curtis opened his mouth, hesitated, then said, "No, no, I don't."

"The zombies see something!" Greta shouted abruptly. She pulled the stick to the left and banked around. "They see something!"

Kevin appeared beside Curtis. The zombies in the clearing banged on the barn, which shook under their assault. A pale hand darted out from beneath the overhang and waved at the helicopter; then a frightened, bloodied face peeked up at them.

"We got them!"

"Curtis, get on the hoist and lower the harness. Greta, move closer." Kevin's voice was clipped.

Obeying despite his reluctance, Curtis watched the safety harness drift down toward the barn.

The zombies were in a frenzy, shaking the old structure. It threatened to come apart at any moment. Curtis hunched down by the open doorway and watched, feeling cold and disconnected from those around him.

Monica grabbed the safety harness and struggled into it. He could imagine Bette telling her, *You first*. He saw their heads draw together in what had to be a kiss; then Bette signaled for them to hoist Monica up.

As Monica swung over the heads of the zombies, they leaped up at her, forgetting the barn temporarily. Curtis couldn't take his eyes off her. He loved how her brown hair swam around her face in the wind. He imagined touching it.

Then Monica was being pulled into the helicopter. She quickly wiggled out of the harness.

"Hurry! Hurry!" Monica clung to safety straps just inside the doorway. "Her arm is broken! She made me come first."

# 4.
## *The Restless Dead*

The zombies had returned to shaking the barn. Pieces were breaking off and it was beginning to list to one side. Bette was holding on for dear life with her one good arm.

"She won't be able to get into the harness by herself," Kevin said. Pleasure washed through Curtis at the thought that they'd be leaving Bette behind.

"No! No! Don't leave her!" Monica screamed.

"I'm not," Kevin said, slipping into the harness and securing it. "I'm going to get her myself." He discarded his headset and inched toward the door. With a thumbs-up to Curtis, he stepped out of the helicopter.

Operating the hoist, Curtis watched Kevin's descending form, wishing both he and Bette would fall to the zombies. Then he and Monica could renew their love . . . and he'd be close to Bill and Travis again, not pushed aside by Kevin and his arrogance.

The zombies again focused on the food dangling overhead. Curtis glanced at Monica, but she didn't acknowledge him. Her gaze was firmly fastened on Bette.

Kevin reached Bette, his feet just barely out of reach of the leaping zombies. Struggling to stand on the rickety structure, Bette reached out with her good hand. Just then, several zombies hit the barn with such force that Bette was knocked off balance. She lurched forward.

Kevin managed to grab her as several zombies seized her booted feet. Flailing about, Bette struggled to break free from the grasp of the undead. Kevin hooked his legs around her waist. Curtis saw that both of them were screaming, but he couldn't hear them over Monica's earsplitting shrieks. She yelled at him to reel them in.

He still hoped the bitch died.

"Fuck this," Greta said, pulling the big bird upward.

Bette felt like she was being pulled in two. Kevin had such a tight grip on her, she could barely breathe. The zombies on her legs were heavy. She kicked at the creatures until she managed to get free of most of the gripping hands.

The helicopter rose, swinging Kevin and Bette over the barn. One last zombie, a woman in a housedress, held firmly to Bette's foot. To the soldier's horror, it pulled itself up her leg. Its desiccated, black lips and toothy grimace made Bette scream with sheer terror. She tried to push the creature off with her other foot, but the zombie grabbed that one as well and drew itself higher.

Both legs imprisoned, Bette struggled. The zombie's teeth gnashed together as it drew closer to her flesh. The young woman could not tear her eyes from the thing's horrible face.

Kevin let go of her with one arm and Bette gasped in terror, feeling as if she was about to fall. The zombie's head exploded; its fingers went slack and it tumbled to the ground. Bette felt Kevin wrap his arm around her again and realized he'd shot the zombie.

She lifted her eyes to see Monica gazing down at her. Bette raised her good arm in victory.

Curtis felt cold and angry, but put a smile on his face when Kevin and Bette fell into a heap inside the helicopter. Monica shoved everyone aside and took Bette in her arms.

"I promised you a happy ending, babe!" Bette shouted before pressing a fervent kiss to her lips.

"Are you bit?" Curtis asked, hoping she was.

"No, no! The car accident banged us up," Monica answered.

"Gotta check," Ed said, then did just that.

Curtis almost wanted Bette or both of them to have been bitten and wasn't sure what he felt when Ed nodded that they were okay.

"Now what?" Greta asked as she swung the aircraft around.

Below, a steady stream of zombies stumbled past the field, heading west. Away from the fort.

Kevin fell into the seat next to Greta and donned his headset.

"Now what?" she repeated.

Kevin hesitated, then said, "Signal the next Durango for phase two."

## CHAPTER TWENTY-SEVEN

## 1.

### *Hordes*

Dale and Ken listened in silence as the drama unfolded on the CB radio. When it was clear that Monica and Bette were both safe, Ken let out a sigh of relief and collapsed against the dashboard. "Oh, God, I was praying so hard, I thought my head would explode."

"Well, at least they didn't get eaten," Dale said. "Guess that proves the Baptists wrong, eh? The hot lesbians live to kiss another day."

"You're really sick, you know," Ken nagged.

"Yeah, I know," Dale answered, winking. "And that's why you like me."

Ken blushed deeply.

Bill and Katarina listened with their fingers intertwined and their hearts pounding. It was far too easy to imagine themselves in the place of the two women. The thought of losing each other was too much to bear.

After, they held each other.

"I love you, Bill," Katarina whispered.

"I love you, Kit-Kat," he answered, giving her a gruff kiss.

"Durango Two, prepare to depart," Kevin ordered.

"That's us, honey," Bill said, kissing her one more time. He stroked her long red braid, then sat back in the driver's seat and steadied his nerves. Shifting into drive, he spotted the helicopter drifting into view. "Let's hope it goes better for us."

"I'm praying something fierce," Katarina confessed. "But if it's our time, I just pray that the Good Lord gives us time to do what we need to."

With sadness in his eyes, Bill nodded.

"Durango Two, depart," Kevin said.

"We almost lost Bette and Monica," Travis told Katie and Juan as his closest friends entered the communication center. "But they're okay."

"Shit," Juan said. "How?"

"Runners. They're on the helicopter now. A little battered, but okay." Travis rubbed his face. "They're okay."

"And they got a lot of zombies moving away from us," Peggy added from her position by the radios. "So that's good."

"So the plan *is* working." Katie sat down in a chair and ran one hand gently over her large belly.

"So far," Travis agreed.

"Shit. I told my crazy-ass cousin not to go." Juan sighed and rubbed his day-old stubble. "Who's the bait now?"

"Bill and Katarina," Peggy replied. One of her well-manicured hands rested against the earpiece of her headset.

Katie and Travis linked hands. Giving her a small encouraging smile, he squeezed her fingers.

"Bill knows those roads. He'll be fine," Travis said, reassuring himself along with everyone else.

Katie gave him a hopeful yet solemn look.

*Don't scream don't scream don't scream don't scream don't scream* . . . Katarina's mantra repeated endlessly in her mind.

The Durango idled at the crossroads, waiting for the lumbering zombies. The hungry dead clogged the road, filled the ditches, and staggered among the trees. Though the air conditioner was recycling the air in the SUV, the stench was growing unbearable.

Thousands of outstretched hands reached toward their vehicle. The marching zombies were mostly gray and sun-blackened. Their bristled hair stood up around their heads. Their clothes were unrecognizable scraps clinging to decomposing flesh.

"Dear God, Bill, one is in a wheelchair," Katarina yelled when she saw a terribly eaten-looking zombie rolling down the road, swept along by the undead around it.

Bill arched his neck to see, then laughed. "Shit, babe, don't that beat all."

A little boy, a baseball cap on his head and a bat in one hand, reached the Durango and banged on the door with his fist. Katarina studied his cherubic face, somehow still cute in death. In another time, he would be any Little Leaguer, begging to enter his mom's SUV after a hard game. But this child was hissing and growling, trying to reach their tasty flesh.

The boy began to hit the Durango with his baseball bat.

"Time to go," Katarina said.

Bill waited for a second, until more zombies were within a few feet of the SUV, then hit the gas. Slowly, the car moved onto the side road, heading west, away from the fort.

Almost in unison, the zombies leading the horde altered their course to pursue the Durango, the little boy dragging his baseball bat on the asphalt.


"So why are lesbians hot to you Neanderthal straight men but gay men aren't?" Ken asked, staring out the passenger-side window.

"Uh, 'cause women are hot," Dale answered.

"I have it on good authority that *I'm* hot," Ken responded. "According to many, many women and men."

"Eh," Dale said with a grin. He enjoyed giving Ken a hard time—the young man was so easily riled. Dale knew Ken had a mad crush on him, and he'd made it abundantly clear to Ken that nothing would happen between them except friendship, but Ken couldn't help but flirt. Teasing him seemed the natural response.

"I'm so not 'eh.' I am anything but 'eh.' I am a *hunk*. Before I came out, I had so many women after me, I was a stud." Ken frowned at Dale. "And I was still a stud after I came out, until the world died."

"I'm sure there are guys in the fort who are gay but aren't out," Dale answered seriously.

"Really?"

"I'm pretty sure," Dale said, shrugging. "My money is that you're not the only Nancy boy."

Ken sighed. "Well, they're so deep in the closet, I can't find them."

"It'll happen. When the time is right," Dale promised.

"Are you sure you're not gay?" Ken arched an eyebrow at him.

"Yep. Tried it . . . kinda . . . once. Well, actually, I thought she was a girl, but she was a guy."

"Real *Crying Game*–ish, huh?"

"Yeah." Dale nodded. "She was damn hot, too. Until, you know, that."

"You brute! You turned her down over *that*?"

"Hey, I tried. I just couldn't." Dale said earnestly, "I did try, really."

Ken let out a soft sigh. "I have the same trouble with women. I love Lenore, and if she were a guy, maybe she'd be my groove thing, but . . ."

"Sometimes love ain't enough," Dale said with another nod. "But at least I got laid last night."

"Did not!"

"Oh, yeah. Sure did!"

"Who? Tell!"

"Peggy."

"No!"

"Yep."

"She's a dirty whore!" Ken frowned, clearly jealous.

"Oh, yeah," Dale answered with satisfaction. He winked at Ken, then caught movement just beyond his friend's window.

"No fair! I didn't get laid! I'm laid-less. No fair!" Dale reached out and grabbed Ken's shoulder. "Okay, if you insist! Take me!" Ken joked, then saw the look on Dale's face. Turning, Ken gasped as he saw a horde of zombies emerging from the trees next to the road.

"They shouldn't be here!" Dale grabbed the radio. "We got hundreds of zombies at our location. A massive horde. Do you read me?"

In a panic, Ken hit the LOCK button, and the doors clicked.

"Repeat that," Kevin's voice answered.

"We got zombies," Dale answered, then uttered, "Oh, shit," and tossed the mouthpiece to Ken. The Durango lurched forward as the zombies moved to encircle it. The vehicle smashed into a few undead, then broke free.

"Zombies everywhere. Coming out of the trees on both sides of us. Oh, shit, and up the road. I thought you got them to turn to the west!" Ken screamed into the radio.

"Shit," Kevin said. "We must have missed some in the recon." His voice got softer—probably he turned away from the mic—as he said, "Pull back."

Dale turned the big vehicle around. The narrow, tree-lined road didn't allow a full U-turn, so he had to back up to adjust his angle.

"We are totally surrounded! This is not good!" Ken shouted into the radio.

Dale was backing up a second time when the wave of zombies hit the truck in an unrelenting wall of flesh, bone, and decay. Moaning, desperate faces filled the windows as clawlike hands scrabbled at the doors.

"Fuck," Ken whispered into the microphone.

Dale tried to back up, but it was as if the truck were pushing through a brick wall. Fear gripped him as Dale realized their situation had gone from bad to worse.

"Dale," Ken cried. "Dale!"

The flood of zombies was forcing the Durango across the road. Sliding sideways, the metal sides of the vehicle groaned from the constant pressure. Ken screamed as the zombie pressed against his window split apart like a ripe melon.

"Shit, oh, shit," Ken whispered, ignoring Kevin's demands for a status report.

Dale cussed up a storm as he fought with the steering wheel, his foot pressing down on the brake, trying to stop the truck.

The truck fell into the ditch at the side of the road, squashing some of the undead in the process. Dale felt the impact to the marrow of his bones. Ken dangled above him from his seatbelt, screaming. Reaching up, Dale unbuckled him and Ken fell into his arms. The two men lay on the driver's-side windows, staring at the zombies swarming on all sides of the capsized vehicle.

"We're not gonna make it, are we?" Ken asked, his voice catching.

"Nope," Dale answered, resigned to their fate. He felt bad for the young man in his arms, wishing he could find a way to save him.

One of the zombies beat against the back window. Cracks slowly spread across the glass.

"Oh, God," Ken whispered, covering his mouth in horror.

Dale cradled Ken's head against his chest. "It's okay, Ken."

Ken sobbed softly. "Lenore is going to kill me."

"At least you know someone loved you," Dale consoled him.

"Yeah," Ken whispered as the glass shattered. "Yeah. I do."

"Ready to go?" Dale flicked the safety off his gun.

Pressing his lips tightly together, Ken nodded.

"I'll do it for both of us," the big man said.

Ken nodded again, unable to speak.

Dale kissed Ken on the forehead, then raised the gun. "Sleep tight, Ken," he said, and fired. Ignoring the bits of brain and blood splattered over him, Dale wrapped his arm around Ken's shoulders and took a deep breath.

"I'm right behind you, buddy."

As the first of the zombies fell into the truck, Dale pushed the gun into his mouth and pulled the trigger.

## 2.
### *The Helpless Living*

Katie didn't remember falling asleep on the couch in the communication center. She'd been feeling drained, so she decided to lie down, but she'd been listening to the radio reports. The next thing she knew, she was waking up because someone had cried out.

Travis looked stunned; there were tears in his eyes. Peggy sobbed loudly, hands over her face.

"What happened?" Katie asked hoarsely.

"Ken and Dale . . ." Travis's voice broke. "We think they're gone."

"No," Katie whispered in disbelief.

Peggy wiped her tears away and pressed the button on the microphone in front of her. "Dale, Ken, please respond. What is your status?"

Static was the only response.

"What happened?" Katie asked, sitting up.

"Zombies came out of the trees and surrounded them. It sounded like they were trying to drive away when they went silent," Travis answered.

"Oh, God!" Katie cried.

Peggy continued trying to raise the two missing men.

"This means the zombies are closer than we thought," Travis said hollowly.

Juan stepped into the room. "We're taking off in the other helicopter. I'll let you know what we find."

"Be careful out there," Travis answered.

"We will be," Juan assured him, then was gone.

Katie wrapped her arms around her belly as though to shield her unborn child. The loss of life in the last few months had been staggering. How much more could they endure?

"I wish Nerit was here," Peggy said through her sobs. "She'd know what to do. No offense, Travis."

Travis squeezed Peggy's shoulder. "None taken. Once we know what's going on out there, we'll figure out the next step."

Peggy wiped her eyes again and turned back to the communication center. "Come in, Dale. Come in, Ken. What is your status? Repeat, what is your status?"

## 3.
### The Pied Piper of the Living Dead

Twisting around in her seat, Katarina looked out the back window at the massive crowd of zombies following them. The creatures were so determined, they had actually increased in speed. Bill had had to press down a bit on the accelerator to keep ahead of the flesh-eating mob.

Her stomach heaved and she tried hard not to vomit. Her fear was so powerful, she was trembling. Her teeth were chattering and Bill kept touching her to reassure her. She was sure Nerit would be sorely disappointed in her, but this was very different from being a sniper. Not since the first day had she seen the dead so close, and she'd never seen so many in one place.

"Bill, how much longer?"

"About ten more minutes," he answered. He was sweating profusely in the unrelenting sunlight that beat through the windshield. Katarina felt sweat trickling between her breasts.

"We gotta get out of here, Bill." Just looking at him made her even more afraid. She loved him so much that she was terrified of what could happen to him. Yes, she was scared of dying in the snapping, tearing jaws of the undead, but Bill . . . She touched his shoulder lovingly. His fingers covered hers.

"We'll be out of here soon enough, darling."

"Bill, we need to leave now!" Her voice cracked as she shouted.

As the Durango went around a curve, Katarina spotted an overturned semi in the road.

"Shit," Bill grumbled as he saw it, then swore again as he slowed down to edge around the crashed vehicle. He grabbed the CB mic. "There's an obstruction in the road. We're going around."

There was loud static; then a voice said, "We're moving up to rendezvous."

Katarina faced front, unable to look at the undead horde drawing closer as the Durango crept around the overturned semi.

"Bill," she whispered, "I'm so afraid."

"Darling, you're going to be okay."

"But if anything happens to you, I won't be able to bear it."

"Kit-Kat, we're going to be okay. We'll get around this truck, then we'll be fine." Bill took one hand off the steering wheel so he could kiss Katarina's hand.

Darting out from behind the truck, a zombie struck the window with a wrench. Reacting on pure impulse, Bill jerked the wheel and the Durango clipped the guardrail, then bounced off and hit the edge of the back of the semi. Fighting to gain control, Bill swore violently. The Durango plowed into a station wagon directly behind the truck. Bill and Katarina were tossed about inside the SUV as it flipped over and slid down the street.

"Get out! Get out!" Bill shouted, fumbling with his seat belt.

Katarina unbuckled her seat belt, shoved the door open, and climbed out. Tumbling onto the road, she dared to turn back and saw the zombie mob coming around the semi. Bill climbed out of the Durango. His forehead was gashed and bleeding.

"Bill!" she gasped, pointing at the wreck.

The accident had freed the undead family from the car, and they were scrambling out of the wreckage, badly decayed and fiercely hungry.

"Kit-Kat, run!"

She raced away on aching legs, Bill at her back. From the corner of her eye, Katarina glimpsed Bill trying to pull his gun from his holster. The zombies pursued them, and though the family and the truck driver weren't runners, they were fast enough.

Katarina saw something lurch up at the side of the road. She ducked away as Bill launched himself at the zombie. They crashed into the brush, the thing under Bill growling and snapping at him.

Katarina lunged toward the wrestling figures, but Bill yelled at her to keep running.

"Keep going!" Bill shouted.

The helicopter slowly descended in front of her like some great bird. She sucked air into burning lungs through bruised lips and headed for it. With relief, she heard a gunshot behind her.

"Keep running, honey!" Bill called as more gunshots sounded.

The helicopter hung over the road. Katarina jumped, then collapsed into Kevin's arms. He swung her into the safety of the chopper. Turning, she saw that Bill was not running for safety; instead he was standing still and firing steadily into the quickly advancing zombie crowd.

"Bill! Run, Bill!"

"He's bit," Kevin said brokenly.

"No! No! Bill, run!"

Bill turned and smiled at her in that special way that made her heart beat faster. Giving a short wave with a badly mangled hand, he turned back to slaying the undead.

Katarina felt her heart throb as she was gently pulled away from the door.

"No! No! We're getting married! No!" She fought to get away, but Monica and Curtis held her. As the helicopter rose, Ed stepped to the doorway and aimed his rifle.

"Ed, please, don't! We're getting married! Bill just fell! We had an accident! He's not bit!"

Ed fired.

Everyone averted their eyes as Ed lowered the gun and the helicopter swung about.

"No," Katarina said again. "No. We're getting married."

In the landing area of the fort, Kevin leaped out of the helicopter, followed by Ed and Katarina. Monica and Ed helped Bette down. Charlotte had brought a wheelchair—Bette was eased into it and Charlotte rolled her away, heading for the clinic. Reverend Thomas, who had come to meet them, whispered a soft prayer of thanks as he greeted each person. He took Katarina in his arms and wept with her.

Travis clasped Kevin's hand tightly before the two men walked on together.

"How does it look?" Kevin finally asked.

"You guys peeled off at least half of the undead. The rest have slowed down slightly, and some of them are also changing direction, following the others into the west. I think we confused them."

"Dale and Ken?"

Travis shook his head, a bleak expression in his eyes.

"Shit." Kevin sighed.

Travis regarded Katarina sadly. "Losing Bill is one of the hardest hits this fort has taken. Everyone is important, but Bill . . ."

"I know what you're saying," Kevin responded with another weary sigh, thinking of Valerie. "Damn. It's good to know a good portion of the zombies were diverted, but losing Bill and the others doesn't make it feel like much of a victory."

As they walked through the gates into the old construction site, the two men realized that people on the street were avoiding them. Word had spread quickly about the deaths in the world beyond the walls.

"We made some tough calls," Travis stated morosely. "And people died."

Kevin patted Travis's shoulder lightly. "It's what we have to do."

In Juan's memorial garden, Katie sat on a bench with Lenore, who was crying silently, clutching a bright pink teddy bear. Peggy sat nearby, dabbing at her eyes and rocking her son. Maddie sat beside Rune, eyes closed, tears staining her face. Rune had one arm around Maddie's shoulders, grief etched into his posture.

"This is just the beginning," Kevin said somberly.

"I know," Travis answered.

The men hesitated at the edge of the garden, feeling as if they were about to enter sacred ground. "We did the right thing," Travis said finally. "We've diverted half of them."

"Doesn't make it feel any better though, does it?"

"No. No, it doesn't, Kevin," Travis agreed.

"Let's get to work," Kevin said.

The two men walked into the hotel.

## CHAPTER TWENTY-EIGHT

**1.**

*The Fine Line*

The room was dark except for a small SpongeBob night-light tucked into a wall socket. Kevin sat beside Nerit, his hand tucked under hers. The Israeli woman's strong features were not what most would call beautiful, but some would dub them elegant. Kevin wondered what she had looked like as a young woman.

It was nearly midnight and the fort was very quiet. Dale, Ken, and Bill had left an impression on the whole community. Reverend Thomas's impromptu memorial service had been standing room only.

Juan's recon mission showed that the SUVs had sent the majority of the zombies off toward West Texas. That had been the good news.

Juan's team had also seen a swarm of zombies milling around Ken and Dale's overturned Durango. Others, apparently splintered off from that group, were drifting off to the west. But a third, large group was heading toward the fort. That was the bad news.

"It's too risky to try that stunt with the SUVs again," Travis had said before he and Kevin parted for the night. "We're going to have to fight them on the outskirts of town. We cannot allow them to reach the walls."

Their plans would take a lot of hard work to pull off, and how effective they would be was yet to be seen. But their choices were limited.

"I need you back," Kevin said, his voice breaking. Tears filled his eyes. "I need you, Nerit. You make me feel less alone. Less afraid. When I stand next to you, I feel strong. I don't know if we can do this without you."

Nerit slept on.

## 2.
### *The Winds of War*

For two days, heavily armed contingents had been raiding every supply store, farm, ranch, and auto shop within a hundred miles, steering well clear of the zombie horde. The fort seemed to be bursting at the seams with stacks of wood, tanks of gasoline, bags of cement, rolls of razor wire, and other materials.

Katie leaned against the rail of the catwalk that stretched along the interior of the wall. The fresh air felt good against her warm face. She was eight months pregnant and her stomach was enormous. The baby was much more active now, and she sometimes felt as if her child were treating her ribs like a treadmill.

"Here you are," Travis said, joining her.

"I'm watching the crews working," she said. "I got tired of not doing anything, so I thought I'd come out here. I'm getting accustomed to the view—I've been assigned to this position as a spotter for the big battle."

"I can't believe Kevin let you wrangle yourself onto the front lines." Travis bestowed a slightly frustrated but amused look upon her.

"The front line is out there," she said, waving a hand toward the city limits. "If our plan works, none of us will be in any danger."

"Fine, fine, Lady Prosecutor. So, how is it going?"

"Take a look. The barricade is almost finished."

In the distance, bulldozers were shoving wrecked houses and downed trees into a barrier between the hotel and the oncoming zombies. The ground on either side of the obstacle had been cleared and plowed for a hundred yards. Small Bobcat construction vehicles were clearing away the last of the brush that had grown up around the exterior walls in the last year. Inside the fort, the sound of chain saws, mowers, and axes resounded as volunteers cleared away any foliage near the interior walls.

"It's coming along impressively," Travis agreed. When he took her hand, his palm was damp with perspiration, probably from nerves, Katie thought.

"Where were you earlier? I looked for you after lunch." Katie watched a crew toss bags of dry grass and firewood onto the barricade.

"I was meeting with the new volunteer fire department."

"We have one of those now?" Katie arched her brows, amused.

Returning her smile, Travis answered, "Why, yes, ma'am, we do. We now have four fire engines and, luckily, we found enough people with previous experience to form several crews."

The fire trucks and firefighters had become essential when, during a long and emotionally exhausting meeting, it had been decided that the most effective weapon against the zombies was fire. The undead had consistently shown an innate fear of fire, and given the large number approaching, it was the best way to try to keep them away from the fort. The trick was not to burn the place down in the process.

"That lets me breathe a little easier," Katie said, relieved.

"I'm sure the fire crews will do a good job." Travis craned his head to watch a bulldozer digging into the earth near the center of the barricade. Massive tanks sat on the back of a nearby truck, waiting to be lowered into the ground. "When the barricade goes up in flames, it's going to be damn impressive."

"And terrifying." Katie glanced over her shoulder at one of the trucks dropping off crews to work on the defenses. There was a narrow alley that led to the hotel loading dock, and the entrance to it was going to be heavily booby-trapped in case the zombies did breach the fire line. "Do you think we've thought of everything?"

Travis lifted his shoulders. "We've ransacked our brains for every contingency. I wish Nerit was awake. She'd spot any flaws in our plans, but I'm not sure what we might have missed. We've created firebreaks to protect the fort, done controlled burns to try to prevent the fire from jumping, and have fire crews ready to go. We have fire traps, razor wire traps, and any other trap we could think of. Hell, we're lucky none of the workers have set off any traps.

"We have catapults and we have our crossbows and spears. If the zombies get past the fire line and we have to deal with them up against the walls, that's when we'll be in real danger." He took a breath, then finished, "We'll stop them out there because we have to."

Katie had let him rattle on, knowing that his speech was as much for his nerves as for her own. She rubbed his arm lovingly and gave him a sweet smile. She knew he was driving himself harder than anyone else to make their plans work. Even though she was afraid, she had confidence in his ability to anticipate every eventuality.

Travis wrapped an arm around her shoulders and rested his hand on her stomach. He loved feeling their baby move and often tried to guess if it was a foot, elbow, knee, or small hand reaching out to the world beyond the womb.

Kevin joined them on the catwalk, clipboard in hand. Dressed in fatigues and wearing sunglasses, he was an impressive sight. "Looks like we're making good progress."

"Barricade should be ready soon," Katie agreed.

"I meant the baby. Girl, you're bigger than you were yesterday. I'm telling you, you're getting close." Kevin grinned.

"I think I'm at the start of my ninth month," Katie said, "so not that close."

"Closer than you think," Kevin said. Sorrow darkened his expression for a moment. "I had three kids. I know how it goes."

"I guess we'll see." Katie heard several shots ring out. Most likely a few zombies had strayed too close to the workers.

"Do you have a minute for me, Travis? I want to show you the new contingency plans."

"More plans?" Katie asked.

"Yeah, for if they reach the walls. We'll have to deal with bodies piling up and creating ramps for the zombies," Kevin answered, his smile vanishing. "I talked to Juan, and some of his people are modifying two of the bulldozers so they can be used to clear away the bodies if we wind up under siege."

Katie didn't want to think about that. Maybe he saw the expression on her face or maybe Travis wasn't ready to think about it either, because Travis put his hand on Kevin's arm and said, "Let's discuss this in my office."

"Okay," Kevin said, tucking his clipboard under his arm. He took off his glasses and leaned toward Katie. "I promise you that your baby will be born into a safe world. We will win this battle."

Katie smiled. Kevin kissed her hand; then he and Travis headed for the hotel.

Alone on the catwalk, she watched the people below busily preparing to defend their home. Fear swept through her. What if their defenses weren't enough? What if the undead made it past the barricade? How many zombies would get through?

"Oh, Jenni," Katie whispered. "I wish you were here. Then maybe I wouldn't feel so afraid."

As they walked, Travis and Kevin spoke quietly to each other.

"What did Greta report?" Travis asked.

"The zombies are still on the way. They'll arrive within two days." Kevin sighed. "I know the timing isn't good, but we're running low on fuel for the helicopters, so we have to ground one of them now. We need to have as much fuel as possible for Greta's bird on the day they arrive and in case we have to evacuate."

"How do we evacuate more than four hundred people with two helicopters? And where would we go?"

"We can evacuate only sixteen people at a time. . . . As for where . . ." Kevin shook his head. "We have to concentrate on winning. We can't afford to lose the fort."

The weariness in Travis's shoulders reflected Kevin's own exhaustion. "Okay, so we outfit the bulldozers to protect the drivers and plan to use them should the zombies hit the walls."

"Hope for the best," Kevin said.

"Plan for the worst," Travis finished.

Together, they walked into the hotel.

# · CHAPTER TWENTY-NINE ·

## 1.

### *Between Two Worlds*

"I always loved to watch you sleep," Lydia whispered.

Katie stirred slightly, her eyelashes fluttering.

Lydia's ghost moved into the circle of light cast by the lamp on the bed stand. Her sad expression was full of love as she sat down on the edge of the bed, folding her long hands on her lap.

"The veil is so thin now, I can almost touch you." Her hand glided over Katie's stomach. "I miss touching you so much."

Katie remained still and peaceful in her sleep.

"I love seeing you this way." Lydia smiled tenderly. "All that has happened has been a curse, yet a gift. I miss you, Katie; I love you and I want you to be happy. But I fear for you. I've done all I can to help you and yours. And now . . ." Lydia sighed. "Now there is nothing more I can do. It's time for us to move on, we who are lingering between the worlds. We've done what we can. It's time for us to leave you to do what you must."

Tears in her eyes, Lydia pressed a hand to her slim throat, composing herself. "You are standing on the brink of a new world. Whether the dead or the living rule will be decided. I know you think of yourselves just as survivors, but you are more than that. You are the new Eden. You are the new beginning. There are other enclaves of survivors, but this is the place that was chosen to give birth to a new world. The choices you make tomorrow have ramifications far beyond what you can understand or see."

Lydia kissed Katie's hand and pressed it to her cheek. "We lived in a world where reality was sharp and clear. We were unaware of how deep and wondrous, how frightening, the roots of our world truly are. But now I know. I've stood in the center of the veil. I've seen many possible futures and many possible pasts. And tomorrow is the one point in time that can change everything."

Standing, Lydia straightened her long skirt, then tucked her hair back behind her delicate ears. Sorrowfully, she leaned over Katie one last time.

"I pray that you live. But if not . . ." Lydia gently touched Katie's cheek. "I will be waiting for you."

In her sleep, Katie sighed.

"I love you, Katie." Lydia kissed her wife.

"Lydia," Katie whispered, opening her eyes.

The room was empty.

Katie rolled over, tucking the pillow under her head. Feeling more alone than she had in a very long time, she closed her eyes and fell back to sleep.

## 2.
### *Danger Looms*

Katie stirred when the first knock came at the door, but did not wake until the second.

Carefully maneuvering her growing self out of bed, she waddled to the door, using her hands to support the weight of her belly. "Hello?"

"Katie, it's Curtis," came the response. "I need to talk to you, okay? I need advice."

"Okay, come in," she said, opening the door to reveal his tearstained face and downcast posture.

He shook his head. "I can't talk about it here. I need fresh air. Meet me on the wall near the hotel loading dock in like fifteen minutes?"

Katie glanced over her shoulder at the clock on the bedside table. "Curtis, it's after midnight."

"Please, Katie. I really need some advice. I'm desperate."

He looked so pathetic that Katie couldn't refuse. "Okay. I'll get dressed and meet you there."

"Thank you," he said with a sigh. "Just don't tell anyone, okay? I don't want people talking about me and my problems."

Katie nodded. "Okay, hon. I understand."

Curtis lowered his red face. "Thanks, Katie. You're a good woman." He turned and walked away. With a sigh, Katie shut the door and rubbed her eyes, wondering what was troubling Curtis. She was exhausted, but sleep would have to wait.

Travis quietly unlocked the door to his room, trying not to wake his wife. He was surprised to find the lights on and Katie struggling into a T-shirt.

"Babe, what's going on?"

Pulling the shirt down so her face popped into view, Katie said, "Curtis came by. He looked like shit. He says he needs to talk, so I told him I'd meet him in a few minutes at the corner of Morris and Main."

Frowning, Travis gently stopped her as she reached for her jeans. "It's after midnight. You're exhausted. Why can't it wait until later?"

Leaning against him, Katie sighed. "He looked so upset. I feel bad for him; I know things have been rough on him since Bill died and Monica became involved with Bette."

Kissing the top of her head, Travis exhaled wearily. He laid his cheek on her soft hair and closed his eyes, enjoying the feel of her in his arms. As tired as he was, he could stand there forever, holding her. "I'll go talk to him."

"Travis, you're tired, too," Katie protested. She gazed up at him in a way that made him feel as if he could fight a million zombies and win.

"I would love nothing more than to lie down next to you and

hold you in my arms as we sleep, but you're right, Curtis is having a rough time right now. I think Bill may have been the closest thing he had to a best friend." Travis pushed her gently down on the bed. "So, you go back to sleep and I'll see if I can offer him some brotherly advice."

Katie started to refuse, then sighed and lay back on the bed. One hand draped over her pregnant tummy, she gazed up at him. "Okay, okay, I won't fight you. I'm too tired anyway."

Travis kissed her belly, then her lips. "I'll be back soon and we'll have a few hours of nice, cozy sleep."

"Yum," Katie said, "that sounds wonderful."

Travis smiled. "You're wonderful."

Running her hand lightly down the side of his face, she whispered, "Hurry back."

"I will." Travis leaned down and kissed her lips again softly. "Love you."

"Love you," Katie answered drowsily.

"Always and forever," Travis added.

She snuggled into her pillow. "Send Curtis my love."

"I will."

He straightened the covers around her, then turned to go. A sudden chill flowed over his body and he froze, feeling the hair on his head stand up on end. Looking back, he saw that Katie was already asleep; the lamp next to the bed turned her hair into a halo.

There was nothing visibly wrong, but Travis couldn't shake the fear that had washed over him. Taking a deep breath, he headed for the meeting with Curtis.

# 3.
## *Vigilante Justice*

It had been many months since justice was dealt out at the fort. For a long time, the Vigilante watched and waited to see what the so-called leaders of the fort would do or say.

The Vigilante had not been satisfied. The time had come for the Vigilante to deliver justice to those who were weak and a burden to the fort.

Yes, the time had come.

The Vigilante hesitated before the communication center and looked in the glass window set in the door. Smiling, the Vigilante studied Curtis's features. The man had obviously been crying.

Curtis was weak.

But the Vigilante was strong.

It was time for justice.

## · CHAPTER THIRTY ·

## 1.
### *The Veil Falls*

Travis trudged wearily up the stairs to the wall. The humidity hung in the air, making him feel sticky. This area of the wall was basically a dead end, and Travis wondered why Curtis had picked such an isolated place to talk. He supposed the younger man wanted to be sure no one would see him discussing his troubled love life with the mayor's wife.

He heard a step on the catwalk and turned to see Curtis moving toward him.

"What's up, Curtis?" he called out.

"Oh, Travis! Hi," the younger man said awkwardly. Looking around swiftly, Curtis shifted uncomfortably on his feet.

"Katie's asleep, Curtis. She's real tired, what with all the hard work and the baby coming. She's almost due. I told her I would offer you a sounding board. I know this is a really rough time for you."

Curtis looked extremely uncomfortable. "Yeah, I guess . . . I just thought . . . Katie could give me some good advice. I didn't know who else to go to. With Bill . . . you know . . ."

"I know," Travis answered. "We're all feeling his loss. And Jenni's, and everyone else's. It feels overwhelming sometimes."

"Really?" Curtis said. "You don't seem to be too affected."

Travis heard an odd tone in Curtis's voice, but replied calmly, "Of course I'm affected. I just don't show it to everyone."

"I guess you're just good at hiding things. I know I'm too emotional."

"Some people might say that I'm not emotional enough. You and I, we're different people," Travis answered carefully, hearing the sarcasm in Curtis's tone. "We deal with things differently."

"Yeah," Curtis said, nodding. "Yeah, we do."

"Nerit," a voice called softly.

Standing on the shore of the Dead Sea, Nerit turned and raised a hand to shield her eyes from the blazing sun while she looked for the speaker. Wind made her long blond hair thrash around her face, and she felt sand and salt in the creases of her uniform, rubbing against her skin.

"Where are you?" she asked.

"Here. Come to me." The voice was on the waves.

Feeling disoriented and afraid, Nerit nonetheless stepped into the sea.

"Deeper," the voice called. "Come to me."

"Ralph?" It sounded like her husband, but she wasn't sure. The water was up to her waist; she felt the warm wavelets lapping around her.

The wind was howling, almost screaming in her ears.

"Don't look behind you, Nerit, just come," Ralph's voice persisted.

Despite his words, she peered over her shoulder. The shore was filled with the screaming, howling undead. A few were wading into the Dead Sea, following her.

Suddenly a hand reached out of the water, grabbed her, and dragged her into the salty depths.

In the clinic, Nerit's eyes snapped open. As her eyes struggled to focus, she ignored the annoying ache of the IV in her wrist. Cautiously, she sat up and was surprised to find that her body responded without pain.

Ralph stepped out of the shadows and sat down in the chair at her bedside. Dressed in jeans and his favorite blue shirt, he looked just as he had on his last birthday. The day the zombies rose. He smiled warmly and laid his hand over hers. "Nerit, you're okay. You're awake." He sighed. "It was hard to get you back, you were so far gone."

"Ralph," she whispered, placing her other hand over his. "I can feel your hand."

"Only for a little bit, hon," he said, giving her a small smile.

"Am I dreaming?"

"No, sweetheart. You're awake. Out of the coma. Lots of prayers were going up for you, you know," Ralph said with a wink.

"What's happening?" Nerit asked cautiously.

Looking sad, Ralph squeezed her hand. "What happens next is gonna be hard. Not to my liking. Probably not to yours. But it is how it is."

"Ralph, please, I know I have cancer—" Her voice broke. Was he here to take her for good?

"Not no more, Nerit. It's gone." He looked grief stricken, and Nerit squeezed his hand tightly. "I wanted you home with me, but you got an extension. They need you here." He sighed, and then a corner of his mouth quirked up. "I even prayed for you to stay."

The relief she felt was overwhelming. To fight on for the fort was all she wanted, and yet she felt sad not to be joining him. "Ralph, I'll always love you."

"I know, Nerit, but your place is here. And your being here changes everything. Some of us on the other side realized that. We saw it all: Past, Present, Future. There are points in time that the future hinges on. This is one of those moments."

Nerit's senses felt sharply focused. "I see."

Ralph stood up. "I hope that the world lives on beyond tomorrow."

"Ralph, there's more, isn't there?" She looked at him evenly. "I can tell by your expression."

With a short nod of his head, Ralph said, "There's trouble in the fort. . . ."

* * *

"When I see people doing shitty things to other people, I want to tell them that they need to shape up and get with the program. I want to tell them, 'This is the law. You gotta obey it.' But lately—" Curtis shook his head. "—I can't find order anywhere, even in my own damned life."

Tucking his hands into his jean pockets, Travis nodded slowly. "Yeah, I know what you mean. We're all just doing our best."

"But people keep dying, Travis."

Measuring his words carefully, Travis answered, "This world is dominated by death, Curtis."

"Yeah, yeah," Curtis agreed. "But some of the living make it harder on the rest of us."

Travis tried to keep his face neutral, but his body tensed. He studied the young policeman's twitchy behavior and flushed face with growing concern. "We're doing what we can, Curtis."

"Yeah, right. Saving people. Bringing them here. Taking a fucking stand against religious people. But maybe they were right, Travis. Did you ever think of that? Your girl got all right and straight—" Curtis laughed sarcastically. "—but my girl went all queer when the mall folks came here. Do you even give a shit about that?"

"Monica and Bette—"

"Don't say their names like they fucking belong together. They don't! Monica, my Monica, was okay before those shitbags from the mall got here, those corrupters. And that nigger—"

"Hey!" Travis's voice was harsh. "Don't go there."

Curtis glared at Travis. "This is the country, city boy. We talk different out here. And why the hell is an outsider leading us anyway?"

"Curtis, you know I'm just one of many people who make decisions—"

"You blew into town all fancy and handsome, got all the girls crazy about you and your fancy ways. Then all this shit hits and you're the fucking king? If the mayor wasn't such a pussy, we might have had a little more fucking luck taking care of our own before dragging every fucking faggot, raghead, nigger—"

"That's enough, Curtis! You need to calm the hell down. I'll drag your ass down to the clinic and sedate you if I have to."

Curtis stepped forward. "Try it," he said in a low whisper. A knife glittered in his fist.

Katie was fast asleep when she felt someone tug on her arm, cajoling her out of her dreams. Opening her eyes, she gazed into Jenni's eyes.

"Jenni!" Katie gasped.

"Hi!" Jenni said with a perky smile and a small wave.

"I'm still asleep!" Katie was disoriented, but thrilled that she was seeing Jenni, even if it was in her dreams.

"Nope! You're awake and I'm here!"

"You're dead."

"I know! I'm a ghost." Jenni was beautiful. Her skin was pale but pink. Her dark eyes were brilliant and her dark hair fell silkily over her red sweater. "Don't be such a stupid dork."

"You're really here," Katie said, "and this isn't a dream?"

Jenni shook her head. "Not a dream. I'm really here, but only for a short time. I've always been nearby, but I was waiting."

Katie flung her arms around Jenni and felt flesh and blood in her grasp. "I can feel you!" Katie was laughing and crying at the same time. "Oh, my gawd, Jenni."

"Isn't it cool? And look at your tummy! You're about to pop!" Jenni snuggled up to Katie. "You look so good, Mama."

Katie sobbed with joy. "Oh, Jenni. I've missed you so much."

"It's okay, sweetie. I'm here now. I'm here to save you and Travis."

"What do you mean?" Katie demanded, hearing the seriousness in Jenni's tone.

Jenni glanced at the clock. Her hand, in Katie's, was beginning to feel thinner, less solid. "It's almost time. Crap. I forgot what time was like. It's different on the other side."

"Jenni, what do you mean?"

"I'm here to save you and Travis," Jenni repeated.

"Jenni, you're scaring the hell out of me! What's going on?"

"Curtis is about to kill Travis! We have to hurry!" Jenni grabbed Katie's hand, but their fingers passed through one another. "Oh, damn! I'm already fading!"

"Jenni, what do you mean Curtis is going to kill Travis?" Katie felt as if she couldn't breathe.

"You need to get help to Travis right away! Curtis is the Vigilante," Jenni replied. "Do it quick!"

Katie scrambled into action as Jenni vanished.

Juan woke to the ringing of the phone on the bedside table. He fumbled for the receiver.

"Hello?"

"Juan, it's Katie! Curtis is the Vigilante and he's going to kill Travis."

"Huh?" Juan couldn't process what he was hearing.

"Juan, you have to help me! Everyone is asleep and Jenni says I only have a few seconds to sound the alarm!"

Struggling to wake up, Juan listened as Katie repeated herself and added the location where Travis was to meet Curtis. "Katie, what do you mean Jenni told you—?"

Katie made an inarticulate noise and slammed the phone down. Juan winced at the sound, his fingers already dialing Kevin's number.

"Curtis," Travis said, "you don't want to do this."

"Actually, I do." Curtis took a step forward, moving with deadly confidence. His expression was calm; his eyes were hard and his jaw set. He seemed more self-assured than Travis had ever seen him.

Travis watched the knife warily. His heart was thundering in his ears as he stayed alert, ready to evade any attack.

Curtis smiled triumphantly. "You know, originally, I was going to push Katie over the wall. Let you see how it feels to lose the woman you love. But you dying works just fine."

Travis took a long breath to calm himself, knowing that he needed to think clearly and not let his emotions get in the way. Taking another step back, Travis felt the catwalk sway slightly. He scrutinized his surroundings with a sinking heart. Curtis had picked one of the best places in the entire fort for an attack. The area was isolated at the best of times. In the middle of the night, no one would notice anything.

"Who knows? Maybe your lesbo wife will hook up with Bette and return my girl to me. That could work." Curtis methodically advanced on Travis.

"Curtis, think about what you're saying. You're speaking about murder," Travis said in a measured voice.

"I call it justice. I got rid of the people when you wouldn't. I took care of the fort when you didn't. You all blamed Blanche, but she was just a stupid whore. *I* did what was necessary!"

"So you killed them? Ritchie, Jimmy, Phil, Shane . . ." Travis tried to push his shock away and focus on the moment.

"And a few others you don't know about."

Travis knew he had to act soon before the younger man backed him into a dead end.

A low moan froze both men in place. A zombie staggered into the alley below.

"Well, that is perfect timing. Guess he heard the lunch bell," Curtis said with a grin. He lunged at Travis.

Travis avoided the knife and smashed into Curtis with his shoulder, knocking him back. Curtis fell, but didn't drop the knife. Travis kicked, aiming for the wrist of Curtis's knife hand. He missed and Curtis grabbed Travis's leg and tried to pull him off his feet. Travis gripped the handrail and fought to keep his balance.

Curtis raised the knife. "It's better for the fort this way."

"No!" Katie crashed into Curtis; the impact pitched Travis over the wall. Somehow Travis remembered to tuck and roll as he hit the ground, but he landed with a shock of pain and bit the inside of his mouth. In a panic, not sure where the zombie was, he struggled to his feet. Moaning filled his ears and Travis kicked out, catching the monster squarely in its torso. The zombie fell to the ground.

Bracing himself against the wall, Travis feverishly searched for a weapon. To his surprise and relief, he saw Curtis's knife glittering on the ground nearby. He kicked the zombie again as it tried to scramble to its feet, then snatched up the knife.

"Travis!" Katie screamed from above.

"Katie, run! Get help!"

The zombie's gnarled, gray hand slashed out; its teeth snapped together as it growled. Circling around it quickly, Travis thanked God for its slowness. He shoved it over. It landed facedown and clawed at the ground.

He heard the sounds of a struggle from the top of the wall. He wanted desperately to look up but knew he had to kill the zombie first.

The creature started to clamber to its feet and Travis rushed forward, kicked it down again, and planted his foot squarely on its brittle neck. He felt the bones giving way under his weight as he rammed the knife into the zombie's eye socket. Its teeth champed just inches away from his hand as he leaned all his weight into the knife and felt the blade push deeper. Working the knife back and forth, he finally felt the undead thing go limp.

Katie screamed and Travis spun around, staring up at last. His very pregnant wife was dangling from the railing. Curtis was trying to pry her hands loose.

"Curtis, stop!" Travis shouted.

Low moans from behind him made his scalp crawl. Slowly, he turned his head and saw at least a dozen zombies lumbering into the mouth of the alley.

He felt completely and utterly helpless.

\* \* \*

With an eerie calm, Curtis worked to dislodge Katie from the rail. "Got some zombies down there ready for ya. I disabled the traps earlier just so they would have a chance to eat you."

"You fucking asshole!" Katie screamed.

Smiling madly, Curtis kept saying, "It's okay, really. It's fine, let go."

The moans of the zombies were louder. Travis was swearing at Curtis, his voice full of despair.

"You're going to die, Katie, just like Jenni did. This is the end of your little *Thelma and Louise* story. No one can save you," Curtis said in a disturbingly soothing tone.

"Hey, fuckface," Jenni's voice said sharply. She was standing behind Curtis, looking very real and solid to Katie. "Why don't you try fucking with me, asshole?"

Curtis spun to face the black-haired woman. "You're dead!" he said, sounding surprised.

"So?"

Just then Katie lost her grip and half slid, half fell down the outside of the wall.

As she dropped out of sight, Katie saw Jenni stare Curtis straight in the eye, grinning.

"Bang," the dead woman said.

"Wha—?" was all he managed before a hole was punched neatly through his brow above his left eye.

Curtis fell slowly to the catwalk, crumpling like a puppet with its strings cut.

Juan reached the catwalk just in time to see Katie fall and Curtis die at Jenni's feet. Startled, he could barely breathe as he stumbled toward the woman he loved.

"Loca," he whispered.

"Hey, baby," she answered with a wide smile. She looked down, yelled, "Shit!" then swung her legs over the rail and dropped out of sight.

*   *   *

Katie fell into Travis's arms, sending them both sprawling. Travis scrambled up and hoisted her to her feet. There were now maybe twenty zombies in the alley, moving resolutely toward them.

Nerit shoved past Juan and stepped over Curtis's body. It had taken her longer than she'd hoped to get her sniper rifle and rid the world of that bastard. Taking up position, she aimed at the zombies shambling toward her friends.

Katie and Travis shouted for help at the top of their lungs. They both flinched when a figure fell from above.

Jenni landed on her feet in front of them and flipped her hair back from her face.

"Hey, Travis," she called.

He gaped at her.

With a grin, Jenni sauntered toward the zombies, her long hair flowing in the night wind and her laughter drifting into the night.

"What the hell?" Travis managed.

"She's back . . . kinda," Katie answered.

Jenni smiled at the undead. She understood them now in a way she could not in life. While they were dreadfully sad and terrible, they were also hunger personified, and her friends were their chosen meal.

That was simply not acceptable.

"Hey, fucktards, why don't you stop right there and wait for the nice sniper lady to shoot your heads off?" she said, then stepped into the middle of the mob.

The zombies grabbed at her, their hands slipping through her arms, neck, and body. They growled in confusion and hunger.

"Good zombies. Now, bang."

The first zombie's head exploded.

Juan could barely believe what he was seeing, but his Jenni held the zombies at bay as Nerit shot them one by one.

The loading dock doors slid open and Kevin emerged with heavily armed soldiers at his side. With the way cleared for them by Nerit's expert shooting, Katie and Travis rushed for cover. Kevin leaped down to help Travis lift Katie onto the dock as Nerit continued to fire; then everyone retreated to safety. The heavy doors clanged shut behind them.

Juan watched in awe as Jenni walked calmly past the downed monsters, pulling the remaining zombies along with her. Jenni shoved a few out of her way as she walked, but whenever they tried to touch her, they failed. They followed her relentlessly, moaning with aggravation.

Jenni squatted down, examining the ground. Finding the broken mechanism hidden in the dirt, Jenni smiled up at the zombies clustered around her, then triggered the trap.

A spring-loaded frame mounted with razor wire sprang upright, slashing through the crowd of undead, dismembering the zombies instantly.

Jenni rose, smiled again, and was gone.

## CHAPTER THIRTY-ONE

## 1.

### *The Time of Choice*

The lobby grew packed with people as word of what had happened with Curtis, Travis, and Katie spread. Katie and Travis huddled together on a couch.

"This is bullshit," Ed declared. "Sorry, folks, but I don't believe in ghosts. Jenni is dead—end of story. And protocol was broken when Kevin opened the loading dock."

"Were we supposed to leave them out there to die?" Peggy asked angrily.

"I'm just saying that this place is going to shit fast," Ed responded.

"I saw Jenni," Juan said sharply.

"Ghosts are bullshit, and if this is how people are gonna act when the zombies come, breaking rules and throwing plans to the wind 'cause someone they really like is in danger, I'm out of here," Ed groused.

"I see ghosts, too," Katarina said from near the elevators. "I saw my mama until Bill and I got engaged."

"How many here saw a ghost tonight?" Nerit's voice broke through the murmuring.

Silence fell over the lobby. People were still stunned by her miraculous recovery. She appeared stronger than ever before. Her keen eyes swept over the faces, demanding an answer. Nearly a third of the people in the room raised their hands. Nerit nodded as if she'd received confirmation of something she'd suspected.

"I saw my dead husband," she said. "He told me what Curtis was trying to do. I saw Jenni, too. Now, I may be an old woman, but that only means I've lived longer than most of you. This isn't the first time I've seen things I cannot explain." Nerit's voice was strong. "The ghosts came to guide us. But they have all passed on now, and it's up to us to deal with what happens next."

"C'mon," a voice said nearby. "That's a bunch of bull. You're sounding as crazed as those Baptists we threw out."

"I saw Jenni, too," Travis said. "Clear as day. She held off the zombies coming for me and Katie. We have the dead walking the earth, why are ghosts so hard to believe in?"

"Ghosts or no, that side door was opened," Ed said, "and there were explicit orders to keep it closed."

"That was my call," Kevin said. "To save Travis and Katie."

Gretchen, who had been a librarian until the zombies rose—and had always been an outspoken woman—stepped up to stand next to Ed. "Ed's right. We've been doing what you said, even when we disagreed, because we want this to work. But would that door have been opened for me?"

Angry murmurs grew loud until Nerit held up her hand. "Kevin did what he felt was right. You may not agree, but the choice was made."

Travis stood up. "This isn't the time to fall apart."

Long-festering resentments were flowing to the surface. Friends and family members were arguing with one another. Everyone was on edge. Everyone was afraid.

"Maybe the Baptists had it right. Maybe it isn't safe here," Gretchen said at last. "Especially if we can't trust our leadership to look out for all of us."

"They've been excluding us a lot lately. They tossed Blanche out without a vote!" someone shouted.

Travis winced. "It seemed like the best choice at the time."

"You cut us out of that decision," Ed said sharply.

Kevin moved to Nerit's side. "Everyone standing here knows how hard it has been on those in leadership roles. We've all suffered losses."

"Maybe looking out for our own best interests is the way to go," Ed said flatly.

"I don't understand where this is coming from," Travis protested.

"A lot of us are tired of feeling that we don't have a choice about what goes on," Gretchen said. "No offense, Travis, but it's damn hard, in this world, to give our lives over to other people."

Ed nodded slowly. "It's nothing personal. I may be a mite angry, but I'm damn scared. What happens if something goes wrong out there and someone opens a gate or a door they shouldn't? I don't like feeling like I'm not in control of my own life. Gimme a truck and some ammo. I'm willing to take a chance out there on my own."

"Let them go," Eric said from near the front desk. "Let whoever wants to leave the fort take what they need and go."

"We need them here. Everyone has a role to play in the upcoming battle," Juan protested. "Everyone has assignments!"

"Some of us don't want to be part of any battle," a man near Juan snapped.

More voices rumbled through the vast room, both disagreeing and agreeing.

At last Travis stood. He said, "Very well. If you want to go, go. We've got some extra vehicles. But you're on your own once you're gone."

Ed nodded. "That's fair."

Nerit observed the room thoughtfully. Katie noticed that Kevin's hand was resting on her back in a gesture that seemed more for his comfort than for hers. "Those who are going must go tonight," she said.

"Why?" Gretchen asked, with an edge in her voice that sounded more like frustration than anger.

"The zombie horde will arrive in the morning. At nine twenty, they will cross the first line."

"How do you know that?" Art asked sharply.

"My husband told me. The battle is tomorrow. If you're going to leave, it has to be now," Nerit said firmly.

"Why are we supposed to believe her?" someone asked.

"Because she knows what she's talking about." A haggard-looking Otis Calhoun strode through the crowd, carrying a small tape recorder. "I've been monitoring the alien transmissions. Got this." He held up the recorder and hit PLAY.

A woman's voice came from the speaker. "If anyone can hear us, we're trying to get to the fort, but ran into thousands of zombies near the junction of 16 and 1456. We got away and are heading back to the Baptist Encampment. Hello? Can anyone hear me? It's Milo and Susan. We were trying to get home but they're everywhere."

Katie felt a chill. The junction they had named was close to town.

"I gotcha," Calhoun's voice said on the tape. "Head back to the crazy Baptists and stay low. Make sure their demon-possessed leader don't do nothing stupid. We'll fight off the zombie-clones and let you know when it's clear."

"Thanks, Calhoun," the voice answered.

Calhoun hit STOP.

The lobby was completely silent for a long minute. Then Ed said, "We leave tonight."

"Can I go with you?" a voice called out.

It was Belinda. Juan's one-time crush and Mike's widow. She pushed through the people to Ed's side. "I want to go, too."

"Okay. You can come. Let's roll within the hour," Ed said.

Arguments sprang up everywhere. People were shouting and crying. Katie watched, sad with the knowledge that there was nothing more she could do.

# 2.
## *Sweet Sorrow*

Three Durangos and three other cars were quickly loaded with ammunition, MREs, and jugs of water—with Peggy setting the limits on what people could take. Families were being split apart as folks carried bags of clothes and personal effects to their vehicles. Some kept arguing; others were saying tearful farewells. Twenty-three people were leaving.

Ed strode through the throng with Belinda in his wake. Ed's sons were already in the backseat of their truck, holding shotguns. It was no surprise that they were leaving with their father; they were a tight-knit family.

A young woman helped her six-year-old daughter into a car's rear seat and buckled her in, then climbed in beside the child. Two men got into the front. The slamming doors seemed to sound a note of finality.

"They're probably all going to die," Juan said finally. He and Travis were leaning against a pallet of bricks, watching the departure preparations.

"Yeah, but it's their choice."

Having seen Belinda to the SUV, Ed walked over. His haggard face was worn and his eyes tired, but his jaw was set firmly. As he drew near, he thrust out his hand. "Boys, it's been good," he said.

Travis didn't hesitate to take his hand and clasp it tightly. "We'll miss you."

"We did good here, but we gotta move on," Ed said.

Juan stepped forward and he and Ed shook as well. "Take care, man."

"I will. Hope you guys make it through tomorrow okay."

"We will," Travis said confidently.

Ed nodded, then headed for his truck. Other conversations

broke up as people followed his lead and climbed into their vehicles.

Juan lifted a walkie-talkie to his lips. "Clear?"

"All clear," was the response.

"Open the gates," Juan ordered.

Travis exhaled slowly as the massive doors opened. In his peripheral vision, he saw Peggy sobbing. A few of the fort's inhabitants called out to their loved ones, pleading with them to stay even as the vehicles rolled out of the fort.

"This sucks," Juan finally grumbled.

"Can't be helped," Rune said from nearby.

"What do you mean?" Travis asked.

"Texans stick together as long as they have a common enemy, but when they feel someone is trying to put the hammer down on them, watch out. Things have mostly gone fine around here, but right now, people are feeling powerless and they're gonna either fight or run. Those folks . . . God bless 'em . . . they're running." Rune grinned, showing all his teeth. "They're scared, so they're outta here. I say let 'em go." He waved at the last Durango.

Travis reluctantly agreed.

"They're just a bunch of ingrates," Peggy said, joining them, her face red from crying.

Calhoun came up to them and said, "Okay, the pussies are gone and the real soldiers are left. So, I gotta know a few things real quick."

"What is it, Calhoun?" Travis couldn't help but smile at the sight of the old man, who was wearing some sort of weird hat with what looked like a miniature satellite dish on top.

"Is Nerit going to have the Amazons come help us tomorrow?"

Travis grinned, then shook his head. "No, they're staying put on Paradise Island."

Calhoun frowned. "They don't live on Paradise Island." With a scornful look, Calhoun stalked off, muttering about Amazons not helping out like decent women should.

"Oops." Juan laughed.

Travis shook his head ruefully. The group turned to leave the paddock and Travis was surprised to see Manny Reyes, the former mayor of Ashley Oaks, walking slowly back toward the hotel. He was pale and short of breath. The poor man suffered from coronary disease, and his medicine stores had run out a few months before. It was clear to Travis that the mayor's time was running out. He caught up to Manny and took his arm to give him support.

"I'm fine," Manny said in a breathy voice. He did not pull away, though, and Travis made sure to match the sick man's pace. "I came down to say good-bye to a few friends."

"Guess they didn't care for our style of leadership," Travis said in a miffed tone.

"Let me tell you something," Manny said. "It doesn't matter if they were happy or not. In the end, you can only do your best. People will agree with you. People will disagree with you. For every person who hates you, there is someone who loves you." Manny sat down on a box and rested his hands on his knees. Rune nodded in agreement as he stopped alongside the former mayor. Juan and Peggy also joined the little group.

"Well, we're doing our best," Travis said. "I guess we gotta be okay with that."

"You do. And you and the council have done things I never could have." Manny waved a hand around to indicate the high walls and the fort in general. "I know you guys did your best by us. Whether we make it through tomorrow or not, know that you have my support. You gave me one more year of life."

Travis took Manny's words to heart.

Juan averted his eyes and Travis knew he was trying to hide his emotions. "We'll win this," Juan said. "We gotta. We don't have what we used to—a whole world to feel free in—but we got this fort and our families."

The former mayor inclined his head. "Worth fighting for, isn't it?"

"Damn straight," Rune declared.

"Do you think we can win?" Peggy appealed to Travis, sniffling loudly.

"I think so. We're gonna try."

"I don't want to get eaten by those things. I don't want my boy to get eaten by those things. I want you to promise me that we'll live through tomorrow!" Peggy exclaimed, jabbing her finger into Travis's chest.

He gripped her arms gently and looked down at her with compassion. "I promise you that we will do our very best."

With an agonized cry, Peggy wrenched away and ran off.

Manny gazed after her solemnly. "She's a good woman, but she's endured a lot. I hate to see her cry."

Juan crossed his arms and surveyed the fort. "We're ready as we can be."

"Time to kill some zombies," Rune said, grinning.

That night, when Travis finally lay down to grab a few hours' sleep, he wrapped his arms tightly around his wife, grateful that they were both still alive. Without waking, Katie rolled over so that their unborn child was nestled between them.

Juan stretched out on his sofa, thinking of Jenni and the kids and all that had happened since the first day and gnawing on his scarred thumbnail. His old, nervous habit was somehow soothing. Jack padded out of Jason's bedroom and flopped down next to the sofa, and the man reached down to stroke the dog's head.

Nerit slept without fear and rose early to join Kevin on the roof of city hall. They reviewed the defense plans one last time. At one point, he took her hand. For a long moment, they gazed at each other, not saying a word, then went back to work.

Calhoun and Jason—and many others—worked deep into the night.

Katarina fell asleep alone in her bed, wearing Bill's shirt. Her rifle was ready at her bedside.

Peggy woke her little boy to give him a glass of chocolate milk laced with strong sedatives she had stolen from the clinic. She sat with him while he happily drank this rare treat, then tucked him into bed and kissed him one last time. She waited until she was sure he was gone, then, with tears streaming down her face, went into the bathroom. She found her own peace at the end of a razor blade and faded from the world knowing that she and her child would never know the agony of being eaten alive.

## · CHAPTER THIRTY-TWO ·

### 1.

### *Final Exit of the Wickedest Woman in Texas*

Politics was a fickle lover.

One moment you were the hero; the next, the villain. But if you were clever, you could become the hero once again. The public was immensely shortsighted and had no memory to speak of. Even Nixon had been memorialized for his virtues when he died.

"It's all going to be okay," Paige Brightman told herself.

Tucked behind the steering wheel of the big Ford truck she had liberated from a dealership, Paige smiled in the gracious way Raleigh had taught her. She wondered what the little faggot was doing now. Probably wandering around half-eaten like the rest, unless the undead had cracked his skull open like a boiled egg and eaten his brain.

It was a shame all the men who had helped her escape from the mall had run off or died. Blessedly, she was a country gal who knew how to handle herself. Even when she'd failed to cross I-35, she hadn't lost her way. She'd simply reassessed her situation and decided to hole up for a while in her sister Blanche's mansion.

After months on the road, it had been good to have a few days of peace. The provisions she'd salvaged along the way had helped restore her, and she'd reveled in the opportunity to use Blanche's grooming products and clothes.

The long days and nights alone had given her time to think. She realized she had come on too strong back at the mall. She should have taken a more motherly approach. Playing into the stereotype would have worked to her advantage.

Driving toward the fort now, Senator Paige Brightman's appearance was dignified and feminine, with a touch of strength. She had discarded her darker suits for one of Blanche's, a soft pink skirt-suit with rose satin lapels. Her shoes were sensible and her jewelry was gold and quartz—understated and elegant. She was ready to present herself as a kinder, gentler, better option.

She checked her gun one more time—a little .22 she'd salvaged at a sport shop. The holster was comfortably hidden under her suit jacket. She wasn't worried—Paige was certain she could deal with the undead.

She planned to approach the fort with a motherly smile in place and a well-prepared speech spilling from her lips as if it were flowing from her heart. Tears would spring to her eyes. They would have pity on her and take her in. She would be humble and repentant before them.

Then she would work her way into their hearts and back to the top of the pecking order. She would be Mother Teresa, the Virgin Mary, and Princess Diana all rolled into one. They would forgive her and embrace her. Soon enough, she would become the fort's leader and they would be on the road to their true destiny, the one she had planned for them. Failure was not an option. Lord knows, if George Bush could win a second term in office, she sure as hell could get her ass into the fort.

Of course, she did not admit to herself that her current plan matched Gordon Knox's advice from the night before the mall fell.

The sun was just beginning to rise; a thin, scattered mist gave the impression that ghosts were wandering across the fields. The senator hummed to herself as she drove.

Cresting the hill, she gasped at the sight of the fort. The walls were a lot more extensive than she remembered from the photos and there seemed to be catapults mounted on several buildings. A lot of the town had been demolished, creating a no-man's-land that ran completely around the fort.

"Interesting," Paige said out loud, hitting the gas.

One second she was cruising along just fine; the next, her truck was nose down in a huge hole in the ground. Luckily, Paige was wearing her seat belt, so she only hit her forehead on the padded steering wheel, but the jolt made her scream. Staring out the windshield, she realized she was eye level with the road. The truck was sputtering, and steam rose from beneath its crumpled hood. *What the hell?* she wondered. There had been no sign of a hole.

Paige got out of the truck slowly. The hole was about three feet deep, and the bottom was a pool of unstable mud that sucked her high heels right off her feet. Panicked, she managed to grab her suitcase and fling it and herself into the truck bed. Catching her breath, she looked down and this time saw what looked like a big piece of cloth, painted to match the road, under the truck's wheels.

"A fucking trap." Probably for outlaws. She opened her suitcase and pulled out a fresh pair of shoes and her least favorite of her sister's blouses, which she used to clean her feet. At least there were no undead fuckers in sight. Tucking her feet into the almost too tight black shoes, she forced herself to calm down. She would walk the rest of the way. It would be fine.

Zipping up the suitcase, Paige decided to leave it with the truck—someone could come back for it later. She twisted around and leaned into the cab to retrieve the bullhorn she'd left there. She'd found it at the same sport shop where she'd acquired her gun; even then, she was planning to present herself at the fort and knew she'd need to attract their attention.

She climbed onto the cab of the truck and then scrambled out of the hole. It wasn't easy and she almost fell more than once before reaching the street. Paige took a moment to pat her bouffant back into place, straighten her clothes, and take a few deep breaths, intent on reclaiming her earlier mood. She had to be positive and glowing.

Walking briskly down the street, bullhorn in hand, she tripped over something and fell. As she reached out to catch herself, she heard a sharp, mechanical clang; then something invisible slammed into her and shoved her off her feet.

The senator found herself lying on the street, gazing at her severed hand a few feet away, still gripping the bullhorn. Her mind sputtered as a cascade of information overwhelmed her.

What was her perfectly manicured hand doing over there? It looked as if it had been sliced off at the wrist. She was having trouble seeing it, because liquid had begun to flow over her face. She tried to move and could not. She felt numb, but beneath the numbness, she sensed excruciating pain.

Senator Paige Brightman had no way of knowing, as she quickly bled to death, that she had triggered one of Jason's traps. A spring-loaded frame mounted with razor wire had snapped upright, slicing deeply into her, easily cutting through muscle, sinew, and blood vessels.

Blood quickly flowed down the street. In moments, her eyes clouded over. Her last thought was, *They don't know I'm here. . . .*

## 2.
### When All That Is Left Is Good-bye

"So this is the day that decides the fate of the world," Katie said musingly. She, Nerit, Travis, Juan, and Kevin were riding up to the ballroom together to grab some breakfast.

"Perhaps," Nerit said.

"Guess so," Travis said as he rubbed her back.

"Sucks, huh?" Juan said with a small smile.

"It feels . . ." Katie struggled to find the right word.

"Normal," Nerit offered.

"Boring," Travis stated.

"Annoying," Juan finished.

Katie laughed.

"It's a good day to die," Kevin said from a corner of the elevator.

Katie flicked her gaze at him and shook her finger. "Oh, no! I'm not dying."

"Keeping it positive, huh, babe?" Travis observed.

"Or just annoyingly optimistic," Juan decided.

"Or she knows something you don't know," Nerit teased as the doors opened to the foyer off the ballroom.

Anyone not involved in the battle would stay here. They hoped that the ballroom—the highest point in the fort—would be safe no matter what happened. At the moment, the room was full of people finishing their breakfast tacos and saying good-bye to their small children and their elderly or disabled friends and relatives. Everyone was tense, but most partings were tender.

As Katie stepped out of the elevator, Jack bounded up to her and she leaned down to hug him.

Jack woofed, then took off. Katie followed him through the crowd to Juan's family. All four children were sitting in a little group around Guadalupe's wheelchair, munching on breakfast tacos. Juan paused a few steps away from his family, and Katie stopped beside him.

"She gave me four kids," he said.

In response, Katie lifted an eyebrow. "Hmm?"

"Loca. She couldn't have any more kids, but she found a way to give me four. Two boys, two girls." Juan grinned. "That woman sure did get her way, huh?"

"Yes, she did."

With a smile, Juan kissed Katie on the cheek. "Thank you for bringing my Loca to me."

Tears sprang into her eyes and she choked up. Juan tightened his embrace, then released her and went to speak to his family

Her husband drew near and smoothed her golden hair back from her eyes. Cupping her face, Travis kissed her lips, then pressed his forehead to hers. "We're going to make it."

Katie nodded vehemently. "Without a doubt."

An ungodly smell hit them. Wincing, Katie searched the room

and saw Calhoun, satellite-dish hat intact, looming in the doorway nearby.

"Calhoun, what is—?" Travis started to ask.

"The main fire trap is disconnected!" Calhoun yelled, waving his hands about as he rushed forward. "Gawddamn mind waves of the clones are disrupting my instruments and—"

Nerit strode over, carrying a half-eaten taco, with Kevin half a step behind her. "What do you mean, Calhoun?" she asked.

"I lost the main fire trap. The controls are dead!"

"Shit," Kevin said. "We need that one to go off to ignite the area in front of the hotel. Lighting it manually will not have the same effect."

"The zombies will not reach the outskirts for another thirty minutes," Nerit noted. "Can you fix it in that time?"

"Sorry, Amazon lady, I don't trust your dead incubus of a husband about the time when the zombie-clones arrive!"

"Calhoun," Katie chided, "that wasn't nice."

"I don't trust ghosts with their mysterious ways," Calhoun retorted.

"Calhoun, that trap has to work. The fire barricade has to ignite or we might get overrun," Travis said sharply.

Calhoun mumbled under his breath nervously.

"We got thirty minutes, Calhoun. Let's go fix it," Rune said, coming up from behind Katie. "Let's do it, dude. I mean it. Let's go!" Clad in his motorcycle leathers, Rune looked ready for war.

Calhoun looked uneasy, then said, "Okay, but I'm not riding bitch."

With a grin, Rune dragged Calhoun toward the elevator. "Oh, yes, you are."

"I'd better monitor them," Kevin said, moving toward the elevator.

"Good idea. I'll get Katarina out there to cover them," Nerit said, joining him.

Katie turned to her husband and took away his half-eaten

breakfast taco. He quirked an eyebrow at her as she began to munch on his food, then turned away to get more. Katie smiled. She felt strangely calm. Maybe it was the golden sunlight of the new day pouring through the windows or the vast expanse of light blue sky overhead, but it felt peaceful in the ballroom.

When the elevator doors closed behind them, Kevin shifted on his feet and looked at Nerit steadily. "I've wanted to tell you something since you woke up."

"I already know. You don't have to say it," Nerit responded quickly.

"One of my men once called you the sexiest old woman around," Kevin said bashfully. "I think he was right." He stepped closer to her.

"You deserve to find a new family, to rebuild, once this is over. I can't give you that."

"But I know you feel it, too. If we were closer in age—"

"Yes," Nerit said simply, meeting his gaze. "But that's not the case, is it?"

"I wish it was."

Nerit looked away and stared at the elevator door. "Me, too."

Moving quickly, Kevin pressed a firm, hard kiss to her cheek. To his delight, Nerit blushed.

The elevator dinged, the doors opened, and Kevin stepped out.

Trailing him, Nerit took a breath. Hopefully, there would be a future for all of them to enjoy.

"And then we shoot them in the head," Holly assured Juan.

"They're not getting in," Jason promised the little girl again.

"*Nieta,* the monsters will not get past the walls," Rosie assured her adopted granddaughter. "It's not going to happen."

"But if they do," Margie said in an ominous voice, "we will shoot them in the head."

"Shoot dem in da head," Troy said firmly.

Juan laughed, loudly and sincerely, and kissed each one of them. "It won't come to that, I promise."

Jason rubbed Jack behind the ears. Troy flopped backwards to pillow his head on the dog's stomach. The utter normalcy of it struck Juan to the heart. Guadalupe had fallen asleep in her wheelchair; his mother was fussing with the kids; the little ones were both impish and innocent; Jason was using his bangs to avoid revealing his feelings; and the dog lay happily in the middle of it all.

Juan would do anything to protect them. Every day, he thanked Jenni—his freaky, somewhat insane, zombie-killing girlfriend—for making this happen. He loved her and missed her, but he knew she was at peace. His children had been her final gift to him. Without their love, he would still be in mourning.

"I need to get going," Jason said.

Suddenly, the little ones fell silent. Rosie looked somber.

"Give me a kiss, *nieto*," she said, throwing her arms open.

Jason went to her, looking embarrassed. She kissed him and hugged him tight. Guadalupe stirred long enough to give him a firm kiss on the cheek.

Juan offered Jason his hand, then drew him into an embrace that said more than words ever could.

"Me, too!" Margie leaped onto Jason, who laughed as he hugged her and his other sister and brother.

Then, without another word, Jason strode away. Watching, Juan thought he might explode from pride.

"He's a good boy," Rosie said through her tears.

"So am I!" Troy shouted as he leaped into her arms.

Rosie laughed and hugged the little boy tightly. "Yes, you are. Now, kiss your Daddy One."

Somehow Juan managed not to cry as the three kids kissed him and hugged him tight. "Go kill the zombies," Margie ordered.

"I will," Juan promised.

"Shoot 'em in the head," Holly instructed.

"I will," Juan answered.

"In da head," Troy repeated.

"In the head," Juan assured him.

He walked away with his heart in his throat.

His children would not die today. They would not. There was simply no other choice but to win.

## 3.
### *And the Clock Winds Down . . .*

Katie stared out the window as the ascending sun pushed away the gloom of the night. She saw her husband's reflection in the glass and turned as he reached her, pulled her into his arms, and fastened a gentle kiss to her lips. Closing her eyes, she relished the moment and felt its sweetness fill her.

"I love you," Travis murmured.

"Yeah, well, good. I'm crazy about you, too."

Ruffling her hair, he winked.

Out of the throng of people eating breakfast Eric appeared, his brow furrowed, followed closely by his girlfriend, Stacey, who was crying. She was holding Pepe, their little dog, who stared up at her sadly.

"What's up, Eric?" Travis asked worriedly.

"We have a situation," Eric said, pain in his voice. Tears glimmered in his eyes. "Peggy's . . . gone."

"What?" Travis and Katie said in chorus. "She left?"

"No, she killed herself and Cody sometime last night," Stacey sobbed.

"Oh, Jesus," Katie murmured, covering her mouth with her hand.

"Shit," Travis said. "Shit!" He shook his head in disbelief. "I knew she was scared, but I never thought . . ."

"She's not the only one. There are about four more, according to reports from loved ones." Eric sighed. "I was really hoping there would be none."

"Peggy was going to run communications," Katie said mournfully.

"Yolanda can do it," Travis stated.

"I'll find her," Stacey said, vanishing into the crowd.

Eric rubbed the bridge of his nose with one finger, shoved his glasses back into place, then shook his head. "I better check in with Nerit." He hurried off.

From the change in the hum of conversation in the ballroom, Katie guessed that people were learning about the deaths. She saw looks of dismay and sorrow on many faces. She remembered something Peggy had said to her once: *There are no secrets in a small Texas town. If you fart, everyone knows what you had for dinner.*

"Oh, gawd, Peggy," Katie whispered. How many more would they lose today? Clasping Travis's arm, she appealed to him. "They need to know that there is hope. You and the reverend need to speak to everyone before those things get here."

As if drawn by her comment, Reverend Thomas approached. "Travis," he said, "the people are in despair. We need to rally them."

Travis sighed. Katie knew that he hated the idea of talking to a crowd, but she could tell that he knew he had no choice. "I agree. Let's head down to communications." He kissed Katie again and whispered, "How do you always know what's needed?" before heading for the elevators with the reverend at his side.

With a sigh, Katie brushed her blond hair from her face and looked out over the desolate swath of land before the fort. She could clearly see the ramshackle wall of debris around the fort. She wondered what progress Rune and Calhoun had made in fixing the main firetrap. If that didn't work right . . .

Suddenly she was very afraid.

## CHAPTER THIRTY-THREE

## 1.
### *Time to Die*

"Move it, Calhoun. They're coming and they're hungry," Rune said firmly. He was unfazed by the reek coming off the crazy old guy.

They'd been lowered to the ground outside the walls on a makeshift elevator—a shipping pallet suspended from a crane—first Rune and his bike, then Calhoun. Now Rune straddled the Harley and motioned for Calhoun to climb on. While the "elevator" was being set up, he'd gotten his bag of grenades out of storage. Now the bag rested firmly against his side. Today seemed like a good day to blow stuff up.

"I ain't as young as you, you long-haired hippie," Calhoun groused, swinging his leg over the bike on his second try.

"I ain't a hippie, Cal," Rune answered.

Calhoun's response turned into a shout as the motorcycle lurched forward, roaring over the rough terrain.

"The fire line is a damn good idea to push back the dead fucks!" Rune hollered over the roar of the motorcycle.

"I know how to deal with this stuff. Years and years of planning for the clone uprising."

"You may be a crazy old shithead, Cal, but you know what's going on, in your own way," Rune almost growled. "You're a mean old codger."

"Not as mean as Nerit," Calhoun said, pouting.

"No one is as mean as Nerit," Rune admitted, stopping the bike.

It had taken only a minute or so to reach their destination, close to the barriers made of dirt, brush, tree trunks, and the bull-dozed remains of houses and buildings. Several gas tanks had been half-buried in the soil and linked to remote detonators. If it worked right, the barrier would go up like kindling.

Calhoun fell to his knees and dug up the device he'd rigged to explode the fuel tanks. He popped open the huge metal box and began to examine it closely.

"What's wrong with it?" Rune asked.

"Don't know yet," Calhoun answered. "Tried to run the start-up sequence remotely and there was no response. Problem's gotta be at this end."

"'Cause, you know, it's almost time," Rune said, arms folded across his chest. "If you don't get this fire going, they're gonna come right over this barrier. Then we'll have 'em up against the walls."

Though the wind was mostly blowing away from the fort, Rune could faintly smell the zombies. It was the all-too-familiar smell of death.

"I know." Calhoun glared down at the device. "Gawddamn gremlins got into it. I knew it!" Calhoun beat the ground with one fist, then controlled himself and adjusted his satellite dish hat. "Okay, I need Jason."

"The kid?"

"Yeah, the kid! You know, our future leader. Our John Connor? Our freaking salvation!"

"Take a chill pill, Cal, I'm calling the fort," Rune said, yanking out his walkie-talkie.

"I don't need a chill pill," Calhoun asserted as he began to sort the wires with his grubby fingers. "I need the freaking gremlins to stay out of my stuff."

"We need Jason down here, Peggy," Rune said.

There was static for a moment, then, "Okay, I let him know," said a voice that was not Peggy's.

"Hey, Yolanda," Rune said. "You pulling a double shift?"

"Yeah, things are not so good with Peggy."

"That sucks," Rune said, and didn't press it. He didn't want to know.

Calhoun rubbed his big nose and frowned. "Whose idea was it to blow up the gawddern fuel tanks?"

"Yours," Rune answered.

"Gawddammit! Why do people listen to me? I'm freaking nuts!"

"And that, sir, is why they listen to you," Rune said, laughing.

Calhoun shot him a disgusted look. Then he, too, began to laugh.

Surrounded by the slowly strengthening stench of death, the two men laughed at the absurdity of life until tears ran from their eyes.

Reggie, a big black man, steadied the pallet as Jason climbed on, tool bag on his shoulder. The teenager took a firm grip on one of the thick cables.

"Ready?" Reggie asked.

"Yeah," Jason answered.

Reggie released the pallet and signaled the crane operator. The clumsy elevator lifted with a sickening lurch and started to swing over the wall.

With a sharp bark, Jack dodged around Reggie and leaped onto the pallet, landing with a yelp. Jason grabbed the dog's collar as the pallet swung sharply due to the unexpected weight and motion. Boy and dog slid across the wood for a moment before the platform stabilized. Tucking Jack securely between his legs, Jason looked down at his startled pet.

"Damn dog, you were supposed to stay with the kids," Jason chided him.

Jack gave him a soulful, apologetic look. As the pallet was lowered to the ground, the big shepherd growled low in his throat and laid his ears back.

"I know, boy," Jason said, fear in his voice. "They're coming."

Calhoun was in a tizzy, muttering angrily to himself.

"Smells worse than you now, Calhoun," Rune said, sniffing the air and glancing over his shoulder at the makeshift barrier.

"Soap is ungodly and unnatural. It poisons you slowly," Calhoun declared.

With Jack at his side, Jason rushed up to Calhoun and fell to his knees beside the old man. He and Calhoun bent low over the detonator. Jack stood guard, staring at the barrier and growling.

Rune turned, following the dog's gaze. "You know," Rune drawled. "I always wanted to die a noble death."

Coming up over the top of the barrier was a lone zombie. When it saw the people, it let out a mournful wail, stretched out its gnarled hands, and limped forward.

"I think he's hungry," Calhoun said.

"Well, boys, time for me to go do the hero thing. Let it be known to all survivors of the fort that I went out like a warrior!" Rune grinned toothily and got onto his bike.

"What are you going to do?" Jason asked, his eyes huge with fear.

Rune shifted his bag around so he could grab the grenades easily. "Not sure yet, but it's gonna be wild."

He gunned the Harley and sped toward the zombie.

Jack began to bark fiercely as ten more zombies crested the barrier.

Then twenty more.

The lone biker aimed his bike at a piece of sloping roof that made a perfect ramp. As he accelerated, he shouted, "Time to rock and roll!" The bike flew over the barrier, vanishing from sight.

The zombies disappeared from view as they followed him.


In the communication center, Yolanda was listening to the various groups check in from all over the fort. She marked off each numbered group on her list, her full lips pursed slightly.

Her reaction to Peggy's suicide was complex. Peggy had become a friend, so Yolanda wanted to feel sad about her death, but for her to leave them in the lurch like this pissed her off. Yolanda was supposed to be up on the wall with Lenore, manning one of the huge crossbows, but instead, here she was, trapped in the windowless communication center. She knew that what she was doing was important, but she wanted to be outside, where the action was.

As she wrote, she tried not to notice her stubby fingernails, coated with bright red polish. Last night, she and most of the fort's other black women had had a kind of party. They'd cut their fingernails short and braided their hair. It had been harder to do than Yolanda expected. It might have seemed silly to some, but having fancy nails and hair made Yolanda feel connected to her old life. But she and the others had snagged and broken their nails during target practice, and flowing hair could be dangerous if the zombies managed to breach the walls. They'd made a night of it and spent hours talking and laughing, trying to scare away their fears.

Rune's voice came through the walkie-talkie. "Yoli, gotta create a distraction."

"What are you talking about?" Yolanda snapped at him. "You're supposed to be—"

He laughed, cutting her off. "Say *boom,* baby."

A second later, she heard a faint explosion in the distance, just as Travis and Reverend Thomas entered the room.

She turned to them in indignation. "That crazy-ass, long-haired biker boy is off doing something stupid," she said.

The tall man's eyebrows shot up. "Rune, what the hell are you doing?" Travis said into the mic.

"Getting the zombies away from the kid and Cal." They heard an explosion through the radio. "Don't worry about me. I got my bike and a bag of grenades."

On another channel, Nerit said, "Rune is drawing the zombies away from the fire line. He's lobbing grenades into the group following him."

"He just called in," Travis told Nerit. "How do you think he's doing?"

"Looks good so far," Nerit answered. "It's a smaller group. The main horde isn't here yet."

"He's a brave man," the reverend decided.

"More like damn crazy." Yolanda couldn't believe the gall of the white-haired biker.

"We're going to say a few words before they breach the fire line," Travis said to Nerit. "Keep an eye on Calhoun and Jason. Pull them back if the zombies get too close."

"Understood," came the reply.

"Yolanda, open up the speakers," Travis instructed. "I need to speak to the fort."

Travis's hand was so sweaty that he almost dropped the microphone. As he tightened his grasp, for the first time, Travis acknowledged to himself just how frightened he was. He'd lived with low-grade paranoia and fear for so long that he barely noticed those feelings most of the time. Now, with an army of the dead approaching, his emotions threatened to swamp him.

The reverend gently patted his shoulder. "You can do this, Travis."

Travis tried not to think of Katie on the wall. Armed with her binoculars and walkie-talkie, she was one of the spotters who would report in to the command center. He desperately wanted her to stay in the ballroom, but she just as desperately wanted to participate, and in the end, he couldn't refuse her.

He closed his eyes, said a silent prayer, then pressed the button and spoke.

" 'Good morning' seems like the wrong thing to say," he began, hearing his voice booming from the speakers mounted throughout the fort. "I don't think we've had a good morning for a damn long time. But . . . hell . . . good morning anyway.

"If we have to fight for our lives, I guess we couldn't ask for a prettier morning."

Lenore was loading one of the giant crossbows. She looked up and found that she agreed with Travis. The sky was brilliant; the sun shone through beautiful white clouds. She wished Felix and Ken were with her.

"We can fight and win. No matter how afraid you are, remember that we're in this together."

Katie smiled as her husband's voice echoed around her. The smell of decay had grown stronger, so she pulled her kerchief over her nose. She watched the dark wave of the undead in the distance, just beyond the fire line. On this beautiful day, the ugly, decaying zombies seemed like a sacrilege.

"I just wanted to say that y'all are my family. I'm glad to know you and I'm proud to stand with you today. And now a word from Reverend Thomas."

Perched on the roof of the newspaper building, Katarina smiled at the sound of the microphone being jostled around. She bent her head to the scope of her sniper rifle. The first zombie to swim into view was vile beyond belief—a large woman, half eaten, her abdomen torn open to reveal the zombie fetus inside her shredded womb, its small limbs moving. Katarina closed her eyes, took a deep breath, then opened her eyes and fired. The dead mother jerked once, then stumbled on, oblivious of the fact that the small form inside her had stopped moving.

"This is the day that the Lord has made. Let us rejoice and be glad in it." Reverend Thomas spoke smoothly, pouring gentle, healing balm on the fevered minds of the fort's inhabitants.

On the command center set up on the wall, Kevin looked down at the map held under heavy plastic on the table before him and took a deep breath.

Nerit stood next to him, her face calm as she gazed out toward the oncoming horde. The dead were flowing out of the trees as they trudged toward the fort.

Near them, Juan smiled as he ran final tests on some of the traps set outside the gates. His cowboy hat was firmly in place over his pinned-up hair.

"Those are difficult words to embrace on a day such as this, but we must do just that. For this is the day the Lord has made for us to fight for our lives and the lives of those we love. This is our home, our fort, our safe haven."

Kevin moved several red markers along the map as another of Rune's grenades exploded in the distance and his spotters reported in.

"We have lost many friends and family members during this plague of the dead. Those we love have fallen. Some have joined the ranks of our enemies."

Margie leaned against her new grandmother, listening to the reverend and playing idly with her doll's tangled hair. She thought of her old mommy and daddy and of the nice lady with the black hair who had saved them. Kissing her doll, she hugged it like Guadalupe was hugging her.

"But we must be strong and stand firm. We must not waver in the face of evil. It may wear the face of humanity, but it is corruption. They are the enemy of life. Be strong and know that the battle you fight today is just and good in the sight of God."

Monica watched the zombies stumbling after Rune's motorcycle. Beside her, Bette loaded a catapult.

"Today we fight for our lives. We fight for the lives of our families and friends. We fight for our future. We fight for life itself. And that is a good and righteous thing."

Rune grinned, feeling satisfaction as he brought the motorcycle to an abrupt halt. He'd succeeded in redirecting the first small wave of zombies, along the outside of the barrier. The big bike rumbled between his legs as he drew another grenade and whistled loudly at the zombies.

Aggravated by his nearness, the zombies let out moans of desperate hunger. Their stench was almost overwhelming at this distance.

"Yep, damn good day to die," Rune said to himself, lobbing another grenade into the undead mob.

He gunned the bike and rode away as the grenade went off with a resounding boom and peppered him with body parts. Rune barked a laugh. The zombies shambled after him.

\*   \*   \*

"Damn gremlins," Calhoun growled, watching Jason.

Jason glanced nervously over his shoulder and was relieved to see that no more zombies had passed the barricade. He hoped they were all following Rune, whose progress was marked by a series of explosions. "The gremlins probably took off when they saw Jack," Jason said, trying to calm Calhoun. He needed the old man's mind working on a solution, not freaking out over invisible opponents.

"Yeah, gremlins hate dogs," Calhoun conceded. "Good old Jack here probably got them running for the hills."

"Yep." Jason tried to concentrate, his trembling fingers moving methodically through the innards of the contraption he and Calhoun had built. Fear gripped his body, and he found it hard to concentrate. For at least the ninth time, he started once again to trace each wire, trying to figure out which one was shorting.

"Jason," Calhoun whispered, "the clones are here."

Jason looked. A lone zombie had climbed over the barrier and was staggering toward them. It was so badly decayed, the teenager wasn't sure if it was a woman or a man. Jack let out a low growl but held his position, waiting for orders.

"It's still far away." Jason returned his gaze to the detonator. "Don't shoot it, or the rest of them will come after us."

Calhoun drew his gun anyway. "I don't like the idea of those things having an all-they-can-eat Calhoun buffet."

Jason kept working, repeatedly glancing up at the zombie, which kept coming, its movements jerky, rigid, and excruciatingly slow. Jason carefully dug deeper into the box. Jack growled again, louder, and bared his teeth. Abruptly, the creature fell backwards and lay still. Calhoun scrambled forward and gazed at the thing.

"Right through the head! *Damn!* That old woman is evil!"

Realizing a sniper—probably Katarina—had taken out the zombie, Jason blew out a breath in relief and kept working. Another explosion sounded in the distance. Jason heard a catapult creaking as it tossed a load of microwaves and TVs into the crowd of zombies approaching the fort.

"That's not good," Calhoun said sharply, scuttling along the ground on his hands and knees.

"They're probably trying to keep them from catching Rune," Jason replied.

"Not that. That!"

Jason looked up and his blood ran cold. Three zombies had clambered over the barrier and were racing toward them.

"Oh, shit!" Jason jumped to his feet and reached frantically for his gun.

Calhoun took a shot and hit one of the runners in the shoulder, spinning it around, but it recovered immediately and kept coming. Jack leaped onto the first runner and sank his teeth into its shoulder. The creature went down, struggling to get free of the growling canine. Like all other zombies, it was not interested in eating animals. Jason saw Calhoun stagger as the runner Jack was battling grabbed the old man's ankle.

Another bullet from above took out one of the runners. Jason aimed at the last one. He saw puffs of dirt kick up around the zombie and realized that someone in the fort was shooting at it—and missing. The zombie screeched as it barreled toward him.

It was on him in an instant. The creature grabbed Jason's long bangs and jerked him toward its mouth. Jason lost his balance and he and the zombie both fell to the ground, Jason on the bottom with the zombie's howling mouth just inches from his face. Shoving his hand under the thing's chin, Jason pushed it away, his desperation giving him strength.

In the next instant, Jack was on the zombie, clamping his jaws on the back of its neck. The undead, howling thing tried to hold on to Jason, but Jack yanked it off his master.

Jason scrambled to his feet. To his horror, he realized that Calhoun was using the detonator to bash the other runner's brains out.

"Calhoun, no!" Jason gasped. He heard a terrible sound—a steady beeping. "Jack! Let go! Come here!"

Jack whirled around and rushed toward his boy. The nearly

decapitated runner pushed itself to its knees just as the sniper finally found the range. The zombie fell over, truly dead.

Finished with his runner, Calhoun blinked at Jason, then stared at the bloody, battered box in his hands. It kept beeping; the light that had refused to come on was now blinking red. "This is not good," the older man said calmly.

"Run!" Jason shouted. "Now!" He raced away from the fire line. The sounds of the fight had drawn more attention from the zombies. About fifty were trudging over the barricade.

Jack growled at the shambling undead, then ran after his boy. Calhoun threw down the metal box and began to run, putting on as much speed as he could. Jack barked at him and darted back and forth between man and boy.

The three of them were halfway to the fort when the fuel tanks exploded. The force of the blast blew them off their feet. A wash of heat, followed by flames, filled the air.

On the fort's walls, people ducked for cover as fiery debris rained down and the roar of the explosion rang in their ears.

Katie hauled herself to her feet and saw that the fire line had roared to life as the accelerant-drenched debris exploded. Flames roared across the top of the barricade, encircling the fort in a wall of fire. Many zombies had been blown into bits; others, burning brightly, had been tossed back into the approaching mob. The horde was splitting apart as the zombies tried to avoid the flames.

Clutching the railing, she peered through binoculars into the acrid smoke and realized that at least twenty zombies were still on the move inside the fire line. *But where are Jason, Calhoun, and Jack?* At last she spotted the dog that was barking anxiously at the zombies who were moving determinedly toward the fallen figures of the teenager and the old man.

"Oh, shit!" Katie grabbed her walkie-talkie. "Jason and Calhoun are in danger near my point!"

\* \* \*

"Right now, don't worry about the two lines that are moving away from the fort," Nerit said over her walkie-talkie. "Concentrate on anything that breaches the outer perimeter. Anything that moves into your hot zone is a target."

"The outer ridgeline is on fire. It's splitting the horde in half just like we hoped." Kevin drew rapidly on the map, updating the battle. "We're going to win, Nerit."

Her reply was a slight smile.

Travis arrived at the wall just in time to see his wife about to slide onto the makeshift elevator. "Katie!"

"I need to get Jason!" Her gun was already in her hand. She looked at Travis with an expression of both fear and determination on her face. "He's Jenni's boy. I have to."

"You're not going down there," Travis said firmly. He saw her jaw setting and he shook a finger in warning. "Jenni wouldn't want you risking the baby."

"Dammit," she said, sighing as she conceded his point.

Travis grabbed her and kissed her. "Now, get back to your post!"

Jason slowly returned to consciousness, coughing. A figure lurched out of the smoke and fell to its knees beside him. The thing's dead, gnarled face moved to bury itself in his soft flesh. Realizing in that instant that he still held his gun, Jason raised it to the zombie's temple and fired.

The thing collapsed.

Blinking, Jason sat up. Jack hurtled out of the swirling smoke and nearly landed on the teen, barking frantically. Jason almost called Calhoun's name, then thought better of it. The zombies would find him faster if they heard his voice. Holding on to Jack's collar, he clambered to his feet, then bent over to whisper, "Find Calhoun," to the dog.

Jack looked up at him with clear brown eyes. Jason saw concern and puzzlement in their depths, but after a moment the German shepherd began to lead Jason slowly through the hot, acrid air and dark smoke.

A moan near him made Jason jump. Jack growled low in his throat, and Jason raised his gun. The stench of decaying burning flesh filled his nostrils and he stared into the smoke in terror.

A woman lurched out of the mist, and Jason instinctively pulled the trigger. The impact of the bullet knocked her back a few feet; then she snarled and started forward once more. Jason fired again, this time aiming more carefully; the bullet punched through her forehead and the zombie fell.

Another one staggered toward him and he quickly swung his gun around to aim at it. Jack shoved Jason's legs hard, knocking him sideways just as the smoke cleared enough to reveal that the new zombie was actually Calhoun, who was still alive.

"Damn clones!" Calhoun grabbed Jason's arm. "They're all over the place. We gotta back up toward the wall."

"Where's your gun?" Jason whispered.

"No clue. Got the living bejeezus knocked out of me by that explosion," Calhoun answered.

The dark smoke began to dissipate; the fires were burning out. The two men and the dog moved a little faster as more and more zombies were revealed.

"This ain't good, boy," Calhoun said quietly.

Another explosion near the barrier showered them with body parts. Then the roar of a motorcycle filled their ears.

"Crazy hippie," Calhoun complained as Rune's Harley drew close to them. The biker looked a bit bedraggled and was covered in soot.

Rune motioned to them. "Get on."

Calhoun shoved Jason onto the bike, then managed to squeeze his skinny butt on as well. Jason wasn't sure what smelled worse: the zombies or Calhoun.

"Sorry, boy, you gotta run back," Jason told Jack as Rune gunned the bike, heading for the fort at top speed. Jason and

Calhoun clung to Rune as the bike weaved around the zombies.

Glancing back, Jason saw Jack running as fast as he could, a big doggy grin on his face. The teenager smiled; he supposed a motorcycle was almost as good as a car when it came to chasing.

The motorcycle reached the elevator just as it hit the ground. Above them, Reggie shouted, "Hurry up!"

Rune lifted his shotgun and calmly blew the head off an approaching zombie. "Gotta leave you here, Charlene," he said to the bike, patting it as he got off. "Sorry, babe."

Rune helped Calhoun off the bike and onto the elevator. Jason followed. Jack leaped onto the crowded platform, and Jason went down on his knees to hold on to the dog as the elevator began to lift.

Just as they reached the top, a shift in the wind blew much of the smoke away from the fort. Jason looked over the wide expanse of land and saw that a lot of the zombie horde had split in two and was moving off away from the town. The fire had spooked them.

"Did we do it?" Jason asked breathlessly, not sure if he could trust his eyes.

"I'll be damned," Rune said with awe. "Watch those fuckers go."

Calhoun sniffled loudly, surveying the two lines of the undead shambling away from the fort. The burning remains of the zombies caught in the explosion smoldered before the barricade. "Well, I ain't cleaning *that* up," he declared.

# 2.
## *Breach*

Peering through her binoculars, Katie kept watch on the fire line. From her perch on the southwest corner of the fort, she could clearly see the retreating shambling forms of the undead. The sheer numbers of the walking dead were astounding. Would the walls have stood against so many?

The flames dancing along the barrier were beginning to die. New explosions reignited some sections, sending huge plumes of fire and smoke up into the blue sky. Katie turned away, the heat and smoke making her eyes burn. Coughing on the acrid air, she lifted the binoculars again.

"Oh, shit," she whispered.

One of the fire-trap detonations had blown a hole in the barrier. Burning bits of debris littered the ground, and the dirt stirred up by the impact had doused some of the flames. A few zombies staggered through the gap. Spotting the people manning the wall defenses, they lifted their hands and shambled toward the fort.

"No, no, no," Katie whispered, lifting her binoculars. "This can't happen."

To her horror, more zombies slipped through the break in the barricade.

Nerit and Kevin watched the retreating mob of zombies with reserved optimism as they continued to monitor the situation.

"It's looking good," Kevin said.

"It is," Nerit agreed.

The walkie-talkie beside Nerit came to life as Katie's voice broke through the static. "Nerit, we have a problem."

Lifting the device to her mouth, Nerit said quickly, "What is it?"

"The fire line is breached. We have about two hundred zombies about to hit the wall on the southwest corner."

"Understood. We'll sound the alarm," Nerit answered.

Kevin somberly handed her the bullhorn that had been resting on the corner of the table. "You should do the honors."

Wrapping her fingers around the handle, Nerit pulled the trigger.

The loud blast cut through the air.

And the fort went to war.

# 3.
## *The War*

It is common knowledge that war is hell. It is not so well known that war is surreal. Hyperreality mixes with moments of feeling disconnected from reality. A sense of fragility is wrapped in a feeling of invincibility. Nothing about war makes sense. Nothing about it registers fully in the human senses.

As the dead trudged over the smoky remains of the barricade, the fort occupants unleashed the fury of their weapons upon them.

The morning air was filled with the creaking of catapults showering the undead with their loads of discarded junk. The sharp twangs of the massive crossbows were followed by hissing whistles as each load of twenty arrows soared through the air in gentle arches before slamming into the battered, mangled bodies of the undead. There came the sudden *whoosh* of gas jets being activated on the field below; the loud bang as they ignited; burning zombies wailing.

The smell was unbelievable. Charred flesh. Rotting flesh. Fire. Human sweat and fear.

The area surrounding the fort had been divided into sections, each of which was protected by specifically assigned crews of defenders, from sharpshooters to catapult and crossbow squads. The walls had been painted in different colors to mark off each zone. If something crossed into an assigned zone, the defenders in that area fired. There was plenty of swearing and shouts of rage as something undead moved just before a toilet smashed to the ground right where it had been standing.

At Nerit's command, Juan activated the traps: the fire jets, the quick-drying cement, the stakes. A shuffling family of four, complete with a toddler, flailed around in the cement until snipers shot them. An armless woman in scrubs turned into a torch when a gas jet ignited right under her. Zombified firefighters, clad in tattered turnout gear, were skewered on the stakes.

Lenore worked with feverish intensity, loading her crossbow, then waiting for something to move into her zone. Every time the shambling dead went down under her arrows, she would grin fiercely. "This is for Ken, fuckers," Lenore said as her crossbow split zombies apart, pouring their putrid innards onto the ground. She pumped her fist in the air.

Jason and other teenagers worked the slingshots, launching Molotov cocktails with startling accuracy. Their T-shirts had the words FOR ROGER written across their backs in Sharpie. Jason's also read, FOR MY MOM.

Rune ran across rooftops, shooting anything trying to come up the side streets. Most of the traps had already gone off with zombies dangling from the razor wire.

Monica and Bette reloaded their catapult countless times. The discarded junk of the old world flew out over the battlefield, causing brutal devastation among the undead. They would high-five at each particularly gruesome death; a favorite was that of a zombie priest who lost his head to a flying toaster oven.

Calhoun, followed by his pack of dogs, ran along the wall, smiling gleefully as he activated more traps. If zombies began to congregate in one area, he would trigger a variety of swinging arms strung with lawn mower blades. These were his pride and joy; swiping through a group of zombies, they'd obliterate anything they hit.

Katarina took out the living dead with terrible accuracy. Being a sniper meant she witnessed their ravaged faces, their empty eyes, their mutilated forms. Every age, every gender, every race wandered into her view, and every single one was given a final rest by her bullets. She was startled to feel peace instead of the fear and dread she had lived with for so long. Instead of feeling rage, she felt sorrow. Every bullet, she realized, was a blessing to those creatures, an exit from hell.

Bulldozers rolled through the battlefield, clearing the edge along the wall. The cabs were heavily fortified to keep the drivers safe. The wicked blades of the large vehicles swept the truly dead corpses out of the fray to keep them from piling up against the walls.

Those who could not fight watched from the hotel's opulent ballroom. They'd been terror stricken when the zombies first swarmed toward the fort. The beginning of the battle had been mesmerizing as the dead were met with fierce resistance. Now it was hard to tell what was happening below. The battlefield was a ruin. Smoke filled the air. Fear and hope filled the hearts of the spectators.

In the communication center, Yolanda listened to a war she could not see. Her pistol lay on the counter. If there was a breach in the wall, she would fight . . . but she would save one bullet for herself.

Katie gagged on the putrid stench. All along her part of the wall, the crossbows and catapults finally fell silent and still. The catapults on the east side were still firing, but most of the rest no longer had moving targets. Relief began to fill her as she surveyed the carnage.

"Is it done?" someone yelled.

"I don't have any in my zone," Lenore called out.

Katie lifted her walkie-talkie. "Hey, what's going on?"

From his point on the wall, Kevin could see most of the west side of the battlefield. A few severely mutilated zombies were trying to pull themselves along the ground; the rest of the corpses seemed truly dead.

"This might be it," Nerit said hopefully..

"Get the copter up," Kevin said into his walkie-talkie.

Moments later, a lone helicopter lifted and began making a pass over the fort, the town, and the hills.

All over the fort, the defenders reloaded their weapons and held position. Some sat in chairs; others collapsed to the top of the wall or to the ground. People tried not to breathe too deeply; the air was full of the stench of warfare and death. Everyone was tired and aching, not daring to think that the battle might be over, yet hoping that it was.

An eerie silence filled the morning, broken only by the sound of the helicopter and the dull hum of the moaning dead as they shambled farther and farther away from the fort.

Nerit surveyed the map of the battlefield as she waited for the word.

There was a burst of static over the walkie-talkie.

"That's it," Greta said through the radio. "Holy God in Heaven, that's it. We see two columns heading away, east and west. As for the ones that hit us straight on . . . boys and girls . . . what you see in front of you is it!"

# · CHAPTER THIRTY-FOUR ·

## 1.
### *The End*

Katie watched in awe as the fleeing zombies skirted around the burning fire line. Rubbing her sore back, she followed Travis as he hurried to the command center. Nerit and Kevin were both talking on their walkie-talkies as the helicopter swooped low over the retreating hordes.

Juan was crouched down, setting off traps remotely. The sound of fire traps going off punctuated the retreat of the moaning undead. The smaller traps would continue to go off and keep the barricade burning until the zombies were gone.

Along the wall, the fort defenders watched the departing zombies in silence, as though unwilling to accept the ease of their victory.

Katie felt tears pricking in her eyes as she thought of all they had endured to reach this moment of sweet victory. Glancing over her shoulder at the zombie retreat, she knew for sure they had won.

"Greta is reporting in that both columns are heading away from the fort and that there are no more zombies heading our way," Nerit said with the most beautiful smile Katie had ever seen.

Kevin picked up his binoculars and peered out at the battleground. "We got them all. The ones that attacked the walls are down."

"So this is it?" Travis laughed in disbelief. "We did it?"

Katie grinned at him. "We did work our asses off to win, you know."

"Planning man! We planned it out and we did it!" Juan whooped. "We were a little late on the 'organize before they rise' part of the *Zombie Survival Guide,* but we were ready when they fucking got here."

With a proud gleam in her eye, Nerit covered Kevin's hand with her own. "Well done."

Kevin raised her hand to his lips and kissed it. "I've learned from the best."

Jason and Jack ran into the command center and Juan swept the boy up into his arms. "My boy did it!"

"Dad!" Jason complained, squirming free, but smiled.

Leaning against Travis's side, Katie watched the two columns of the shambling undead disappearing into the countryside.

Half an hour later, Travis hugged Yolanda tightly. He and Katie had gone to the communication center to make a final announcement. Tears glittered in Yolanda's dark eyes as she stepped aside to let him reach the microphone. She flipped the switch to bring the speakers to life.

"Ladies and gentlemen, one hour after reaching our defenses, the zombie horde is gone. You did one helluva job," Travis said, his voice breaking. "God bless us all."

Beaming with joy, Katie flung her arms around his waist and he kissed her soundly. When he drew back, he was surprised to see a shocked look on her face.

"Honey, what is it?"

"My water just broke," she answered, her eyes widening.

"Holy shit!" Bette shouted when their victory was announced. Whooping, she tossed her hat into the air as Monica screamed with joy. Grabbing Monica close, Bette gave her a smoldering kiss.

\*   \*   \*

Rune sat down on the wall and dangled his feet over the edge. Surveying the open space in front of him, he admired the smoking clusters of body parts.

"Well, hot damn," he said, and grinned at the sight of his Harley, standing unscathed right where he had left it.

Katarina began to cry, cradling her rifle in her arms. "We did it, Bill. We did it."

Rolling onto her back, she stared up at the sky, hoping he saw her smile of happiness from heaven.

Lenore leaned back in the chair next to her crossbow and stretched. Nodding to herself, she pulled a soda out of her pocket and popped the top. "Damn zombies shouldn't have touched my best friend." Raising the can in a toast, she said, "For Felix and Ken. Rest in peace, my brothers."

Eric was serving as a spotter on the far wall. He'd been awestruck, watching the steadily receding stream of zombies disappear into the west. The official announcement was the most beautiful news he had ever heard.

"Eric!"

Lowering his binoculars, he saw Stacey and Pepe rushing toward his sentry post. He clambered down the ladder and caught his girlfriend in his arms. Kissing her deeply, he cherished the softness of her lips.

Drawing back, she grinned up at him. "We won!"

"I know! It's the greatest news ever!"

"Oh, no, Eric," she corrected. "I'm about to tell you the greatest news ever."

The zombies were vanquished, the fire line was a smoldering ruin, and the fort was once more secure. After a long day of cleanup, the night had been full of celebration. Katie's greatest joy was reserved for the moment when Charlotte laid her baby daughter in her arms for the first time.

Later, their family of friends came to gush over the newest member of the fort. Exhausted and proud, Katie felt the promise of the new world come fully into being as the people she loved best crowded into the room. Travis sat beside her, holding her hand with a blissful expression on his face. Nerit held the new baby as Kevin and Juan vied for the infant's attention, making goofy faces and laughing. Eric and Stacey took turns holding the baby, sharing smiles that seemed to hold a secret. Katarina cried throughout her visit but insisted it was because she was happy. Even Lenore came, staring at the little one with something close to a smile on her lips.

"It ain't ugly," she said at last.

Finally, Nerit shooed everyone out of the room. She kissed Katie's cheek and whispered, "Well done," before leaving.

Alone at last with her little family, Katie cuddled her daughter. She admired the little face peeping out of a pink swaddling blanket and felt as though she would never stop smiling. The baby had a mushed-up, funny look about her, but she could see Travis in the shape of the wee one's nose and eyebrows. The small feet that had pushed against her bladder at the worst times were now wiggling under the blanket. The little hands that had made bumps under her skin now clutched her fingers.

Travis gently touched his new daughter's cheek. "She has your mouth," he murmured.

"And your nose," Katie replied.

"It's amazing—we're parents at last!"

"Yes, we are, and don't you forget that," Katie said, her eyes bright. "I'm not changing diapers alone."

"What are we naming her, Mommy?" Travis asked, touching one little fist.

Katie had had plenty of time to think about this in the days since they'd returned from the mall. "Bryce Jennily Kiel-Buchanan."

Travis smiled in understanding. He said, "To honor Bruce, Jenni, and Lydia. Perfect." He kissed the baby on the forehead. "You're the first, Bryce, but soon there will be others. You will be the first generation in a new world."

Katie regarded Travis curiously. "Others?"

"Eric told me Stacey is about three months along."

Katie found herself weeping tears of joy. "We did something amazing today, didn't we?"

Travis laid a soft, passionate kiss on his wife's lips. "Yes, we did."

They would continue to rebuild, to bring a new world out of the ashes of the old. It was a wonderful world to bring their daughter into.

The new parents gazed down at their newborn in awe. Bryce yawned—a tiny pink sigh—as she dozed off.

"Welcome to the new world," Katie said to her sleeping infant.

## AUTHOR'S NOTE

If you have jumped to the end of the book to see how it ends, I suggest you stop reading now. While I hope you're eager to know who lives and dies and if there is a happily ever after, you really shouldn't spoil things for yourself.

Trust me.

Go back to the front of the book and read this last leg of a journey that started with tiny little fingers reaching under a door. . . .

## AUTHOR'S SECOND NOTE

Welcome back.

By now, you know that the death toll in this novel is high. Of course, in *The First Days,* I killed off the entire world except for a few survivors. And if I kept to zombie tradition, no one would be standing at the end of this novel. But, you see, I think the doomsayers have it wrong.

As the World Dies was inspired not only by the heroics of 9/11, but also by people's reactions to other disasters. Journalists and writers of fiction love to concentrate on the terrors and evils of natural and man-made disasters, but I find myself fascinated by the heroism and selflessness of many people in times of crisis. Watching ordinary folks scrambling to save complete strangers is inspiring. I've sat mesmerized in front of the TV, watching brave people try to dig through rubble, mud, and debris to save others; or dive into the ocean to rescue someone who has been attacked by a shark; or scramble to get supplies to desperate survivors they don't even know.

It is popular to buy into the concept that if our world went to hell, people would become barbarians. I think that would happen to some people, but I believe that a greater number would work hard to rebuild their communities.

Together we stand or alone we die.

Looking over humanity's long history, I can say that we have not always been the noblest of God's creations, but we have managed to rise above our faults to build families, communities, vast cities, and nations. We aren't perfect, but we're doing a much better job than we give ourselves credit for.

As the World Dies is the tale of a human settlement being founded in the middle of a hostile environment—a situation human beings have faced over and over again throughout history. And like history, As the World Dies is a story about people.

It's been one hell of a ride with Jenni and Katie. I hope you enjoyed it as much as I did.

Eternally,
Rhiannon